PRAISE FOR

DEATH ALONG THE SPIRIT ROAD

"A mystery novel that grabs you by the lapels and refuses to let go . . . This is storytelling at its best and C. M. Wendelboe is a new author to watch."

—Margaret Coel,
New York Times bestselling author of *The Perfect Suspect*

"The pacing of the novel . . . is distinctly native, something I haven't read since the departure of the old master, Tony Hillerman."

—Craig Johnson,
New York Times bestselling author of *Hell Is Empty*

"Wendelboe paints a vivid portrait of life on the reservation and deftly mixes history with a satisfying mystery."

—*Kirkus Reviews*

"The absorbing first in a new . . . series."   —*Publishers Weekly*

"*Death Along the Spirit Road* is a fantastic read . . . C. M. Wendelboe is a fabulous writer with an eye for detail and the ability to express it perfectly. This is a definite must-read."

—*The Romance Readers Connection*

"This Native American police procedural is a strong whodunit because of the powerful backdrop in which Tanno investigates."

—*Midwest Book Review*

DEATH WHERE THE BAD ROCKS LIVE

C. M. WENDELBOE

BERKLEY PRIME CRIME, NEW YORK

THE BERKLEY PUBLISHING GROUP
Published by the Penguin Group
Penguin Group (USA) Inc.
375 Hudson Street, New York, New York 10014, USA
Penguin Group (Canada), 90 Eglinton Avenue East, Suite 700, Toronto, Ontario M4P 2Y3, Canada
(a division of Pearson Penguin Canada Inc.) • Penguin Books Ltd., 80 Strand, London WC2R 0RL,
England • Penguin Group Ireland, 25 St. Stephen's Green, Dublin 2, Ireland (a division of Penguin
Books Ltd.) • Penguin Group (Australia), 250 Camberwell Road, Camberwell, Victoria 3124, Australia
(a division of Pearson Australia Group Pty. Ltd.) • Penguin Books India Pvt. Ltd., 11 Community
Centre, Panchsheel Park, New Delhi—110 017, India • Penguin Group (NZ), 67 Apollo Drive,
Rosedale, Auckland 0632, New Zealand (a division of Pearson New Zealand Ltd.) • Penguin Books
(South Africa) (Pty.) Ltd., 24 Sturdee Avenue, Rosebank, Johannesburg 2196, South Africa

Penguin Books Ltd., Registered Offices: 80 Strand, London WC2R 0RL, England

This book is an original publication of The Berkley Publishing Group.

PUBLISHING HISTORY
Berkley Prime Crime trade paperback edition / September 2012

Library of Congress Cataloging-in-Publication Data

Wendelboe, C. M.
Death where the bad rocks live / C. M. Wendelboe.—1st ed.
p. cm.
ISBN: 978-0-425-25611-4 (pbk.)
1. United States. Federal Bureau of Investigation—Officials and employees—Fiction. 2. Indian
reservation—South Dakota—Fiction. 3. Dakota Indians—Fiction. I. Title.
PS3623.E53D46   2012
813'.6—dc23   2012014771

PRINTED IN THE UNITED STATES OF AMERICA

10 9 8 7 6 5 4 3 2 1

*To those who have become ill and lost loved ones
in the place where the bad rocks live.*

Acknowledgments

Again I would like to thank my editor, Tom Colgan, and my literary agent, Bill Contardi, for their patience and professionalism leading me through this maze that is the publishing world. I am thankful to my first publicist, Kaitlyn Kennedy, and Penguin's sales and marketing staff, especially Eric Boss and Kaccy Pfaff. I am grateful for my mentors, Judy and Craig Johnson—especially Craig for keeping me and "Big Elvis" up on two wheels. I value the input of my Lakota friends, especially Oglala Lakota Ernie LaPointe for sharing his knowledge of the Old Time as it relates to present attitudes on Pine Ridge Reservation. I am most thankful for the support, untiring help, and love of my wife, Heather—who absolutely never tells me what to do.

Since the creation of the Turtle Island (The North American Continent), the first Nations always knew all things have a Spirit. The four-legged, those that fly, the green growing things, the water, the rocks (stones), and the Earth. The first Nations lived with all these entities as relatives, because we are all born from the Earth, our true Mother. There is not anything bad or evil from these living entities, but are labeled as such from people that do not have any knowledge, by the two-legged that create controversy.

ERNIE LAPOINTE
Great-grandson of *Tatanka Iyotake*: Bull Who Sits Down
(Sitting Bull; Hunkpapa Lakota)

CHAPTER 1

The faint whisper of wind grew louder in Moses Ten Bears's ears as the throp-throp-throp of a large aircraft cooking off speed neared. Snow, mixed with cottonwood seeds that made their own breed of snowstorm, swirled around the car as the bomber passed overhead at treetop level. If there had been any trees in the Badlands.

"You're sure they're not bombing here today?" Ellis Lawler's eyes darted between Moses and the aircraft, which was shrinking in the distance. The frail, little man with skin the color of dirty snow shivered inside the frigid Buick, and his teeth clicked together as he rubbed his hands for warmth.

Moses chuckled. Here on the reservation, people would say the Buick they huddled inside was a Big Ugly Indian Cow Killer.

"You think that's funny?" Ellis blew into his gloves. "They came pretty close that last pass."

"They have not bombed here since last year. Those Army Air Corps flyboys have used this part of the Stronghold for practice so long they could make the run in their sleep. Besides"—Moses snatched a glove from Ellis and held it just out of his reach—"they stopped using cars for targets last year."

Ellis reached for the glove, but Moses kept it away, finally allowing Ellis to grab it. He craned his neck out the window in the direction the bomber had flown. "Just the same, I'll feel better when Clayton gets here. This place gives me the creeps."

But it didn't give Moses the creeps. It rejuvenated him every time he came here. The Wanagi Oyate, the spirits of those that have passed on, called to him from this place. This was the Stronghold, for so long a Lakota sanctuary, for so long a place where warriors fled to seek safety from invading enemies, for so long a place where spirits of those gone before him still roamed. This was *Oonagazhee*, the Sheltering Place. And he decided this would be the final time he'd guide any *wasicu*, White man, here.

Ellis uncapped a mason jar of corn whiskey, the odor permeating the car. Moses retched, as much from the revolting smell as from what revolting things whiskey had done to the Lakota, draining their will, draining their history, like the cold draining the heat from him this frigid afternoon. Ellis took a long pull and wiped his mouth with the back of his hand. He passed the whiskey jar to Moses, but Moses shook his head. Ellis shrugged and took another drink before capping it and setting it on the floorboard. "Where the hell's Clayton?"

Clayton promised to meet them here an hour ago. Ellis's car had no heat and even Moses shivered as he fought to stay warm from the *Waziya*, the killing North Wind, which seeped through the cracks in the side window. "He must have had car trouble. He is always on time. He is close, though."

"How the hell you know that? More of your medicine man mumbo jumbo?"

Moses ignored Ellis the Ignorant, as he called him, and shoved his hands in his jacket pockets. When Clayton had asked him to ride here with Ellis, Moses had refused at first, but Clayton persisted. Moses relented, not because Clayton was a sitting U. S. senator, but because Moses never refused his friend. He had agreed to guide the geologist here, an act Moses was growing to regret. He had always suspected the greedy little bastard could not even carry on an intelligent conversation. Now he had his proof.

The biting wind whistled through a crack in one side window, bringing snow and fine dust inside, accompanied by that same roaring engine sound that grew louder. Moses turned in the seat to look out the fogged-over back window. The B-17 flew even lower this pass, heading straight toward them, following the jagged terrain of the Badlands. "They're flying too low."

"What?" Ellis turned in his seat to look out the back window. His eyes widened and his mouth dropped as he spotted the bomber bearing down on them.

"I think they are going to drop their bombload," Moses said, matter-of-factly.

Ellis screamed and yanked on the door handle, while Moses watched the bomber coming closer. The aircraft was near enough now that Moses saw the turret gunner fog the inside glass with his hot breath, heard the engines drown out Ellis's screams, smelled the avgas exhaust from the quad motors as strong as the odor of Ellis's moonshine.

Ellis hit the starter button on the floorboard with his foot and the Buick coughed to life. He ground gears and double-clutched just as the first bombs exploded fifty yards behind them. Pressure ruptured their eardrums. Moses cupped his hands to his bloody head and prayed silently to *Wakan Tanka*, the Great Mysterious, praying that his journey to the Spirit Road would be successful.

Another bomb exploded closer to the car. Overpressure blew out the windows. Ellis screamed, but Moses could not hear him or the other bombs detonate. All was silent. All was peaceful. All he heard was the prayers in his head, silent and chilling as the killing North Wind.

The aircrew did not score a direct hit, but that mattered none. Ellis lay slumped against the steering wheel, blood flowing freely from his nose and mouth and lifeless eyes. Moses looked down at the large piece of windshield glass protruding from his own chest. His hand feebly grabbed for his medicine bundle on the thong dangling around his neck. *Soon*, Wakan Tanka. *Soon I'll meet you along the Spirit Road.*

CHAPTER 2

Willie jerked the wheel, skidding the Durango on the loose dirt, the back end of the SUV dropping off the edge. Manny yelled. Willie screamed. The wheel spun in his hands. He stood on the brakes, dust engulfing the Dodge, obscuring the two-hundred-foot drop-off. It rocked to a stop, and Manny opened his eyes. He chanced rolling his window down, chanced a look at the drop-off that could kill them both. Scrub trees on the floor of the Badlands looked like tiny weeds. The alkaline floor below looked like an unwelcome grave, sagebrush sitting like tiny headstones.

"Now what do we do?"

Willie smiled, but the sweat rolling down his face betrayed his fear. "We can pray."

"You better pray we don't get out of this in one piece." But Manny's idle threat revealed his own fear. He chanced another look out his side window. The Durango teetered over thin air that Manny had no intention of stepping into.

"Got any ideas? You're the one that got us into this fix."

"Not my fault this road's so narrow."

"Would you rather have brought my bureau car?"

"Not with you driving."

"Like I could do worse?"

Willie put the Durango into four-wheel drive and tapped the foot feed. Tires spun without catching, the back end swaying in empty air.

"Stop! You're making it worse."

Willie put the Dodge in PARK and sat back in the seat, closing his eyes and breathing hard. "The winch," he said, opening his eyes and looking around. "There."

"There what?"

He pointed to a large boulder off the path away from the drop-off. "If I can run the winch cable off the front bumper around that rock, we might be able to ease it back on the road."

Willie opened the door and started to step out. The SUV tilted more to the open air and Manny grabbed his arm. "You step out and this thing's gonna drop over the edge. With me in it."

"Well, we got to do something."

"How much you weigh?"

Willie shrugged. "Two forty. Give or take."

"Well, I'm one eighty . . ."

"Diet's not working, huh?"

Manny ignored him. "If I slide behind the wheel when you step out, it might not change the balance much."

"Worth a try."

Manny crawled over the radio console and slid behind the wheel as Willie opened the door and stepped onto the road. The Dodge rocked, threatened to tip off the cliff before it settled back into an uneasy silence. Manny held his breath as Willie unbolted the winch cable from the front bumper and slowly ran it out. He reached the boulder. Manny breathed.

Willie circled the rock and secured the hook end to the cable itself. He walked back to the Durango. "Hand me the winch remote from above the visor."

Manny grabbed what looked like a garage door opener and handed it through the window.

"When the cable tightens, I'll signal you and you stick this baby in LOW."

"And it'll get dragged back onto the road?"

Willie laughed. "Either that or the cable will break, and you and the outfit will do a double gainer off the side."

"You don't seem too worried about it."

Willie grinned. "I'm not the one inside. Here goes."

A steady whirring reached the inside of the Durango, and Manny took several deep breaths, his hand on the gearshift, foot on the brake, ready to stick it in LOW.

"Now."

Willie stepped away from the Durango, remote in hand, cable tightening. Manny stepped on the accelerator. Play in the cable gone, the front tires bit into the dirt, rear tires still dangling over the Badlands. The back tires jerked, the SUV jolted ahead, back tires back on hard ground. Manny skidded to a stop inches from the boulder. He put it in PARK and sat back in the seat. Sweat had flowed freely, staining his shirtfront, and he grabbed his bandanna and wiped his forehead.

Manny stepped out and walked to the edge of the drop-off. A chill ran over him as he fought down a vision of him and Willie and the Dodge caroming off the cliff and coming apart in a hundred pieces before reaching the floor of the Badlands. He backed away and joined Willie, who had reversed the winch and stood watching the cable run back on the spool. "Another few inches and we'd be in the Happy Hunting Grounds."

"Spirit Road," Willie called over his shoulder.

Manny sat on a rock and closed his eyes, aware once again

that he had a heartbeat, and that it slowed to normal. If he were a better driver, he'd demand Willie let him take the wheel. But Manny drove crappy, which only recently had been upgraded from driving shitty.

"Whenever you get around to it, feel free to drive a little slower." Manny wiped his face and the inside of his Stetson with his bandanna. "The victim's been dead for years. It's not like we got to race to get there. Hell, you've been racing around all morning. Look at yourself—didn't even shave. And what you got on your shirt, last night's pizza?"

Willie rubbed his hand over his stubble that hadn't been shaved yesterday either, and he picked at some kind of food dried to the front of his uniform shirt. "Been having things on my mind lately."

Manny suspected Willie bordered on full-blown depression, his life teetering over the ledge like the Durango had just been, threatening to drag Willie down. Even his recent appointment to Oglala Sioux Tribal Police investigator hadn't rescued him.

Willie shut the remote off and slipped the hook over the cable, securing it. "I got to see a man about a horse." Willie stepped away from the Dodge to relieve himself. Manny suddenly felt the urge as well, surprised he hadn't peed his pants as he sat teetering over the edge a few moments ago. As he turned and unzipped, he realized the whole place was his urinal.

As Manny did dust control on his own side of the car, he marveled at tawny sandstone spires towering a hundred feet above the Badlands floor that had lured people to their deaths in this remote part of the reservation that George Custer dubbed "hell on earth." Most people would agree with that assessment. At first glance, nothing could exist in this desolate landscape, no one could survive here for long, in this land that hosted barren hilltops overlooking a million years of change. The siltstone and sandstone and mudstone makeup of the

Badlands caused it to change daily, adding to the danger of getting swallowed up and never being found by anyone. As if the Badlands wished it that way.

"Come back tomorrow and you will get lost," Uncle Marion had told young Manny every time they ventured here to search for fossils, or pluck herbs for the upcoming winter, or harvest smelly skunkbrush sumac for making the baskets that Unc sold.

But the Old Ones knew this place teemed with life. The Old Ones only had to walk dry creek beds and gullies to locate the rabbitbrush the elk and deer grazed on to feed their horses, or locate yellow-waving sunflowers to harvest their nutrient-rich seeds. The Old Ones recognized that golden currants grew only on north-facing hillsides and where to pick them, using the summer-blooming plants in making pemmican. Most people saw the Badlands as an unforgiving place. Most people dared take only day trips and counted themselves fortunate to have made it out at the end of the day.

But to the Lakota, this was the Sheltering Place, the Stronghold, and it had sheltered and protected their ancestors well for hundreds of years. But this Sheltering Place demanded payment for those not strong enough—or savvy enough—to decipher her riddle of survival.

Thirty feet above them on the side of the hill some ancient Lakota woman had dug a cooking pit. Unc would send Manny scrambling up such a hillside, where he would filter the dirt through his fingers, filter remnants of charcoal from such stone-lined fire pits. And sometimes Manny would be rewarded with a bone scraper, sometimes with potsherds that had survived the centuries. Sometimes he found only a fire pit abandoned in haste.

Finished with their duty, Manny and Willie climbed back in the SUV and drove slow along the narrow trail. "How do you suppose those ordnance techs found that body?"

Manny shrugged. When the bomb disposal technicians had called it in, they were certain the skeleton in the car had been there since the Army Air Corps had bombed there during the war. "I'm anxious to find out how a man ended up in a bombing range he must have known was hot."

"Unless he died long after this part of the range closed after World War II."

They'd get their answer soon enough as they drove over a rise and down the other side, inching their way between two enormous hills consisting of millions of years of volcanic ash and sandstone topped by dried mud shale the consistency of popcorn. A solitary fifty-foot spire, eroded at the base by shifting winds and flash floods, seemed to teeter like a giant mushroom defying gravity.

Manny thought back to one of the first times he had been there. "Look over there," Uncle Marion had pointed out when he had brought Manny here to gather herbs. "That's where Kicking Bear led his band after Big Foot's Minneconjous were killed at Wounded Knee."

Manny squinted, shielding his eyes from the bright sun fighting to stay alive just above the jagged ridges. "Do people drive down there?" he had asked.

"Why do you ask?"

"There are cars down there."

Unc shook his head. "Practice targets for the Air Corps during World War II. They drug old cars down there to bomb when they ran out of dinosaur fossils to obliterate."

Manny turned back. Unc's mouth had assumed that downturned look he always got when he was saddened. "What's wrong, Unc?"

"The government. Kicked a hundred families off their land to use it for that bombing range," Unc explained as he looked away. "Paid them little or nothing at all, and most never moved back after the war. Nothing ever changes—the government takes from us Indians and leaves little more than a memory of what we had."

Manny remembered—or thought he remembered, though those days grew somewhat cloudy as he aged—that he had seen Unc cry for the only time.

The Durango dropped into another rut right before the road took a sharp turn away from the venerable sentry and revealed a three-axled van idling beside the rusting hulk of a bombed-out car. Three men sat in the shade of the van, one smoking and staring at the car while the other two slept, ball caps pulled low, feet outstretched. A long boom extended in front of the contraption like the long snout of a dinosaur that swam in the warm waters once flowing here. As the Durango approached, smoker nudged sleepers, and they all stood.

Willie stopped his tribal SUV a dozen car lengths away from the old car. Sand had drifted in broken windows through the years and covered the heap up to the top of the doors. Weeds and dirt had taken up residence inside the passenger compartment, and a scorpion scrambled out from under a dirt clod. Wind had blown one fender clean of any semblance of paint, and Manny counted three rusted, chrome bullets on the fender: a 1940s Buick. Willie and Manny approached the car, and the three men moved away as if relieved of guard duty.

"Senior Special Agent Manny Tanno." Manny extended his hand to the man who stepped closer, speaker for the other two whose eyes darted from the car to Manny and back to the car.

"Damn glad you made it. It's over there." Mark Weber pointed to the car.

"What's over there?"

"The body."

Manny stepped closer to the Buick.

"We're not used to seeing this in our business. But when we found that arm . . ." Weber shuddered and stepped back. Manny bent and peered inside.

"An arm all right," he called over his shoulder, and used the car to stand. "Tell me how you found it."

Weber divided his attention between Manny and staring at the arm. "We're subcontracted by Native American Environmental to work the bombing range. Cleaning up UXOs."

Willie had briefed Manny on the Oglala Explosive Ordnance Disposal company the tribe had contracted for locating and disposing of unexploded ordnance in the Badlands Bombing Range, remnants from bombers that had dropped a variety of ordnance, some of which never detonated. For the past five years, Oglala bomb techs had been working to locate and diffuse the danger, and had recently brought in nonnatives to help.

"How'd you find UXOs here?" Willie studied the ground as if expecting something to detonate in front of him. "This is pretty remote. You just didn't happen on to this."

"You ever see helicopters flying around Pine Ridge, with big booms going out from the sides?" Weber asked.

"Crop dusters."

Weber shook his head. "Those booms house magnetic detectors. We need the choppers to fly over rough terrain like this." He swept his hand in a circle. "When we pick up a magnetic anomaly, we throw a GPS marker on our map and return to it once we're on the ground. That's how we found the skeleton in the car—he was thirty feet away from a hundred-pound practice bomb that didn't go off seventy years ago."

Weber joined the other two bomb techs staring wide-eyed at the car like they expected the hand to animate. Willie dropped beside Manny. On his knees, he was even with the top of the car, the dirt of a thousand wind storms having all but buried the Buick. A whitened arm and hand with a single finger remaining jutted from the dirt, as if the corpse was flipping the world off, final and defiant. Bits of white cloth clung tenaciously to the wrist bone and fluttered against the wind.

"What'll Pee Pee do once he gets here?"

Manny stood and arched his back, stretching. Precious Paul Pourier was the Oglala Sioux Tribe's evidence technician. Although he had no degree, Pee Pee had worked with Manny many times. And Pee Pee was a talented tech, if a bit eccentric. "After photos he'll start excavating the remains. Then we'll decide if we need an archeologist from the state to join us. For now we can release those ordnance techs."

"Kind of creepy, huh?" Willie whispered.

Manny smiled. "Guess this is your first old body call."

Willie shuddered.

Manny slapped his back. "You'll do just fine. Start by getting their info."

Willie turned to the bomb techs and jotted the names of each before releasing them. They wasted no time in leaving the scene, their six-wheeled-drive bomb disposal unit easily climbing out on the two-track. Willie joined Manny already sitting in the Durango. The morning frost had disappeared, and soon the sun would bake dangerously hot. Manny flipped on the AC and leaned back. He closed his eyes, opening them just long enough to tell Willie to wake him when the evidence van arrived, and began checking for light leaks in his eyelids.

>‹›‹›‹

Whistling awoke Manny and he cracked an eye open. Pee Pee had backed the evidence van close to the car and moved sand and thistles out from around and inside the Buick. Manny got out and stretched. Precious Paul, as his parents jokingly named him at birth, whistled while he moved dirt with a trowel that looked more at home weeding a garden than moving dirt from around a skeleton. He grabbed a whisk broom and half crawled into the car, his thin legs jutting from the window opening. He tossed dirt back over his shoulder like a skinny badger digging for grubs, moving dirt away from the body until a complete skeleton began to emerge. He backed out of the car and dusted off his coveralls.

"Just like a sculptor," he said as he stood with his hands on his hips, admiring the bones. "That work of art's always been there. At least it's been buried for a very long time. It's just my job to chip away the dirt, reveal the body for what it is. Or was. I'm like the Michelangelo of the croaker world."

"Could you sculpt a little quicker, Michelangelo?" Manny said as he took off his Stetson and wiped his forehead with a bandanna. "It's getting hotter than hell down here."

"Not as hot as it's going to get," Willie said. He'd materialized soundlessly beside Manny and chin-pointed to a black Suburban bouncing on the trail toward them.

"What? Just your acting chief."

"And my new partner."

"What new partner?"

"Chief Looks Twice's niece. She's going to be a burr under my saddle."

Manny watched the Suburban sliding on the loose gravel. "She's not going to be that big a pain, is she?"

"Is Chief Looks Twice a big pain for you?"

Manny groaned. "That big a pain?"

"That big."

Since childhood, Manny had collided with Leon Looks Twice. They'd wrestled in rival schools, got into fights on weekends. They'd clashed when Manny and he had both worked for the tribal police department, and butted heads during the Jason Red Cloud murder case. Now Lumpy was the acting police chief, and in a position to be an even bigger pain. Apparently, like his niece would be for Willie.

Lt. –Acting Chief Lumpy Looks Twice had come to a skidding stop. The dust cloud continued in their direction and engulfed Manny and Willie, as if punishing them. A petite woman wearing a starched Oglala Sioux Tribal Police uniform emerged from the cloud like an avenging angel, her gold buttons winking in the light. "You forgot me." She smiled at Willie, and dimples popped out on her cheeks. "But I'm sure you didn't mean it."

Willie stuttered to answer when Lumpy shouldered his way around her. He stopped with his hands perched on pudgy hips inches in front of Willie. "Forgot my ass. You disobeyed an order."

"Had to pick Manny up at the White River Visitor's Center and . . ."

"I don't care about Hotshot there. You were ordered to take Janet along and snap her in."

"So she can take my place?"

"What, like you're the only one on Pine Ridge with a college degree? Janet's more than qualified, and with her academic achievements and natural abilities, she'll be an excellent investigator. And soon, if the current investigator disobeys another order. Besides, this is a tribal case."

"Not the way I see it." Manny stepped around the Durango and stood next to Lumpy, still with his hands embedded somewhere on his hips. "Major Crimes Act makes this an FBI case."

Lumpy snorted. "What major crime? Some dumb White guy got himself lost and died of heat exhaustion sixty-five, seventy years ago? Not uncommon here in the Stronghold."

"Homicide falls under federal jurisdiction."

Lumpy smiled. "If you think there's a homicide waiting to be solved in that old heap, hop to it. Until then"—he turned to Willie—"you and Janet give Pee Pee a hand."

Lumpy shook his head as Janet followed Willie over to where Pee Pee was busy excavating the body. "Thought if I'd pair them up together, they'd have some solidarity. Make them both better investigators. Lord knows they both need experience."

"That's why Willie brought me along." Lumpy had thrust Willie at Manny during the Red Cloud case, never dreaming Manny would welcome an opportunity to teach a rookie officer the ropes. "And he's coming along just fine."

Lumpy tilted his head back and laughed. "So he's learning from the Great Manny Tanno, the one who failed to solve the most important homicide of his career?"

Manny bit his lip, itching to confess to Lumpy that he *had* solved the last homicide he'd worked on Pine Ridge two months ago. Jason Red Cloud's murder had been the one homicide in Manny's career that he hadn't solved. At least not publicly. He wanted to confess that he had solved the case. He wanted to scream at Lumpy that he had solved Jason's murder, that the killer had acted in self-defense, when Pee Pee rescued him.

"We have a winner!" Pee Pee called out as he backed out of the car on his belly. He stood and brushed dirt from the front of his coveralls. Dust and dried gumbo, slick mud and half-wet alkaline dust caked his sweaty face and clustered around his eyes, giving him the appearance of an unkempt raccoon. Pee Pee looked in their direction and smiled. A solitary tooth peeked out from gums devoid of other teeth. Pee Pee had forgotten his dentures again. "Contestants—come on down."

"What the hell you hollering about?" Lumpy gathered the hood of his Windbreaker around his face, making him look like a customer at one of those peep shows on East Colfax in Denver. Manny wondered where Lumpy's towel and quarters were stashed. "Do you have to be so happy digging up dead people? What you got?"

Pee Pee turned to Manny. "You got your homicide." He brought a whitened skull, replete with a patch of blond hair still clinging to one temple, from behind his back and thrust it at them. Dirt filtered out of an empty eye socket like an hour-glass swapping sand. Janet Grass ran to a clump of sage and got rid of her breakfast.

Pee Pee's grin showed even the skull had more teeth left than he did as he placed the tip of his pen in a hole in the skull. "I believe this is a bullet hole."

Manny hefted it and turned it to the light. There was nothing unusual about the skull except a clean hole the size of the tip of Pee Pee's pen in the back of the skull.

"No exit wound," Willie said, taking the skull from Manny and turning it over. "Small caliber."

"Good eye." Manny smiled.

"You get a prize." Pee Pee grinned and shucked out a PEZ candy into Willie's hand from an Elvis PEZ dispenser. Pee Pee waved it around so Lumpy saw it before he put it back into his coveralls pocket. Pee Pee had outbid Lumpy on eBay for the original 1960s PEZ dispenser, and Lumpy drooled over it the first time Pee Pee brought it out. Even though Pee Pee was no Elvis collector, he'd refused Lumpy's offers to buy it. Pee Pee got more mileage out of waving it under Lumpy's nose.

"So nearby bombing practice had nothing to do with his death?"

Pee Pee shook his head and his thin, gray ponytail flopped against the side of his face. "There's no evidence that a direct hit on this car killed him. I'd say this man died stopping a bullet to the head."

Lumpy grabbed the skull from Willie and laughed as he turned it over in his hand.

"Something funny?"

Lumpy handed the skull to Pee Pee. "This is what's funny, Hotshot. This guy's been dead for a long time, probably since bombing practice in the forties. And like you said, this is your jurisdiction—just identifying him is going to take up a lot of your free time, time you could be using for something else, like being a pain in my butt. I'll have a nice vacation from your tired ass. Happy investigating."

Lumpy turned to Pee Pee. "Help out our federal friend all he needs, though to hear him tell it, the FBI doesn't need help from us locals. When you finish processing the scene, you can remand whatever you find in that rusted old heap to Agent Tanno here. I mean"—he winked at Manny—"the renowned Senior Special Agent Tanno."

"You about done?" Janet asked. She stood and maneuvered around so she stood in Willie's shadow, looking up at him. "If this were my case, I'd have things underway by now. Guess I'm just a little more organized than you." Her nose came even with a large stain on Willie's shirt. "And it looks like whatever organizational skills you had went south."

Willie's face reddened, but once again Pee Pee came to the rescue. "Just freed the long bones of the leg," Pee Pee called over his shoulder, backing out of the car holding a shin and anklebone with shoes still intact. He handed it to Manny, who turned it over in his hand.

"Looks like late sixties, early seventies," Manny said.

Pee Pee stepped back, and Lumpy grabbed the bones. Pee Pee talked to Manny with his single tooth sticking out of his upper lip. "What, you got Psychic Friends on speed dial?"

"Yeah, what makes you think this body's that recent?" Janet had recovered enough that she was able to act like she knew what she was doing. "Maybe his *wanagi* told him."

Manny shuddered as he thought of the victim's spirit remaining close behind. He handed the leg bone back to Pee Pee. "Look at those tennis shoes."

Pee Pee turned the shoes over and matched Willie's shrug. "So he wore Keds. They've made them since my dad was a youngster."

"But not with those closures." Manny pointed to the Velcro securing the shoe to the foot bone.

"You're right." Lumpy rarely admitted Manny was ever correct. "Velcro didn't come out until late sixties, early seventies. This stiff's fresher than we figured." Lumpy laughed again and slapped Manny on the back. "And with a stiff fresher than we thought, you might just be able to solve this one. At least this croaker will tie you up for a while. That means I won't be dealing with pain-in-the-ass Manny Tanno for a while. Be like a vacation for me."

"I understand with you being the front runner for the appointment to permanent police chief, you've had a lot of pain in your ass lately. I'll bet you can suck start every car driven by the selection committee."

Lumpy turned his back on Manny and spoke to Pee Pee. "Make sure you help our federal friend here all you can. We're just country yokels here, but we're all he's got." Lumpy turned to Janet. "And stick with sloppy boy here like flies on a gut wagon."

Janet looked Willie's uniform up and down. "That won't be hard, Uncle Leon."

Willie shot her a glance and she shrugged. "Family's got to count for something."

Lumpy grabbed the oh-shit handle and struggled to get into the new Suburban with ACTING CHIEF plastered across the hood. He tromped on the gas, kicking up dirt, pelting the old Buick where Pee Pee still worked bent over, sharp dings from rock hitting the car echoing off the steep canyon walls. Just before Lumpy disappeared over the ridge, he hit sagebrush that knocked a wheel cover off. It caromed off a rock and sailed over the side and into the deep canyon like a silver Frisbee. Another victim lost to the Stronghold.

Manny bent to help Pee Pee, but he waved Manny away. "I'll holler if I need you guys. No sense for all of us to sweat our asses off in this heat."

>‹›‹›‹

They sat in the shade of the Durango. Manny wiped the sweat from his face and neck and draped the damp bandanna on top of his head to catch the breeze. *Badlands in August. Just where I want to be.* Shimmering heat waves floated off shrubless spires and turtleback mounds that had eroded with the wind and rain that came upon the Stronghold with sudden anger and chipped away at the land, always angry when men invaded her privacy. *Welcome to the wonderful world of National Parks.*

But the Badlands had been wonderful, back when Unc and he would travel to the rim and leave the car on top, walking down to the bottom in one of their yearly pilgrimages. "It's so desolate down here," Manny said on one of their hikes. "Nothing can live in this heat. And there's no water, Unc. No food."

Unc smiled and chin-pointed to silver and red and yellow blooming flowers crowding each other in the shade of a dead cottonwood tree. "Pick those wild onions and bee plants so we can eat."

They had eaten over a fire fueled with sacred sage, eating cottontail Unc had snared. He thought then that Unc was the smartest man he'd ever met even though he'd never completed school. Unc had run away from the boarding school in Rapid City so many times they gave up dragging him back.

It had all been an adventure for young Manny. In retrospect, he now knew it wouldn't have mattered if he and Unc had done nothing except walk until they dropped, as long as they were together, for Unc always knew where to lead them to show Manny the secrets of the Badlands. As if Unc talked with the spirits that Manny felt even now might be watching them. He rubbed the hair standing on his neck.

That was a lifetime ago, before Manny's brother Reuben was sentenced for an AIM-style murder. That was before Manny vowed to do what was necessary to escape Pine Ridge. That was before Manny's assignment to the FBI Academy as an instructor, and before his fall from grace this summer when he'd failed to solve the Red Cloud homicide case. At least publicly.

"How did the Old Ones ever survive in this heat?" Janet wiped her face with a handkerchief and dabbed at sweat dripping down her neck. "Especially with no water."

"They knew of water holes." Willie took off his Stetson and wiped the inside with his bandanna. He set the hat on the ground, careful not to dirty the pheasant feather hatband. "They passed on that information to other generations."

"Like travel guides."

Willie smiled. "Sort of. We Lakota had to rely on each other for survival, and locations of water holes were primary."

"But the water in this part of the reservation is alkaline. Undrinkable. Clay can't settle to the bottom. Uncle Leon tells me nothing good ever came out of the Stronghold, including water."

"Old Ones sliced prickly pear cactus and dropped them into their full water bladders." Unc's teaching came back to Manny at odd times such as now. "It cleared the water enough they could drink it. And survive."

Janet rolled her eyes and Willie caught it. "It's true. If you'd gotten a degree in Lakota history you'd know some of these things. Which brings up: Just what *is* your degree in?"

"Sociology. Straight 4.0."

Willie laughed. "Just what we need on the police force—a social worker."

"I'm no social worker!" Janet stood and kicked pieces of volcanic rock and alkaline pebbles as she stomped away from the Durango.

"See what I'm stuck with? A damned rookie."

Manny nudged Willie. "Is that your vast experience talking? Seems like you don't have much more experience than she does."

"Well, she bugs me. Always asking questions. Getting underfoot."

"Almost like she's trying to learn?" Manny hadn't minded Willie being underfoot. Working reservation cases with Manny, Willie had shown a desire to be a top investigator. He'd asked appropriate questions during the investigations that Manny had been happy to answer. "Like another officer I work with did recently?"

"Damn it, you know what I mean. She wants to learn so she can take over my job when Uncle Leon decides he wants to stick me back on patrol."

"Over here!" Pee Pee yelled.

Before Pee Pee's words died out Willie had jumped to his feet and ran to the car, with Janet and Manny close behind. "What's the yelling about?"

Pee Pee popped a PEZ into his mouth and gummed it as his one fang shone through his wind-cracked lips. "Bonus round!"

Pee Pee used the car to help himself stand and pointed to the windowless opening. "Bonus round. Some lucky contestant will have the pleasure of investigating two more croakers." Pee Pee gave them a come-hither gesture with his finger and dropped back onto his knees. Red flannel fluttered, still attached to an arm bone jutting up from the exposed sand. Beside the white cloth a brown muslin shirt clung to the remains of a breastbone.

"When I got to stiff one"—he turned to Janet—"that's what we call our customers, 'stiffs'." He winked at Manny and turned back to Janet. "When I finished digging stiff one out of the dirt, I saw an arm bone with red cloth still attached to it underneath him, buried to the wrist. Now, I got no fancy degree like you three, but I suspected stiff one didn't come from the factory with three arms, the other two which I had already carted off to the evidence van. So I got to sculpturing some more and uncovered two more lovely souls. My uneducated guess is those two would be that sixty-five- or seventy-year-old case that the chief mentioned. I'd wager they've been here since the bombing range was active, given the amount of dirt that's blown into the car."

"Sixty or seventy years," Janet said under her breath. "How will we ever figure out who they are, let alone what or who killed them."

"FM," Willie said, brushing dirt from his uniform trousers.

"FM?"

"Friggin' Magic. We can do wondrous things nowadays," Pee Pee said, meeting Manny's stare as if he were defending his years of evidence experience. "Stuff like DNA profiles, missing persons records, dental records."

Janet turned away from the two skeletons. "But if we don't know who they are, how are we ever going to find out who their dentist was?"

"If you'd gotten a degree in criminal justice instead of sociology"—Willie smiled—"you'd know these things."

><><><

"When's he going to be done with that mumbo jumbo?" Janet chin-pointed to Willie. He stood beside the Buick, his black uniform shirt coated with white alkaline dust, settling heavier around the armpits and middle of his back where the sweat broke through, his singing rising and falling in time with the gusts of wind that coated the Durango with dirt.

"He needs to do a Sending Away ceremony for the spirits that still linger." Goose bumps grew on Manny's arms, and he wished Janet hadn't asked.

"That's old superstitious stuff they tried to teach us in school. We've evolved beyond that now."

Three months ago Manny would have agreed with her, before he'd experienced visions of Wounded Knee, and visions of Jason Red Cloud that screamed for Manny to find his killer and allow Jason's *wanagi* to travel south along the Spirit Road, the *Wanagi Tacanku*. He had denied his Lakota heritage then, as Janet did now. He knew how she felt, knew she tossed aside the old ways, just as he had, forgetting where he came from as he lived comfortably in the White man's world to the east. Now he wasn't sure, and a part of him sympathized with Janet's rejection of tradition.

"What's he doing now?"

Willie dipped into his *wopiye*, his medicine pouch, and tossed *peji wacanga* into the air. The sweetgrass seemed to hang on the breeze for solemn moments before being carried away. "He's praying to the four winds. Have you never heard that a man has four *wanagi,* four spirits? Those victims' first spirits—their *niya*—are gone, but the other three are there. Willie's wishing them well as they travel along the Spirit Road."

"Right." Janet sat back in the seat, arms crossed, looking out the side window. Willie's voice—singing the *Lowanpi*. The *wakan* songs rose and fell with an eerie staccato captured by the ashen rock formations comprising the Badlands. Nothing escapes the Stronghold.

><><><

Manny dozed, his head falling back against the headrest, lulled by Willie's voice as he performed the Sending Away ceremony under the blistering noonday sun. Manny dreamed of long ago times when the Oglala were one with others of the Oceti Sakowin, Seven Council Fires, strong and able and capable of driving their enemies from this place that sheltered them in times of crises. Old Ones came to this Sheltering Place to pray to the Great Mysterious. And so many would be buried in this Sheltering Place where their spirits would be helped south to the Milky Way.

Manny sat upright when Willie's voice stopped, realizing he was here in the Durango, with Janet snoring in the backseat. Sweat beaded on Manny's forehead and he wiped it with his shirtsleeve. He breathed deep to ease his heart thumping in his chest. Had he been dreaming just now when he felt someone tug at the corner of his sleeve? The hairs stood on the nape of his neck just like they had when he came here with Unc, feelings a boy could never explain, any more than the grown man could now.

Willie climbed back into the car. Janet leaned over the seat and started to speak, but Manny shook his head and she dropped back, arms crossed, glaring at Manny. Willie started out of the Badlands bottom and was nearly to the top when he stopped and grabbed his cell. "Shit! No signal."

"You calling pizza delivery or something?"

"I wanted to tell Pee Pee to tow that car for evidence."

"Don't you think he knows to do that?"

Willie shrugged and drove slowly toward the rim. "Even damn cell signals don't escape the Stronghold."

"Then how do those people living down there call out?" Janet had leaned back over the seat and her arms brushed Willie's neck. He made no attempt to pull back from her.

"What people?"

"Those ones living in that cabin down there." She pointed to a cabin a quarter mile away nestled between a steep cliff and a creek washout. A shallow dirt road led to the cabin.

Manny grabbed his binos. The sun-bleached cabin showed gaps in the logs where mud chinking had fallen out over the years. A single smokestack leaned at an awkward angle, as if the constant wind had caused the metal to grow that way as scrub junipers did here. But the cabin itself stood straight and proud. "Just an old shack. Doubt if anyone lives there."

Willie looked through the field glasses and handed them to Janet. "That's Moses Ten Bears's old cabin."

Janet grabbed the binoculars. "Shit—that the cabin that belonged to that old dude who was such a good artist?"

Willie frowned at her while he took the binoculars and eyeballed the cabin again. "Moses Ten Bears was one of the last of the great Oglala sacred men, the last of the great *wicasa wakan*. Not just some old dude." He put the glasses back under the seat. "Margaret Catches and I tried to find the Ten Bears cabin last summer."

"Why would you do that?" Janet asked.

"We thought his *Sicun*, his spirit, might still linger."

"If a sacred man performs the proper rituals," Unc had told Manny one night huddled around the fire on the lip of the Stronghold, "the *Sicun* of another holy man will enter him, make his own power stronger. Sacred men need other *Sicun* to build their power. Only then can they give it away to help others."

Manny had shuddered with the thought, as he did now, thinking of Willie studying with Margaret Catches to be such a sacred man, to possess power that would allow him to help those with Indian sicknesses, sickness of the spirit. Perhaps Moses Ten Bears's spirit had lingered for so many generations waiting for the right holy man to take possession of his *Sicun*.

"Let's hike down there and see what's left inside." Janet grabbed for the door latch, but Willie stopped her.

"That'd be trespassing. That cabin's on deeded land that belongs to Marshal Ten Bears—Moses's grandson."

"How you know so much about it?"

Willie shrugged off Janet's arm against his neck and started driving up the two-track. "The Heritage Committee tried to pressure Marshal to move his cabin into Pine Ridge Village last year. They wanted to make it part of their Heritage Exhibit, display it directly across from Billy Mills Hall. But Marshal told them to stay off his land or else."

"That so?" Janet asked.

" 'Fraid so," Manny said. "Marshal told the committee he used the cabin now and again. Said his grandfather would have wanted it left right where it sits, there at the edge of the Stronghold. Or so my brother, Reuben, told me one night after a sweat. Marshal said if the money were right he'd sell it, though."

"I take it the Heritage Committee told him to pack sand?"

Manny nodded. "In a polite way. They figure history they have to pay for isn't history worth displaying."

As they made their last half-mile ascent out of the canyon, Manny looked back down at the shack. Angry heat waves fought the wind for control of the valley, and for just a heartbeat the cabin disappeared. When it reappeared once more, a feeling of peace overcame Manny, as if he were welcomed to this place, as if Grandfather Moses welcomed them all and offered his protection from the Stronghold's brutality.

CHAPTER 3

Pee Pee shucked popcorn into his mouth as he waltzed through the swinging autopsy room doors. He stopped midstride, mouth agape. He looked odd standing there with his full set of teeth, bad fitting with a pronounced overbite, gawking at Manny. "You look like hell."

"I feel like hell," Manny said.

"Bad night?"

"Long night. Let's just say there were no sheep left to count."

"Clara?"

Manny nodded. "I think she's trying to make me into an Indian Johnny Stud."

"Poor baby." Pee Pee handed Manny the bag of popcorn. He grabbed a handful, and Pee Pee flashed Janet a toothy grin. "How about you sweetcheeks?"

Janet shook her head, her eyes transfixed on the sheets covering the skeletal remains of the three victims on the autopsy tables.

"Might help your green."

She ignored him and continued staring at the sheet.

"I'll take some." Willie sank an enormous hand into the bag and came away with half the popcorn. Some spilled on his uniform shirt but he made no attempt to brush it away, or cover the butter stain it made on one pocket. He leaned over and whispered to Manny, "This is my first autopsy. Do we help the doc or anything?"

"Just watch. Doc Gruesome will record everything." He jerked his thumb over his shoulder. "But you might keep an eye on Janet so she doesn't hit her head when she faints."

Janet jumped when the medical examiner came whistling through the doors. Doc Grooson slapped Pee Pee on the back and tipped an imaginary hat to Janet. He smiled at the sheet. "And who will we be talking with this fine morning?"

No wonder we call him Doc Gruesome.

"Don't we have to mask up or something?" Janet stammered, moving away from the examination room when Doc Gruesome tossed the sheet aside. "Put on robes?"

Doc Gruesome grabbed the last of the popcorn and looked at the clipboard hanging from the end of the stainless steel table. "We would if we were talking with fresh bodies, but these have decomposed long before you were born. And gowns and masks would interfere with our snacks. Besides"— he winked at Janet—"I got a cultural anthropologist coming in from University of South Dakota after we talk with these three lovely souls."

He crunched down on an old maid as he turned to the first pile of bones on the table. "Since you're the first one found," he addressed the body under the sheet, "You'll be the first we visit with."

He turned on the microphone hanging from the ceiling and smiled at Janet. "Just in case this fella says something memorable."

>‹›‹›‹

Manny stood beside an elderly couple at the Burger King order counter. They glanced his way, bent and whispered to each
other, then looked his way again. At one time, Manny would
have felt flattered that they had recognized him, perhaps from
a *Newsweek* article, or a CNN interview concerning some
high-profile case he was investigating at the time. Now it just
felt as if they talked in hushed tones about the Great Manny
Tanno, solver of all homicides. Except the Red Cloud case and
the one that dragged him away from his FBI Academy position and landed him this lovely transfer to the Rapid City
Field Office.

Willie slouched beside him and ordered a Whopper and
fries, ignoring Janet standing in line beside him, pale and silent since the forensic autopsy. Manny caught the wonderful
odor of hot grease wafting past his nose, grease that all things
tasty would be cooked in. He was about to match Willie's order of a Whopper when Clara popped into his mind, and he
ordered the chef salad instead. Extra pounds sneaking upon
him to match his diabetes diagnosis made him think twice
about ordering the good stuff. That and Clara's scowling face
popping into his head.

Pee Pee followed suit and grabbed a salad. "Out of solidarity for Johnny Stud." He smiled as he drowned his salad with
four packs of full-fat ranch dressing. "Going to eat yours?"
He motioned to Manny's cheese and crouton packs.

"And invoke the wrath of the Health Nazi?"

Pee Pee shrugged and grabbed the packets, doubling the
cheese and croutons smothering his greens.

Willie picked at his hamburger and looked at it, nibbling
at the outside. Even though he still presented an imposing figure, his trousers were now a size too big and his shirt hung
loose over shoulders that slumped more often now. The old

Willie would have wolfed the burger down in two bites and ordered another. The new, depressed Willie just picked at it. Even visits to his aunt Lizzy in the state mental hospital couldn't bring Willie out of it. And neither could Manny.

Janet nibbled at her Chicken Tenders. "How long will DNA take to come back?"

Pee Pee licked dressing that had leaked out of the small pack and settled on the web of his hand. "Depends. We'll have it back from the FBI lab in a couple days if Manny can grease the wheels."

Grease again. "I'll overnight the samples today. DNA takes a while to come back, but I've still got some pull with the lab." Manny stabbed his salad with the flimsy plastic fork/spoon combination, the spork, jail being the only other place in the civilized world where you had to eat with one of these fast-food instruments of torture. Manny prayed the spork wouldn't break like it usually did when he stabbed salad. Greens always reminded him of cows grazing. *Wakan Tanka* had made him a Lakota, a carnivore, and he couldn't imagine his ancestors sitting around the campfire and diving into a Caesar salad. But the ancients didn't have Clara's line of questioning to contend with at the end of the day. "I intend to wrap this up quick."

"Why the rush?" Janet finally spoke. "The first body's been in that car longer than I've been alive. And the other two longer than any of us."

"I just want to piss Lumpy off." Manny smiled at her. "I mean, Uncle Leon. He's got it in his mind that this will keep me tied up for some time. For the record, I'd just as soon be a pain in his behind." Manny knew that whatever he said in front of Janet would get back to Lumpy. That in itself was worth having Janet around.

Willie left the rest of his burger on the plate and stood for a soda refill. "That draft card we found in the first stiff's wallet should get things rolling."

"I'd just like to know what caliber the poor bastard was shot with," Pee Pee said as he heaped more cheese onto his salad, making it slightly less calorie-dense than Willie's Whopper. "Doc Gruesome said gray matter hadn't leaked out, which meant the guy lived for some time before he died. A small caliber projectile, most likely."

At the mention of gray matter leaking out of the victim's skull, a young couple in the booth beside them squirmed in their seats. Looking like twins, with their cardigan sweaters and tweed gray golfer hats, they shot Pee Pee a worried look as if they shared a booth with Charles Manson or Jeffrey Dahmer.

"Do they usually mummify like that?" Janet was coming around, shaking off the effects of watching her first autopsy. Or first three. "You'd think the badgers or coyotes would snack on them."

The couple behind them left their remaining food on the table and hurried out, eyes darting to the booth they'd just escaped from. Manny eyed the burgers the couple left. Even used hamburgers appealed to him. "The dryness of the Badlands often causes bodies to mummify." Janet leaned across the table listening to Manny and her hand brushed against Willie's arm. "Probably the reason they weren't snacked on was they all died in that car. Or at least all three ended up inside. Made it hard for predators to get to them. We'll know when we look it over, but I suspect not every window shattered from the bombing nearby. By the time the elements ate enough of the car away where critters could get to them, the victims were too decomposed to be appealing to scavengers."

Janet shook her head. "But I still can't figure out the oldest two—how was it they were lying under the guy with the tennis shoes?"

"What's puzzling?" Pee Pee finished his salad and patted his stomach. "Great to be eating healthy." He got up and returned within moments carrying a triple-decker hot fudge sundae. Manny eyed the sundae, envious of Pee Pee, not for his single tooth, but because he could eat anything and stay rail thin.

Pee Pee sat beside Manny, the ice cream inches from Manny's salivating mouth. "The last two—or should I say the first two that died in that car—were long dead before passenger number three came along. By the looks of that whiskey bottle busted on the floorboard, I'd say those first two drove out there to pass the jug. Wouldn't be the first time one of our people whiled away an afternoon sucking the sauce."

"But why way out there?" Janet asked.

"It was as illegal to have booze back on the reservation then as it is today," Willie said. "They didn't want to get caught then any more than young folks do nowadays."

Manny eyed Pee Pee's sundae, with chocolate and caramel dripping over the sides of vanilla ice cream. If only Pee Pee would leave for a moment, go to the bathroom or something, even for just a second. "But that doesn't explain the White guy with the Indian. Whites didn't need to sneak drinks back then—they could drink any time they wished."

"Maybe Doc Gruesome was wrong about the one being Caucasian," Janet said. "Maybe both those bodies were Indians."

Pee Pee stopped the spoonful of sundae midmouth. "Doc wasn't wrong. Pelvis and facial bones clearly show one was *wasicu*."

Willie said, backing away from Janet's touch, "Maybe he wanted to show some solidarity with the Indian."

"Sure." Pee Pee licked his chocolate-covered lips as if to emphasize Willie's point. "Just like I just did with Manny when I ordered a healthy salad."

><><><><

Manny jotted on his pocket notebook and thanked the person on the other end of the phone. "That partial draft card came back to Gunnar Janssen. DOD will fax a copy of the original when they locate it in the archives."

Willie slowed to allow two skateboarders to cross the road, jeans sliding over their pale butts, exposing their tighty-whities. "You were living on the rez in the seventies. Gunnar Janssen ring a bell with you?"

Manny shook his head, more to clear it from the memory of the death that lingered over the autopsy table than anything else. Intellectually, he knew the bones Doc Gruesome examined were too old to smell anymore. He'd just never gotten used to the imaginary odor hovering over old bodies. "Never heard of him, but his Social Security card has a 504 number—South Dakota. Homegrown—and buried—boy. We might track the name through DMV."

"Can I help with something?" Janet gazed into a small pocket mirror as she reapplied lip gloss, the last having been abraded when she lost her breakfast at the autopsy.

"We do need help." Willie batted his eyes at Janet.

She smiled. "Anything."

Willie motioned to Pee Pee sitting in the backseat beside her. He held his dentures and picked food out of them with a pocketknife. "You mind dropping Janet off at the *Rapid City Journal* office?"

Janet snapped her compact shut. "What am I supposed to do there?"

"Research."

"Research what?"

Willie stopped beside Pee Pee's truck in the morgue parking lot. "I need you to find all the missing persons reports from the years 1964 through 1972, the years the draft was in effect. And"—he winked at Manny—"missing persons from the early forties, when the bombing range was most active."

"Where will you be?"

"Investigating."

Janet glared after Willie as he pulled out of the parking lot even before Pee Pee fished his keys from his pocket.

"What's the chance of Janet finding something?" Manny asked as he looked out the back window at Janet fuming, hands on her hips, staring at them as she stood beside Pee Pee's truck.

"Slim. But it'll keep her busy. Do you know what Doreen will do if she even suspects I'm messing around with Janet?"

"That Big Eagle girl from Ft. Thompson?"

Willie nodded. "Your typical mad Lakota woman. Things haven't been going so good lately even before Janet was assigned to me."

"You still got the nightmares?"

Willie nodded. "I can't seem to shake the image of Aunt Lizzy cooped up in the loony bin."

Manny had encouraged Willie to talk about his aunt Lizzy. He had been as close to his aunt as a son is to a mother, and he struggled daily with her spending her time these days doing macramé and tatting doilies in the South Dakota State Mental Hospital.

"It was best for her and it was best for the tribe. You did your job."

Willie snorted and set his hat on the seat divider. "Sure. I did my job, and now where the hell do I go? What the hell do I do—Aunt Lizzy's still locked up. Now this fight with Doreen. She'll have my jewels on a skewer if she thinks I'm messing around with Janet."

"Don't let that happen. Clara's got mine and look what a mess I am."

Manny dialed the Department of Motor Vehicles. After explaining he needed Gunnar Janssen's information, he had his answers within minutes. "The address he used when he had a valid DL was the men's dorm at Black Hills State in Spearfish. Let's take a drive up there."

"Anything to put distance between me and Janet," Willie said and turned onto I90 for the thirty-mile drive.

>○○○<

"Maybe the police department can help us."

"Maybe." Manny climbed into the Durango parked in a visitor's slot at Black Hills State. Students crossing the lawn on their way to summer classes stared at the Oglala Sioux Tribe markings on the door. "Their records didn't help much."

Manny shrugged. "Might when we find out why Gunnar left school midsemester in '69."

Willie drove through the campus and onto Jackson Boulevard. "It makes no sense that an honor student would slip academically so far that he was failing most of his classes."

"Obviously something else had been going on in his life. Maybe something that he needed help with."

"Such as?"

Manny shrugged. "Can't say. But might have been something a good counselor could have helped him with."

"Don't start that shit again!"

"Maybe if you just talked with someone. I know the man that does post-traumatic counseling for officers at the Rapid City PD. I know he'd . . ."

"I'll talk with someone in my own time."

Willie had resisted Manny's attempts to line him up with a good depression therapist. Perhaps Willie was right. Perhaps in his own time he would break down and talk with someone. Manny was just grateful Willie had spoken of it in passing this morning. Perhaps Willie was thinking along the lines of a therapist.

Willie pulled into a parking spot at the Spearfish PD. A patrolman gawked as he got in his cruiser and motored away.

Willie looked after the cruiser and shook his head. "You'd think no one ever saw us Skins before. Or an Oglala tribal vehicle."

"Probably not one without whiskey dents."

"That's 'cause I haven't let you drive."

They entered the Spearfish Police Department and Manny badged the receptionist. She buzzed them through the security door and directed them to the records section. Down the hall a blond woman wearing headphones around her graying temples pec-pec-pecked at a computer terminal. When she noticed them leaning on the half door leading into her office, she hit a foot pedal and stood. She smoothed the skirt covering her thick thighs that ran all the way down to lace-up clodhoppers with dried cow dung on the soles. She smelled like she'd tramped around a recent rodeo and forgotten to change shoes before work. Manny was certain she'd not forgotten to change, and just as certain she was comfortable coming off the farm to work in the office. Her name tag proclaimed her Helga, and Manny imagined her straddling a three-legged stool, wringing the last milk from some hapless Holstein's teats.

He fought to suppress the odor of cow crap and explained why they were there. "Gunnar would have lived here in the late sixties when he attended Black Hills State."

"Long time ago," Helga said as if, in voicing it, the request would fly out the window, like the odor that flew past Manny's nose.

He turned away. "Long time, indeed."

She turned her attention to Willie and smiled. Willie blushed. When it became evident to her that they were going to actually wait until she found the records, she turned on her heels and returned to her computer. She sat behind her terminal, and Manny thought she'd returned to transcribing her report. "How do you spell Janssen?"

Manny spelled Gunnar's name and she continued typing.

After several minutes, she stood and walked to a rotary file cabinet and reached high. A sizable clump of hair sprang from her armpit, and Manny knew he'd just met his first granola head. He had heard Spearfish was full of them. She handed him a microfiche roll. "This can't leave the office."

"Of course." Manny wanted to reassure her he was privy to any number of documents affecting national security, that a roll of microfilm was safe in his hands. "You have a reader?"

"Follow me." She sighed and led them to a cramped office with archive boxes piled inches from the ceiling. She cleared boxes off a railroad chair missing one arm, and blew dust off the ancient microfiche screen. She hiked her skirt up and polished the screen. She only managed to move the dust from one side of the reader to the other. "Just slip the roll in here."

"I've used these before"—Manny smiled—"back when I was a rookie at the Pine Ridge PD."

"Did I detect some condescension in her voice?" Willie said when Helga's footsteps faded down the hallway. "Almost sounded like you."

"I think she was angry because I wouldn't leave you two alone in the office. I think she might be sweet on you."

"Whatever."

Manny adjusted the focus and started his search in 1966, working forward. "Shit."

"Shit what?" Willie stood from the chair and leaned over Manny's shoulder.

"Got it. Gunnar went missing in the fall of 1969. Look who filed the missing person report." Manny canted the screen so Willie could read it.

"Alex High Elk."

"So?"

"Maybe you should watch something on the tube besides sports once in a while."

"So some High Elk reported Gunnar missing. So what?"

"Alexander Hamilton High Elk. Federal appellate judge out of Sioux Falls. And recently nominated for the U.S. Supreme Court. Went by Alex during his college days."

"Shit!"

"That's what I said." Manny read aloud the missing person report. Alex High Elk had reported his college roommate missing in the fall of 1969. High Elk told the investigating officer that Gunnar's parents lived in Iowa, but that he knew little more about his friend. The report concluded that another roommate, Joe Dozi, was the only other person who might have useful information.

"Maybe Judge High Elk will remember something more about Gunnar. Do you think the tribe will fly me to Washington to interview him? I understand Senate confirmation hearings on him are about to convene in two weeks."

"See, you do watch something beside sports now and again. But even the bureau wouldn't fly *me* to Washington to interview someone on a forty-year-old homicide. I'll ask someone from our D.C. office to talk with him."

"An all expenses paid trip to Washington down the drain. What else is in the report?"

Manny scrolled the microfiche reader and read an attached arrest report. Gunnar had been arrested just a week before he disappeared, along with his roommate Alex High Elk. "Too coincidental."

"What is?"

Manny took off his reading glasses. "It's too handy that Gunnar disappears a week after he was arrested fighting with the very guy that reported him missing."

Manny walked into the hallway and found Helga typing at her desk, oblivious to anything except what came through her headphones. She noticed him standing by her door and shut the dictation machine off. She stood and tossed the headphones on her desk.

"Now what is it?"

"The arresting officer on Gunnar's arrest—Frank Willis—still around here?"

"You missed him by ten years."

"Quit?"

"Quit life. You can find him in the Veterans Cemetery outside Sturgis."

"How about the officer who took the missing report, Micah Crowder?"

Helga stepped closer. The office was heating up and Manny could tell she wore no deodorant. Or was that her boots? "Micah Crowder left the department right after that incident to run for sheriff. Lost big, from what the old-timers said."

"He still around?"

"As in alive?"

"Alive and around."

She shrugged. "He raises hell over at the retirement home, Parkside Manor. You'll find him ruining shuffleboard games, or organizing protests against the food, or looking up some old gal's skirt. Old-timers said he turned into a horse's patoot after he lost the election."

"Can I get a copy of this report?"

Helga smiled and Manny noticed a large gap between her front teeth. "For a price."

"Don't tell me—something like dinner?"

She frowned. "Not with you. Him." She jerked her thumb at Willie standing in the hall looking absently at courthouse construction photos hanging on the wall. "It'll take a lot of work to copy a report on microfiche. But I'll have it ready for you Wednesday, say around suppertime?"

Manny forced himself to smile at her as he led Willie out of the station. What he had to sacrifice for the success of a case—promise her Willie.

>‹›‹›‹

An elderly woman with a decided leeward limp scowled at the Durango when Willie parked in an empty spot in the Parkside Manor. "Can't read?" she screeched.

Willie nodded to the sign in front of the Durango. "Sure, it's R. Head's parking spot. But he's not here and this is official police business."

"Suit yourself, sonny, but if Richard catches you in his spot, you'll get a tongue-lashing you won't soon forget."

"Fair enough. We're looking for Micah Crowder."

"You arresting that old bastard?"

"We just need to speak with him." Manny read her name tag, which like her gimp, was slightly askew. "It's pretty important, Joey."

She softened at the sound of her name and stepped closer to Manny, her sheer, static-laden blouse attracted to his Dockers. Her wide smile reminded Manny of Pee Pee without his dentures. "This way."

She led them into the Manor and down a long hallway. "You spoken for?"

Manny avoided Willie's grin. "The government. You could say I'm married to my job."

"Ever think of cheating?"

They arrived at a sliding glass door at the end of the hallway, and Jocy pointed to a patio outside. "That's Micah."

A man teetered on the edge of a lawn chair as he trained a garden hose on two women twice Manny's age. Their clothes drenched, they laughed as the man played a stream of water over their chests.

"Micah!" Joey turned the spigot and the water flowed to a trickle.

"Oh, Joey." One woman gathered her top in her hands and

wrung out the water. Her boobs drooped decidedly south through the wet shirt. "Micah was just showing us what a wet T-shirt contest was."

"Yeah." The other woman, younger and thinner and one time attractive, stepped closer to Joey. Manny felt like a pervert for watching her chest. "He was just cooling us off. He's just being a sweet guy. Besides, it's hot today."

"Go inside where it's air-conditioned."

"Air went to hell a month ago," Droopy Boobs said. "Richard promised he'd get it fixed."

Thinner laughed. "About Christmastime when we're knocking icicles off our asses he will." She grabbed Droopy Boobs by the hand and disappeared through the sliding glass doors.

Joey looked after them as she talked to the back of Micah's head. "These officers are here to see you."

Micah stood easily and turned toward them. With his full head of thick, black hair flecked with white around the temples, he could have passed for a man in his fifties, and reminded Manny of golfers on those Florida retirement commercials. "You must finally be taking my complaints seriously." He grinned at Joey. His perfect teeth contrasted with her snaggletoothed smile. "Or maybe they're here to cart you off."

Joey turned and stomped through the door. Micah waited until her footsteps had died down before extending his hand, firm and well manicured. "Please sit."

Micah motioned to a green glass-topped table with chairs situated around a center hole for an umbrella to cut the sun. If there had been an umbrella. "Know why this dump is called the Parkside?" He didn't wait for an answer. "Me either. The closest thing to a park is where I park my wrinkled old ass in one of these rusty chairs. Now tell me what you want to see this old man about."

"Gunnar Janssen. He went missing . . ."

"In '69. Kid was failing school and just took off."

"You remember?"

"Quite well."

"He's been found." Manny explained that Gunnar had been interred in an old Buick Roadmaster at the Badlands Bombing Range, and that he'd been found with a bullet hole in the back of his skull.

"I'd lay my next Social Security check that damned Judge High Elk is behind it."

"What makes you think that?" Willie leaned close enough to Micah that he leaned back in his chair.

"Could it be that Judge High Elk is Lakota?"

Micah's eyes narrowed, his brows coming together as he glared at Willie. He still had some fire left in his makeup. "Hell no, it don't. I don't have a bigoted bone in my body, bigun. It's 'cause High Elk and Gunnar got arrested fighting each other just a week before High Elk reports his buddy missing. That didn't pass the smell test."

"You ever get any leads on Gunnar?" Manny cut in. The last thing he needed now was a source of information to take offense and clam up. "You find any reason he just up and left?"

"None," Micah said, but continued to stare Willie down. "I went into his apartment—he'd moved out of the dorm he shared with High Elk two weeks before he disappeared—and found some topo maps of the Badlands. Had notes over it like he was doing some prospecting there."

"Didn't think there was anything worth prospecting for in the Badlands."

Micah laughed. "None of us did, and we got a good chuckle out of it at the station house. But I thought I'd follow up on a long shot and go there, poke around. But I never found Gunnar or where he might have gone."

Nothing leaves the Stronghold. "Not even a SWAG."

"SWAG?"

"Scientific Wild Ass Guess."

"Judge High Elk," Micah blurted. " 'Course, he wasn't a judge back then."

"You don't like him much, do you?"

Micah shook out a Marlboro and lit it. *Not a Camel, but it would do right about now.* Manny patted his pocket out of habit for one of his beloved friends that he'd abandoned three months ago for the healthy lifestyle. He suppressed the urge to bum one from Micah. "When Alex High Elk was being considered for the federal bench, one of your FBI agents looked me up on a background investigation. Asked what I thought of him. I told them I thought High Elk was dirty, that he'd had a hand in Gunnar's disappearance. Made no difference, though. He still got appointed the judgeship."

"You aware he's been nominated for the Supreme Court?"

"Sure I am. The president's making a big deal out of it. First Native American Supreme Court Justice. Guess I'll have to fire off some letters to the editor before his confirmation's final, not that my bitching will have any effect."

"How about this other friend of Gunnar's"—Willie thumbed through his notebook—"this Joe Dozi?"

Micah sat back in his chair and looked away. When he spoke, he did so slowly and deliberately so as not to lose effect. "That Joe Dozi's a dangerous SOB. He's always lived on the fringe."

"So you remember him?"

Micah's eyes narrowed and he leaned closer to Willie. "Sure, bigun, I remember him. He hung around with High Elk and Gunnar, though I don't know why the hell he ever went to college. He fell flat on his ass academically, what with the boozing and partying. We'd arrest him once a week back then and he always had some surprise for us." Micah rolled his shirtsleeve up to expose a four-inch scar that ran from his shoulder to his bicep. "Son of a bitch knifed me in the Bon Ton one night when I went to slap cuffs on him. Before I even saw the knife he cut me."

"He get sent up for the assault?"

Micah laughed and pulled his sleeve down. "Damned circuit judge Wainwright gave him the choice of the army or state penitentiary."

"I take it the army was blessed with his warm body?"

Micah nodded and flicked his cigarette butt into a flower box that was more like a weed box, with shriveled plants and cigarette butts stuck in it like people expected them to grow into cigarette plants. "Son of a bitch did three tours in 'Nam. Ended up being a bonafide hero."

"Made it back?"

"Unfortunately. Owns a motorcycle shop in Sturgis that specializes in vintage iron. But he won't talk to you about the judge."

"Attitude?"

He frowned at Willie. "You got it, bigun. He hates authority, though I always thought that kind of ironic, hating authority while being the judge's best friend."

"All the same to you, I think we'll visit with him." Manny stood and stretched.

"Suit yourself, but you watch your ass. He's still a coyote."

Willie followed Manny to the parking lot just as a blue MINI Cooper, complete with the Union Jack splattered across the hood, skidded to a stop behind the Durango and hemmed it in. A wafer-thin man, pale toothpicks jutting from pocketed tan hiking shorts, sprang from the car and blocked Manny's way to the Durango. "Can you not read, man? You're in my parking spot."

Willie stepped close to him and looked down. The man

came to Willie's breast pocket. "You weren't here when we pulled in. I had to park someplace. We're leaving now."

He eyed the OST decal on the side of the door, and eyed Willie's sloppy uniform. "Maybe I'll call our local police."

"Look Mister Head." Manny motioned to the RESERVED sign the Durango was parked in front of. "Can I call you Richard? How would it look if the papers mentioned their very own Richard Head was an antilaw administrator? I'd bet the state office overseeing retirement homes would take notice. Probably even pull a surprise inspection, not that this Shangri-la of a retirement home couldn't pass muster, with no air-conditioning. Poor upkeep. See what I'm getting at here, Richard? See what could happen if one makes himself noticeable? The state inspectors are absolutely the Untouchables."

Richard stepped back, his mouth agape, showing uniformly stained and uneven English teeth, before climbing into his MINI and moving so Willie could pull away. As they pulled out of the parking lot, Richard Head had gotten out of his car and looked after them as if he expected a squad of inspectors to come roaring up, clipboards in hand as they descended on the Parkside.

>◇◇◇◇<

Janet Grass cursed Willie the entire three miles from the *Rapid City Journal* offices to Clara's house on Skyline Drive. "Don't ever send me on some frickin' wild duck chase . . ."

"Goose." Willie smiled. "It's wild-goose chase."

"Whatever. It was terrible, being down in that musty basement all alone with those dusty archives." She scratched her arm, then her head, then back to her arm as if she'd been infected with bugs.

"Just tell me what you found out about Gunnar."

"He was reported missing . . ."

"In the fall of 1969."

"How'd you know that?"

"I had a vision."

"Bullshit." Janet slugged Willie on the arm. "You just wanted to get rid of me for the day."

Willie feigned pain. "Why would I send my girl Friday away? Or is it Monday today? Anyway, the chief wants me to snap you in, teach you the tricks of the investigator's trade. That musty archive office is part of our job."

"Do you want to hear the rest?"

"We're on pins and needles and my behind hurts just waiting for your report."

"What did you find out?" Manny pushed.

Janet unbuttoned her top two uniform buttons and withdrew a notebook. She left it unbuttoned as she flipped pages, cooling her neck off. "Gunnar Janssen was president of the Black Hills State Geological Club, even though he was just a junior. Guess all the money his parents sent him had something to do with that."

"Money?" Manny turned in the seat. "What money?"

"Gunnar came here from Des Moines—his parents owned a string of catering businesses throughout Iowa. When his freshman year ended, he stayed in Spearfish. He was fascinated with the Badlands. Guess they don't have any fossils in Iowa."

"Only those like Micah Crowder."

"Who's Micah Crowder?"

"I'll explain later. What did the newspaper say about Gunnar's money?"

Janet thumbed to another page and waited for a long moment, drawing out the drama before she explained. "Nothing direct, except the reporter who interviewed students after he went missing claimed Gunnar always had money, always bought the beer when they went out partying. And they quoted a Spearfish policeman as saying he doubted Gunnar had gone into the Badlands. What's that all about?"

Manny explained Micah Crowder searching Gunnar's room and finding Badlands maps and trail guides, and how he'd gone there looking for Gunnar, but had been unsuccessful. "It's doubtful, but his folks could still be alive. Might be a place to start, looking them up."

Janet laughed. "Maybe Mr. Holy Man here might be able to look them up—they died in a boating accident the year after Gunnar disappeared."

"One day, you'll see the importance of harmony with the spirits, with keeping the circle unbroken," Willie said.

As if to punctuate his argument, they reached the top of Skyline Drive, and an eerie orange glow cast by the sun threw long, erratic shadows across the houses. Manny felt Janet shudder through the seat, and she leaned farther over closer to Willie. "Maybe Clara's not awake."

"Fat chance. She's probably waiting for me with whip in hand."

"Why'd you move in with her in the first place?" Janet's arms brushed Willie's neck, leaning even farther over to peer at Clara's house as they pulled into the driveway. Sometime between retrieving her notebook and now, another shirt button had opened up, and Manny averted his eyes. He'd see enough of that tonight. "Guess I just fell in love with her."

"Why?"

"Why what?"

She rolled her eyes. "There must have been some overriding reason you love her."

Manny had often thought of that, of the feelings he'd experienced that first day at the Red Cloud Development Corporation when acting CEO Clara Downing greeted him. She'd treated him with honesty and dignity from the start, and

Manny didn't have to pretend he was someone else with her. "I just do."

"Then you should welcome her romance, her stamina." She nudged Willie, who sat straight ahead so as not to stare at Janet's shirt.

"At this stage of my life, I welcome BENGAY and Tylenol more than anything else. See her?"

Willie winked at Manny. "She's waiting for you with that whip and chair. Go get 'em tiger."

"Thanks for the support."

Manny started for the door when he noticed the headlights reflecting off the eyes of a calico cat hunkered down in front of the garage door, ears laid back, tail flicking side-to-side. Manny bent down with his hand out when Willie stuck his head out the window. "I'd leave him alone. He doesn't look like he wants to be bothered."

Manny shook his head. "Poor homeless kitty, I think he's hurt. But don't worry—I've always had a way with critters. Haven't you heard, we Indians talk with animals."

"Then you'd better listen to this one and stay away."

Manny ignored Willie and squatted in front of the cat while he held out his hand for the animal to sniff. It hissed and the hair stood on the back of its bony spine. "He looks injured."

"Then let's call animal control."

Manny waved the offer away and extended his hand again. The cat retreated until it had the garage door at its back. Manny offered his hand once more, and the cat came alive. Or came psycho. It leapt on Manny's pant leg and started clawing its way higher. Manny howled, grabbing the cat by the back of the neck as Clara burst through the front door, headlights shining through her flimsy teddy.

"What's going on?" She looked at Manny battling the cat, prying the claws sunk into his leg.

"Open the garage door."

Clara punched the combination on the outside key pad just as Manny pried the cat off his leg. Blood soaked through his trousers and he held the hissing, clawing, crazy cat at arm's length, but it turned its head and sank its teeth into the web of Manny's hand. He gritted his teeth and grabbed an old comforter off a garage shelf and threw it over the cat. The moment it released its grip to breathe, Manny dropped the cat and ran for the door, hitting the closure button on the way out with the cat struggling to get free of the blanket.

Manny bent over, hands on his knees, breathing heavy. Clara grabbed his hand and held it to the light. "I think we ought to get you to the ER. What do you think, Willie?"

Willie stood with his back to Clara, hand covering his mouth. "Willie?"

Willie's hand came away and he bent over laughing.

Clara stood apart, hands on her hips. "I don't see this as funny."

Willie nodded and coughed, under control. "It is if you'd have seen Mister 'We Lakota Talk with Animals' there as he tried prying that thing off his hand."

"We'll, I still don't think it's funny. I think Manny ought to go to the ER."

"For a cat scratch?" Manny had wrapped his bandanna around his hand and rubbed his trouser leg that the cat had shredded.

"I guess Clara's right." Willie and Janet stood beside Clara as if ganging up on him. "Cat bites can be pretty infectious."

Manny pulled his trouser leg up and turned to the garage light. "I'll clean it up with some peroxide. Douse it with Neosporin. It'll be all right."

They waited until Willie and Janet backed out of the driveway before starting into the house. "You sure you're going to be all right?"

Manny jerked his thumb toward the Dodge backing out. "Sure, but I'm not so sure about Willie." Janet had moved to the front seat and scooted herself as close to Willie as the seat organizer between them would allow. *Maybe she's got a whip of her own reserved for Willie.*

CHAPTER 4

JULY 5, 1920

The wagon wheel fell into a hard, dried mud rut, and Clayton Charles yelled in pain. Moses glanced over his shoulder at Clayton clawing at the sides of the wagon to sit up. Moses whispered to the team and the horses pulled the wagon out of the hole.

"Damn it, stop this thing! Can't you see I'm hurt."

Moses tickled the reins and the wagon rocked to a stop. He set the brake and stepped off the seat, the wagon rising several inches, the springs groaning in relief. He reached under the seat and came away with a deerskin water bladder.

"Where the hell am I?"

Moses ignored him and sipped the water

"Hey, I'm thirsty as hell, too."

Moses handed Clayton the bladder.

"Where the hell *am* I? And who the hell are you?"

"Moses Ten Bears."

Clayton drank long and started to tip the water bladder over his head when Moses snatched it away.

"Water is scarce in the Badlands this time of year. We will need some for the rest of the trip."

Clayton started to argue and winced in pain. He gingerly dabbed at his head, his fingertips stained with dried blood. "What happened to me?"

"Me."

"What?"

Moses's laugh shook his great bulk. "I did not think that you would remember last night."

"Last night? Last night I was at the Fourth of July Dance in Imlay and having a damned good time, but that doesn't explain this." He probed his head and jerked his hand away. "Damn this hurts. If I didn't know better, I'd say someone stomped the dog shit out of me."

Moses took a last short pull from the water bladder and stashed it back under the wagon seat. "You remember picking a fight with two Lakota boys at that dance?"

"No."

"About half your size?"

"No."

"And putting the boots to them after you knocked them to the dance floor?"

"No, damn it, I don't remember anything past that first jar of moonshine." Clayton stood and teetered on rubbery legs, then fell back onto the wagon tongue and held his head with both hands. "You didn't answer me—who the hell *are* you?"

"I am the one that stopped you from killing those two Indian boys. I pulled you off them."

He pointed to his head, careful not to touch where it hurt. "That still doesn't explain this."

Moses smiled. "Sure it does." He leaned against the wagon and pulled a red stone pipe from his pocket. He began filling the bowl from a Bull Durham pouch he'd grabbed from the pocket of his patched brown muslin shirt. "When I pulled you off them, you came after me."

Clayton groaned and his hands came away from his head. He looked up at Moses. "You telling me I was drunk enough to want to fight someone your size?"

Moses nodded and lit his pipe, watching smoke rings float higher until they were as nebulous as the sparse afternoon clouds. He sat on the wagon beside Clayton, the springs creaking under the weight of both men, and one horse looked over its shoulder and nickered in protest. "You gave me no choice, what with you being so drunk and the crowd egging you on. They wanted to see those boys take a beating—or worse. A cowboy warned me to stay out of it, said that you were a mean drunk and would be more than a handful, you being as big as you are."

Clayton looked up at Moses seated beside him. "I take it I wasn't quite the handful they thought I'd be?" Clayton probed his face. Dried mud caked with blood crusted his cheeks and scalp. "I think I lost a couple teeth."

Moses reached into his shirt pocket and handed Clayton a pair of pearlies. "Like I said, I could not allow you to kill those boys. When I pulled you off them, you sucker punched me." He rubbed an eye that would be closed and blackened by tonight.

"And that was all she wrote?"

Moses smiled. "That was all she wrote. I will hand it to you—you did not give up easily. But when it was all over, no one came to help you—they just let you lie there while they went back to the party. I had to carry you away and patch you up. No one else would."

"You did this? You some kind of doctor? Never knew there was a Sioux sawbones around here. You one of those medicine men my dad talks about?"

Moses tamped his pipe on the heel of his moccasins and

pocketed it. "My mother was a *waphiya winyan,* a medicine woman, and she taught me some of the ways of the Old Ones. But I am not a medicine man. People say I am *wicasa wakan.* A sacred man."

"You're my age—you aren't old enough to be a holy man."

"Suit yourself, but I do know a little of Indian healing. Now do not pick at that poultice or you will infect those wounds."

Clayton jerked his hand away. "You said we were in the Badlands?"

"Northern part of the reservation. About five miles from your father's ranch. Be there by sundown."

"You know my father?"

Moses shook his head. "Never met him, but everyone knows about Randolff Charles."

Moses stood from the wagon, and Clayton grabbed his arm. "I know you said you're Moses Ten Bears. But what were we doing at the dance together?"

"It was not like we were there as a couple." He grinned as he grabbed the bladder and poured water into his massive hand for the horses. They slurped the water up and Moses refilled his hand. "I hired out to the McMaster Ranch west of Conata. Been there since planting time, and the dance was the first relief I had for months."

"And I spoiled it." He stood and doubled over in pain.

Moses shrugged. "Your ribs are bruised. I tried not to hurt you more than necessary, but things happen in a fight."

Clayton grabbed on to the side of the wagon. "Can I ride up there with you?" he gasped. "I don't know how much more of your hospitality in the back of this wagon I can stand."

>‹›‹›‹

The road smoothed as they neared the Charles Ranch. Wagon ruts and gouges made by those new rubber-tired machines had been bladed over, with fresh pea gravel having been laid down to soak up water and allow passage over the slippery gumbo underneath. Clayton reached under the seat for the water bladder and took a long pull before handing it to Moses. "My father is going to be furious that I got into another fight. You're not going to tell him about the dance?"

Moses spit dust that had blown into his mouth and gritted his teeth. When he grinned, those teeth were as white as any sun-bleached cow or buffalo bones on the prairie. "I am not going to tell him anything."

Clayton sighed. "Thanks."

"You will tell him."

"What?"

"You will tell him how close you came to killing those two boys at that dance, and why I had to beat you."

"I am not."

"Of course you are."

"My father will have a fit. He hates it when I drink. What makes you think I would cut my own throat?"

"You will," Moses laughed. "Trust me. Eventually, someone at that dance will mention to one of your father's hands, who will embellish it by the time he tells your father. You will want him to hear it straight from you. Besides"—Moses tapped Clayton's cheek, and he drew back—"he will know you did not come by this from dancing with some pretty lady."

They drove the last mile along the winding road that snaked around to the west and passed through a huge log entryway proclaiming this as Charles Town. Moses nodded to the sign. "Little pretentious, isn't it?"

Clayton leaned back. "Big word for . . ."

"An Indian. Just because I am Lakota does not mean I am stupid."

"Sorry." Clayton dropped his head for a moment. "Didn't mean . . ."

Moses waved it away. "Of course not. But tell me about this place."

Clayton sat straighter in the seat. "My father worked his tail off to make a go of this ranch. Even though we're in the middle of hard times, he still turns a profit, what with his government beef contracts."

"I see he is doing well." Moses nodded to a large corral a quarter mile ahead. A dozen ranch hands leaned over the railing watching two others trying to get a halter on a bucking, kicking, sundancing sorrel kicking up a cloud of dust over the hands. A few cowboys glanced over their shoulders at the approaching wagon before returning their attention to the entertainment in the square pen. One man looked up a second time as the wagon was within earshot of the screaming ranch hands whooping and waving their hats at the rider glued to the bronc. He nudged the man beside him and whispered. Soon, ranch hands peeled themselves off the railing and stood watching the wagon as it passed, oblivious to the two men wrestling the horse in the corral.

One of the hands broke away and ran to the two-story ranch house. Within minutes, a large man that looked to be an older Clayton Charles appeared on the veranda. He ran his fingers through thick, gray hair before setting his Stetson at a rakish angle and stepping off the porch toward where the wagon rocked to a stop.

Moses set the brake and counted the ranch hands as they surrounded the wagon. The gray-haired man peered up and cocked his head, stepping around to look closer at Clayton's injuries. "Looks like you been on the bad side of a rough bronc, Clay. From the rodeo in Imlay yesterday?"

Clayton shook his head. "Got into a fight, Dad." He looked at Moses with surprise in his eyes that he had admitted to the fight.

"What kind of fight?"

Clayton grabbed onto the wagon brake and eased himself to the ground, holding his ribs and wiping sweat from his face and neck with a snotty bandanna. "Got stomped at that dance."

"Who were they? This something we need to follow up on?"

Clayton nodded to Moses. "He kicked the shit out of me."

Two hands stepped closer to the wagon, their fists clenching, their eyes darting to Moses.

"Step down from there," the old man ordered.

Moses wrapped the reins around the brake and stepped down, the wagon creaking and rising several inches. The two men closest to Moses stepped back as they craned their necks up. Another man that had approached from the back of the wagon stopped. Randolff Clayton stepped to Moses and looked up at him. "It'd take some hoss as big as you to get the better of Clay. Thanks for bringing him home, but that don't mean you're going to walk away from here in one piece. Grab some ax handles, boys. This big bastard needs special attention."

Moses watched as the men circled him. He showed no emotion other than a distant amusement.

"You don't seem too worried, hoss."

"You will not hurt me." Moses spoke so softly Randolff had to cock an ear to hear him.

"You think what you will, but my boys are about to beat the lumps till they're smooth."

"You will not hurt me."

"No?"

"Trust me."

The runner returned from the barn with an armload of ax handles. He handed one to each of the three men gathered around Randolff and tossed the others to four hands lingering at the back of the wagon. One man tapped his hand with the ax handle. The one beside him smiled, letting the handle rest on his shoulder like a ball bat. Moses turned to sounds behind him. Two men stepped close. One bladed himself, one leg moving back. A boxer's stance setting himself to toss a punch. Or swing an ax handle. He spit his chew on the ground.

Moses faced the men in front of him. The smaller of the three shuffled close as he cocked the ax handle. Bigger moved to Moses's side.

Shuffling in back as the men stepped within striking range.

"Okay, boys," Randolff said, "get it over with."

Clayton stepped between Moses and the men. "Don't touch him, Dad. I got what I deserved."

The men stopped. One breathed a sigh and his ax handle drooped beside his leg, relief etched on his face as he rubbed a misshapen nose that had already taken one for the team sometime before.

"It was my fault. I got liquored up on some shine someone was foolish enough to bring to the dance. I beat the hell out of two Indian boys from the Rosebud that were unlucky enough to be there, too. Moses here stepped in."

"Three Indians against just you?"

"Not like that. I had the two down on the dance floor putting the boots to them when Moses pulled me off. I came after him. Big mistake. But he could have beat me worse than he did."

Randolff turned his attention from his son to Moses. "That so? You could have beat him worse?"

Moses nodded. "I could not help it. He will need a little rest to nurse himself back into shape. I think the booze hurt him worse than I did."

Randolff turned to Clayton. "Like hell you'll get any rest. First light, you'll be sitting your sorry ass in a McClellan and joining the line crews mending fences." Clayton kicked the dirt with his toe, and Randolff turned back to Moses.

"Getting late. You eat yet?"

"Yesterday."

"We're fixing to have supper. You can join us if you wash up."

"I wash up pretty good." Moses smiled. "Trust me."

><><><><

Randolff waited until his house woman ladled stew into each bowl before telling her, "Carmel, go see what's keeping Clay."

She set the stewpot on the table and disappeared upstairs without speaking. "Don't mind her. She's not rude; she just doesn't talk much."

Randolff poured wine in a glass and handed it to Moses. He waved the wine away. "It would embarrass her."

"How that?" Randolff asked.

"She is Lakota. Standing Rock. I talked with her while I washed my hands. Many Lakota are ashamed to speak English."

Randolff laughed. "She's got nothing to be ashamed of. She's Hunkpapa, claims to be a descendent of Sitting Bull. But then every Indian from Standing Rock claims that."

Moses held his tall crystal glass to the light. *Sacred* mni. Water bounced around the inside, reflecting light from the window behind him, making odd shapes against the white-washed walls of the dining room. He swirled the cool liquid around in his mouth, savoring the life-quenching flavor of sacred *mni* before swallowing. "Sitting Bull had many wives. She could be related."

Clayton stumbled down the stairs, holding onto the railing for support, and disappeared into the kitchen. Randolff looked after his son and shook his head. "Looks like he's suffering for squeezing that rotgut jar, but then Clay always was wild. He's been especially restless since returning from the war."

"Army?"

Randolff nodded. "He wanted to go into aviation. I got some connections in the War Department from these beef sales, and thought it'd be better for him if he flew. But his eyes weren't good enough, so they stuffed him into an infantry uniform and sent him to the front."

"That where he picked up that wound in his leg?"

Randolff put his wineglass down and leaned closer. "You don't miss much. He's still got shrapnel from an artillery shell that gives him trouble now and again."

"And he drinks to forget."

"That and fighting when the effects of the drink kick in. You ever serve?"

"No."

"You're about Clay's age. How is it that you never went?"

"I am not fee patented. I do not own land. Like many Indians, I am not even a citizen of this country. They told me this at the Induction Center right before they sent me home. Besides"— Moses smiled—"the induction officer said they did not have uniforms my size."

Carmel backed through the door carrying a tray. She set fresh bread and butter in a crystal dish in the middle of the table.

"Where the hell's Clay?"

Carmel spoke to Moses in Lakota before disappearing back into the kitchen. "She is putting fresh tape on his ribs."

"You must have given him a real thrashing." Randolff laughed. "But it looks like he might have gotten a lucky shot in."

Moses rubbed his eye that was swelling, making it harder to see out of that side as he eyed the butter bowl. Clayton pushed it closer and handed him a butter knife. "Help yourself."

Moses sliced through crust, the aroma of fresh pumpernickel drifting past his nose. The butter slid off the bread and pooled on the tiny plate as Moses took his first nibble, then a full bite. He closed his eyes, savoring the brown bread, the fennel seeds crunching, sliding down his throat greased by the melted butter. "What was Clayton like before the war?" he asked after he'd swallowed the first piece. "What did he enjoy doing?"

Randolff cut his own slice of bread. "He used to live to hunt, back when there was actually game hereabouts. That's another thing he drinks to forget, his mother."

Moses remained respectful of Randolff's silence until he was ready to continue.

"Sylvia and Clay were out scouting for a trophy mule deer they'd spotted the day before. Sylvia's horse stepped in a prairie dog hole and threw her. Broke her neck. Once in a half-moon Clay talks of going out and finding that mulie, though he's never gone hunting again."

"That fence detail—how bad do you want to teach him a lesson?"

Randolff dabbed at the corner of his mouth with a napkin. "He needs to be taught a man can't just beat two helpless boys, Indian or no. No offense."

Moses waved it away. "Does he need healing more than he needs to be taught that lesson?"

"What you getting at?"

"Hunting. Game is plentiful on the reservation, if one knows where to look. If you can spare him for four or five days, I'll find that trophy mulie for him."

"What about your job? I thought you were ranching for Sal McMaster."

The corners of Moses's mouth drooped and he looked away. "After the fight with Clayton last night, McMaster's foreman fired me."

"But why?"

"He said he did not want Randolff Charles as an enemy once you found out one of his hands beat Clayton."

"Sorry to hear that."

Moses shrugged. "It is all right. We Indians are used to it."

"You want your job back, I'll talk to Sal."

Moses shook his head.

"Then why don't you come work for me?"

Moses took a respectful time before declining the offer. "I need to get back to the reservation anyway. People need my help, but I thank you for the offer." *I have to get back to the Stronghold. Dance in the sun. Get pierced. Sacrifice for* Wakan Tanka. *If I could explain this to all* wasicu, *perhaps they wouldn't be so fearful of the Sun Dance. And perhaps they would make it legal to dance in the sun as did our ancestors.*

"If you change your mind . . ."

"And you? Will you change your mind about letting Clayton go for a few days?"

Randolff closed his eyes, and when he opened them, he grinned wide. "It might be good for Clay to get away and hunt again. And thank you." He stood and thrust his hand out. Randolff's hand disappeared in Moses's grip.

"It will be good for him. Trust me."

CHAPTER 5

"When Clara offered to take you to the ER in Rapid City last night, you should have gone. Now we gotta sit here waiting for who knows how long before you can get in." Willie waved his hand around the waiting room at the Pine Ridge Hospital. They sat surrounded by two dozen patients waiting to see the one ER doctor. "I have half a notion to leave you here all morning."

"Thanks for your compassion." Manny held his throbbing hand away from the chair. His hand hurt worse by the hour. His only distraction was the growing infection in his leg, which vied with his hand for attention. He'd broken down this morning and let Clara call Willie to give him a ride to the ER. "How would you like an infected hand?"

Willie tossed a Styrofoam cup in the waste basket. "Serves you right. We all told you not to touch it. But no, the Great Manny Tanno always knows better than anyone else. I don't feel sorry for you."

"Give me a break already, I only meant . . ."

"And we'd be out working this case, instead of sitting here."

"We'll be working the case soon enough. Sometimes a person just has to let the facts set in his mind for a time."

"How long?"

Manny shrugged. "It's like pornography—you'll know it when you see it. When you get some more experience under your belt."

"Well, I still hate hospitals. And doctors."

Manny looked sideways at Willie. "The voice of experience there. How would you know about doctors—I'll bet you haven't been sick a day in your life."

"I wish. I had to go back to the doc just last week."

"Sick?"

Willie leaned closer and whispered, "Prostate problems."

"You? You're twenty-three. Too young to have prostate troubles."

"I got a prostate as big as a bagel. Doc gave me some meds to shrink it. Now, I got to go back once a month for a blood draw and the finger wave to check if the med's working."

Manny groaned. His own physician had donned a finger glove and checked him once a year since he turned forty, and it was no fun. "I hope you at least found a woman doctor."

"No such luck. I drew the old Greek doc here, the one with fingers like sausages, and a huge ring that I swear he leaves on during the wave. I hate doctors, and now I'm stuck here with you instead of out working the case."

Manny had once shared Willie's enthusiasm. He recalled his first homicide call as a rookie tribal cop, and the excitement he felt as he dug into the circumstances. A drunk had been rolled at the powwow grounds for the price of a six-pack of Falstaff and been left propped against the fence. Except someone had run a blade across his femoral artery and the old man had died where he slept. Two punks from Cheyenne River, visiting Pine Ridge for the festivities, had drunk themselves out of money and killed the old guy. Manny had been as excited as Willie to solve a murder back then.

"At least you don't have to look for the guy that broke out your truck window."

Willie shook his head. "I'd feel better with someone besides Janet looking for the suspect."

"You got to admit it was decent of her to volunteer to look into it, and to stick by your truck until Glass Doctor came."

"The guy almost didn't come. He thought it was a joke. He said the side glass was worth more than my truck when I explained what I drove."

"All the same, it was nice of her to offer. You should trust her a little more."

"As far as I can throw her."

"Depending on what she was wearing at the time, that might be a pleasant proposition."

Willie turned his face away. "Not if Doreen finds out."

"Hey Officer Tanno."

Henry Lone Wolf stumbled through the ER door, teetering on delicate legs that were purposely bowed. For those who had a hard time remembering faces, Henry's would be the exception. His cheeks glowed with that same florid look and broken, blue capillaries of the perpetually drunk, and he reeked of stale brewskies.

Henry glared at Willie and turned his back on him. He smiled at Manny. "Mind if I sit with you?" He grabbed onto the sides of the chair and eased himself down. He gave a pain-filled grunt when he'd settled in.

"What happened to you?"

Henry closed his eyes, and he ground his teeth together with a gnashing sound that didn't bode well for what teeth he had left. "I got scalded on my backside. Mostly my butt." As if to punctuate his pain he winced as he stood.

"Must be some story behind this," Manny said.

"There usually is with Lone Wolf McQuade." Willie smirked.

Henry jerked his thumb at Willie. "It's officers like him that did the damage." Henry fidgeted, pulling his trousers away from his legs.

"What's wrong?"

"Rapid City Police Department," Henry said. "They washed my ass."

"Come on Henry," Willie said. "What the hell's the problem with the PD up there this time?"

"I said they washed my ass. Waxed it, too."

"I'll bite," Willie said. "What did they wash it with?"

"The car wash." Henry pulled his trousers down over his butt, oblivious to the other patients watching his behind in the waiting room. One mother covered her infant daughter's face with her shawl, and her two boys laughed. Blisters were intermingled with beet red skin on Henry's legs, and he pulled his pants back up over his bony butt. "A couple officers took me to the car wash."

Willie laughed. "Don't tell me—you were so dirty they had to clean you up?"

"You're one to talk." Henry nodded to Willie's shirtfront, which hosted samples of whatever Willie had for breakfast this morning.

"What happened?" Manny pressed.

Henry turned his back on Willie. "Two White cops arrested me for public intox in that little park by the Civic Center. There I was examining the bottom of a muscatel bottle when they rousted me. I wasn't doing nothing but they arrested me anyway. Pissed me off."

"So they took you to the car wash?"

Henry smiled. "Right after I crapped myself. I figured if they was arresting me for a chickenshit public intox charge, I was going to make them pay. So I crapped my pants in the back of the cruiser. And that pissed *them* off."

"As I recall," Willie said, "that's not the first time you pulled that stunt. You did that to me a time or two."

"But you didn't take me to the car wash. These guys were pissed. Said that was the last time I was going to crap in their cruiser—I guess I've done it before there as well, but I don't remember. Anyway, they took me to the Soap and Suds there on LaCrosse. Bent me over the hood of the cruiser. Gave me a wash and wax."

"Doesn't explain how you got those burns," Willie said.

"Sure it does." Manny shook his head. "My guess is that car wash water is about a hundred and fifty degrees, hot enough to scald anyone, drunk or not. I'm sorry, Henry."

"What you sorry for?"

"Them," Manny answered. "Not all cops are like them. That was uncalled for."

The receptionist called Henry's name and he hobbled toward the examination room door. "I'll make a few calls for you, Henry," Manny called after him. "Make sure this doesn't happen again."

Henry stopped and faced him, his mouth downturned with a sadness that overrode his physical pain. "Don't matter, Agent Tanno. Nothing's going to change. We Skins aren't exactly treated like kings anywhere off the rez. Besides, it'll get the officers in trouble, and next time they won't call for a ride to get me back home like they done today."

The receptionist held Henry's arm, guiding him through the examination room doors.

"So much for White-Indian relations." Willie pinched Copenhagen into his lower lip and rubbed the excess off on his pant leg. "That's shit they did twenty years ago."

"Let's hope we've evolved a little more in dealing with the *wasicu*. Still, I'll call the PD patrol lieutenant tomorrow. I'm certain it won't happen again. But right now I got my own troubles." Manny fought the urge to scratch his leg. He sat back in the chair and gritted his teeth.

"I don't feel sorry for you. I'll bet that little girl over there's got more sense than to grab onto a wild cat." He chin-pointed to a four-year-old huddled beside her mother. The child tapped feet shrouded in beaded moccasins, and played with the collar of a white muslin top that had multicolored geodetic designs painted on the front and spilling onto the sleeves. The girl looked up from the floor and spied Willie and Manny across the room. She broke away from her mother and ran toward them, arms as wide as her grin.

"At least kids like me." Manny held his arms out to catch her, but the girl ran around him and jumped into Willie's lap. She eyed Manny suspiciously as she peeked around the safety of Willie's arms.

He smiled at Manny. "Guess she knows quality. How are you doing, Morissa?"

The child buried her face in Willie's chest as her mother walked across the room and sat beside them. "Morissa's not doing so good," she said. At the sound of her name, Morissa grinned and showed a dozen new teeth before she started coughing into Willie's shoulder. Willie introduced Manny to Adelle Friend of All, and the woman eyed him as suspiciously as her daughter did. *Guess the FBI's just not the most popular folks hereabouts.*

Adelle took Morissa from him and cradled her against her chest as she stroked her head. "She's been awfully sick these past weeks."

"Flu?" Manny winked at Morissa, who turned her head away and covered her face in Adelle's shirt.

"The doctor can't figure it out. Morissa's been having diarrhea and vomiting. Now this." She pulled Morissa's top up to show a misshapen sore the size of a quarter that was spreading across her back. "*Maku mi yazan* is what the last doctor told me. Upper respiratory infection. I don't want Morissa to be like my two oldest, always sick and nothing the doctors can do about it. I'm just grateful I can get Morissa in today." She waved her arm around the crowded waiting room. "Just don't get sick the last half of the year—Indian Health runs out of money about then."

Willie nodded. "Ain't that the truth."

Manny popped a piece of Juicy Fruit gum in his mouth. Morissa eyed him and he offered her a piece, but she turned away. "You'd think something would tip the doc off as to what it is. Maybe something they've been eating. Maybe bad spores. The Old Ones tell us *wakan sica* sends us bad things now and again." Manny recalled Unc telling him the same thing.

Adelle forced a smile and brushed a lock of hair out of Morissa's eyes. "This goes beyond anything the evil spirits could send. Besides, *wakan sica* afflicts us with Indian sicknesses. This is a White man's disease."

A nurse appeared at the door and called out to a hunched old man slumped against a teenage girl. "You're next."

She helped him stand and they shuffled through the examination room door. Adelle looked after him and hugged Morissa tighter. "I'm afraid for my children."

"I would be, too." Manny stroked Morissa's head a moment before she burst into a coughing spasm. Her eyes kept fixated on Manny's pocket, and he grabbed his pack of gum. This time she smiled and snatched a piece. "Has something been different, like Willie said—change in eating habits, lifestyle changes, anything out of the ordinary?"

Adelle shook her head. "We've been on the same routine for the past couple of years. I take my kids to my sister's outside Red Shirt Table every morning, before heading for the Visitor Center. You know, that's been a good job since the tribe and Park Service started running it together."

"What do the doctors say about Morissa?"

Adelle frowned and her eyes darted to the examination room door. "That new one that came in from Chicago says my kids are malnourished. He says I don't care for my babies. Maybe we don't eat prime rib every night over a glass of fine Chianti, but we make do. And it sure isn't whooping cough like he said the last time."

"Do your sister's kids have problems, too?" Manny asked.

Adelle looked away. When she turned back, tears had formed at the corners of her eyes and she held Morissa closer, rocking her gently on her lap, stroking her hair. "May's only child, Julie, died two years ago. Docs couldn't figure out what was wrong with her, either. May said she wished she'd had Julie autopsied—maybe that'd help figure out what's wrong with my babies. But it's just not our way to autopsy an eight-year-old."

"May must enjoy watching your kiddies," Manny was quick to say. "Bet she dotes on them."

"Big time." Adelle smiled and dabbed at her eyes with the sleeve of her top. "May takes them swimming every day, since she lives right at the Cheyenne River. Takes them for hikes. Does things with them, like they were her own. If hers were still alive."

"Morissa Friend of All." A nurse in multiflowered scrubs stood in the doorway holding a clipboard and smiled when she spotted Adelle.

"Wish me luck." Adelle carried Morissa, coughing into her mother's shoulder, into the examination room.

Willie picked loose strands of Morissa's hair from his lap. He looked around for a wastebasket, then stuck the wad of hair in his shirt pocket. "Adelle's right, she's a good mom. Never knew her to neglect her kids."

"Sounds like she might have fallen on hard times." Manny rubbed his leg and flexed it to work out the numbness caused by the spreading infection.

"Most folks on Pine Ridge have fallen on hard times— started about one hundred and fifty years ago when the *wasicu* took our land and made us beg for the food they gave us. But that don't mean Adelle's kids are neglected. Anyone that'd drive as far as her to get her kids medical attention can't be a bad parent."

"How far?"

"Fifty miles. Just west of Cuny Table. East end of Blindman Table. Lives on a section of trust land her father managed to hang onto until he died young. That's what made the job at the White River Visitor's Center so attractive to her—it's only four miles from her house."

The nurse reappeared at the examination room door and called out another name. A couple in their seventies, perhaps their eighties—it was difficult to tell with elder Lakotas— helped each other as they followed the nurse. "Damned assembly line."

"Treat 'em and street 'em is how the nurses put it," Manny said. "Run patients through as fast as possible so they can see everyone before the end of the day."

"Still sticks in my craw they can't—or won't—do anything for the Morissas on the reservation." Willie stood and spit his chew into a trash can by the door. A woman holding a swollen arm glared at him. Her eyes followed his black uniform and settled on his embroidered badge until he sat back beside Manny. "Maybe if the docs stuck around and got to know the people, they'd take more of an interest."

Manny rubbed his leg, which seemed to throb in time with the pulsating hand he held away from the chair arm. "Average rotation time here is a year for doctors."

"Sure, they get their student loan forgiven and they hightail it off the rez." Willie grabbed his can of Copenhagen and pinched another lip full. Some spilled on his shirtfront but he ignored it.

"It's you the doctor will be seeing for lip or throat cancer."

"Nothing worse than a born-again tobacco addict. But here's the deal—these guys come here from the trendy parts of the country and the first look they get of Pine Ridge, they figure they've been beamed to some third world country. They equate what they've studied happens in those places and figure it's the same here and presto! He's got him a handy diagnosis. Malnutrition. Poisoning. Something he's read about in med school, or seen in the Philippines or Kenya and presto! Morissa will be out the door with a brand-new prescription for something else that won't help her. Presto! Next patient please."

Manny bumped his hand against the chair and winced in pain. "So you think there's no chance malnutrition or some type of neglect could be harming those kids? Something else that warrants a police investigation?"

"No way. Adelle runs a few cows, and always plants a big garden every spring. She's a single mom and takes good enough care of her kids. There's nothing we need to investigate."

"Manny Tanno."

The nurse moved aside to allow Adelle and Morissa to leave while she waited for Manny. Morissa's sad eyes followed him as she passed, Adelle clutching a new prescription form. Manny held his hand and stumbled toward the exam room, dragging his injured leg like a Lakota Quasimodo. "We'll see what kind of ER doc this guy is. In the meantime, get hold of Pee Pee. We need to go over those last two autopsies with him."

><><><><

Manny limped into the justice building, gauze wrapped tight around his leg, the cat gouges throbbing through the bandages. He thrust his hand inside his trouser pocket to conceal his wrapped hand, but his pants were too tight and his fingers were the only part hidden from others. *Better hit the road and cut down on sweets or Clara will have my ass.*

Willie keyed them through the door and Manny followed him down the hallway to Lumpy's office. CHIEF had been painted in foot-tall letters across the top of the door, and Janet Grass sat close to Uncle Lumpy at the conference table. He ignored Manny, his attention on Pee Pee seated across from him. Pee Pee sported a fringed leather vest with the likeness of Elvis painted on the lapels, and a picture of Graceland embroidered across the back. He leaned backward, his chair legs off the floor as if accentuating the King's throne.

"That's some vest," Manny said, hiding his hand while he stirred the pot. "Where'd you ever find it?"

Pee Pee winked at Manny. "Roadside stand across from Mother Butler's in Rapid."

"It original?"

"If it were it'd cost Pee Pee a month's pay." Lumpy turned sideways to Pee Pee, but he sneaked a look at the vest out of the corner of his eye.

Manny ran his hand over the vest. It folded under his touch with the supple toughness of elk hide. "Sure it's not vintage?"

"Hell no," Lumpy repeated.

"Oh chill out, boss." Pee Pee lowered his chair. "You're just mad 'cause they were sold out when you got there."

"They said they never had any."

"Well, they had this one. You just had to pour on the old charm, like I did, to get them to sell you one."

"If I'd have been a little quicker, I'd have got the bid on one that came up on eBay."

Pee Pee chuckled and popped a PEZ from his plastic Elvis into his mouth. He offered one to Manny. "The chief's just mad 'cause someone else collects Elvis memorabilia."

"Uncle Leon just collects the finer things." Janet scooted

her chair close to Lumpy and draped her arm around his shoulder. "I can understand why he's mad—everyone on the rez knows he's a big Elvis fan."

"Let's just get on with this." Lumpy slid a manila folder across the table. With his stubby arms and potbelly, he barely slid it far enough for Manny to grasp, and Willie got to it first. He turned his chair around and leaned across the table as he opened the folder. *Chairs never seem to fit Willie, even as thin as he's become these last couple of months.*

"Looks like that old Buick in the bombing range was owned by an Ellis Lawler. Who's he?"

Janet smoothed her uniform shirt. "He was a geology professor from the School of Mines. The school had archival files that indicated he might have been cheating on his wife."

"They keep records on stuff like that on professors?"

"Got you stumped there, Hotshot?" Lumpy leaned back and crossed his arms as he grinned at Manny. "We country Indians—mainly Janet—managed to dig that up."

"His infidelity was only speculation," Janet volunteered. "He failed to come home to his wife a week before Christmas in 1944. Lawler was a ladies' man, from what the missing person report says. The investigator thought it too much of a coincidence that he'd leave right before Christmas, especially since he was known to have affairs with students."

"This Lawler got relatives for DNA testing?"

Janet shrugged. "The Rapid City PD's missing person report doesn't list any."

"But it did say he had a house where Dinosaur Park is now, if that helps."

Lumpy tipped his head back and laughed. When no one else did, he looked around the room. "Tell me no one else finds this funny—the guy lived at Dinosaur Park and we dug him up in the land of the dinosaurs."

"A real riot." Manny took the file from Willie and thumbed

through the forensic autopsy report. "One of those guys found in that car was Indian."

"And big." Pee Pee popped a PEZ. "The anthropologist from USD said he was much bigger than the White dude."

Lumpy snatched the report. "Where's it say that?"

"Just read it," Manny smiled. "We city Indians can."

Lumpy scanned the report and tossed it back onto the table. "Doesn't mention anything about size differential."

"Sure it does." Pee Pee turned slightly so that twin lapel Elvises faced Lumpy, the leather rippling and giving the impression that the King winked at him. Pee Pee spread the report on the table. "Says here, Doc Gruesome had a hard time matching one arm bone. They'd been scattered, but not by predators. Time and wind did their work. The damned Badlands weather. But some critter got inside the car at some point, and Doc said there were two large femurs but only one small leg bone. That critter I mentioned had a snack when he could have had a meal."

"It's still just an accidental death case." Janet dabbed lip gloss on her finger and ran it across her lips as she eyed Willie. "As much as Uncle Leon would like you to be tied up with this, it's still just a case of two guys driving into the Stronghold and getting knee-walking drunk, probably died of carbon monoxide poisoning. Old car like that was sure to have some exhaust leak."

"The car was in gear," Pee Pee added.

"So. That just tells us they were getting ready to pull out," Lumpy said. "They had one last pull before the exhaust got to them. But we still got to identify the remains. We know Ellis Lawler owned that Buick. That should be easy enough to verify."

"And the Indian?"

Lumpy shrugged. "If I were White, I'd say he was just another Indian went into the sticks to get loaded and never made it out. Not much chance that any lawman back then would work very hard locating an Indian."

"Sometimes, relations aren't any better now." Manny recalled Henry Lone Wolf's scalding burns.

"How's that?"

"Nothing." Manny closed the folder. "We still got to try."

"Janet's already checked missing persons reports in Rapid," Lumpy said. "She narrowed the year down to 1944. Ellis Lawler was the only one reported missing that year."

"Now if we find out just who Lawler's partner was in the car," Willie said, "we'll be a step closer to finding out what happened."

They all turned to Janet, who continued buffing her nails. "I'm a jump ahead of you. I already poured over files in the tribal office from that time period. There were four Indians missing from the roles in 1945 that were listed in early 1944. Two of the four had been killed in the Pacific with the Third Marines, and another with the army in North Africa."

"And the last one?"

Janet remained mute as she put her nail kit in her purse.

"Come on," Lumpy said. "You got an idea who our croaker is, you tell us."

Janet smiled, playing the room like a comedian about to deliver the much-anticipated punch line. "The only man not accounted for on the books is Moses Ten Bears."

"Moses Ten Bears the painter?" Lumpy looked with disbelief at his niece.

"Moses Ten Bears the artist and—as Willie will point out—Oglala holy man." She nodded to an oil painting hanging on Lumpy's office wall. It was a mass-produced copy in subdued colors, and shared the wall with a copy of a Charles Russell print of a branding. Both looked as if Lumpy had liberated them from the Honeymoon Suite at the Motel 6.

"That's one of Ten Bears's paintings?" Pee Pee winked at Lumpy.

"You know it's a reproduction."

"I know," Pee Pee smiled. "If it were an original it'd cost you a month's pay."

"More like a year's." Manny stood, his leg cramping from the bandages, and walked to the painting, standing in front of it as if it could speak to him. It did. "If my memory serves me, legend claims Moses Ten Bears disappeared someplace between his cabin on Cottonwood Creek and the Stronghold around Christmastime in 1944. Unc told me stories—or rumors of stories—that Moses must have slipped and fell off one of those steep cliffs while he hiked there to pray."

"Folks figured that was the only explanation," Willie said, joining Manny at the wall, "that he would ever leave his Victory Garden untended, what was left after the first snow. It's said he gave away most of his garden to others during those years of World War II. Folks said the water was bad and his garden never produced much, but that he did the best he could to feed the hungry."

"Was he artist or holy man?" Janet asked.

Willie tapped the picture with his finger. "He was both—he couldn't have been such a spiritual inspiration without his artistic ability, and he couldn't have such talent without *Wakan Tanka* guiding him."

"He painted what he saw in his visions," Lumpy said. "People would visit him, and he'd tell their future with his paintings."

Manny eased himself back into the chair, hiding the wince of pain as his hand bumped the table. "Unc said people rarely took their paintings with them, once Moses showed them their vision he'd had of them, so frightening were they."

"And most of the paintings were never found," Pee Pee added, smoothing Elvis. "But you know the Badlands—it would be impossible to find something there unless you got lucky."

"About as lucky as Moses being in that Buick with Ellis Lawler all these years," Lumpy said. "Moses got any relatives living around here?"

Willie frowned. "Just his grandson, Marshal Ten Bears."

"That guy with the firewood business?"

Willie nodded and dropped in a chair across the table from Janet. "And he guides hunters during the season."

"Then put the habeas grabeas on him." Lumpy bent and flipped through the autopsy report. "I understand there's enough DNA in bones to make a comparison. If we could get Marshal to submit a sample . . ."

"He won't give us a sample."

"Why the hell not?"

Willie stuffed Copenhagen in his lip and puffed out his cheek to Janet. "Marshal hates law enforcement."

"Then why haven't I heard of him before now?"

"He keeps a low profile. Keeps to himself."

"And if you'd work the street now and again"—Manny stirred the pot even more—"you'd be able to listen to the moccasin telegraph and know who Marshal is."

Janet popped her compact from her purse. "Shouldn't be hard for an FBI agent to get a search warrant for his DNA."

"You've been watching too much *CSI*," Manny said. "Hard enough to get a judge to sign off on a recent case, let alone one older than most judges."

Lumpy ignored him and turned to Willie. "Somebody's got to interview Marshal and get consent for a sample. At least try."

"Janet." Willie turned to face her. "You being my gal Friday—or Tuesday morning now—why don't you hunt up Marshal. Charm him into giving a sample."

"Not me. I'm going to Rapid City this afternoon to go

over that missing person report on Ellis Lawler. Besides, J. C. Penney in the mall's got a huge sale going on."

"Then that leaves you or Hotshot there." Lumpy smiled and hooked his thumbs somewhere behind his belt, under his overhang.

Willie sighed at Janet. "Then Manny and I draw the assignment. But we'll miss your company."

"Will you really?" She smiled at Willie, but Lumpy rescued him.

"You two line up a date later. Right now I want to know what you've found out about the first stiff—if you want to keep your investigator position."

Willie's face reddened but he kept quiet as he retrieved his notebook from his back pocket and flipped pages. Manny noted Willie didn't read from his notes, but kept it open as a distraction. The kid was learning after all. "Alexander Hamilton High Elk reported Gunnar Janssen missing in the fall of 1969."

"High Elk the Supreme Court nominee?"

Willie nodded. "And there's more. Gunnar and the judge were arrested just a week before Gunnar disappeared."

"I'll have someone interview the judge in Washington," Manny said. "I imagine he's there preparing for the confirmation hearings."

"You're in luck, Hotshot." Lumpy grinned through a full set of perfect choppers. "He's taking a leave of absence from the bench in Sioux Falls. He's in Rapid City today giving a talk to the Rapid City Bar Association. You can catch him there and interview him after the presentation. A high profile case like this might shoot you back to Quantico—leave us yokels without the benefit of the Great Manny Tanno. Somehow, we'd survive. Maybe Janet should interview the judge after all."

Manny held his hands up and his injured one throbbed in

the movement. "Suit yourself, Lieutenant. But you want your niece eaten alive by some federal judge—or worse, make a mistake in interviewing that will come back to haunt this agency—then be my guest, have Janet talk with the judge. Just let us know what he says when you get through recovering from the ass chewing he's bound to give you for sending a rookie."

"Wait a minute you chauvinistic . . ."

Lumpy stopped her. "This one time, he's right. Besides, you're going to be tied up looking into that missing person report between mall shopping. Go right ahead, Hotshot, interview the judge till he makes you bleed."

Lumpy left Manny gathering the autopsy reports on all three bodies, and he stuffed them in the manila folder. As he started out of Lumpy's office, the Ten Bears painting drew him close as if it had powers that wouldn't let him leave. The muted colors shimmered yellows and grays and tans, bouncing off Badlands spires and undercut erosions and Devil's Corkscrews rising higher than anything else in the picture.

Off to one side, crows fed on a dead and bloated coyote while scraggly cows looked on, their ribs poking through their mangy hides. Manny pinched his nostrils shut, but the stench crept through, the odor overwhelming him, along with the maggots crawling from the coyote's nostrils, ears, eyes. Amid the sounds of the crows pecking on carrion, and of maggots consuming flesh, the waves of heat put off by the insects rose in rippling waves against the already intense Badlands scorching heat. Manny swayed on precarious legs. His hand shot out to the wall to steady himself. He jammed his hand and the pain brought him back to the land of the living.

He looked around. He was still alone in the room. Sweat dripped from his face and forehead, and he wiped it out of his eyes with the back of his hand. He stared back at the painting, now just a cheap imitation with none of the sounds or smells or sights he'd just experienced. Had he had a vision of sorts, or was Moses telling him something? *No wonder people didn't want to keep their paintings.* But somewhere deep in the recesses of Manny's mind, in that special file reserved for "Things Needing an Explanation," he knew Moses had had a purpose for such a vision painted on canvas seventy-five years ago.

CHAPTER 6

Manny hobbled to a tree stump opposite Reuben's lawn chair and dropped onto it. A piece of bark cut into his butt and he picked it away. "I should have let you doctor me. My leg and hand feel like crap."

Reuben shook his head. "I'm a sacred man—not a medicine man. I can treat Indian sickness, but I can't doctor this. But that's all right, *kola*. What's the worst that can happen—these cat scratches get infected to the point where you get blood poisoning. Or worse."

"I didn't come here to be lectured about getting to the hospital sooner."

"Then why did you come, *misun*? Just to be close to your big brother?"

Manny patted his shirt pocket for cigarettes that would have been there three months ago. Before he quit. Whenever his stress level was under siege, he needed one badly. Like now. His stress level was always under siege whenever he visited with his brother the felon. "I need some information."

"That's usually why you come around. What is it this time?"

Manny grabbed a soda from a cooler sitting on the ground between the tree stump and the lawn chair Reuben sat in. Manny handed him a Diet Coke, dripping with water, but Reuben waved him away.

"I don't want any of that diet stuff." Reuben's shorts bound up his crotch and he pulled them down for comfort. "When I journey to the Spirit World, I want the Old Ones to know I went out in style."

Manny nodded to Reuben's shorts. "Some style." He kept the Diet Coke for himself and handed Reuben a full lead version. He shook off the water and popped the top. It fizzed over onto his hand and he flicked the cola droplets into the dirt where they made tiny mud balls when they hit.

"Must be something important for you to come limping way out here."

Manny rubbed his leg, feeling the itch, and he struggled to ignore it. "We found three bodies in the Stronghold District where the Air Corps had their bombing range during World War II."

Reuben laughed. "I'm surprised that you found only three. That's some rugged terrain up thataway. More than a few corpses have been tossed over the edge or left to the mercy of the coyotes and mountain lions."

"Personal knowledge?"

Reuben's face reddened. "You know better than that shit."

Manny nodded. "I do. Old habits die hard, or some philosophical crap like that. Sorry."

"None taken," he replied, though Manny knew Reuben had taken offense. When Manny was working the Jason Red Cloud homicide on Pine Ridge two months ago, he'd accused Reuben of knowing where so many dead and missing bodies could be found on the reservation.

"You were an AIM enforcer back then," Manny had blurted out one day when the investigation had stalled.

"I never killed anyone like your FBI said I did."

"Bullshit. The kids in school had you pegged . . ."

"The kids you went to school with got their rumors from their parents, who got them from Wilson's goons. I never murdered anyone."

"You murdered one."

Reuben had turned away then, but Manny pressed his point. "You confessed to killing Billy Two Moons. Shot him to death in his car outside Hill City. Spent twenty-five years in the state pen for it. Don't tell me you never murdered anyone."

"I tell you, I never murdered anyone!"

And before Manny's assignment was finished, he learned he'd been wrong about Reuben in so many ways. Manny dropped his head." I didn't mean . . ."

"Of course not." Reuben waved the comment away as he eased back in the lawn chair, his butt poking through missing plastic slats, sipping his soda. Reuben—with his love for Manny—had a way of deepening the guilt Manny had felt for so long, making it harder to deal with his feelings. For most of his life, Manny had fought against having any kind of relationship with his brother. And it had been an easy fight, with Manny representing every federal lawman and Reuben representing what every AIM member could achieve if they committed the right crimes. Now as Manny feebly played catch-up, he knew he'd missed Reuben's love for these many years. And that had hurt them both.

Reuben licked the side of the soda can. "These bodies—anyone we know?"

Manny shrugged. "We think one is a Spearfish college student who went missing in 1969."

Reuben whistled between teeth that shone bright and unblemished, remarkable considering what he had been through in life. "How you going to solve a case that old?"

"Oh, it gets better. There were two others that we unearthed buried in dirt underneath the student. We think they died in that car during a bombing practice run as most of the windows were blown out, and it appears as if one of the victims died by a piece of windshield sticking into his chest. He may have been Moses Ten Bears."

Reuben became silent and his head dropped onto his chest. Manny remained quiet, unsure if Reuben prayed to God of the Christians or to *Wakan Tanka* of the Lakota. "That would shoot down that old theory of Moses falling off some steep cliff as he prayed," Reuben said at last. "You certain it was Moses Ten Bears?"

"Reasonably." Manny wiped the sweat from his face and neck and pocketed his handkerchief. "We'll know for certain when we get a DNA sample from his grandson."

"If that was Moses Ten Bears in that car, I've got to send him off to the Spirit World properly."

"Willie already did that."

Reuben nodded his approval. "I appreciate you coming here to tell me. Being a *wicasa wakan* I've always felt a strong connection to other sacred men, particularly Moses."

"That's why I came here, to ask your help."

Reuben smiled. "I knew it, little brother. But shoot—what you need help with?"

Manny stood and stretched his leg, as he massaged his hand. "That part of the bombing range they were found at is pretty inaccessible. It takes a four-wheel drive or a car a person doesn't care if they beat to hell to get down there, but a person can get there. Is there another way down to the Stronghold?"

Reuben stood and reached inside a leather portfolio. He came out with a Bureau of Land Management map and spread it on the ground, weighting the corners with rocks.

"You always have maps handy."

Reuben knelt beside the map. "This shows where Old Ones gathered herbs."

"For what?"

Reuben shook his head. "Maybe if I hadn't driven you away from tradition you would have remembered."

"You didn't drive me away from anything."

"Didn't I?" Reuben's eyes softened as he sat on the ground in front of the map and looked up at Manny. "If I hadn't been such an outlaw back in the day, you wouldn't have felt you had to leave. I know you were ashamed of me and . . ."

"Nonsense." But Reuben was right. When Manny was growing up on Pine Ridge, the turmoil between the American Indian Movement militants and Chairman Dick Wilson's Guardians of the Oglala Nation was bolstered by the people's mistrust of federal law enforcement, particularly the FBI. Reuben had been on the forefront of AIM violence, enforcing their strict code of adhering to traditional ways, of keeping one's mouth closed to any lawman asking questions.

Uncle Marion had discouraged Manny from idolizing his older brother, discouraged him from even seeing him. But Manny always managed to sneak out and meet with Reuben, sitting for hours outside Billy Mills Hall with other schoolkids, listening to Reuben regale them with AIM's interpretation of the Good Red Road. The Red Road, where a man took back, with violence if necessary, that which the government has taken. At least that's what Reuben espoused. And that's what Manny thought until Reuben was sentenced for the Billy Two Moons murder. Then the Red Road became the Black Road and Manny had to find another way to travel his own Red Road of truth and honesty and courage in his life.

Manny felt his temples pounding and he put the cold can of soda against his head to fight the rising headache. Manny always felt he left the reservation for the FBI in Washington,

D.C., because it offered so many more opportunities for a Lakota. Since he'd returned to working Pine Ridge cases, and talking with the brother who had walked his own Red Road on the other side of the line, doubts had crept into Manny's logic. He had come to realize those opportunities weren't for the Lakota but for Manny Tanno himself. "Do we always need to have this conversation every time I come here?"

Reuben held up his hand. "You're right. Just pointing out that many Lakota gather herbs for ceremonies there. But let's get back to that other route you wanted to know about." He pointed to the south end of the Stronghold Unit. "Take Route 2 out of the White River Visitor's Center about twelve miles, past the Cuny Café about a mile." Reuben ran his finger over the route. Manny put on his reading glasses and squinted against the bright sun.

"If you park on top of Battle Creek Canyon you can look to the northeast and see the Stronghold Table. Down the south side of the table is a trail that will get you to Cottonwood Creek. It's easy to find Moses's cabin from there."

Manny brought the map closer and studied the route. "Looks like it would be a pretty healthy walk."

"It is. Believe me." Reuben patted his stomach, which, Manny noticed, had not grown much over the years, and his brother had remained a trim 240 with just a hint of the Lakota paunch. "It takes a damned mountain goat to get down there even with horses. Why?"

Manny opened a manila envelope and took out a map hand drawn on stained parchment. "On loan from the Heritage Committee. Shows how things looked back during the time the government seized the Stronghold for the bombing range." Manny laid the map next to Reuben's. "See how things have changed there since that time. If this were the 1940s, it would be near impossible to get to those cars the way we went."

Reuben turned the map a quarter turn and nodded. "A person would have had to take the Battle Creek Canyon trail. That'd take someone who knew the area well."

Manny agreed. "Then it looks like I have to take a hike down that way." He dreaded the hike ahead. He could still walk down a deer in winter, but Manny knew it would be hard descending that trail. But it might give him a better understanding of who might have trekked into the Stronghold during the time the bombing range was in operation. And right now, he had little else to go on.

"What do you hope to accomplish?" Reuben asked. "You're able to get four-wheel drives down the other way to Marshal's cabin."

"I got to go down that other trail, just to get an idea who might have walked it. By the looks of our maps, that trail you showed me is the one alternate route down to the bottom."

Manny folded his map and slid it carefully back in the envelope. He started to sit, but pain shot up his leg, centering on the places where the cat had dug its claws in. Instead, he walked a tiny circle, working the stiffness out.

"At least Willie had enough sense to haul you to the ER."

"I felt bad calling him so early. He looked like he didn't get a wink of sleep. He certainly hadn't showered and changed clothes since yesterday." *Why am I telling Reuben this, he's not my priest.*

"Lizzy again?" Reuben asked while he dug for his cell phone. "Willie's still guilt-tripping himself over that?"

Manny nodded. "Wouldn't you if you betrayed your only aunt? He won't talk with anyone about it. Just seems to slide deeper into himself."

"I'll pray for him my next sweat."

"There's something else." Manny hesitated, tossing over in his mind how much he should tell an ex-felon. But Reuben was his brother. And his *kola.* "I got other troubles in this investigation—Judge High Elk's personal friend and protector, Joe Dozi. He's a genuine bad one."

"Problems with this guy?"

Manny nodded, the hair on his neck standing. He was worried—and serious—about Dozi.

"Your FBI have anything on this Dozi?"

"Just that he was drafted in the army in '69. I had him checked out, but the army wasn't helpful at all. Said they had no record of a Joe Dozi being in Vietnam, though I learned he spent three tours in country."

"So much for interagency cooperation."

"Tell me about it."

Reuben leaned over and grabbed another Coke and sat back on the lawn chair. "My guess he was SF."

"Special Forces?"

Reuben nodded. "They were often hidden from rosters. We had some operating up by Con Thien. Nasty bastards. They did the same thing we did in CAG." Reuben explained that the Marines Combined Action Group operated much like the SF A-Teams, living and fighting among the Vietnamese natives. "We'd go out on two- and three-man killer teams, always with a couple indigs. If this Dozi was doing that—and survived three tours with SF—he's very good. And DOD may have buried his records so deep you'll never find them. You want me to pay this Dozi a visit?"

Manny shook his head. "I don't want to give him the satisfaction of thinking he spooked me."

"How about I tag along when you make your hike into the Stronghold."

"Thanks anyway."

"Give me an excuse to pick herbs."

"No."

"Well, I got to look out for my only brother."

Manny sighed, put his hands at the small of his back, and stretched, the pain increasing in his leg as he sat back on the stump to wait for Willie. "We've had this discussion before, too. You don't have to look out for me."

"You need spiritual guidance. Besides, dealing with someone like this Dozi that sounds a little out of your league, no offense to you or the bureau. Now if you walked with the Great Mysterious . . ."

Manny held his head in his hands, the headache now a raging migraine. "I chose to leave the reservation, and what I remember of the culture here. If I get back to Unc's teachings, it'll be because I want to."

"You want to."

Manny laughed.

But Reuben didn't smile. He used the lawn chair to pull himself up. His soda disappeared in his enormous hand. "You've been dreaming again."

"No."

"Sure you have. The headaches are coming back. Driving you nuts figuring out what they mean."

Manny leaned over and rested his elbows on his knees as he pressed the cold can to his temple. "I thought Jason's *wanagi* was done with me when we solved his case this summer." Manny shook his head as if warding off the thought. "But dreams are coming back. I thought I dreamed of Moses Ten Bears even before we suspected it was him in that car. At least I think it was him. I just don't know."

Reuben stood and motioned to the creek bank where Manny knew he kept a sweat lodge erected permanently. "Perhaps it's time to get right with *Wakan Tanka* again, *misun*. Perhaps we should sweat once more."

"I don't want to sweat."

"Still afraid?"

"Of what?"

"Of those visions you experience when you get right with the *Wakan Tanka*."

Manny wanted to tell Reuben that he had visions even when he wasn't right with the Great Mystery. But Reuben was right. He needed to sweat, to get right with himself even if he wasn't sure there was any Great Mysterious to get right with.

Manny followed Reuben over the bank to the creek running in back of his house, and slid on his butt to get the ten feet down to Reuben's *Initipi*. Reuben had started a fire and stood in front of the sweat lodge and began praying to the four winds while Manny began stripping off his clothes.

Manny remained silent until Reuben finished praying to the earth and sky. "You expected me?" Manny pointed to a hot fire in front of the lodge where stones heated, awaiting the coming of life.

Reuben smiled. "Just say I figured you'd need cleansing by now."

Reuben grabbed a wicker pitchfork and scooped hot rocks from the fire, then ducked low and disappeared through the lodge entrance. He repeated this three more times until all the rocks had been placed inside, in a dug out hollow of the ground in the center of the lodge to awaited sacred *mni*, water that brought life where none was before.

"It's time again to confront your fears, little brother." Reuben dropped his shorts and entered the lodge naked.

Manny felt in his jacket pocket for the pouch of Bull Durham. Why had he brought it? Because he wanted a smoke so bad he would even roll his own? Or because he knew he would be purified inside the lodge this day and would need something for offering when finished?

He palmed the pouch and bent low—for humility—and entered the canvas-covered dome structure with just enough room inside for him and Reuben. Reuben trickled water on the hot rocks with a buffalo horn. Steam erupted, activating the creative forces of the universe.

"*Yahapo!*" Reuben said, and Manny closed the flap door, plunging them into darkness except for the glow of the rocks in the center pit.

Reuben handed Manny an eagle feather and together the two passed burning sage smoke over their bodies.

More water.

More steam, hissing, angrily at first, but mellowing out as the two men grew purified by the smoke.

The heat from the rocks and the steam rising with nowhere to go but around the lodge intensified. Every pore in Manny's body opened, the impurities leaving him, the aches he'd felt the last few days subsiding. But he suspected this wasn't the work of anything the Great Mysterious did, for he had felt these same things when he went inside the sauna at the FBI gym back in Virginia. There was nothing mysterious about this.

"Feel Him enter you," Reuben said as he squatted cross-legged on a bed of sage. "Feel what He can do for your spirit, *misun.*" From a small pouch at his feet Reuben pinched *peji wacanga* and tossed it into the darkness.

Manny sat back, sage poking his butt, yet he continued passing the eagle feather through the smoke and the steam, over his body, wishing the feather were a giant fan he could flap to make the heat go away. The intense heat, burning his nose. Manny tried breathing through his mouth, but that burnt as well.

Reuben dribbled more water on the rocks, the heat as stifling as anything the Badlands had to offer on its hottest day. How had Moses Ten Bears ever survived living there all his life?

"Because I had *Wakan Tanka* guiding me along the way."

Manny rubbed sweat from his eyes. He strained to make

out Reuben in the darkness, the rocks illuminating his face, eyes closed, rocking back and forth as he chanted softly. It hadn't been Reuben talking to him, but a voice so soft he knew he imagined it.

"The Great Mystery is always there for us. He can help us in our journey."

Through the steam, a figure rose in his mind's eye, a figure as solid as anything within the lodge, a figure that towered over Reuben, a figure that had to stoop so as not to rub his head on the lodge. Manny had never met him, yet he knew he faced Moses Ten Bears sitting cross-legged opposite him, naked, smudging himself with his own eagle feather. "You have to cleanse yourself for the journey ahead."

More steam, more heat, the sweat stinging Manny's eyes. "I'm here to find out what happened to you and Ellis Lawler and Gunnar Janssen."

Moses looked confused for a moment.

"The other body found in the car."

After a long pause, Moses nodded.

"What can you tell me about them?"

Moses shrugged. "I cannot tell you anything about them."

"But you said you're here to help me with my journey. And finding Gunnar's killer and what happened to you and Ellis is my journey."

Moses smiled. "You got a bigger journey than that, little brother. You got that journey of your own that you struggle to walk. You got that journey within you that you keep denying."

"I won't ever find it."

"You will," Moses said, his form fading away, riding with the steam, his voice fading over the hissing of the rocks and Reuben's faint chants. "Trust me."

CHAPTER 7

JULY 7, 1920

"We going to sit here all afternoon or are we going to hunt? The old man wants me to kill something bad, so let's get it over with. I got better things to do back at the ranch."

"Like what, bossing your father's hands around?" Moses peeked around the easel at Clayton pacing the cabin like a chained wolf. "If you want to go out in this weather, help yourself." He nodded to Clayton's boots sitting just inside the door. Gumbo had caked the boots as high up as the mule ears. When they had rushed inside to escape the storm, Clayton had complained his boots weighed forty pounds apiece. "We are lucky we made it inside when we did."

"Bullshit." Clayton cracked the door and hard raindrops pelted his face and neck. He slammed the door just as a clap of thunder, near and high and bouncing around the Badlands' steep crags and pinnacles, shook the cabin walls.

"You better keep the door shut unless you want to wind up a Wakinyan."

"A what?"

"Thunderslave."

"More of that superstitious crap? What the hell's a Thunderslave?"

Moses ground brown earth pigment between the steel muller and the thick piece of plate glass. He dribbled water on the glass, grinding and working the thick paste into the center of the glass, mixing until he got a consistency he could use in his painting.

"I said, what the hell's a Thunderslave?"

Moses mixed the brown with the gray already on his palette before he spoke. "Men and horses that get struck by lightning become Thunderslaves. From then on, you must obey the Thunder Beings."

"Now you're talking a foreign language."

Moses smiled. "The lightning is the flashes from the eyes of the Wakinyan Wakaya, the thunder is the beatings of their wings."

Clayton laughed and cracked the door, looking out for a moment before being driven back by the hard rain. "So just where the hell are they?"

"We cannot see them." Moses added more subdued tans to the sky. "They hide themselves in the thick, dark clouds. It is dangerous to look upon them."

"Superstitions." Clayton snickered and chanced a last look out the door. "Just tell me this storm'll be over soon."

"What do I look like, a fortune-teller?"

"You claim to tell the future in those visions you have."

"You do not sound convinced."

Clayton laughed. "If they're anything like the visions I get when I have too much rotgut, they're scary."

"I cannot say—I have never drank."

"Then conjure me up a vision and tell me how long this storm's going to last."

Moses stopped painting. He set the badger hair brush on the palette and closed his eyes. *Ignorant* wasicu *who knows so little of the scope and powers of Wakan Kin. If Clayton were not so in need of an education, I would have left him in one of those fast flooding gullies.* Moses opened his eyes. "Perhaps one day you will ask me for a vision."

"And you'd paint something like that, wouldn't you?" Clayton walked around and bent to the crème colored muslin encased in a hasty wood frame propped against the easel. Clayton cocked his head to both sides, moving so as to study every inch of the yet unfinished painting. "This what they call an abstract? Don't look like anything we have hanging back at the house."

Moses covered the palette with a damp cloth and draped a wet burlap sack over the painting. He stepped back and filled his pipe from a stone urn on the table. He studied the bone skewer he tamped his tobacco with. How could this wealthy *wasicu* ever understand the ways of the Lakota? If he told Clayton the skewer he tamped tobacco with once pierced his chest muscles until it tore loose the first time he had danced to the sun at twelve, Clayton would not understand.

"You know, you get me a nice mulie buck and I'll buy you a nice ivory tobacco tamper."

Ignorant man.

Moses pocketed the sharpened bone. He leaned back in his chair as Clayton cocked his head at the other paintings adorning the walls, others propped against the table and cupboard in the one-room cabin. The paintings hanging on the walls moved eerily in time with the wind whistling through the cracks in the mud chinking. At just twenty years old, Moses had as little experience with the *wasicu* as Clayton had with the Lakota. Moses had been told many things about the Whites from his father. Kills Behind the Tree had walked with a bitter limp the rest of his life from a 7th Cavalry trooper's bullet to his thigh at Wounded Knee. He had clung to his low opinion of White men until the day he died from the White man's consumption disease. Moses constantly fought against his father's opinion of the *wasicu* so it did not skew his own judgment. "This painting is abstract because you are not willing to learn the meaning of the vision."

"What meaning?" Clayton pulled the cloth covering away. "Looks like some crows feeding on a dead coyote."

Moses sighed. "If I tell you, will it help you understand the Lakota better?"

"Might." Clayton sat on a chair beside Moses and scooted close. "Try me."

"See that sunrise?" Moses gestured with his pipe to the top of the painting. "That represents my people rising after the flood."

"Like the one Noah went through?"

Moses shrugged. "Could be. And below the flood, on the banks of the river it left behind, beside the dead coyote, there are soldier's uniforms that have been trampled into the mud when my people rose again."

"What's with the cows? Looks like they haven't eaten in a coon's age."

"They have the sickness of the rocks."

"What sickness?"

Moses ignored him. "The coyote in this vision represents the enemies of the Lakota that have been brought to atone for their injustices against us by the Great Mystery. And the cows looking on are witnesses to these atrocities against us."

"You saying Indians are going to rise up and trample us Whites?"

"It is what I saw in a vision."

Clayton stood and backed close to the door. "Sounds pretty hostile to me."

"It is not. Trust me."

He covered the canvas once more and stood. The rain had stopped, and the only water Moses felt when he opened the door was rain trickling off the roof and dripping onto his head. He breathed deep, holding it as long as he could before he let it out. He always loved that time right after a summer rain, loved the smell and what it did to nourish the land. It was times such as these he most appreciated the Thunder Beings' power, when their terrible violence was replaced with life-giving rain and a newness it brought. But he knew that within an hour, perhaps less, the Badlands would soak up the rain like it soaked up everything else that lived here. And little trace of the Thunder Beings' work would remain.

Clayton joined Moses in the doorway and he turned his head and held his breath. Clayton was *sicamna*, bad smelling. Moses found Clayton's odor offense, yet here was another opportunity to understand the *wasicu*. Perhaps he'd find some way to convince Clayton he needed to cleanse daily, both physically and spiritually.

Clayton pointed to stars peeking around from the Thunder Beings shifting wings, dark clouds passing by. "The Big Dipper's most visible clear after a rain. What do you Indians have to say about it?"

"Sure you want to know? The answer is not simple."

"What the hell else do we have to do until we go hunting in the morning?"

Moses chin-pointed to the night sky. "What you call the Big Dipper has seven stars. That is why there are the Seven Council Fires of the Lakota. They were given to us—along with all the stars—by *Wakan Tanka*. We say they are the breath of life, the *woniya*, of *Wakan Tanka*."

Lightning flashes in the sky to the south where the storm had escaped lit Clayton's face for a brief moment before burning out. "And over there?" Clayton pointed to the west.

Between flashes of light, a tall butte jutted up out of the floor of the Badlands, dark and ragged and uninviting. "What's that?"

"That is Galigo Table, what the Old Ones called Escape Mesa." Moses wrapped his lips around the catlinite pipe and inhaled the tobacco mixed with sweet sage, exhaling it so slowly so as not to frighten the smoke away. He allowed the fragrance of sweetgrass to linger just a moment longer. Good spirits like *wacanga*. "Some say that is where Big Foot's Minneconjous fled to escape capture after Wounded Knee, and where they danced the *Wanagi Wacipi*, the Ghost Dance, before meeting their fate on Wounded Knee Creek."

"My father talks about that sometimes. Says those Indians picked a fight and ran off to Galigo Table."

Moses paused, closing his eyes, and breathed deep, his chest filling with air. And sadness. The *wasicu* version of the tragedy was far different than the Lakota's. "They actually fled to the Stronghold table just beyond, the place of many Ghost Dances leading up to the . . . battle."

"Can we ride over that way sometime?"

"Sometime. But tomorrow is the last day to hunt. I got to get you back to your ranch before your father puts a bounty on my scalp."

"That's if we even see anything worth killing."

"We will."

"I'm not so sure there's even any game here like you claim. I don't even see any heads hanging on your wall. Only thing resembling something you killed is that mountain lion hide on your bunk." Clayton pointed to a tawny, thick-hided cougar pelt that served as a blanket.

Moses tamped his pipe against his heel and the burnt ashes fell outside. "There is nothing hanging on my walls because we do not kill for trophies. We kill to survive, killing with great reverence for the animal we hunt."

Clayton laughed. "Did you have reverence for whatever we ate last night?"

"The rabbit? Sure, and I will kill a squirrel, maybe a badger, before I get you home, all with equal reverence and thanks for sacrificing its life for us. But we will get your prize to hang on your wall. Now we better get some sleep so we can get up early so the sun can bake your white skin one more day."

>◇◇◇<

"No wonder Dad forbade me to come here." Clayton's hat fell off as he craned his neck up to look at the high canyon walls. He dismounted and grabbed his hat, holding it to his chest as he squinted to look at scrub junipers clinging tenaciously to shale cliffs a hundred feet above the floor of the Badlands. Even at this distance, exposed roots jutted out of rock as if stretching to catch whatever moisture might happen to fall. A hawk hunting in the morning lit on one of those junipers and looked down on them. "Nothing grows here. It's ugly."

Moses dismounted his mule and wrapped the reins of his packhorse around his hand. He led them along the narrow half path snaking down toward the floor of the Badlands, a one-animal path. Clayton led his own horse. It snorted and pulled at the hackamore and kicked up loose rocks that plummeted down the cliff.

"There is beauty here. My people used this place for sanctuary for longer than even the winter counts tell us. That alone makes this a beautiful place. Besides, things grow here if you know where to look."

"Well, I'm looking and I see nothing worth writing about." Clayton leaned over the edge and jerked back. Loose rock careened off siltstone outcroppings. The sound bouncing off the floor below made the hair stand on his neck. "You trying to get me killed?"

Moses smiled. "If that were the case, you would be gone now."

The trail broke out into a large flat of dirt and they stopped in the shade beside an overhang of volcanic rock. There they tied their horses and Moses's mule to a large boulder. The packhorse shook its head and the sound of antlers clanging together on the pack saddle echoed like gunshots. Clayton ran his hand over the enormous mulie rack tied to the saddle, and grabbed the water bladder from the packhorse. "This'll look great over the fireplace—it's even bigger than the one Dad got eleven years ago."

Moses grabbed a handful of sparse gama grass and began rubbing his mule's withers. The air was too dry, too hot, and whatever sweat the animal created instantly evaporated. Rubbing the mule's muscles would help with circulation, and ease the animal's soreness. They had miles yet to go before the mule could drink at the cabin, and Moses had no desire to carry the critter back. "We took the life of the deer, but we did so with reverence, as we do for every living thing here."

Clayton stopped midswig. "As ugly as this place is, there's something about it that makes me want to come back." He took a last drink before capping the bladder. "Keeps my mind off the war. And off Laren."

"The girl at the dance?"

"Does it show?"

Moses nodded. "I figured it would take a girl to distract someone like you have been."

"She wanted me to leave the dance with her, but all I wanted to do was stay and get drunk. She made me drink a lot more than I wanted to."

"No man can make another do anything."

Clayton's smile faded. "A woman can. She told me that night she'd be leaving for South America. Missionary work. So remote she couldn't even send me a letter. And all I wanted to do is get in the missionary position with her."

Moses took the water bladder from Clayton. "Know her long?"

Clayton sat on a sandstone table, eroded by wind and water, and dried the inside of his hat with his bandanna. "Since school days. I think I always loved her. Now I put the run on her with my wild ways."

"You did not tell your father you had broken up."

"How'd you know?"

"Intuition. Trust me, he thinks the world of Laren, and he will be upset when he finds out."

Clayton kicked a rock with the toe of his boot. "He thinks she's too good for me, but figures she could straighten me out. He keeps talking about having a grandson to bounce on his knee. He'll be furious when he finds out I drove her away."

"I know how he will feel."

Clayton spit on a centipede scurrying across the ground. "You? How could you possibly know how he'll feel?"

Moses leaned back against the outcropping and grabbed his pipe from his pocket. "I looked forward to being an uncle once, to having a baby nephew to bounce on my own knee. But brother Trusty died at the Marne. He was fee patented. A citizen. His wife tried to talk him out of enlisting, but all Trusty would say is that we Lakota have a warrior tradition to uphold. That he was *akicita*, and he enlisted in Pershing's army. He was sent to the front in France with the first wave of doughboys. He never made it past that first forest of barbed wire the Krauts strung for our men."

Clayton became silent and hung his head and, for a moment, Moses heard sobbing. When Clayton looked up, the corners of his mouth drooped with the sadness of a man holding the world inside his heart. He wiped his eyes with his shirtsleeve. "I've been there. Seen more than my share of men die in those same barbed wire traps, stuck while the Germans machine-gunned them. Tell me, did Trusty have children?"

"He did not have time. He married Hannah a month before the war."

"How'd she take it?"

Moses shrugged. "She is Oglala—used to such sorrows, especially death. It was not the first time a Lakota woman was widowed because her man died an honorable death in battle."

"She ever remarry?"

"No." Moses stood and stretched. "A shame, too. She is a good woman. And most beautiful."

"How come you didn't bring her along on this hunt?"

Moses laughed, then stopped when he recalled Randolff's account of Clayton's mother dying on a game hunt. "Our women do not hunt. They stay at home and await the triumphant return of their men back to the teepee and all that."

"Maybe she'll come along next time. Maybe I'll get a chance to meet her."

Moses smiled again, and for the first time in recent memory, his heart was happy for his brother's wife. "You would like her. Trust me."

CHAPTER 8

A hotel guest, gaudy in his Bermuda shorts and flowered shirt, elbowed past Manny getting through the entryway of the Hotel Alex Johnson. *I wonder if that fool knows how ridiculous Hawaiian garb looks in South Dakota.* The man ran to a set of double doors at the end of the lobby and disappeared inside. The clerk behind the desk looked after the man before doing a double take, watching Manny as he walked around the lobby. *Guess the Alex Johnson will have two celebrities today: the first Lakota Supreme Court nominee and the first Lakota FBI agent.* He cursed the *Rapid City Journal* for pasting his picture over the front page with the Red Cloud homicide two months ago. He'd prayed his notoriety—as the FBI agent that had failed to solve the Red Cloud case—would fade. But it hadn't, and Manny often felt people's accusing looks as he walked by or entered a room.

It surprised Manny that so few people occupied the lobby today during the height of the tourist season, and he figured most folks were here to listen to Judge Alexander Hamilton

High Elk. But that was all right: that gave Manny the freedom to wander the hotel lobby without others gawking at him.

He looked about in awe at the grandeur of the historic hotel and wondered at the vision to build such a place in the middle of the west. Starting the day before Mt. Rushmore construction began in 1927, Alex Carlton Johnson had spared no expense in incorporating Indian and German themes into the architecture of the building. Journalists of the day proclaimed the Alex Johnson the Showplace of the West, while people in modern times echoed that sentiment.

Manny stepped onto bricks laid by craftsmen seventy-five years ago, the bricks hand fired, many with Indian symbols painted on them. The bricks with the swastika particularly fascinated Manny, and he could only guess about the artist who had painted them. The symbol had special meaning to the Navajo, though he had forgotten what, like he had forgotten many things Indian since leaving the reservation. Far too many things lost over the years of living in the east.

Judge High Elk's secretary had instructed Manny to wait in the lobby where the judge would meet him after his talk to the local bar association. Manny dropped into an overstuffed paisley chair that wrapped its enormous arms around him as it had others before him for three-quarters of a century. He closed his eyes, imagining the people that had enjoyed the chair's comforting embrace, imagining what stories they had whispered to the old chair as they sought solace in it.

Clapping from the large conference hall snapped Manny awake. The applause subsided, but grew again until it bounced off the walls, and came full around to where he sat: the judge getting a standing ovation, he was certain, as he did wherever he spoke. Or so the press reported always happened whenever Judge High Elk honored people with an appearance.

Manny turned his attention to one wall spanning the length of the lobby. Lakota artifacts, quivers and arrows and

lances, weapons of war, adorned that wall, along with artifacts of peace: a ceremonial pipe of red catlinite, and framed
copies of broken treaties between the Lakota and the government. The artifacts shared the wall with railroad memorabilia.
Alex Johnson had been vice president of the Chicago and
North Western Railroad, and had been as proud of his connections with the railroad as he was fascinated with Indian
life.

The applause stopped and a small, pale man in a black suit
too large for him threw open the conference room door. He
pushed his long sleeves over his wrists and stood there as if he
were a movie usher directing young neckers to leave. Manny
caught the man in the Hawaiian garb in the middle of the
crowd, jostled around while being pushed from behind as the
crowd filed out of the room.

Manny averted his eyes, his gaze drawn to a wall, not to
the two enormous buffalo heads standing guard on either size
of the oversize mantel, but to the painting hanging between
them. He had heard that the Alex Johnson had acquired an
original Moses Ten Bears piece—only five of which were
known to have survived the Oglala sacred man—but this was
the first Manny saw of the painting since its unveiling last
month. Manny took in the subdued colors, almost an abstract,
and the nebulous meaning of the painting. The *Rapid City
Journal* article claimed the hotel had bought the painting in
honor of the nomination of Alexander Hamilton High Elk to
the Supreme Court.

"Remarkable, isn't it?" A voice spoke so softly behind him
Manny barely caught it, yet the tone and timbre sent goose
bumps scurrying across his forearms. A tall Lakota with sky
blue eyes, kind eyes, met his gaze. The eyes were set on either
side of a nose so straight one could set a ruler along it, and an
angular, muscular neck sported a bone choker. "Did you know
Moses Ten Bears and my grandfather were best friends?"

"Grandfather?"

"Clayton Charles. The senator from South Dakota."

"Of course. Died in office at the tail end of World War II. A pleasure to meet you, Judge High Elk." Manny cursed himself. He wasn't used to being caught so flat-footed. *I'll be up on High Elk family history the next time I talk with the judge.* "I didn't connect your grandfather with Moses Ten Bears."

Judge High Elk smiled easily. "Most folks don't remember that part of local history. And I'm not so certain I do either. Grandfather died long before I was born."

"Folks will remember seeing a Ten Bears original, I'll wager."

The judge chin-pointed to the painting. "People would ask Moses for a vision and he would go into the hills—he favored the Stronghold—and pray. Sweat. Have his vision and paint it when he returned to his cabin. But most people weren't strong enough to accept their fate. People didn't want to be reminded it might come true. After all, an Oglala holy man painted it." He turned away from the painting. "You must be Senior Special Agent Tanno."

Manny nodded and accepted Judge High Elk's hand, rough, chapped, not soft as Manny expected an attorney and judge's to be. To his chagrin, Manny realized that his own hand was soft enough to be in a Palmolive commercial.

"My secretary didn't say what the nature of your interview was, only that it was important. I speculated there's something the FBI needs to clarify prior to the Senate confirmation hearings."

"It's important for the family of a man murdered forty years ago."

Judge High Elk's eyes darted to the crowd closing in around him, wanting to be close to the next Supreme Court justice. "Perhaps we can adjourn to the balcony. I'm assuming this is something I won't want others hearing."

The judge took the steps to the second floor two at a time

and waited for Manny to catch up. Though fifteen years his senior, the judge wasn't the least out of breath as he motioned to a pair of occasional chairs overlooking the balcony. Manny dropped into one that was twin brother to the strong, protective chair that had comforted him earlier in the lobby.

The chairs were close enough to the balcony railing that sitters were rewarded with a panoramic view of everything happening below. A leather-garbed biker, squat and bald with a connected look to him that matched his menacing air, stopped two couples starting up the wide staircase. He whispered something and both couples retreated back down the staircase as they shot looks over their shoulders at the man.

"So tell me about this victim."

Manny turned in his seat and took out his notebook, not for reference, but because people expected it, as if he had to finger it to listen to them. "Judge High Elk, we . . ."

"Ham. Call me Judge High Elk if you ever argue a case in front of me or testify in my court. Out here, it's just Ham. Now about a murdered man . . ."

Manny nodded. "Gunnar Janssen."

Ham drew in a quick breath. "Gunnar's finally surfaced?"

"He was found murdered in the Stronghold."

"Murdered?"

"In that area of the Badlands the Army Air Corps used as a bombing range during World War II."

"Gunnar," Ham breathed again, sitting back in his seat and covering his eyes with his hand. The bald man started up the steps, and Ham caught his movement. "It's all right," he called to the man. "We're just discussing some sad news."

Baldy sat back on the steps and surveyed the crowd below him. He was the oddest Secret Service agent Manny had ever seen. If he were Secret Service.

"This is bizarre—Gunnar found after all this time. How did he escape capture after all these years?"

"Capture?"

"Draft dodger. I wonder how he hid out this long."

"Nature's hideaway—he's been dead all this time."

"All this time?" Ham slumped in his chair. "Please tell me how he died."

Manny flipped a page and pretended to read from it. "Small caliber gunshot to the head. I thought you might shed some light on his disappearance, since you reported him missing in 1969."

"So long ago. Let me think a moment." Ham closed his eyes and rubbed his forehead. When he opened them after several minutes, he spoke in that same soft, composed voice. "Gunnar and Joe Dozi and I were roommates at Black Hills State back in the day. To say we were all inseparable would be to slight our relationship. We did everything together. Scouted around the Black Hills together. Hiked the Badlands together. Partied together." He smiled. "So when Gunnar disappeared, I filed a missing person report with the Spearfish Police Department."

Manny studied Ham, but detected no deception, no faltering in his voice. But then, Ham had suffered more pressure as a sitting federal judge than Manny could ever put on him. "I've read the missing person report. What did you think happened to Gunnar?"

"Gunnar lost his school deferment when his grades went south. Joe and I always figured he fled to Canada rather than be drafted."

"Was he afraid of service?"

"He was anti–Vietnam War; organized protests here, and across the state. We knew that he'd never allow himself to be drafted and risk fighting in 'Nam. Besides, he had an aversion to killing. Loathed the thought of killing anything."

Manny jotted notes in his book. "We know now that didn't happen. Tell me, what reason would he have to go into the

Stronghold? He could have picked other places in the Badlands easier to travel around in."

Ham took a long-stemmed red clay pipe from his pocket and filled it with tobacco from a pouch. Stalling? "There's no smoking here, but I suspect no one will say anything if I do."

Manny smiled. "I suspect you're right."

Ham blew smoke rings upward. When they neared the ceiling fan, they were sucked upward to the coppered ceiling. "Gunnar had just come back from Pine Ridge the week before. He said he missed a trophy buck, and we figured he went back the next weekend to fill his tag. That was the only other thing I thought might have happened to him—a hunting accident."

"I thought he had an aversion to killing anything?"

"That was the odd part of his story to me." Ham held the smoke before releasing it. "Seems like Gunnar acquired a taste for hunting somewhere along his road."

"He knew Pine Ridge well enough to hunt there?"

"Few people know the Badlands well enough to get in and out in one piece. He hired a guide."

"His name?"

Ham leaned back in his chair and rubbed his eyes. "I never knew his name, but Joe might. I'm sorry, Agent Tanno, but it was thirty years ago."

"Understood. Perhaps the name will come to you. Did you try to find out what happened to Gunnar after he disappeared?"

"Heavens, yes. The other place we thought he might be hiding out besides Canada was the Badlands. He was into geology and he'd been there numerous times. I knew the Stronghold area well enough we traipsed around the reservation for a week after he left trying to locate him. When we failed to find him, we assumed he fled north across the border. Or someone got to him."

"For what reason?"

"As antiwar as Gunnar was, there were pro-Vietnam students on campus as well. They were as vocal for the war as Gunnar was against. We thought maybe someone decided to shut him up."

"No proof to that, either?"

Ham shook his head. "Not a shred. We just racked our brains figuring out where Gunnar may have gone and concluded dodging the draft was the most plausible."

"Can anyone verify you were on the reservation?"

Ham looked sideways at Manny. "Am I a suspect?"

"A person of interest."

"I hate that term. A *person of interest* is Cindy Crawford in a G-string."

Manny smiled. "Either I verify your week on the reservation in 1969, or the pit bulls your Washington opposition send to root out dirt about you find it."

Ham nodded. "I stayed with my mother for that week."

"I have to ask this, is she . . ."

"Alive?" Ham laughed. "Still alive and mean and independent as always." Ham wrote her address on the back of a business card and handed it to Manny. "Knock hard, she's half deaf. And you're right—I'd rather have you question me than whomever my enemies sic on me."

Manny pocketed the card. "Let's get back to Gunnar's deferment. You certain he lost it?"

Ham nodded. "He was failing every class except geology—his only passion. When I found out he was failing his other classes, I offered to tutor him, but he was too busy with a new girlfriend and being the Geology Club president to take time out for his studies. When I suggested he could avoid losing his deferment if he picked up his grades, he just laughed. Said he knew enough people who would hide him out until he could cross into Canada. But we still looked in the Badlands for him."

"We?"

"Joe Dozi and I." Ham watched the smoke rings dissipating near the ceiling as if gathering his thoughts from the hazy cloud. "Joe got his notice the same week as Gunnar to report to the Induction Center in Omaha. But Gunnar was so frail, he didn't want anything to do with the military, not like Joe, who took to it naturally. Joe and I were both hurt when Gunnar left without even saying good-bye. Hadn't even contacted us after the war ended. Now I know why."

"Did he get his draft notice before or after you two were arrested in Spearfish?"

Ham dropped his eyes. "You know about that?"

"Public record."

Ham sighed. "It is, and I might as well practice my response. It'll come up in the hearings anyway."

"It will."

"You're right, so here goes. Gunnar's girlfriend—Agenta Summer—was a beautiful girl, and she had needs, shall we say."

"She was horny?"

Ham laughed. "Very much so. When Gunnar started failing classes, he hung around campus less and less, and Agenta became more and more frustrated. She told Gunnar she wanted him to stick around more, tend the fire, so to speak. But he didn't."

"That's when you started tending that fire?"

Ham nodded. "That's when I started stoking it. Agenta and I started spending time together. We were an odd couple, the Indian and the Swede, odd enough that other students commented how opposites attract, that we'd get hitched before the end of the semester. One night when Agenta and I shared a pizza and pitcher of beer at the Bon Ton, Gunnar came in and jumped me."

"That was the fight that you were arrested for?"

"Wasn't much of a fight." The sides of Ham's mouth downturned and he shook his head. "Like I said, Gunnar was frail. Even when he planted a pool cue across my back, I was willing to let it go. But when he went after Agenta . . ."

"The cops were called."

"In force. Every one of them. I even held Gunnar so the officer could get the cuffs on without hurting him. The officer had the one set of handcuffs, but I went along peaceably." Ham stood and leaned over the balcony. "The fight wasn't what it seemed, like many things aren't what they first appear. Take those swastikas down there."

Manny joined Ham at the railing. Out of his periphery, Manny saw the bald biker stand from his seat on the staircase. Ham nodded to him, and Baldy sat. Ham pointed to the Hawaiian-garbed man he'd seen earlier, now joined by an equally gaudily dressed, portly woman with two cameras draped around her wattled neck. They pointed to the bricks embedded in the floor. "Did you know some native craftsman painted that symbol in the brick when they built this hotel?"

"My uncle Marion told me that once when we came to Rapid City to see *Bigfoot*."

Ham's eyebrows raised. "Bigfoot? Here in town?"

Manny laughed. "Not quite. Uncle Marion thought there were Bigfoot creatures living on Pine Ridge."

Now it was Ham's turn to laugh. "I remember those local legends."

"That's all they are, legend, but Unc thought otherwise. When he heard the Diamond Theater would be showing *Bigfoot*, he just had to see it. For three months he saved the money he got for selling baskets he'd woven so we could come here. The flick was so bad we left ten minutes into the film and wandered around Rapid. We ended up sightseeing here, Unc showing me the swastikas on the bricks, which was far more interesting than John Carradine and that awful film."

"I imagine it was terrible moviemaking." Ham clasped his

hands behind his back and turned to Manny. He stood a full head taller, but didn't appear to be looking down on him as he spoke softly, slowly, as the judge and educator Alexander Hamilton High Elk, and Manny felt as if Unc were there teaching him. "The painting on the brick is the Whirling Log of the Navajo. Another legend— more credible than the Bigfoot rumor— has one of the Navajo outcasts hiding in a hollow log floating down a river to a safe place. Four deities had sealed him in the log, and only when he'd suffered through the ordeal of a mighty whirlpool did they rescue him. Am I boring you?"

"Not at all." Manny had to remind himself why he was interviewing Judge High Elk, mesmerized by his tale.

"The deities gave our wayward brave some corn," he continued, "which he planted, and eventually harvested. And he was taught to paint with the sand, to return to his tribe and tell of his fortune. So the Whirling Log represents prosperity, not death as many White men associate it with. I guess you can say I am much like the Navajo Whirling Log."

"How so?"

"I represent the best in jurisprudence, not some nominee that will say anything to win the appointment. Not at all like the newspapers have been reporting."

"They haven't been very supportive of you."

"At least the *Rapid City Journal* wants to do a spread of my accomplishments. I'm to meet a Sonja Myers for an interview this afternoon."

Manny frowned. "A word of advice—be cautious what you say to Ms. Myers. She has a way of twisting the truth around."

"I'll remember that. Now if we're finished, I really do have to meet her."

"Will you be in the area for a few days, if I have any more questions?"

Ham smoothed his jeans. "I have a cabin in view of

Roughlock Falls in Spearfish Canyon." He jotted the address on another business card and handed it to Manny. "I'll be there for most of the week prepping for the hearings."

Ham had started down the steps when Manny stopped him. "One last thing—where could I find Joe Dozi?"

"The business card," Ham said. "That's his shop address."

Manny turned the card over. A drawing of a biker on a lowrider engulfed by smoke proclaimed VINTAGE IRON.

"Joe's there most of the time when he's not helping me prepare for the confirmation hearings."

Manny followed Ham down the steps, and Baldy stood and walked beside Ham. People in the lobby stared, and a couple close to the door stepped aside to allow them to pass. Ham nodded to Baldy. "This is Joe, by the way."

Baldy gave Manny a menacing stare and went back to studying the crowd. "Call him anytime, except tonight. We're rehearsing questions over a pitcher of Moose Drool at a local watering hole."

Manny followed them out the door ahead of the crowd that watched as Ham and Joe Dozi straddled their motorcycles that were parked in front of Willie's Durango. Dozi swung his leg over a Harley Panhead, restored to perfection, while Ham sat astride a bright red Indian Chief. Naturally. Just as he kick-started his bike, he turned to Dozi. "You remember that hunting guide Gunnar hired on the reservation the week before he went missing?"

"Marshal Ten Bears."

Ham paused putting on his helmet and turned to Dozi. "You sure? That was Moses Ten Bears's grandson?"

"I ought to know." Dozi rotated the kick lever to stop dead center in preparation to kicking the bike to life. "I talked with him while you hiked around Red Shirt Table back in '69."

Before Manny could ask more questions, vintage motorcycles roaring to life drowned him out, rapping up as they rode east on Sixth Street. He got out his notebook and wrote the name of the hunting guide, not because he would forget, but to remind him how coincidences rarely happen in real life. Marshal Ten Bears.

>()()()<

"I thought you wanted to sit in when I interviewed Judge High Elk. Last we spoke, you were going to finagle a parking spot close to the hotel."

"Fat chance." Willie turned onto Main Street on his way to Clara's house. "As soon as I started up the stairs, that Secret Service guy blocked my way. Told me the stairs were now closed and to take a hike."

"The one in leathers looking like a squat Mr. Clean or a bald fireplug?"

Willie nodded.

Manny laughed. "He's not Secret Service—he's Judge High Elk's personal friend. I made the same mistake myself."

"You? Make a mistake?"

Manny ignored him. "Doesn't answer where you were."

"Well, the biker got a little personal there. Wouldn't let me come any farther into the lobby. Said the judge was in a special meeting upstairs. If I'd known he wasn't government, I'd have put a boot in his rectum."

"He would have planted one back. Remember what Micah Crowder said: three tours in 'Nam with Special Forces."

Willie nodded in recognition. "Either way, I wish I would have stayed with the vehicle and not hung out in the lobby. Some SOB keyed the side of this outfit."

"What SOB?"

Willie shrugged. "Don't know, but I'd bet money it was that bald-headed SOB."

>()()()<

Willie turned into Clara's driveway. "Where's Norman?"

"Who?"

"That psycho Norman Bates of the feline world."

Manny looked from the garage to Willie to the garage. "If he's still in the garage I'm going to make friends with him today."

Manny climbed out of the Durango and punched in the code for the garage door. It whined as if protesting the door opening, protesting Manny's access to Norman. Manny squatted on his heels and looked under Clara's car. "Kitty. Kitty."

"I'd leave him alone."

"He's all right. I think he's warming up to me."

Manny spotted the cat curled under Clara's car and reached in to ease the cat out. It came alive, hissing, leaping on Manny's bandaged arm. Manny shook his arm violently and the cat lost its hold, skidded into the far wall, and retreated back under Clara's car. It squatted on its haunches, hissing, demanding a rematch.

"Looks like he's warming to you just fine."

"Give him time," Manny said as he walked away, all the while expecting Norman to leap again.

"Speaking of time, what time will you be on the rez tomorrow?"

Manny, his eyes darting to the front door of the house, whispered to Willie through the open window. "All depends what time my Viagra loses its potency."

CHAPTER 9

OCTOBER 8, 1927

"I would aim two inches over his back." Moses studied the four-by-five mulie through his binoculars. The buck's wide rack peeked through heavy sagebrush, the deer's body hidden by the brush. "Yes. Two inches. He is two hundred yards."

"I think he's farther than that." Clayton snuggled behind the rifle stock.

"Things seem farther away here in the Badlands. Two inches. Trust me."

The .45-70 barked and the muzzle flew up. It settled back down onto the dead juniper where Clayton had rested the gun. Clayton recovered just in time to point at the deer disappearing over the embankment. "Shit! Right over the top of him."

"Maybe next time you'll listen." Moses stood and cradled his rifle as he started through sagebrush.

"Where the hell you going?"

"Get supper."

"With a .22?"

Moses smiled. "I have killed most game with a .22. Trust me."

>‹›‹›‹›‹

"We should be eating venison."

Moses prodded the rabbit roasting over the fire with his knife; the fat dripping down onto the flames crackled and hissed. "We would be if you had listened. We will go out again tomorrow morning and find your trophy buck."

Clayton sat cross-legged on the ground in front of the fire and wrapped his saddle blanket around his shoulders. "Gets colder than a well digger's ass here at night."

"Cold and clear." Moses pointed up to a sky that never ended. As far as he could see, *Wakan Tanka* had provided the two-leggeds with wonderment they could never fully comprehend.

"Big Dipper is full tonight." Clayton shivered and inched closer to the fire.

"The Old Ones would have said the Seven Council Fires are alive tonight, talking and deciding what they will do tomorrow." The constellation seemed to move, to wink and to gyrate as it fought to remain free of low clouds obstructing their vision.

"All I know is a man could freeze to death here in the middle of summer. If we get lost, we're done for."

Moses sliced off a piece of rabbit breast and put it on a plate beside wild turnips and onions. He nodded to the sky as he handed Clayton the plate. "See *Wachpi Owanhilla*? What you *wasicu* call the Big Dipper? He will never lie to us, he will always show us the way home as long as we can see him. So do not worry about getting lost."

Clayton cut his rabbit breast in two and speared it with a fork, blowing on it as he talked. "We've got tomorrow to hunt, then I got to get back to the ranch, and you got that job in Rapid City in three days. If you'd let me drive you we could shave a day off both our trips and have an extra day to hunt."

"I hate riding in that car of yours. It is noisy and it smells bad, like you *wasicu*."

Clayton tossed a rock at Moses that bounced off his moccasins. "At least sleep on it."

"All right," Moses said after biting into a rabbit leg. Juice dripped onto the back of his hand and he licked it off. "But you sleep on something as well."

"What?"

"Hannah. When are you going to marry her?"

"This again? I know your sister-in-law expects me to tie the knot. But I'm a slow starter."

"Not so slow that you did not already have a son with her. Samuel is a fine boy, but he needs his father close. And my Hannah needs a husband."

Clayton stood and tossed the rabbit bones into the sagebrush before untying his bedroll from his saddle. "I just have to wait. I intend to marry her just as soon as this election is over."

"Whose brilliant idea was that?"

"Dad's. He likes Hannah well enough. Thinks she's a beautiful woman and will make me a fine wife. But he figures it'll hurt my chances if, well, if people . . ."

"If people knew you married an Indian? Is it your father that feels that way, or you?"

Clayton kept his eyes on his bedroll. "This election's just too important for me to lose. Too important to the Sioux. To all Indians suffering on reservations. You want some politician pushing for assimilation to land the Senate seat again?" Clayton tossed his bedroll beside the fire and grabbed a mason jar of whiskey. He dropped onto the ground and sat warming his feet by the fire. He handed Moses the jar and snatched it away just as Moses reached for it. "I know what you'd do with it— you'd smash it."

"And rightly so. You do not need that."

"It's the good stuff."

"Not like the bathtub gin you sell us Indians?"

"Look, I've been selling to Indians since I started coming here hunting with you. Your people want it. I can supply it. And not rotgut that will kill them. Can they help it if the politicians outlawed booze?"

"It has always been outlawed here on the reservation. The stuff you sell them *is* that cheap crap. We Lakota cannot handle the good stuff, let alone that panther piss."

Clayton lit a Chesterfield with an Ohio Blue Tip and tossed it into the fire. "At least people know what I sell them won't hurt them."

"Sure it does. Look at all the broken homes, the failed families because of that. Besides, the cheap stuff has the most profit margin."

Clayton laughed. "Guess you have been studying other things than being a medicine man."

"Sacred man. I know some things of healing the body. What I heal is Indian sickness—things that come out of the night and whisk a person's soul away. Like that rotgut that whisks a man's will away, steals his ambition to be more than another drunk passed out under a rock."

Clayton shivered and wrapped his blanket tighter around him as he stared wide-eyed past the fire into the night. "You're too busy studying the old ways that you forget there are new ways to be understood, new things coming down that will affect your people. The best thing that could happen for you Oglala is for me to get elected to the Senate. Then I can introduce legislation that'll help all the Sioux. And allow me the freedom to marry Hannah."

"And be a proper father to Samuel?"

"Of course."

"Spend time with him like a father should?"

"Look—I'd love to take Samuel to the movies. To ball games."

"But you can't risk being seen with an Indian son?"

Clayton kicked a dirt clod. It skipped once along the ground before it bounced off a boulder as big as a Buick. "Dammit, people just don't see you Lakota like I do. People would judge me by the Indian son I had and there goes the election. At this point I can't risk people knowing Samuel's my son, both for my election and for what I can do for the reservations."

Moses thought of the *wasicu*, of their need for status, their need for money. "And if people knew you had a *atkuku wanice*, a son without a father, people would not give you the money you want."

"Elections cost money—more than even my father's willing to invest—and my liquor sales go into that election fund. Now how about that extra day hunting? I promise to drive you to work on that warehouse project."

"It is a hotel," Moses corrected. "The Alex Johnson, at least it will be when it is finished. That railroad man sent a man all the way to Pine Ridge just to ask me to paint for him. That is money I will come by honestly that will help my people more than your moonshine."

Clayton shrugged and took another short pull of whiskey. "You going to paint one of your visions for this Alex Johnson?"

Moses shook his head while he spread his own bedroll by the fire. "No, but he said I could paint anything that comes to mind on those bricks they are laying on the lobby floor."

"So?"

"So what?"

"What the hell you going to paint?"

"A Whirling Log."

"You sure you haven't been tapping into my jar here?"

Moses laughed. "Never." He drew in the dirt with a twig. "This is the Log." He drew opposing right angles in the dirt. "See how the hands point clockwise—it is the Navajo's powerful solar symbol."

"You think anyone will know what this means a hundred years from now, when they trample on the bricks as they're hauling their luggage into the hotel?"

"Someone will. Trust me."

><><><><

Clayton bolted upright and his head hit the side of the cabin beside his cot. "What the hell's going on? What're you doing?"

"Painting."

Clayton fished his pocket watch out of his trousers draped over a chair at the foot of the bunk. "I can see that, but at friggin' five o'clock in the morning?"

"And?"

"And it's too damned early."

"You said you wanted to get an early start on that mulie."

"But not this damned early."

Moses laid his palette beside the partially finished muslin cloth and covered it against the rising morning heat. "The Old Man is Dancing. Or as you White men say, daylight is burning."

"What old man?"

Moses laughed and handed Clayton a cup of coffee to help shake off the sleep. He pointed to the rays of light coming through the cabin's solitary window. "Those rays of light every morning is the Old Man Dancing. He signals another day, another adventure. I love this time because you can see the Old Man and the Anpao Wichanpi."

Clayton swung his legs over the bunk and cussed as he spilled hot coffee on them. "I don't want to go out and spot the Morning Star again. If I get up at all it's to have some breakfast."

"Fair enough." Moses bent and opened the trapdoor under the cabin that contained his perishables protected from the Badlands heat by cool sand. He grabbed bacon he'd cured last week and sliced off enough for Clayton. He added wood to the cookstove and waited for the stove to heat. Shimmering heat rising upward and sideways from the wind whistling through chinks in the cabin made the paintings leaning against the walls seem to live, to move. Moisture popped off the skillet as he slapped the bacon into a frying pan. "Hand me those eggs."

Clayton grabbed four eggs that Moses had liberated from a sparrow's nest yesterday. "What the hell's this supposed to be?" Clayton had tossed the cloth covering the painting back and stood, head cocked, scratching his testicles while he eyed the painting. "Looks kind of spooky."

Moses snatched the cloth from Clayton's hand and covered the painting again. "It is Hiram Crow Foot's vision. And it is personal."

Clayton backed away as he threw his hands up. "Sorry."

"No harm." Moses turned back to the cookstove.

"You know you could make some serious money selling your paintings."

"They are not mine. They belong to others."

"But you said most folks don't want them when you're done. That they throw them away when they see them, right?"

The wind carried the odor of bacon and eggs past Clayton's nose. "What else good would they ever be?"

"They will help my people. One day they will."

"How?"

Moses shrugged. "Not sure. Just got the feeling."

CHAPTER 10

Manny reached over and turned off KILI. The powwow music gone, his headache instantly subsided.

"Not much different than that Scandinavian hip-hop you're always listening to. Even Janet would agree with me."

"Polka is not hip-hop. And where's your trainee this morning?"

"I convinced Uncle Leon she should do some background research on Marshal Ten Bears." Willie smiled and turned off BIA 18 toward Oglala. Once, this part of the reservation had been particularly hostile to law enforcement. In the 1970s, FBI agents Ron Williams and Jack Coler were murdered here trying to serve an arrest warrant on an American Indian Movement member. Manny recalled that day when he and his school chums huddled around the police scanner blaring outside the gas station, listening to U.S. Marshals and BIA police rush to the scene. Even now the people here shunned and distrusted authority. And Manny represented all that was hated about the federal bureaucracy. They wouldn't hesitate to spit on the Great Manny Tanno like any other federal law-man.

A three-door Mercury, a passenger door missing in action, passed them. Black smoke spewed over the Oglala Sioux Tribal Durango, and Manny tasted the oily exhaust as the Merc limped around them. The old driver brushed a fallen headliner out of his face as he clutched the wheel tightly with one hand and dragged on a cigarette with the other. The car looked like every rez rod on Pine Ridge, with its FREE LEON-ARD PELTIER bumper sticker in support of the only man convicted in Coler's and Williams's deaths.

"Don't expect the red carpet here."

Manny groped his shirt pocket for a pack of cigarettes that he no longer kept there for such stressful emergencies; a Camel moment, as he referred to such times. "Tell me about it. People here find out an FBI agent is snooping around and things might get interesting. At least they don't hate you tribal cops as much."

"That's some consolation. That just means they'll kill me last."

They passed the hamlet of Oglala and continued eight miles farther north, past Reuben's trailer.

"We could stop for a neighborly visit, since you get along so well with your brother now." Willie's disgust was strong in his voice, his sarcasm biting, his unsaid accusation of Manny associating with a convicted murderer hanging in the air.

"Reuben and I are trying to work things out. Got to—he's the only family I got left." Willie drew in a quick breath and he became silent, morose as he drove, and Manny wished he could take back his words. Willie's aunt Lizzy had been the only family he had left, and now he didn't even have her. It hadn't helped when Manny had pointed out that he *did* have family, that Reuben was his uncle by marriage to his aunt Lizzy. That reinforced Willie's belief that Reuben's criminal influence had been his aunt's eventual downfall. All Willie had were the monthly visits she was allowed since being admitted to the psych ward at the state hospital.

Manny wanted to give some words to ease Willie's pain, but he had none. All Manny could do was empathize with him. Manny felt his own guilt that he'd betrayed Reuben for the past twenty-five years, believing his brother guilty of the murder that sent Reuben to the state penitentiary. Since returning to Pine Ridge to work the Red Cloud homicide two months ago he learned the truth about Reuben: He might have been a violent enforcer for AIM, but he was innocent of the murder that sent him up. Manny wanted to tell Willie all these things, tell him he knew how it felt to betray one you loved, but he could not. Reuben's secret was destined to remain locked inside that safe that only he and Reuben could unlock.

"Tell me how things are going with Doreen," Manny said, quick to get Willie's mind off his aunt Lizzy. "Last you mentioned, you two were getting pretty serious."

Willie stopped in the road to allow a skunk family to cross. Three kits waddled behind their mother, her tail high and defiant in the air, challenging anyone to come near her brood. "She suggested I move in with her."

"What's the holdup?"

"Me. I'm kind of set in my ways. Women always want to change a guy."

"Is that something you've learned in your vast twenty-three years? Or did you read that in *Maxim*?"

"You know what I mean."

Manny knew. Since moving in with Clara, she had led him down the domestic path, a trail that was both unfamiliar and frightening to him. But a path that just might have more rewards than not, if he gave Clara a chance. "Maybe you should give Doreen a shot at domesticating you."

"And do what? She's already griping about the way I've been dressing . . ."

"Well it wouldn't hurt you to change clothes once a week." Manny flicked dried egg off Willie's shirtfront.

Willie slapped Manny's hand away. "Then she wants to know wherever I go. It's none of her business."

"It is if she cares about you."

Willie cranked up the music again and Manny knew their conversation was ended for now.

They continued in silence on the road toward Red Shirt Table. Willie slowed when he found the two-track that led to Sophie High Elk's house. Deep ruts remained from when it last rained, and Willie fought the wheel to keep the Dodge on top of them. Milkweeds and cocklebur bushes had claimed the road, but a few pushed into the dirt showed a vehicle had recently driven these ruts.

"I'd feel better if we could have called her first."

"Protocol?" Manny shrugged. "All that would have done is alert her we were coming, and she'd be gone when we got here. Or have her story rehearsed about Judge High Elk's whereabouts."

"Think she'd lie for him?"

"Would your mother have lied to protect you?"

Willie shrugged. "Don't remember her. I was too little when I came to live with Aunt Lizzy."

"Then Elizabeth? Think she'd lie for you?"

Willie frowned. "She would have before I put her in the loony bin."

Manny touched Willie's shoulder. "You didn't put her there. She's sick and needed help. Point is, she'd lie to protect you as surely as Sophie would lie to protect the judge. Besides, it's not our fault she doesn't have a phone."

"Maybe when the judge gets the Supreme Court appointment he'll buy his mother one."

"Be my guess, Sophie High Elk is old-school enough she doesn't have a lot of use for luxuries like a phone."

Willie slowed as the Dodge kicked up dust that swirled around and cut down on visibility. A sudden gust of wind blew thick, dark dirt across the road, obscuring Sophie's house. When the wind died down, it left the house in front of them as if it had just floated down from the dust cloud. Or crashed. The tattered tar paper-roofed shack swayed with the wind in the middle of a prairie dotted with junk cars. A rusted Cadillac and wrecked Hudson in Sophie's yard had sunk into the ground, their tires covered axle-deep with Dakota dirt, standing guard on either side of her front door. Montana Mini Storages, Unc often called them. He thought that was people's rationale for leaving them scattered along every reservation in the west, that they were cheaper than buying storage sheds. Healthier for the environment. A person could even gut one, fill it with dirt and flower seeds, and make a giant terrarium out of it, though Manny had never seen one.

Willie pulled up beside the Hudson, which was missing all its windows. Indian air-conditioning. "*Unci*," he called, using the term of respect for *grandmother* as he stepped from the Durango.

Manny caught movement at the back of the shack, and he started through thick jaggers that stuck to the legs of his Dockers. He cleared the far corner of the house when a shriveled, stooped old woman thrust a rifle barrel into his face, her knuckles whitening through dark liver spots as she kept pressure on the trigger. "What you want?" she hissed through ill-fitting teeth that clacked together.

Manny chanced a look to his side. Sophie High Elk spoke through teeth so bright and straight they could have been in a Polident commercial, one for ill-fitting dentures. She stooped with a pronounced dowager's hump, a head shorter than Manny, with a fire in eyes more rimmed with age lines than

Manny had ever seen. But they were no laugh lines. Her weathered, leathered face was a road map of where she'd been in life, what she'd done. From what Willie told him, Sophie had been alone and independent most of her life and expected help from no one. Including protecting herself.

"I didn't catch that, mister. I said, what you want?"

"We need to talk with you, Grandmother." Willie had walked up on them soundlessly and stood beside Manny.

Her eyes shifted to Willie even if her gun did not, taking in his black OST uniform, and she finally lowered the pump .22. "Hamilton said you'd be coming here to ask questions about his past. He said for me to answer truthfully, that things would come out in the Senate hearings anyway. Don't mean I have to like you snooping around about him."

"We're not here for that, Grandmother," Willie said, taking off his hat. "But we do need to speak with you about your son."

Sophie let the hammer down on the rusty Remington .22 pump and cradled the gun in her arm. She said nothing as she brushed past them and into the house. They followed her into the small, stucco house the color of last month's curdled milk. Sophie motioned through the doorway to a living room and a sweat-stained couch missing one cushion before disappearing into the kitchen.

"That was close," Willie whispered.

Manny smiled. "I doubt that old rifle could even shoot as rusty as it is. She just wanted to make sure we didn't take what's hers."

"This?" Willie gestured around the tiny room. Sophie's house consisted of this room, a kitchen, and another small room missing a door that housed a bed and milk crates piled three high acting as a dresser. Dingy muslin skirts identical to the one Sophie wore took up space in one milk crate, the other two housing socks and what looked like frayed bloomers.

He turned his attention to the living room decorated in gaudy, faded brown paisley wallpaper that had been popular decades ago. A water leak from the roof had trickled down and stained one wall, lifting plaster from it and exposing the chicken-wire underlayment. Wind ruffled through loose wallpaper.

Willie nodded to newspaper sticking out of the wall. "What with the paper?"

"Insulation." Manny lifted a corner of the wallpaper away. Sophie had stuffed newspapers between the plaster and the outer wall. Unc had done the same thing to the log cabin he and Manny had lived in. Unc would scour garbage cans for discarded newspaper to shove between the inner and outer walls, plugging the chinking and preventing wind from whipping through. "People used to stuff most anything behind their walls for insulation, rags, newspapers, even old canvas and burlap they'd scrounge. It wasn't the most efficient, but it kept some of the cold out."

But Manny wasn't interested in the damaged wall. His eye was on the one across from it. He fished inside his pocket for his reading glasses and stepped closer. Photos of Ham adorned the entire wall, which was free of wallpaper and painted a pleasant robin egg blue. The pictures showed Ham in various stages of development, from when he was eight, perhaps nine Manny guessed, through his law school days, each photo unmistakably Alexander Hamilton High Elk, with his prominent nose and intense blue eyes.

Sophie shuffled out of the kitchen carrying a pot and cups. She set them on a cedar log coffee table in front of the couch. "Don't have coffee. All I got is *cheyaka*."

"Tea is fine, Grandmother."

Willie poured the tea and handed the cup to Sophie, but she waved it away. "You men drink. I only got those two cups."

She used the edge of a cushioned chair to ease herself down and grabbed a bowl from the floor and balanced it in her lap. She took out a leather loop, porcupine quills adorning half the loop, and put several more quills in her mouth to soften. "What do you wish to know?" she said between sucking quills.

"Gunnar Janssen, Mrs. High Elk."

Sophie showed no signs of recognition as she continued quilling. "That college pal of Hamilton's? He brought him here a couple times, him and that other roommate of his from college. He disappeared—Gunnar, not the scary one—and Hamilton thought he might have hid out from the draft board or had some hunting accident."

"He was found murdered in the Stronghold a few days ago, in the old bombing range."

Sophie put her quillwork down and stared over her glasses at Manny. "Hamilton brought him here a few times when they were in college. That's all I know."

Manny tasted the tea, weak and bitter and tepid. He set the cup on the table. "Tell me about that time when Gunnar went missing." Manny scooted to the edge of the couch to watch her eyes. "Ham said he stayed with you for a week back then, looking for Gunnar. Do you recall that?"

Sophie flattened a porcupine quill as she pulled it between clenched dentures loose enough they threatened to come out. She pushed against her lip to seat the dentures. "That what Hamilton told you, that he looked for Gunnar for a week?"

"He did."

"Then that is what happened." The wattle under her chin swayed as she spoke. "You think he'd lie to you about that?" Her stare bore through him, defiant and unwavering, her mistrust of authority apparent, thick like a curtain that Manny needed to peel back.

"Sometimes a person forgets when they get on in age."

Sophie used the arm of the chair and stood. Willie leaned over to help her but she brushed his hand away. "Hamilton stayed here for the entire week, just like he said. A federal judge and a Lakota, and you question his words?"

She walked hunched over to her I Love My Son wall and tapped a picture with a gnarled finger. The eight-year-old boy Manny was drawn to earlier stared back through blue eyes set on an angular face and had a pleasant, natural smile. A trusting smile. A smile that beckoned a person to stop and talk with the boy. Ham's smile that he never lost. He clutched a tiny bow and a quiver slung loosely across his back. "Hamilton always saw the good in things. Always happy despite his life here at home. This was Hamilton's last day with me. His father, Samuel, was a drunkard of the worst kind. Did you know that has always been the curse of our people?"

Manny nodded. The curse of the bottle had been the curse of so many Manny knew on the reservation. It had been one of the reasons he had fled Pine Ridge to the safety of the White man's world. Right out of college the bureau had offered him a special agent position and he'd grabbed it, never looking back to the poverty, along with the rampant alcoholism, on the reservation. He often wondered if he should have taken the fork in the road that Lumpy had, stayed right here and tried to make a difference. "You said this was his last day with you." He pointed to the photo. "Where did he go?"

"The Jesuits." Sophie straightened as best she could and her jaw jutted out, a proud mother remembering her only child. "Hamilton was eight when Samuel died, leaving me with no job, no source of income. I was lucky to do some hunting for meat, and plant a garden every year, not that it grew well here in this dry heat. I had little enough for one person, let alone a growing boy. Holy Rosary Mission was a godsend for Hamilton. They did him right."

She chin-pointed to another picture taken when he was a teen. Ham stood beside grandstands, a multicolored medal draped around his neck under his disarming smile. "This was the year Hamilton set the state record in the cross-country."

Willie pointed to a set of pictures of Ham wearing ill-fitting suits. "Law school?

"The dorm in Vermillion. He couldn't find a suit to fit him so we went shopping at the Salvation Army. Made no difference— he still came out top in his class."

Sophie smiled for the first time. "His last day of law school, and his first day starting for Whitney Glover."

"The Rapid City firm?"

Sophie nodded.

"High profile," Willie said, squinting to get a better look.

"As I recall, Ham defended Calvin Wolf Guts in a 1979 homicide. Made a name for himself when he got an acquittal." Manny remembered the case from his Pine Ridge days. AIM enforcer Cal Wolf Guts had been arrested for killing Marjorie White Plume. Whitney Glover assigned his junior attorney, Alex High Elk, to defend Wolf Guts. The press had already convicted Wolf Guts and were salivating over the sentence even as the jury acquitted him. After that, the press consumed stories of the new bright shining star in the Glover law firm. But Whitney Glover hated being replaced in the company spotlight, and assigned Ham piddly cases thereafter until a law firm in Sioux Falls scooped him up.

"Glover expected Calvin to get convicted, like everyone else," Sophie whistled through her dentures. "Thought Hamilton would plead it out, but he didn't. He stood his ground and went to trial." She faced Manny. "And you question a man with that kind of integrity? If Hamilton said he was here for a week looking for Gunnar, he was."

"It's information we had to verify." Manny backed away from Sophie when she put a porcupine quill in her mouth. The last thing he needed was a trip to the ER to dig a porcupine quill spit by an irate senior citizen out of his face.

"You don't know anything about my son, do you?"

"Just what's in the *Judicial Quarterly* and *Indian Law Review*." *And the dossier the bureau sent me.*

"The magazine ever mention his grandfather, Clayton Charles? Samuel's father?"

The dossier had a single brief line about the judge's famous grandfather. "Not much."

"How the good senator abandoned Hamilton's father, Samuel, and his mother, Hannah? Of course, your history whitewashes that." She pulled the quill between her teeth, looked at it, and popped it back in her mouth to soak more. "Sam never got over Clayton abandoning him and Hannah. Hannah was a strong woman, never letting on there was anything wrong with Clayton living apart from them.

"But Sam—it ate on him. Bad. He never forgave his father for shunning him and his mother. So when Hamilton was born, my husband insisted on naming him Alexander Hamilton. Know why?"

"Because the original Alexander Hamilton's father abandoned him when he was only eleven," Willie answered. "In a place called Charles Town."

Sophie's eyes narrowed. "You know your history, Officer. Charles Town. Just like the Charles family ranch that Hannah and Sam wasn't good enough to ever set foot on. Samuel thought it would be funny if he named his son after the first Alexander Hamilton. But it was anything but humorous, and it ate on Sam until the day he died."

Sophie dropped back into her chair and her head bobbed on her chest. She had told them things she may never have told anyone else, just to protect her son, to parry some of the painful questions that were going to sling his way during the Senate hearings. When it appeared as if she had dozed off, her head snapped up and once again her fiery eyes met Manny's. "Hamilton's a good person and a good son. Leave him alone."

Sophie slumped farther into the chair then, and her head rested on her chest. Gentle snoring rose from the old woman, and Willie and Manny tiptoed out the door. As they started toward the Durango, Manny felt eyes watching him. He turned to the house, but saw no movement.

"I'd have hated to get on her bad side back in the day."

"I'd hate to get on her bad side now," Manny said, watching the house until they drove away.

Manny and Willie walked into the house just in time to hear Pee Pee Pourier shout out "thirty-four ninety-nine!" Drew Carey, his arm barely able to drape over the massive, shaking shoulders of the woman in the muumuu, gave the lucky contestant the choice of the winning prize. Pee Pee waved them into the living room and dropped back in front of the television. He turned the volume down and divided his attention between the TV and them.

"Watch this. Drew Carey's going to lead this schmuck into picking door number two."

"You certain?"

"Just watch," Pee Pee smiled and rubbed his testicles as if it would bring the woman luck.

Drew Carey gave the fat lady on stage the choice of three doors, the crowd chanting, working themselves into a failure frenzy following Drew's lead. "Door number two! Door number two!"

"Door number two!" she shouted out and the curtains

rose slowly as if in mourning. Gone was the new Chevy Impala. Gone was the entertainment center, complete with surround sound, and vacation trip to Disney World's Epcot Center. The contestant wound up with two tickets to the Rose Bowl.

"At least she won something."

Pee Pee laughed and turned the television off. "That damned fool lives in Connecticut. You think she's going to plunk down change to go all the way to Pasadena to smell a bunch of flowers and watch a football game?"

"I see your point."

Pee Pee faced them and leaned back in the chair. His T-shirt wore more breakfast than his plate had as if he were competing with Willie for most sloppy. He rubbed his crotch waiting for an answer. *At least Willie doesn't fondle himself.* "You didn't come here to hang out with old Pee Pee or watch Drew Carey put the screws to someone else. You want to know about that car."

"Give that man door number two!" Manny did his best to imitate the *Price Is Right* host.

"That's pretty good," Pee Pee laughed. "But you sounded more like Bob Barker. Remember when he was the host?"

"For years. A hometown boy."

"Close. From the Rosebud." Pee Pee checked his watch. "Wait a sec while I check some bidding." He moved to a chair in front of a computer that took up most of the kitchen table and was the only thing in the room that didn't have food dribbled on it. He played the keyboard like a sloppy Liberace and eBay popped on the screen. Pee Pee entered a bid a dollar higher than the last bidder.

"What you shopping for?" Willie leaned over his shoulder. "I've picked up some good deals on eBay myself."

"Boots." Pee Pee winked, his finger poised over the mouse pointed to the bid button. "The pair that Elvis wore in his last concert in Sioux Falls in '68."

"Think you'll get them?"

"Only other bidder is Lumpy."

Now it was Manny's turn to look over Pee Pee's shoulder. "How you know it's Lumpy?"

"Deduction, Watson. I told him about this pair of Elvis boots that was nearing the end of the auction and how I'd like to bid on them. I also told him I needed to go to Hot Springs and see my dad in the VA home. So Lumpy was real generous and gave me the day off. Said take all the time I need." Pee Pee tilted his head back and laughed. "All he wanted is for me to be away from my computer so I couldn't bid on them."

"That's not very smart. You know Lumpy will bid them up."

Pee Pee chuckled. "I'll recoup my money in the end. Lumpy will hound me until I finally relent and sell the boots to him for more than I paid for them."

"Kind of cold," Willie said. "Staying here bidding instead of visiting your dad."

Pee Pee smiled. "Didn't they teach you anything about deception at the police academy? My dad hit it big time at the Prairie Wind Casino last year—biggest haul in the quarter slots they ever had. He took his winnings and moved to Daytona Beach; lies around all day looking at babes in thongs and getting a tan."

"Didn't anyone ever tell him we Skins already have a natural tan?"

Pee Pee checked his watch again, his finger poised above the mouse, checking the time left, then hit it. His bid went through, and the time ran out on the auction. "There, fat ass! Take that."

"Won?"

Pee Pee nodded and sneered. "Be here overnight. I can't wait to see Lumpy's face when I come waltzing in wearing those fancy Tony Lamas."

"The car," Manny pressed.

"The car. Sure." Pee Pee moved onto the couch and grabbed a manila folder from the end table. "Car was a 1940 Buick Roadmaster. Damned near new in 1944. But bombs definitely did the old girl in. I found fragments of bomb casings imbedded in the sheet metal, and the pattern of the broken windows indicated overpressure blew them out."

"You sure?" Willie sat beside Pee Pee and flipped through the folder. "No one would put a new car out there for bombing practice."

Pee Pee took his teeth out and started picking at them with a screwdriver he'd found under a mound of junk on the coffee table. He spoke to Willie, speaking slowly and deliberately, as if instructing a class of new recruits. "I had the brake drums pulled. Back then, people had to put new brake pads on every two thousand miles. By the looks of the rotors on that baby, they'd been turned once. Twice at most."

"That only means the owner couldn't afford brakes."

"I thought of that." Pee Pee scratched his testicles, rubbing his magic lamp. Manny hoped Pee Pee's genie wouldn't come out with him and Willie there. "That's what took me so long. I also tore into the motor. Know how much dirt and rust accumulates in seventy years?"

"What did you find?"

Pee Pee opened his mouth, and Elvis spit out an orange PEZ. "The rings of that engine had just started to seat in the cylinders. Even though it would have been three or four years old at the time of the bombing, that was a pretty new car."

"That makes no sense." Willie stood and paced the room. "No one leaves a new car someplace like that when they know there's bombing practice going on."

"It does if those two drove there never expecting aircraft from Rapid City Air Base." Manny reached for the Elvis PEZ, then thought better. Pee Pee's scratching hand played with the plastic flip door, and Manny knew where that hand had been the last few minutes. "What we got to do now is figure out how this ties in with Gunnar's body being found on top of the other two inside that car."

"Why do they have to be connected at all?" Pee Pee gummed his PEZ. One tooth was stained orange. "And we sure don't know they were murdered. Looked like they were just in the bombing range at the wrong time."

Manny leaned closer to Pee Pee. "Didn't they teach you anything about investigations in the police academy? I don't believe in coincidences, and those three being interred in that car in that place all together would be stretching the laws of the Coincidence God. No, they're connected somehow."

Pee Pee reached over and played with the remote volume. The television powered on and he adjusted the volume as he scooted his chair closer to the TV. "I'd wager you two got a big job—finding out who wanted those other two dead as well as Gunnar Janssen."

As Drew Carey's assistant called for another contestant, Manny thought how right Pee Pee was. And Pee Pee *was* a wagering man.

>○○○<

Willie pulled into the Cohen Home and parked between a pickup missing the bed and a Volkswagen missing one fender, sitting up on blocks. "Sure you want to go in alone? The way I hear it, he's a bear in the morning."

"Chief Horn's a bear anytime"—Manny grinned—"but at least he tolerates me. If I bring you along, you might have to arrest him."

"Arrest a retired cop?"

"Retired and continues being a crotchety old fart. I'll be all right." Manny tried to sound as confident as he entered the retirement home and stopped at the receptionist's desk. The twenty-something girl looked up from her Harlequin romance and frowned as she recognized Manny.

"You going to get Chief Horn stirred up again."

"How so?"

"After you visited him two months ago, he went into a cleaning frenzy."

"Thought that's what you people wanted—for him to take better care of his apartment."

She shook her head. "It is, but he took it upon himself to be the cleaning police for the home. Insists on daily inspections. Raises hell with the other residents if their rooms aren't cleaned like he thinks they ought to be."

"I'll visit with him about it."

"Wipe your feet."

Manny walked the hallway toward the last apartment, past two-occupant rooms on either side to the room occupied by one person: Chief Horn. The first time Manny had visited his old police chief was while he was working on the Jason Red Cloud murder. Chief Horn's room had been a poster child for every ghetto flophouse that Manny had ever been in: messy and dirty and unkempt enough that no one would ever want to return for a visit. When Manny came away from his visit with the chief, he wished he'd packed a can of Black Flag and hand sanitizer.

But the chief's granddaughter, Shannon, had convinced him that he'd get more visitors if his room were clean. The last visit Manny paid, Chief Horn's apartment had been cleaned so that, with a good imagination, Manny could just about make out furniture uncluttered by trash. But he wasn't prepared for this.

"Come in kid," Chief Horn bellowed and stepped aside. It took Manny a moment for the shock of the chief's white shirt and bow tie to wear off before he took in the apartment. The cases of beer—both empty and waiting to be emptied—that did double duty as end tables and places to set trash were now gone. Manny studied the room trying to locate the beer, but found it nowhere on the varnished wooden floor. And he could actually see the kitchen table with a bouquet of wild flowers in a Budweiser bottle doubling as a vase. "Let me take your coat."

Like a polished butler, Chief Horn helped Manny with his coat and hung it on a bentwood coatrack beside the door.

"Iced tea? How about a soda?"

"No beer?"

Horn smiled. "Got no time for that now. I've been too busy enforcing the house regulations on keeping things cleaned."

"So I've heard. Tea would be nice."

Horn grabbed a glass from the cupboard, held it to the light, and polished it with a dishcloth before filling it with ice cubes and tea. "So why the visit?"

"I just wanted to check out rumors." Manny smiled, waving his hand around the apartment.

Horn tilted his head back and laughed. "Bullshit, kid. I know you. You need some info. 'Bout the only time you come to visit your old chief."

Manny nodded. "I'll correct that in the future. I'm working on a couple deaths that happened in the bombing range."

"Three bodies to be exact."

"Moccasin telegraph clued you in?"

Horn nodded. "Quicker than cell phones—at least there's no dead zones with the telegraph. You want to know if I recall anything about missing people during that time?"

Manny nodded. "Two homicides—at least I'm treating them as homicides for now—happened at the bombing range in the Stronghold we figure happened in 1944. One was Moses Ten Bears."

Horn sat on a chair and rested his enormous arms on his knees. "I heard they found him, and I've been studying on that this last week since I heard. When I hired on with the tribe as a snot-nosed nineteen-year-old wanting to arrest bad guys, one of the standing procedures was to give the rookie the Ten Bears file and a week in the Badlands to find him. I didn't find him, of course, but I looked, using maps other officers had used unsuccessfully to find Moses. I might have walked right past that car he was in. There were so many old bombing targets left there. Never thought one would be a dumping ground."

"There was also a geologist—Ellis Lawler—from the School of Mines in the car beside Moses."

Horn sipped his tea delicately, his glass disappearing in his hand. "Years after he went missing, Lawler's wife hired a private investigator out of Chicago to find out what happened to her husband. Guess she wanted him proved dead or something. Anyway, I hiked into the Stronghold with the PI and we had as little luck as everyone else. Last I heard, after a couple years the widow got the money Lawler had salted away."

"Why would a geologist have been interested in the Stronghold? That's miles away from the annual Pig Dig the School of Mines sponsors—geologists accompanied archeologists even back then."

Horn shook his head. "The PI either didn't know—or wouldn't say—but I always thought it odd. There's little there to interest a geologist. Now some other parts of the Badlands . . ."

"What do you know about where the bad rocks live?"

Horn frowned. "Now where the hell did you come up with that?"

Manny set his empty glass on a tooled leather coaster on the kitchen table. "Uncle Marion told me about a place in the Stronghold where the bad rocks live, whatever that meant.

Warned me not to go there. That bad *wakan* lived among the rocks."

"Legend."

"More than legend. Unc was convinced there was something to the stories."

"Marion often had an overactive imagination. When we were kids . . ."

"When you two were kids, you got into a lot of trouble, or so he said."

Horn laughed. "See, his imagination was even overactive about that. But don't put too much store in those legends Marion spouted. He'd tell them to me and I'd just laugh. There was nothing to it."

Manny recalled asking Unc things, all sorts of things, every question that a young boy had for the man raising him as his own. And every time Manny's question was answered, Unc always explained it by saying, "I just know things."

Horn checked his watch. "Sorry kid. I'm overdue for morning inspection." He stood and grabbed a small notebook.

"For violations?"

"Damn straight. Now if I can just talk the management into authorizing actual citations for rule violations, I could issue those at the same time. I'm getting to hate residents letting their rooms get so messy."

Chief Horn shut the apartment door, but Manny stopped him before he could wander down the hall. "There was another body placed in that old car—years after Moses and Ellis went missing—in 1969. He was shot in the head."

Horn stopped and scratched his chin whiskers. "Don't recall anyone missing during that time."

"He was the roommate of Judge High Elk when they went to college."

Horn nodded. "Sure. I recall Spearfish police wanting us to

keep an eye out for some college kid. Said he might be here, though they also thought he fled to Canada to escape the draft. We looked all over hell for him, but no luck. Sorry I can't be more help, but I got inspections to conduct now."

Manny hurried ahead of Chief Horn down the hallway, making his exit before the chief issued the first stern warning of the morning.

CHAPTER 12

After his phone lost contact, Manny redialed Willie's number, dropped the phone, and veered toward Spearfish Creek. As he bent to grab it under his heel, he jerked the wheel back just as a car passing in the opposite direction laid on its horn. The driver gave him the single finger wave in passing.

Manny dialed Willie's number again. "You figure out what the judge wants to talk with you about?"

"Haven't a clue," Manny answered. "All he said was it was important."

"Did you get to the judge's turnoff yet?"

"Just coming up to Savoy now. You sound exhausted."

"Worse," Willie breathed into the phone. "She's driving me nuts."

"Doreen?"

"Janet. Chief Looks Twice—she even has me saying it now—ordered that I take her along, take her under my wing. Whenever she winks at me like she does, I get the feeling she wants to be under something besides my wing."

"That's love."

"That's a pain in my behind. She asked me—no, told me—to put on a clean shirt this morning. A clean shirt when I'll get sweaty and dirty today anyhow."

Willie had been wearing more dirty shirts than clean ones lately. Manny recalled the neat, young tribal officer he'd first met, his uniform pressed, his shoes shined, his gun belt polished as if he intended to use it. That was before he helped put his aunt in the loony bin. "You must have ditched Janet for a little while at least."

Willie's voice broke up as if he were looking over his shoulder as he spoke into the phone. "We're at the White River Visitor's Center. She's in the ladies' room. Her hair was mussed up, and she wanted to touch up her makeup."

"You could always drive off. She'd hate you forever for that, but it'd solve your dilemma."

"And risk being animal control officer for the duration of my career?"

"I told you before the bureau would love to have you."

There was a long pause before Willie answered. "Thanks for the offer. Again. But I'll stay on the rez. I don't know if you've noticed lately, but I've been a tad messed up. I'll just have to suffer through Janet's company."

"You'll pull through, whatever's bothering you." Manny tried convincing himself as much as Willie. "Does Marshal Ten Bears know you're coming?"

Willie's voice faded, then came back clear. Reception in the Badlands was sketchy, at best. "We couldn't find a phone number for him, not even a cell, though one wouldn't work where his cabin is located anyway."

"How do his customers contact him if they need wood?"

"They tack up a note on the bulletin board at Sioux Nation Grocery. Oh crap, here comes Miss Lakota Nation all fixed up. Gotta run."

"Go get 'em tiger."

Manny closed his phone and laughed at the thought of Willie and Janet alone in a remote part of the Badlands, alone away from anyone, alone with Janet sporting fresh makeup, and alone with Willie sporting a declining will to resist her. And sporting morning wood. He laughed again until he realized Janet did Willie no good. He had enough going on in his life without having to referee Janet and Doreen.

Manny came to the turn leading to Ham's cabin, passing the Latchstring Inn on one side of 14A, and the Spearfish Canyon Inn on the other. He took the gravel road heading west up into the hills. Four hikers waved as Manny passed them on their way to Roughlock Falls. The falls had developed into one of the true scenic spots in the Black Hills. Marriages took place against the backdrop of the waterfall, and families went there to renew relations.

Unc had taken him to the falls once as a boy, at a time when tourists hadn't yet discovered it; at a time when picnic areas hadn't yet been built; at a time when the access to the falls was by a narrow hiking trail. They had entered the sacred Black Hills, the spirits of their ancestors yet moaning among the trees, or so Manny had thought at the time and he'd huddled closer to Unc. They remained four days, praying and offering sweetgrass and sage to those *wanagi* that lingered awaiting the Black Hills to be returned to the Lakota. Even then, Manny felt a connection to the Old Ones, especially here in the sacred He Sapa.

The road cut between ponderosa pine and Black Hills spruce narrowed, and Manny drove past Ham's driveway. He backed up. A tiny mailbox proclaiming HIGH ELK was set apart from aspen and birch trees. A flowering lilac bush hid half the mailbox. The driveway was even narrower than the road and he slowed. He didn't need a tree to jump out and hit him right now.

Manny stopped to allow a whitetail doe and her fawn to cross. They watched him intently until they reached the sanctuary of trees across the driveway before they bent their heads and continued their foraging. *They'll be even more skittish when hunting season opens in a couple months.*

Ham's cabin loomed out of the tree line, and Manny stopped in front of Ham's red Indian Chief parked on the other side of his black Suburban, complete with twin silver feathers painted on front fenders and dark tinted windows. It reminded him of every cheesy movie where black government 'Burbs were armored and every world leader riding inside got shot at. Except Ham wasn't getting shot at. He was seated in a sun-faded Adirondack chair protected by a covered porch, smiling under a large dream catcher, the colored feathers keeping time with the wind chime that kept time with the easy breeze that blew from the west. Ham closed his book and stood.

"Glad you could come, Agent Tanno."

"What choice did I have when a federal judge requests my presence? But I wanted to come anyway, just to see your shack, as you called it."

Ham smiled and waved his hand around like those game show hosts Pee Pee Pourier was so obsessed with. "Took the builders two years to figure out how to squeeze two thousand square feet of log into this space so I'd have a view of Roughlock Falls from my porch. Please sit and enjoy the view while I get refreshments. Beer? Wine cooler?"

"Tea?"

"Sugar?"

Manny yearned for calorie-dense, nutrient-bankrupt sugar, but he wanted to survive Clara's inquisition when he came home. And survive his next diabetes screening. "Sweet'N Low?"

Manny nodded, and Ham disappeared inside.

Manny positioned another weather-beaten Adirondack chair

so he could watch the falls. This had been a wet year for the Black Hills, and the water gently rumbled as it dropped over the top and collected in a frothy pool below on its way along Spearfish Canyon.

Ham emerged with a beaker of iced tea and set it on the cedar table in front of Manny, then sat in his chair next to him and cradled a Corona Light. The sun jostling through the trees played off the slice of lime stuck into the top of the beer bottle, which Ham squeezed while he gestured to the waterfall. "Did you know Roughlock Falls got its name from pioneers?"

"Like Ralph Roughlock or something?"

Ham laughed and sipped his beer. "In the winter, early freighters used to rough lock their wagon wheels—roped logs around them to keep them from turning, then hitched their horses to the rear of the wagons and slid down the slope. That's how they got back down this hill in deep snow."

Manny stirred the sweetener into his tea and wrapped his hand around the glass. The water sweating the sides felt cool in the intense heat, and he brushed his forehead with his wet hand. "You didn't call me up here for a history lesson."

Ham smiled and set his beer on the table. "You don't beat around, Agent Tanno. I like that. No, I'm curious how your investigation into Gunnar's death is progressing."

"It's advancing."

"Any leads?"

"Some."

"Am I still in your suspect column?"

Just like an attorney, beat around the juniper bush until coming to the real question. "Don't have a choice but to put you there—you're the last one that saw Gunnar. But I find it awkward that someone from the suspect list wants to talk with someone from the investigator list."

Ham laughed. His eyes laughed, like the photos on Sophie's wall. Disarming laughs, able to put one at ease sitting
next to him on his grand porch. "On the other hand I'm quite
comfortable talking to someone I have solidarity with."

"How so?"

"We're quite alike, you and me. We were both left without
parents at an early age—me when my father died of exposure
and mother couldn't afford to feed me, and you when your
folks died in that car wreck."

"You have a habit of checking into investigators' lives?"

"We're alike." Ham ignored the question. "You were the
first Lakota to be hired by the bureau, and I was the first Lakota to be appointed to the federal bench." Ham dropped his
lime slice into a wicker basket between the chairs. "I just want
you to solve this before the Senate hearings convene. The last
thing I need is to go on Capitol Hill with the shadow of Gunnar's murder hanging over my head. I can pull some strings if
you need help."

Manny shook his head. "The tribe's assigned two investigators to work with me." He could have added that the two
tribal investigators were a criminal investigator with two
months of experience who was on the verge of a breakdown,
and a snotty, arrogant hottie who had been little help except
to distract the criminal investigator. These were his army of
assistants, but it wouldn't hurt to stretch the truth to the good
judge. "Some things just take time: lab tests need to get analyzed. Identification of next of kin. I hope to have this wrapped
up by the time of the hearings."

"Thanks." Ham nursed his beer. "I have what the *New
York Times* calls a plethora of detractors. Enemies that want
me to fall on my face in those hearings. Many my own people."

"I recall you've caught flak for your repeated opposition to tribal sovereignty. Last thing you ruled on was denying giving the entire Badlands back to the tribe."

"That was over a year ago."

"Right before your mining rulings."

Ham stood and leaned against one of the huge timbers holding up the porch. "I just didn't feel it necessary to mine parts of the Palmer Creek and Stronghold Unit that that Canadian company wanted." He smiled at Manny. "And I see you do some checking of your own."

"Nature of my job."

Ham nodded and sipped his beer. "If we let the tribes handle their own affairs completely, they'd allow mining there. The environmental disasters would do irreparable harm to the park, and the tribe."

Manny swished ice cubes around in his empty glass. "Mining would give the tribe the shot in the arm it needs to get on its feet."

"All the tribe needs to get back on its feet is a shot in the butt. Besides, there's never been proof there's anything's worth mining in the Badlands."

"The School of Mines would disagree."

Ham waved the air as if dismissing the comment. "I know. They filed an amicus brief that last time it came before my bench. Some professors were upset they didn't influence me."

"And the letters supporting mining the Badlands? My agent in Sioux Falls said there were a thousand sent to your Sioux Falls office."

Ham turned to Manny and a frown hung on his chiseled face like storm clouds filtering the sun. "Do you know how many of those letters call me an Uncle Tomahawk? Or how many threatened my life because I stood up for what I believed was best for our people? Come inside."

Ham led Manny into the cabin. They walked under an elk head larger than any Manny had seen hanging over the door, past cedar log tables guarding either side of a sofa with deer antlers as armrests and a buffalo robe draped over the back. Ham stopped at a rolltop desk situated in a small alcove and opened it. A Glock—like the one Manny was supposed to carry at all times—held down a shoe box, and Ham caught him eying the gun.

"Like I said—I have enemies. Joe insisted I keep it handy." He took the lid off the shoe box and shoved it toward Manny. "That's how many vile letters I've received just since it was announced I'd been nominated for the Supreme Court. I keep them close in case someone carries out their threat. And for every one of those that's arrived at my office, I've received a hundred angry e-mails."

"You want me to take these and start a threat investigation? The last thing we need now is a federal judge assassinated."

Ham shook his head. "At least I've risen enough in importance that I might be assassinated and not just murdered. But I wouldn't want to give the bastards that much credit, knowing I whined to the FBI. The investigation I'm concerned about is Gunnar's murder—having it completed before the Senate hearings. His and Moses Ten Bears's."

"You know about that?"

Ham nodded. "Moses and some other guy were found in the same car as Gunnar. Poor souls just happened to be on the bombing range at the wrong time. How they all happened there is beyond me."

"We didn't release anything to the press. Who told you about Ten Bears?"

"I have my sources with the moccasin telegraph, too. Or maybe it's because I have such a strong connection with Moses. I told you he and Grandpa Charles had a special friendship, didn't I?" Ham chin-pointed to a painting hanging on the wall opposite the elk, a painting that hung guarded by shadows that parried light getting to the canvas. Manny stepped closer and craned his neck upward. And gasped. "An original?" The second original Ten Bears work Manny had seen this week. He felt honored.

Ham nodded. "That was one of Moses's early works. Right now you're thinking I'm on the take for owning an original Ten Bears painting."

"It is priceless."

"Hardly. Everything has its price." He took Manny's glass and refilled it with tea from a gallon jar on the granite counter, drawing out his explanation, once again the attorney. He handed the glass back to Manny and continued sipping on the same Corona. "My father, Samuel, resented Grandfather Charles. Bitterly. He'd abandoned Dad and Grandmother Hannah to pursue his political career, and his false promises of marriage and a family broke her heart, though Grandmother never let on, from what mother said. Only once did Grandmother Hannah mention that Grandfather Charles's political career meant more than his family, and it appears as if she handled it well, despite her poverty.

"No so my father—his hate drove him into a fresh bottle every day of his life, and he remained a bitter drunk until the day he died."

"So your mother told me."

"You've spoken with her?"

"I had to verify your whereabouts on the reservation the week Gunnar went missing."

Ham shook his head. "Mother. She would have told me you stopped if she had a phone, but it wasn't until last year that I talked her into getting power run into her place."

"I saw she could use a home makeover."

"Don't judge me by the looks of her place."

Manny nodded. "I apologize. People tell me I get down on folks now and again."

Ham waved the comment away. "She won't allow me to help her. Except for her dentures—that's the one thing she wanted when I became successful."

"I noticed that, too."

Ham laughed. "How could you not? They're white enough to be a lighthouse beacon. And they don't fit well. I told her I'd take her to the finest dentist I could, but she threw a fit. Said it was too pricy, and she found a dental school that I won't name to pull her teeth and give her choppers. Looks like they got the teeth from some donor horse, but she's happy with them, and I'm stuck wearing sunglasses whenever I visit her."

Ham set his empty bottle on the coffee table. "But you wonder about the painting."

Manny nodded.

"Moses gave that to Grandfather Charles after a terrible vision he had of Grandfather, terrible enough that Grandfather didn't want it around after he saw his fate."

"What happened to those other paintings that people didn't want?"

Ham shrugged. "There was the rumor that an art critic from New York found and stole them after Moses disappeared. Who knows. But Grandfather Charles said this was Moses's vision for him—frightening though it was—and said he'd beat the vision. That sounded like Grandfather Charles—reckless and unafraid of the devil himself."

Manny set his tea on the table and donned his reading glasses as he stepped close to the painting hanging above eye level. Subdued browns, burnt umbers, and grays dominated the work, the edges ragged, undefined, cruel. The harsh Badlands under a dirty burnt brown sky. An orange sun blazed too-large for the picture, heating cows with matted, motley, mangy hair, skinny range cows looking as if they'd lived their last season. "Frightening."

Ham had soundlessly come to stand beside Manny. "And this was also Moses's vision for himself, or so Grandfather always thought. Moses was a poor rancher, starting with the few cows the government gave him when he became fee patented. He tried to make a go of it—some ranchers in the Badlands became successful, but not Moses. Those cattle represent his sick herd, or so Dad said."

"Still doesn't explain how you came by it."

Ham looked sideways at Manny. "I'm even a suspect in the theft of a painting."

"I didn't mean . . ."

Ham held up his hand. "Just being facetious. Grandfather Charles left the painting in Moses's cabin because he spent time there every year hunting and knocking around the Stronghold. I think Grandfather always intended bringing it home, but he died three years after Moses did. Eldon—Moses's son—gave it to my father one summer, who tossed it into the garbage in a drunken stupor one night when I was a little kid. I waited until dad passed out and rescued it. I kept it at Holy Rosary Mission until I graduated."

Manny gestured around the cabin. "I don't see a security system. Aren't you afraid someone might steal it, since you're away so much?"

Ham smiled. "I have my own kind of security system. Joe stops often when I'm away."

Manny recalled the heavy-handedness with which Joe Dozi parried the people at the Alex Johnson lobby. "Where could I find him?"

Ham took a tarnished railroad watch from his front trouser pocket. It chimed when he opened it. "My Waltham here says Joe should be at his bike shop. Sturgis Rally Week is the first week in August and he's prepping two bikes to show."

"Then I'll visit him there. I'll keep you posted on those things that don't conflict with the investigation."

"In case your prime suspect pans out?"

Manny shook his head. "I'm hoping my prime suspect ends up being no suspect at all."

CHAPTER 13

Manny veered to avoid hitting an oncoming car that had drifted into his lane. Or was it Manny that drifted into the other lane as he punched a number into his cell phone? He recognized Helga's grating voice right away, sharp and short and sounding as if she'd stepped out of a *Hogan's Heroes* episode. Manny asked if Gunnar and Ham's arrest report was ready to be picked up. "I thought all you guys worked together," she cackled into the receiver.

"What guys?"

Her long pause annoyed him, even more than the look she'd given him over her long nose the previous day when he asked to view the archival reports. "You federal guys. The Secret Service is federal, last I knew."

"What *are* you talking about?" Another car dodged his government Malibu and laid on the horn, missing him by a foot. Manny pulled to the side of the road and stopped. "I'm not working with the Secret Service."

"Well, one breezed in here yesterday. Asked—no, demanded—

I give him the arrest report, the same one I copied for you. At least you asked."

No small compliment from someone that didn't even shave her underarms. "Can you make another copy?"

The cackle again. "He took the microfiche roll the report was stored on, along with the arrest report I'd copied for you and that good lookin' fella with you. I told him you'd be picking up the report today, but he said he'd save you the trip."

"What makes you think he was Secret Service?"

"I thought he was some scary bastard off the street at first. You know the kind whose portrait is painted by a courtroom artist."

"What made you finger him as Secret Service?"

She paused dramatically. "His photo on his Secret Service credentials."

"What was his name?"

Helga exaggerated her sigh over the phone as if to punctuate her annoyance. "How should I remember? When the Secret Service demands I hand over all the files, I do."

Manny did his own deep breathing. For being connected to a law enforcement agency, Helga was unusually naive. Didn't she ever jump on the Web? Didn't she know how easily fake bonafides could be bought for any agency with a stroke of the SEND button? Including the Secret Service. "Do you at least recall what he looked like."

"Of course," Helga snapped. "He was stocky and short. Wore those funky heavy shades you government types wear. Not your average guy. Kind of scary."

"How so?"

"You know—charming as a carbuncle. Women's intuition and all. Like if I hadn't given him the report he would have broke a kneecap or an elbow. That kind of charming."

Manny forced a thank you and started disconnecting from the phone when Helga shouted, "Maybe you can tell that bald-headed son of a bitch to stay away from this agency if he's going to act like that."

><><><><

Manny pulled in front of that bald-headed son of a bitch's Sturgis motorcycle shop, ironically situated between the Jolly Funeral Home and Gunnar's Lounge. As he stepped out of his car, hair on Manny's arms stood at attention beside large goose bumps. Helga wasn't the only one with intuition. Manny had felt anxious the other day when he spotted Joe Dozi in the lobby of the Alex Johnson, anxious and wanting to be anywhere besides close to him. Those same feelings came over him now and he took deep breaths before starting for the shop.

Tiny bells over the door announced his entrance, but he doubted anyone inside heard him. An engine roared as the throttle cracked from the shop area. Manny took in the tiny office in a glance: the black suit jacket sticking out of a green nylon dry cleaner's bag. He bent and opened the drawstring. The jacket was wadded around a pair of black slacks, white shirt, and red tie. Manny set it back beside a captain's chair shoved under the desk.

The motor noise coming from the shop drowned out Manny's footsteps as he walked through the door into the shop. Joe Dozi sat on a short, wheeled stool, his ear cocked too close to the motorcycle engine, one hand on the carburetor throttle, the other clutching a screwdriver. He let off the throttle and the motor smoothed to an idle. "No need to sneak around," he called over his shoulder, never looking at Manny but concentrating on adjusting the carburetor primaries.

Manny shut the door behind him. "Did Judge High Elk call and tell you I'd be visiting?"

Dozi grounded the spark plug against the engine and the motor died. "What was that?"

"We need to talk."

Dozi stood and wiped his hands with a shop rag sticking out of his pocket as he gestured to the motorcycle. "Ariel Square Four. Getting it ready to show at the rally."

Manny bent and ran his hand over the seat, which smelled of recent reupholstery. "Cast iron heads. But this is a midproduction motor. '39?"

"So?"

"This is a '38 Square Four? They had cast iron heads in '38, but switched to aluminum heads the next year."

"You know your bikes. Ride?"

Manny laughed. "I have a hard enough time keeping four wheels between the lines and out of the wrecking yard. My uncle used to take me to the rally every year to watch the races and drool over the bikes." Unc would save up for a month before coming to Sturgis for the rally, saving a little gas every week so he and Manny could make it. Manny hadn't been so interested in motorcycles then: he'd been more interested in spending time with Uncle Marion. And with the double-decker ice cream Unc always managed to have pocket change for. "You might have trouble if the judges spot the switch in heads."

Dozi's high-pitched laughed bounced off the confines of the small shop. "Even the most stringent purist won't spot the difference."

"I did."

Dozi's smile morphed into a deep frown as he scooped GOJO from a bucket and began cleaning his hands. "Maybe you won't be around for the races." Dozi worked the cleaner into knuckles swollen by fights, into fingers that had grown calluses from years of hard work. Or wet work in Special Forces, if Reuben's assessment was correct.

"That a threat?"

"Naw." He smiled. "It's just you FBI types are most likely

to be assigned anywhere. Now what is so important you have to come all the way up here to see me?"

"Your Secret Service credentials for starters."

Dozi shrugged. "Let's talk in the office. As much as I love the smell of oil and gas, I'm sure you don't."

Manny followed Dozi into his office, careful not to step onto the GOJO that was dripping grease off his hands and hitting the floor in tiny, brown orbs. He wiped his hands on the shop rag still sticking from his back pocket and dropped into a captain's chair behind a gunmetal gray desk. He wadded the rag and tossed it into a cardboard trash can beside his chair. "Now what's this shit about Secret Service credentials?"

"First let's start with that Oglala Sioux Tribe Durango getting keyed in front of the Alex Johnson the day I met with the judge there."

"That supposed to mean something to me?"

"It means something to Officer With Horn."

"That big, dumb Indian that was eye humping me there in the lobby, the one I put the run on?"

"Don't sell Willie short. He'd be your match, should you decide to push the issue. And it's important to him 'cause his police chief's going to make him pay to get it repainted. And Willie doesn't make a whole lot."

Dozi tilted his head back and laughed, the high pitch almost a squeal. "If I wanted to screw with him, I wouldn't do a juvenile thing like key his car. If I wanted to mess with him I'd stomp a mudhole in his ass right there in the lobby." He rubbed his flattened nose as if to emphasize his threat. "Now we got that bullshit out of the way, tell me the real reason you're here."

"I'm investigating Gunnar Janssen's death."

"Ham said he'd been found with a bullet hole to his head someplace in the Badlands." Dozi chuckled.

"You don't sound too upset."

Dozi shrugged. "Gunnar always was a chickenshit. I always thought that bastard fled to Canada when he lost his school deferment."

"What do you know about his death?"

"Nothing."

"Judge High Elk said Gunnar may have upset some hawks with his anti-Vietnam activities. That piss you off back then?"

"Not enough that I would hurt the little bastard for it. We argued now and again, but we always parted friends."

"I understand you hiked that part of the Badlands where Gunnar's body was found back in your college days. Even Judge High Elk said you were both on Pine Ridge looking for Gunnar the week after he went missing. You with the judge all that time? Maybe Gunnar was alive when you found him back then."

Dozi dropped the feet of his chair onto the floor and stood. He was several inches shorter than Manny, but put together like he could safely walk Harlem or Watts at night. Even Pine Ridge during a powwow. "You accusing me of offing Gunnar?"

"Maybe you found him in 1969. And he was alive then. Or maybe you're protecting someone else that found him alive."

"Why would I have wanted Gunnar dead?"

Manny scooted the chair away from the desk. "Who knows. But it's more than coincidental that you and the judge went to the reservation the same week he went missing. Too coincidental, like someone fitting your description waltzed into the Spearfish PD and seized the arrest report along with the microfiche. I don't believe in coincidences."

"What arrest report?"

Manny had gotten used to interviewing people who lied for a living, professional criminals who could weave tall tales while they wept, or feign anger as they swore on their mothers' graves or to God on Bibles. Manny recognized Dozi had evolved beyond that category of professional liar, into the realm of someone who was comfortable lying and believing it. His expression remained flat until a slight grimace broke across his face. "You sure it was me?"

"Sure enough that we could take a ride to the police department in Spearfish and let the records clerk eyeball you."

"What makes you think it was me? She mention grease?"

"Why would she?"

Dozi jabbed his thumb in his chest. "The way I reek, someone could smell grease on me a block away. Hardly what a Secret Service man might smell like. And these." He pointed to his oil-soaked combat boots.

"Let's say you clean up pretty good."

"How's that?"

"Looks like a black suit waiting to go to the cleaners." Manny kicked the laundry bag under the desk, and the shoes beside it. "Nice pair of polished wing tips. I'll bet you look just fine in your black suit and shoes, dark aviator glasses that're around here somewhere. I'll bet you could fool any secretary at a small police department."

Dozi's hand went to the bulge in his shirt pocket. "Got no time to waste driving to Spearfish. Sturgis Bike Week starts in two weeks. And I have to help Ham prep for Senate hearings before that. Besides, Ham don't like his friends being harassed."

"You saying Judge High Elk would interfere with an open homicide investigation? Now how would that look in front of the Senate hearings?"

The smile fled Dozi's face and his brows merged into a menacing stare. This must be the scary look Helga referred to, Manny thought, because a tingle of fear crept up his spine, and his elbow brushed his Glock in the holster under his jacket. Dozi leaned across the desk and his thick, callused hands rested on the edge as if he intended to spring over it.

Thoughts of being locked in an angry gorilla's cage kept creeping into Manny's mind. "I don't want any of this entering into the hearings. Got it, Agent Tanno?"

"I'll do my job. If it lands on the steps of the Capitol during the Senate confirmation hearings, so be it."

Dozi stepped around the desk, and Manny felt the pistol with his forearm, gauging if he could draw it before Dozi had him by the throat. He concluded he couldn't. "Maybe I did make that arrest report disappear. Maybe I can make most anything disappear."

"Maybe you made Gunnar disappear."

"And maybe I can make weasels that fabricate lies about Ham disappear."

"*Now* you're threatening me. Maybe I go to the federal prosecutor and get a warrant out for you. They don't take threats on federal agents lightly."

Dozi sat on the edge of his desk, his eyes narrowed, fists clenched, and Manny expected him to spring over the desk. Let him, he thought, his hand falling on a crescent wrench at the corner of the desk. *The son of a bitch might get a meal, but I'll take a good bite out of him on the way down.*

"Do what you need to, but I don't expect Gunnar's death to taint Ham's chances of that appointment."

His eyes locked with Manny's for a long moment before Dozi turned on his heels and disappeared into the shop. Manny wasn't aware he'd been holding his breath in anticipation of Dozi's attack. He breathed deep now, knowing he'd come close to fighting for his life. He'd wanted to tell Dozi he had nothing that would come out in the Senate hearings, no proof that he or Ham knew about Gunnar's murder, a murder apparently swallowed by the Stronghold, a place that kept all its secrets safe.

CHAPTER 14

FALL 1934

Senator Clayton Charles drew in a deep breath, holding it for a long moment before letting it out. His horse snorted as he stood in the stirrups glassing the Badlands with his binoculars. "It's great to be out of the city."

"Too many people, huh?" Moses Ten Bears looked down into the valley, scouting for the telltale movement of antlers among the cactus and sagebrush and dead cottonwoods dotting the dry creek bed below.

Clayton massaged his backside and handed his binoculars to Moses. "As hard as this is sitting the saddle for the last week, it beats being in D.C. People make me nuts there. I tried driving there, but all I manage to do is go in circles and get lost."

"Maybe you legislators should straighten out the roads there. Pass one of those cockamamie laws you rush through when it benefits the *wasicu*."

"Now don't get started on that again. Roosevelt has appointed John Collier secretary of the Interior. Good man. Very pro-Indian. He'll push for laws that'll help the tribes. Besides, the traffic in D.C. is a local problem—not one for the U.S. Senate. But let's find that buck out there with Samuel's name on it."

"Where is Samuel?" Moses looked around for the boy, finally spotting his roan gelding picketed beside a rock outcropping. "There is his horse, but where is he?"

Clayton accepted the binos and let them dangle by a leather thong around his neck. He pointed past the gelding to a large mesa, large and lifeless like the rest of the Badlands. "Renaud spotted a nice buck grazing with some does close to your cows. He and Samuel took off across country."

Moses cursed under his breath. Wakan Tanka *keep me from hurting that ignorant White man from New York when I catch up with him.* "I knew I should have refused to let that blowhard come hunting with us."

Clayton exaggerated a pained look, his mouth drooping down sadly. "He only wanted to bag a buck he could hang in his office. What did he do wrong?"

Moses ignored Clayton and dismounted, tying his mule to a clump of sagebrush. "Leave your horse. Quickly." Moses slung his rifle across his back and started on a steady trot toward the saddle of hills Clayton had pointed out, looking at the ground as he turned toward the sun, reading shadows, imperfections, places that pointed where Samuel and Renaud had gone.

Clayton ran to catch up. "Slow down."

Moses glanced over his shoulder but didn't slow. Clayton was a running back in college, but he struggled to keep pace with the steady gait Moses set.

Moses came to the crest of a hill and shielded his eyes from the light. Clayton stopped beside him, doubling over for breath as he held his side. "What the hell's the rush?" Clayton sucked in air, wheezing. "Samuel knows how to get back to the cabin. He won't lose Renaud."

"I'm not worried about that. They are headed toward where the cows go when they thirst. They are going to the place where the bad rocks live."

"What the hell you talking about, where the bad rocks live?"

"The place where *wakan sica*—the evil sacred ones—live. There." Moses pointed to two tiny figures walking up a hillside leading to a saddle of dirt. Moses started toward them when Clayton grunted. Moses glanced back as Clayton stumbled over a cactus before losing his balance on the popcorn shale and tumbling to the ground.

"Catch up when you can." And Moses disappeared over the hill.

Moses caught movement to his right. Samuel and Renaud had crawled to the rim of the saddle nestled between two high hills. Renaud struggled to get the rifle off his shoulder, the sling hung up on his shirt that was more suited for an African safari than a Badlands hunting trip. Samuel shouldered his own rifle, taking aim at a deer in the distance, when Moses yelled, clamoring up the dirt hill beside them, waving his arms. The buck eyed them for a brief moment before darting over the ridge.

Samuel took his rifle from his shoulder. "What did you do that for? That's the best buck I've seen all year."

Moses glared at Renaud, the fat man with the marked French accent still extricating himself from his rifle sling. "The cows." Moses chin-pointed below to four cows that gathered around an alkaline watering hole near where the deer had disappeared.

"We wouldn't have shot your cows. I know better than that."

"I know you would not have." Moses ran his hand through Samuel's hair and looked into the boy's ice blue eyes. Other children taunted him, Moses had heard, because of those blue eyes. Clayton's eyes. Moses had wanted this hunting trip to be special for Samuel, something he could keep and hold aloft for the other boys to see when they were being mean and vicious to him. But he had to protect Samuel. "You cannot come to this place."

"Same as any other in the Badlands."

Clayton stopped beside them and bent over, gasping to catch his breath as wind-kicked white alkaline dust swirled around him and clung to his sweat-drenched face. He looked askance at Renaud LaJeneuse still wrestling with his rifle sling. He leaned over and moved it off the fat man's shoulder. "You're not going to frighten us with that old legend about the rocks again."

Moses frowned at him. "This is where the bad rocks live and you should not—we should not—be here. Bad things happen here."

"What bad things?" Renaud watched the hills wide-eyed as he fingered his rifle. "Only bad things around here are Indians that don't like us White men, *n'est ce-pas*?"

"There is at least one Indian here that is growing a dislike for a particular White man." Moses put on his best sneer and towered over Renaud. He moved away, his eyes darting between Moses and clumps of sagebrush high enough to hide a man. Ever since Clayton had showed up at the cabin with the Frenchman from New York, the man had been looking over his shoulder. Indians, he said, were still on the warpath, hunting and scalping White men wherever they found them. Or that was the claim around his New York law office. All the man could do since coming here to hunt was worry about a raiding party. And sweat. Kills Behind the Tree had told him stories about French traders, honorable men, decent men,

men that treated the Lakota with respect in their dealings with them. Men unlike this fat, unkempt man from New York City.

"Is that true about the rocks?" Renaud's fear was rubbing off on Samuel. His eyes darted to the underbrush as if expecting something to jump up and pounce on them.

Moses bent low and draped a hand around the boy's shoulders. "There is truth to every legend, even one as old as that. You must promise me never to come here again. Never go to that land between those large buttes."

"I promise," Samuel said solemnly. "But where will I find a buck as big as that?"

"I will show you another place. We will eat venison tonight."

Samuel's face lit up.

"How about we shoot one of those scrub cows." Clayton had marginally recovered as he continued gasping for breath. "There's not much to them, but we could have some thin steaks, though we'd get more meat out of a mulie. Those critters yours?"

Moses nodded. "What is left of them. I never said I was a good rancher. Just said I tried my hand at it."

One cow raised its head and looked in their direction as if knowing they were talking about them, then hung its head in shame once more as it lapped at the murky water in the pool. Flies clustered around the critter's face, yet it didn't even have the strength to swat them away with its tail.

"There's something wrong with them. Copper deficiency maybe. Sulfur or iron in the water. Supplements might help. Or mineral blocks."

Moses shook his head. "Maybe you did not notice it 'cause you live in Washington, but there is a Depression going on. And this is one Indian that cannot afford supplements for his cows. This is not exactly the Charles Town Ranch."

"No shit." Clayton sat on a rock and shook out a Chester-field. He offered Moses one, but he shook his head.

"I'll take one." Clayton gave Renaud a cigarette that the fat man slipped into a brass holder before lighting.

"Up until the day he died Dad never had to give cows sup-plements at Charles Town—the grazing at the ranch was that good."

"Made no difference, though, when the bank foreclosed on him." Moses saw the pain in Clayton's face, and he regretted bringing up the foreclosure that had driven Randolff Charles to slip a rope around his neck and step off the barn loft one overcast afternoon.

"Still, those critters lack something," Clayton said quickly as if expelling the bad memories. "They're pretty sluggish."

"The bad rocks make them sick."

"What's with these bad rocks?" Renaud watched smoke rings filter skyward. "Rocks don't live, let alone hurt people."

Moses took off his Stetson and wiped the sweat inside with a bandanna. "Everything lives: the rocks, the trees, Mother Earth. Everything you see has a soul. Everything you see lives. The bad rocks live. And they live to make their revenge on men who cross their path."

Clayton laughed and flicked his cigarette butt into a clump of sagebrush. "Will you leave that legend alone for one day and find Samuel a decent-sized deer. I'm starving for some-thing besides rabbit and porcupine."

>‹›‹›‹

Samuel picked up the burlap firewood sling and shut the cabin door behind him. Moses watched him leave before he returned to the painting propped on his easel. He mixed beef tallow with the earth paste to bind it to the muslin cloth.

"I would like to spend more time with the boy."

Moses flicked his match into the woodstove and shut the metal door. "Then why do you not?"

Clayton shrugged. "Been busy."

"You are his father." Moses mixed yellows and dark purples until he got the nightshade he wanted and began dabbing it on the canvas. Renaud had brought pigments from his native France, and canvas as a peace offering to Moses, and Moses used them sparingly.

"You know what the other boys call Samuel? They call him *atkuku*. Bastard. And if you ever cared enough to ask him, you would know he got that shiner from taking on half the school bullies that call him that. The boy needs a father."

"I've been tied up lately . . ."

"And Hannah needs a husband. She is a very good woman."

Clayton flung his cigarette butt into the stove. "Damn it, we've been over this a hundred times. I don't have time for a family right now."

"But you got time to plan for one of those socialite weddings you politicians are so famous for."

"Keep your voice down," Clayton said, his eyes darting to the door. "Renaud will come back any moment and I don't want him hearing about any wedding. How'd you find out?"

"Maybe I had one of my visions about . . . what is her name, Heaven?"

"Heather."

"And she is White, so my vision tells me. I am sure that will help your political career in Washington, even though it will leave no chance for a family here with Samuel and Hannah."

Clayton turned, his fists clenching in time with the tensing of his jaw muscles, and Moses recognized the fire in his eyes he saw that first night he met Clayton at the dance, the fire that forced him to beat two Lakota boys senseless. "Haven't I done all I could for the Sioux? You know Pine Ridge has more than its share of WPA projects. That's my Washington political clout making that happen."

Moses set aside the badger brush, and mixed burnt ashes with blueberry stain on his palette with a thin knife. "Your influence is all over the reservation," he said as he peeked around his easel at Clayton. "You are selling more *mniwakan* on Pine Ridge than ever before."

"I haven't sold whiskey here since Prohibition ended."

"I know you do not—you have Alan Brave Heart Bull running shine for you."

"Shush. I told you I quit," Clayton whispered, his fists clenched into balls as he watched the door. Clayton could snap at any moment, and Moses had no desire to hurt him again. They'd been friends too long. "Set the table while I see if the *wahanpi* is done."

While Clayton set mismatched plates and forks on the table, Moses lifted the lid from the stewpot and tested the venison stew, adding more salt just as Samuel came in from the cold with a carrier full of firewood.

"Smells great," he said and stacked the firewood in the log holder beside the stove. Clayton was a fool. Moses would have given all the visions in the world for a fine son like Samuel. *Perhaps Betty and I will one day have a son like him.*

The door flew open and Renaud stepped in, buttoning the fly on his dungarees as he elbowed the door shut. The front of his pants were wet where he'd pissed into the wind. Again. "What's for supper?"

"Venison," Moses answered. "If you wash your hands."

Renaud shook his head and trudged to the washbasin. Moses looked down his nose in more ways than one at the dirty, fat man from New York. Many White men that Moses encountered were dirty and unkempt. Renaud was more so, something that surprised Moses. He'd heard attorneys— particularly those preying on people in the big cities—always dressed like they were going someplace. Right now, Moses wished Renaud was going someplace beside the dinner table.

Renaud dried his hands on the flour sack and stepped around Moses to the painting. He tossed aside the cloth covering the painting and gasped.

Moses reached over and grabbed the covering, but Renaud put his hand on Moses's arm. "Just a moment." He stepped back and cocked his head, examining the painting from different angles. "Your technique is everything Senator Charles said it was."

Moses threw the cloth over the painting and motioned to the table. "I did not realize Clayton was an art critic."

"Just an amateur," Clayton volunteered. "Nothing like Renaud here."

"Thought you were an attorney?"

Renaud laughed and took out a snifter. He took little sips of the whiskey. "I make my money as a lawyer. Art is my hobby. My passion. Now if these were for sale . . ."

"They are not."

"So Senator Charles tells me, *mon ami*. But at least you might be willing to accompany some of your work to New York, maybe D.C."

"Why?" Moses began ladling stew into deep bowls. "What possible reason would I have to do that?"

"Just think of what you're keeping from the public, man. People have a right to know that the Sioux have great interpreters in canvas equal to anything the Europeans have ever had."

"Still does not answer my question—why would I want to go there?"

"My friend," Clayton said, draping his arm around Moses's shoulder, "like Renaud here said, he's a great appreciator of art. If he says people would clamor to see your work, he means it. And it'd give you a chance to see places you've always heard about."

"And it would mean money," Renaud added.

"I got all the money I need."

"Then for the tribe," Renaud pressed. "I could arrange for a substantial donation to the tribe in your name."

"For doing what?"

"For bringing some of your work to New York and showing people what this reservation has produced. For meeting the very man that could produce work like this."

"It'd go a long way to help the tribe meet expenses," Clayton pressed. "Times are tough for everyone."

"Let me ponder this after supper. And after Mr. LaJeneuse washes his hands again."

CHAPTER 15

"Do you have to go to Pine Ridge tonight?" Clara's low-cut negligee rippled and bounced as she crossed the room to where Manny stood between twin eagles perched on either side of the fireplace mantle. "I had something special planned for tonight."

"Willie and I have to hit the ground running tomorrow morning. Early. I'd hate to make the drive there in the morning with just a few hours sleep. You know how tired I've been lately."

Clara blew out the candles. Thin, faint tendrils of smoke rose upward. "Well it's not like I've been keeping you up. I haven't even been able to *get* you up. When will you go to your doctor and get a prescription for Viagra?"

"I already have," he blurted out, moving away from Clara and dropping onto the couch. "Don't seem to make any difference."

"That why does the doctor's office keeps calling?"
Manny looked away.

"His office left a message for you to make an appointment right away." Clara came and sat beside him. She kissed the back of his hand and held it in her lap. "We need to talk."

"We do talk."

She forced a laugh. "Sure, small talk, like what you and Willie had for lunch, or what's playing on HBO to help you fall asleep. Small talk. We need to talk about us." A breeze through the open window brought a whiff of Clara's cologne drifting past his nose, subtle yet intoxicating. From what he remembered Clara's intoxication to be.

"We have a pretty good life together."

"Sure, the hour or so a day we see each other."

"I've been kicking bushes on this case . . ."

"Not that excuse again. You were kicking bushes when we first met, and you had enough energy then. Is there something else?"

Manny looked away, and inside he kicked himself in the ass. For a trained interrogator, he had little success in concealing his lies.

"There is something else, isn't there? That's why your doctor keeps calling and leaving messages for you to see him?"

Manny brushed her hand off his arm and stood. "He thinks I have diabetes. Wants me to come in for another checkup and more blood work."

Clara stood and slipped her arm around his neck. "Your folks had diabetes. Your Uncle Marion died of it. And about half the reservation's got it. You're bound to get it at some point."

Manny shrugged her arm off his shoulder and turned toward her. "I'm too damned young. I've dropped ten pounds since we've been together, and I run my ass off every night, when some damned Norman Bates of a cat doesn't attack me. No way I should have diabetes. The doctor's wrong!" Manny thought back to his academy assignment, to his home in Virginia he'd fled to after leaving Pine Ridge eighteen years ago. He didn't have diabetes back there. He kept telling himself city living—away from the reservation—had protected him, had kept the disease at bay. Yet he knew the doctor was right, even if he fought against the reality.

"So you're not going to make an appointment with him?"

Manny shrugged. "Too busy right now."

Clara backed away and crossed her arms as she leaned against the fireplace mantle. "Well, perhaps a few days away will show you if you're too busy to see your doctor. And too busy to salvage us."

Manny nodded. "Look, the Senate hearings are only a week away. I owe Indians everywhere a chance to have a Lakota Supreme Court justice."

"And you owe me some time to just sit and talk about us. Maybe you haven't noticed, but neither of us is getting any younger."

"Just as soon as the investigation's over, I'll see the doctor. Then we'll have our talk."

Clara remained with arms crossed, watching Manny throw together clothes in an overnight bag. He tossed in his shaving gear and started for the door when she stepped in front of him. "Promise to talk?"

"Honest Injun." He smiled and held up his hand in mock swearing.

Her lips brushed his cheek, and she held the door for him. "I'll hold you to that."

CHAPTER 16

Manny turned off Highway 385 and drove past Oelrichs, Clara's concern still nagging him. She was right—Uncle Marion had died of diabetes, and many people he knew on Pine Ridge and Rosebud had also. But would that diagnosis and treatment give him back his desire, his libido? Or was something else nagging his relationship with the woman he'd grown to love?

He flicked his high beams at an oncoming pickup, but the truck kept blinding him with its bright lights. In desperation, he left his own high beams on. He cupped his hand over his eyes and squinted against the bright lights as the truck passed him, flipping his middle finger at it. Like the driver could see it in the dark.

What the hell am I doing? Back in Virginia, he would have never thought to flip off another motorist. Back in Virginia. Back a lifetime ago before he was reassigned to work reservation cases as the resident Indian in the Rapid City Field Office.

He popped Jimmy Sturr's *Polka Disco* CD into the player

and cranked up the volume. *Who the hell ever used disco and polka in the same sentence? Jimmy Sturr did.* But it didn't matter to Manny. He liked Jimmy and his band. The heavy bass drum and full accordion cords reached the inner workings of his mind, strangely soothing him. For all the cacophony that was polka music, he thought best when he was either running or listening to the polka. He had been so tired of late, skipping running for early bedtimes. So that left polka, with its heavy beat so much like traditional powwow music, without causing Manny to commit to being a Lakota through and through.

He tapped the steering wheel in time to the bass tuba between stanzas of the "Too Fat Polka." *"I don't want her, you can have her, she's too fat for me."* His thoughts turned to Judge High Elk. It was natural for Ham to be concerned about Gunnar's homicide investigation. It wasn't natural for him to have such a conflict of interest with the chief investigator in the case. But this would be Ham's one shot at the Supreme Court—perhaps the only shot for any Indian—and if the case wasn't resolved by hearing time, Ham's confirmation would be in serious jeopardy.

Oomp-bah. Oomph-bah-bah. Oomp-bah. *"She's so charming, and she's so winning, but it's alarming when she goes swimming."*

Manny had gone out of his way to believe Ham was being truthful. He'd studied Ham's judicial rulings since being assigned the three homicides in the Badlands, and nothing in those decisions indicated Ham was anything but an impartial jurist. Even when Ham had taken heat in the Indian press two years ago for opposing tribal sovereignty; he had defended his position logically with court precedence that dated back a hundred years. And garnered much hate on the reservations in so doing.

Then there had been Ham's opposition to mining in the

Pine Ridge Badlands. Half of the enrolled members wanted mining to open up, arguing it would be an economic boon to the Oglala Lakota. The other half fought to allow the reservation to remain closed, to stay as it had for the last hundred years, fearful that uranium mining and its aftermath would harm the reservation for the next hundred. That left about twenty thousand Lakota thanking Ham for his ruling. And about twenty thousand pissed at Judge Alexander Hamilton High Elk.

Oomp-oomp. Oomp-bah. Oomph-bah-bah. He imagined short, stocky men dressed in kneesocks and wearing colorful shorts dancing around blond maidens at some Swiss beer garden. Short stocky men like Joe Dozi. Except nice, short, stocky men. Manny's bureau queries had been unable to unearth any background on Dozi past his college days before being drafted. It was as if he entered the army and the army just swallowed him up. Nothing had been found about his Vietnam service, and thoughts of clandestine missions entered Manny's mind, missions so secret that Joe Dozi's name had been expunged from military records. The one thing Manny was certain of was Dozi's total loyalty to Ham.

Oomph-bah-bah. Manny nodded, the thump-thump-thumping lulling him to sleep. Nod. Two whitetail spring fawns stepped onto the road. Nod. Head dropping on his chest, snapping awake in time to lay on the brakes. They froze and looked directly into the headlights, that same look the Spearfish records clerk had when he asked her about Ham and Gunnar's original arrest report, when they'd been arrested in college for fighting in a Spearfish bar. She'd produced the microfiche, and copied the report, so Joe Dozi seizing them made little sense. Manny had already read the report.

Manny popped over a hill, and another truck kept its high beams on. *Didn't anyone ever tell these guys the headlight dimmer's there for a reason?* He flipped his headlights from high to low, but got no response. He started to flip them to high again when he shielded his hand from the lights and saw the truck was stopped on the road. The driver had popped the hood, and Manny squinted to see anyone. He slowed and rolled his window down, sticking his head out the window, just as a rifle shot erupted, his windshield spiderwebbing, the round traveling and embedding itself in Manny's headrest.

He ducked in the seat as two more quick rounds pinged off his hood, another and the windshield shattered, safety plastic sandwiched between the glass holding it together. Manny floored the Malibu into a bootleg turn, swinging the back end around. Shots came fast, bullets hitting the back window as the car lurched away from the shooter. He thrust his head out the window, spotting his escape through a hay field on one side of the road, and he turned the wheel toward that field.

A front tire flattened, steel wheel biting into the asphalt with a shudder. He hit his head on the doorjamb and pulled inside as the car veered toward a steep ditch just before the field. The steering wheel jerked in his hand, rapping his knuckles. The car went off the road and nosed down into the ditch into dirt. The seat belt tightener bit against Manny's shoulder, the trunk sticking skyward like the tail of an injured gooney bird, steam rolling from under the hood.

He craned his neck around. The shooter, silhouetted against the bright lights of his truck, walked toward him, the rifle cradled in the crook of his arm as a hunter carries his gun.

Gasoline odor reached him then, strong, steady dripping too loud from a punctured gas tank. Manny hit the seat belt release. The shooter neared, bending to the pavement. When he stood he had lit a highway flare.

The seat belt caught on Manny's shoulder and he wiggled to clear it.

The shooter drew back the flare.

Manny cleared the seat belt and dove out the window.

The shooter tossed the flare at the car.

Manny scrambled on all fours, keeping his car between him and the shooter, dirt catching in the cuts on his hands.

The gas tank exploded.

Manny flung himself over the bank.

The fireball lit up the night, heat washing over and singeing Manny's neck and face and arms.

He threw himself at a fallen cottonwood, hitting his head on a gnarly branch, and rolled to his right. He yanked his gun from the holster, peeking around the tree. He swiped blood from a scalp laceration, expecting to see the shooter. Intense heat forced him back behind the cottonwood and he hugged the cool dirt, waiting, vision blurred, lungs seared. He started backing away from the tree and tried standing, intending working his way around to get a shot at his attacker.

He stumbled against soft dirt and fell, fighting his way to one knee when the world around him swirled. Before he lost consciousness, he thought how he felt like he had fallen in a toilet and someone had hit the handle, forcing him swirling down the drain.

>()()()<

Manny woke to the sound of steady beeping above his head, and he cracked an eye. Monitors on a rack at the head of his hospital bed kept time with a nurse walking past his open door.

"Welcome back." Clara sat on the edge of his bed stroking his forehead, her eyes settling on the IV tube taped to the back of his wrist. A forced smile shone through eyes baggy from lack of sleep. She bent and kissed his cheek. "Welcome back to the land of the living."

"This is the land of the living?" Manny tried sitting up, but pain shot through his chest and he eased himself back onto the pillow.

"The doctor said you had a mild concussion. Hair gone from your neck and arms. Minor smoke inhalation, but nothing you'll be able to burn up all that sick time for."

"Great. I'll catch hell for wrecking another car."

"At least this accident wasn't your fault." Willie rose from where he'd been lying across chairs lined up at the head of Manny's bed.

"Did I crawl here from the accident?" Manny's memory faded about the time he passed Oelrichs.

"It wasn't an accident."

"You sound pretty certain."

Willie nodded. "A couple drunks found you. Two goofballs from Hot Springs had been on the rez doing some teepee creepin' in Manderson. They were freshly horned up and tanked up as they drove their dates toward Hot Springs for some more beer. Remember a one-ton dually passing you?"

"I don't remember much."

"Thankfully for you, you didn't dim your lights when you passed them and it pissed them off. They jacked their liquid courage into high gear along with the truck and turned around on you. They were running down the road hell-bent on kicking the shit out of you, but someone beat them to it."

Manny shook his head. "I don't recall the truck. You talk with them?"

"Janet did. They told her when they caught up with you, there was another outfit just parked on the road watching you burn."

"Guess the shooter figured I didn't get out of the car alive."

Willie turned a chair around and sat, draping his arms over the chair back. "That's what they figured, that you were trapped inside. They grabbed their deer rifles when they saw your shooter with his gun alongside his leg, picking up empties from the roadway, not caring if they watched him. They said they nearly shot themselves when you groaned from behind that tree after the shooter left."

"And the shooter's outfit?"

Willie shook his head. "They said just drove off casual like."

"Tell me they got a license number."

"Wish I could." Willie stood and cupped his chin in his hands and twisted his neck to either side, stretching. "Their description was a black or dark-colored Suburban. They were certain the 'Burb had some funky feathers painted on the fenders."

"Judge High Elk's."

"So it seems."

"Driver?"

"Damned tinted windows. The 'Burb took off as they approached and sped past them. They didn't see who was driving."

"Joe Dozi."

"Sure?"

Manny struggled to sit, and Clara propped two pillows behind his back. He waited until the pain in his side subsided and caught his breath. "Judge High Elk's Suburban has feathers painted on it. But this isn't his style, I'm thinking. Remember Helga mentioning Joe Dozi drove away from the Spearfish PD in a black Suburban?"

Willie nodded. "Makes sense. But we still can't rule out anyone. Including Judge High Elk."

"True. But Dozi threw some not-so-veiled threats my way earlier today." Manny told Willie about stopping by Dozi's shop and about how the Secret Service imposter made it known Manny wouldn't throw a monkey wrench into Ham's Senate hearings.

"I'll talk to Ham again just as soon as I get sprung from here."

"That might be pretty soon," Clara said. "The doctor is making his rounds now. You want coffee while you're waiting for the doctor to grace the room?" Clara asked.

"That'd hit the spot."

Manny waited until Clara had left before delving into his non-accident. "She was getting kind of hinked talking about the shooting. She worries a lot."

"Understood."

"Now, did you recover any bullets from my car?"

"It burned up. Mostly. I doubt we could."

"You need to try. Go to the impound lot and go over what's left. If you could even recover some bullet jacketing mate-rial . . ."

"We can get a match with just a jacket?"

Manny shrugged. "Maybe not a match if we find a suspect gun, but we may be able to eliminate guns we suspect. If we find any of Joe Dozi's guns."

Willie jotted what Manny told him on his notebook and pocketed it as fitful coughing in the hallway became louder. An old man staggered into the room, holding his chest and spitting blood into a towel. He started around Willie before he collapsed into a chair. Willie struggled to hold the man from falling onto the floor.

"He went into Tanno's room," someone shouted from the hallway.

A nurse slightly smaller than Willie burst through the door-way, made even larger in appearance by the full mask and long protective gloves she wore. "Frederick! I told you to stay in your room."

Another nurse, young and wearing the same protective garb as the first, pushed a wheelchair into Manny's room. She didn't speak as she wrapped her arms around Frederick and helped load him into the wheelchair. She turned and disappeared with him safely strapped in.

"Frederick slipped by us again." The big nurse's voice was muffled behind the mask.

"What's wrong with him?" Manny jerked his head toward the hallway where Frederick and his wheelchair had disappeared.

She shrugged. "Most likely TB by the way he's coughing. But who knows."

Before Manny could grill her further, she turned on her heels and left the room.

"If he had TB . . ."

"Then we both will have to get tested," Willie answered.

"One more trip to the doctor," Manny groaned. "Take my mind off Frederick—tell me how your date with Doreen went yesterday."

Willie scooted his chair close so he could keep his voice low. "Things were going pretty well. We hit the Olive Garden by the mall. Low lights. Soft music. Nice glass of wine . . ."

"Thought you didn't drink?"

"Doreen likes a glass of Chardonnay now and again."

"Doreen does or you?"

Willie looked away. "I do, too, now and then."

"Thought you didn't drink?"

"I'm in training. Anyways, we patched things up. Or so I thought."

"Don't tell me—she got on you again about quitting the force?"

Willie nodded. "She said with my college degree, I could be anything besides a cop. She suggested I continue and get my master's in public administration. Land a job running Tribal affairs."

Manny grabbed his glass of ice water and sipped from the bent Mickey Mouse straw. "But that's not for you."

Willie shook his head. "I'd die of boredom. She can't understand the reason I went to college in the first place is to become a law officer. Help people on the rez."

"I thought she resigned herself to be the girlfriend—and eventually wife—of a policeman. What made her change her mind?"

"Someone broke into my truck in the parking lot."

"Again?"

"When we came out of the restaurant, some SOB had busted the window out. Stole that new SureFire I just paid two hundred bucks for at Neeves. She went through the roof. She wasn't upset that my light was stolen. She went off because she figures someone's got a hard-on for me."

"Besides her?"

"Different kind of hard-on. She said—and she was spot-on—that someone's escalated their hatred for me. She said it started with keying my Tribal unit, then moved to my personal truck. She's scared for me. She wants me out. Said I could manage a business. Teach elementary school until I got my master's. I told her it could have been worse. I leave my keys in the ignition, and someone could have stolen the whole truck."

"You ought to know better than that, as many stolen vehicles as you've investigated."

"But my truck's antitheft device is its condition. No one would want to steal that beater. Anyway, she's convinced public administration is for me. Or worse, elementary school. She said I could get my teaching license this summer."

Manny laughed, and his hand shot to his ribs. "Oh, that'd go over well with the kiddies, you in your double-breasted Western shirt a size too small. Wearing one of those funky bolo ties with some kind of cheesy bone clasp. They'd figure you came straight out of a Gene Autry movie."

A smile crossed Willie's face for the briefest moment, then he hung his head once more.

"Look, I know what you're going through. I almost lost Clara because of the attacks and that truck running me off the road a couple months ago on Pine Ridge. When she finally figured out there's nothing else I can do except investigate crimes and put bad guys away, she learned to live with it."

"How'd you convince her?"

Manny smiled, and winced in pain as stitches in his forehead pulled against one another. He glanced at the door but Clara hadn't returned yet. "I pointed out how dangerous other jobs are, like construction work or oil field rig hands. And she mentioned my degree like Doreen did."

"What did she suggest for you?"

"The funeral business. Clara actually thought I'd be a natural for managing a funeral home."

Willie laughed. "Mister Compassion in a black suit? I take it you got her off that notion."

"I did. When I pointed out I'd be coming home every night smelling like forever juice and making love to her with perpetually cold hands, she reeled. Said that was sick, but she dropped it."

"That's one angle I haven't tried yet."

"Aside from that little tiff with Doreen and the loss of your flashlight, how'd the rest of the night go?"

"A disaster." Willie stood and paced at the foot of Manny's bed. "When I told her I intended to remain a criminal investigator with the tribe, she clammed up. Didn't say a word until we crossed the reservation line. Then she let me have it about Janet, as if I hadn't got my ass chewed enough."

"What about Janet?"

Willie looked at the door and leaned closer. "Before dinner, we stopped at the mall. Doreen wanted to get some of that smelly stuff at the bed and bath shop."

"Enough already, tell me about Janet."

"We saw her in the commons area at the mall. She ran up to me and gave me a huge bear hug. Pinched my butt. Right there with a hundred people looking on. Including Doreen."

"Bet that went over like a fart in church."

"Tell me about it. Doreen's look bore a hole right through me, and through Janet. It didn't help that Janet was dressed to the nines, like she was coming off some escort assignment. She had so much damned makeup, you couldn't tell if she'd blushed. I swear she goes out of her way to get between Doreen and me."

"Don't you think it's time to have a serious talk with Janet? Insist your relationship with her remain professional. And to give you your space, especially when you're with Doreen."

Willie shook his head. "I got to be careful. Being the lieutenant's niece, she could get me checking parked cars at pow-wows instead of real police work. Besides, telling Janet to leave me alone would be like you telling Clara to give you some rest. It'd just egg her on."

Manny looked at the door as if expecting Clara to come back any moment. "Clara's everything I've always wanted, and twenty years ago I could get it triweekly. Now I try weakly to get it up just once. Even that wears me down. But Clara's at her peak. I hate to admit it, but this accident will give me an excuse to back off from the loving. Give me a little recuperation time from the bedroom."

"You won't be recuperating long." A tall, blond doctor looking more at home in a health club commercial than at the Pine Ridge Hospital entered the room. An equally young nurse, her white dress showing more leg than a nurse ought, sashayed behind the doctor. Clara trailed them as they entered the room.

The doctor unfolded a stethoscope from around his neck and opened Manny's pajama top. He put the cold scope against his chest. He dropped the scope and it dangled around his neck. He snatched a clipboard hanging from the foot of the bed and nodded to the monitor above Manny's head. "I was worried about the concussion, but you're coherent enough." He extracted a penlight from his pocket and shined it into each of Manny's eyes. "How do you feel?"

Manny glanced at Clara hovering over the bed. "I feel good enough, except it's hard to breathe. Like maybe I shouldn't exert myself too much for a while."

The doctor smiled. Either he'd heard the discussion he and Willie had just had or Clara had paid him off. "You should be able to do anything you did before the accident. After all, your ribs are bruised, not broken. You may have to adjust some things." He winked at Clara.

Manny forced a smile. "Thanks, doctor."

"Yes," Clara said, stroking Manny's forehead. "Thank you so much."

"I understand you had a visitor here a moment ago."

"Some old man," Willie said. "Coughing like he had a foot on the banana peel. Nurse said he has TB."

"I can't discuss another patient with you, but I'm not sure it is TB."

"Come on, doctor," Manny pressed: "Frederick there looks and sounds a lot like those kids of Adelle Friend of All's, hacking like he was and paler than the Lone Ranger. He looked terrible."

"You know HIPAA and hospital regulations won't allow me . . ."

"At least tell me where Frederick lives."

"Why?"

"So we can get hold of his relatives," Manny lied.

"That's mighty white of you. Since when is the FBI so compassionate?"

"Where's he live," Manny pressed.

"He lives somewhere around Cuny Table."

"Where around Cuny Table?"

"North along the Cheyenne River," the nurse volunteered.

The doctor gave her a stern look. "We can't discuss another patient with you."

Manny swung his legs over the bed and tested his ribs. "Then at least do this for me, doctor—at least compare Frederick's symptoms with Adelle's kids' and see if they're similar."

"What are you getting at?" The physician's tone rose an octave, as if irritated that Manny had thought of something medically he had not. "Whatever the symptoms, I won't be able to discuss them with you."

"Fair enough. But please, do it."

The doctor began signing the medical release form so Manny could leave. He handed him a slip with a fax number on it. "Make an appointment this week and have your physician get back to me."

"Appointment for what?"

"Frederick," the doctor said. "Like I said, we're not sure what he has. That's why the nurse got so flustered when he left isolation. And until we know, you and Officer With Horn will have to get tested for TB."

Manny waited until the doctor had signed the release form and left the room before he stood. He gasped as the pain of bruised ribs reminded him how close he had come to being killed in the crash. He hobbled to the closet and grabbed his trousers, holding the back of the insane hospital gown to hide his butt. "Tell me what you learned from Marshal Ten Bears when you talked with him yesterday."

"Janet interviewed him inside his cabin. He didn't cotton to me much."

"What were you doing while she took notes?"

"Getting an eyeball around his cabin."

"Why *did* you take Janet along again?"

"Remember? Uncle Leon."

Manny understood but he didn't remember much prior to the accident. "Put out a BOLO for the judge's black 'Burb, and for Joe Dozi. Call Janet so we can meet up with her."

Willie sighed and held the door for Clara and Manny. "I can hardly wait."

CHAPTER 17

Clara ran red-faced from the bedroom, tossing her scarf off as she dropped into the couch in the living room. Manny followed her and started sitting beside her, but her scowl warned him away and he pulled up an occasional chair. "I can't help it. My ribs are killing me."

"You heard the doctor: You'll be able to do anything you did before. At least what I remember what you did before, once when you had an attack of romance."

"I can't help it."

"Then get some more Viagra or something." Clara shook her head. "Maybe this was a mistake, you moving in with me. I've known women before that had a spectacular love life until they got married or had their boyfriend move in, then it petered off. Forgive the pun."

Manny scooted the chair closer and put his hand on Clara's arm. She jerked it away and turned her head to avoid looking at him. "I got other problems." Sometime ago, he'd decided to tell Clara about his checkup, how he had been diagnosed with diabetes. He had hoped to be able to put it off, but knew he must say something to salvage their relationship. "I've been diagnosed with Type II diabetes."

Clara looked back over her shoulder. "So you said before. That's what your doctor keeps calling about. When did you find out?"

"Last month, though the doctor said it's been developing for some time."

Her look softened and she inched closer to Manny. "How'd you find out?"

"The yearly exam the bureau requires of us. Besides, I was experiencing terrible numbness in my legs and feet."

"Your Uncle Marion had numbness, didn't he?"

Manny nodded. "About thirty years sooner than he should have. But not before they amputated both legs and made him sit in a wheelchair looking at rabbit ears that barely received one channel." Unc had vegetated in the nursing home in Rapid City. Manny made it a point to fly back from D.C. every other month. But each time, Unc slipped further and further until he wished to fly to the Spirit World. Manny's big regret was that he was off on another reservation case when Unc's time came. *No man should have to die alone*, Unc had often told him.

Clara turned to him and patted the couch. Manny sat beside her, and she hugged him. "What kind of medication does the doctor have you on?"

"I'm not on medication."

"But you just said . . ."

"I want to get a second opinion before I commit to shots, if that's what it'll take."

Clara's face became red once again, and her brows came together in what Manny had come to recognize as a pre-tongue-lashing. "Your doctor diagnosed you with diabetes a month ago and you haven't seen him since? What kind of

bonehead maneuver is that? Why haven't you talked to another doctor?"

"No time."

"No time? I've been nonexistent in your life for months
now, and there might be a way to fix it? Might be a way to
give you back some of your libido? Remember what that was,
back when you came home all horned up?"

Manny dropped his eyes. "I'll make an appointment next
week."

"You'll make an appointment tomorrow unless you want
to be bunking with Willie."

"I'll make the appointment tomorrow." The last thing he
wanted was to babysit Willie and his problems. He had his
own right this minute.

CHAPTER 18

Janet started to slide into the booth next to Willie at Big Bat's. She frowned as he got up and moved across from her next to Manny. Philbilly came over to their table carrying three sodas, one spilling onto his forearm and onto the floor. He set the sodas down and rubbed the soda into the floor with his foot.

"Thought you were quitting, Phil?" Phil Ostert had lived on Pine Ridge since his folks had abandoned him in his teens. Legend around the rez was that his folks pulled up to Big Bat's to fuel as they were passing through on their way back home from working lettuce fields in Oregon. When teenager Phil went to use the bathroom, they'd seen their chance and skied off. Even Phil didn't know much about his past, other than he was a hillbilly from Arkansas. And acted like it. Manny had run out of fingers long ago counting the one- and two-week jobs Phil had quit when he thought he was being slighted. Manny always suspected the jobs lasted just long enough for Phil to get his fill of sweating and he'd quit. "Thought you were fed up with working here?"

Philbilly squatted beside the table and lowered his voice. "They did me wrong two days ago."

"Now what'd they do to you?"

"They made me help the women unload a semi of frozen chicken patties and corn dogs."

"What's wrong with that?"

Philbilly choked. "I was hired as part-time cook. Unloading trucks ain't in my job description."

Willie looked after Philbilly disappearing through the kitchen doors. "If Philbilly got any dumber, we'd have to water him."

Manny agreed, and he turned to Janet. "Tell me what Marshal Ten Bears said yesterday."

Janet fished in her purse for a spiral notebook. "Marshal hires himself out as a hunting guide in the winter months. Deer. Coyotes. Mountain lion if the customer has enough lucky bucks. For Marshal to take you somewhere, you got to have the cash. Swears he claims it on his income tax every year"—she shrugged—"but he's a little bit shady."

"In your vast experience?"

She glared at Willie. "Intuition."

Manny elbowed Willie, and he let it drop. "We knew he was a guide of sorts, but what's he do in the off-season?"

"Firewood," Willie said. "Sixty-five a cord, stacked and delivered. He went out of his way to tell me it's just a summer hobby. Says he makes more than enough guiding hunters; he doesn't have to do much in the summer unless he wants to."

"And did he give a sample for DNA?"

"He didn't want to." Janet smiled at Willie and made a point to bat her eyes. "It took some persuasion but we got it."

"You?"

Janet nodded.

"Good job, huh Willie?"

"Wasn't the easiest thing for Janet to do—persuade Marshal. But I think they got something straight between them that convinced him."

Janet swung at Willie's head but he pulled back before she could draw blood.

"What? I didn't know what you two were doing when you went back inside the cabin."

"Well, we didn't do what you think we did while you were roaming around outside."

"What *did* you do while Janet was doing her . . . convincing?"

Willie sipped his soda. "I walked around the cabin. Saw where Marshal's been using worn deer trails to get places in the Stronghold."

Manny recalled his days with Unc, when they would travel the game trails interfingered with washout gullies to get around that nearly impassable part of the Badlands. He imagined Marshal shared that same innate knowledge of the area with Uncle Marion.

"On one side of his cabin Marshal had a porcupine hide stretched and drying. With one very small caliber hole that I almost missed spotting. And hanging beside the porcupine was what would have been a nice mountain lion pelt if it had been killed in the winter. Thing was mangy. You know how they get in the summer when they're not haired-up."

Manny nodded.

"That's one of Marshal's side businesses—supplying porcupine quills to local artists. Sells some to the Prairie Edge in Rapid," Willie added.

"Quilling is something Oglala women do." Willie leaned across the table and smiled at Janet, drawing out his words, accentuating his condescending tone. "They're involved in traditional things, like quilling and beading. They don't go off on some tangent, wanting to be a criminal investigator."

"I had a belly full of traditional crafts when I was in school.

They were boring as they are now." Janet's face reddened, and her jaw tightened, then she relaxed and flashed a toothy grin that showed off her dimples. "Now I like things that excite me more."

"Does Marshal think the body in the car is his grandfather?" Manny said quickly to diffuse the looming storm at the booth.

"He's hoping it's not." Janet turned to Manny. "He's made something of a living being the grandson of Moses Ten Bears. People are anxious to buy porcupine quills, take guided tours of the Badlands, book game hunts from the grandson of a genuine Oglala holy man. He's even sold photos of himself for five bucks to tourists wanting a photo with Moses's grandson."

"Marshal will stand to lose a lot of that business if it is Moses," Willie said. "It's more profitable to continue the legend that *Wakan Tanka* took Moses Ten Bears one night when he prayed to the four winds in the Stronghold instead of him dying liquored-up in a car with some White dude and getting bombed to death."

"And just where is the DNA sample?"

"Pee Pee is overnighting it to Quantico." Willie finished his soda and started toward the soda machine for a refill. "Along with two molars from that bigger corpse we think is Moses," he called over his shoulder.

"Still doesn't answer what he's doing at his cabin this time of year. The porcupine quill business doesn't warrant staying all the way out there."

"Herbs."

Manny wiped soda from his lips. "Herbs, like for cooking?"

Willie shook his head and played stare-down with Janet, who sat unblinking across the table. "Ceremonial. He dabbles at being a sacred man like his grandfather."

"Someone teach him, like you're learning from Margaret Catches?"

"It's not polite to ask a sacred man where he gets his powers." Janet smiled at Willie. "I do know some traditional things."

Willie ignored her and slid back in the booth. "Every sacred person has a favorite spot to gather herbs he or she uses in their ceremonies. Mine, I go to a special bank of the Cheyenne River and pick them. It's like they wait for me every year. Marshal picks his *peji hota*—his sage—close to the cabin. One of the things I was doing outside while my partner was busy doing her thing inside with Marshal."

Janet slid from the booth and went to the soda machine for a refill.

Willie nodded in her direction. "She's driving me nuts."

"I would be nuts, too, if those long bedroom eyelashes were constantly batting at me. She bats them any more and she'll start hovering."

Willie leaned closer and lowered his voice. "If Doreen sees us together, it'll be the end gate for us."

"Thought it already was."

"She gave me one last chance. Just keep me and Janet separated."

"I'll do what I can."

Janet returned to the booth, her smiling eyes locked on Willie with lashes long enough she could almost hide those eyes. She started to speak, but Manny interrupted her. "Tell me about Marshal's cabin. I understand it's untouched since Moses lived there."

"That's one of the reasons the Cultural Committee wanted Marshal to move it so bad—it's just how Moses left it the day he went into the Stronghold and fell from that cliff."

"Or got himself bombed in that car." Manny watched out the window as a rez rod pulled up to the gas pumps. An old man stumbled out, put two dollars of fuel in. He rolled a smoke and lit it, tossing the match on the ground beside the pump before coaxing his car onto the street amid billowing smoke.

"People in the tribe believe the cabin where Moses lived is sacred, but I don't buy it," Janet said.

"Of course it's *wakan*." Willie brushed his drink glass with his arm, but he snatched it before it toppled over. "Moses Ten Bears was one of the great Oglala sacred men, and not just of this century. He's talked about like those sacred men we Lakota had even before the time of winter counts."

"But Marshal won't let the tribe move the cabin into Pine Ridge for display. Does he want money for it?"

Willie shook his head. "As important as the almighty dollar is to him, he'd never take even a dime for it. I think he gets more mileage with the cabin during his tourist and hunting business. It adds to the persona of Marshal Ten Bears—grandson of Moses."

"He's stupid stubborn," Janet said, back at Willie. "Like someone else. It would be a good thing for our people to have the cabin moved to a place people—and historians—could look at it. Though I don't buy it, it's significant in that it'd make people come and visit and leave wondering how Moses could live in a one-room shack like a pauper when he could have sold his paintings for tons of money."

"Some people just don't understand honor." Willie emphasized *honor* as he matched Janet's stare. "Marshal thinks it's one more thing of his grandfather's that will be exploited."

Manny shook his head. "But it's all right that he cashes in on Moses's reputation?"

"Not the same, according to him," Janet said. She dug a compact mirror from her purse. She ran a bead of pastel lip gloss across her thin mouth, checking around the mirror to see that Willie watched her.

"He said the tribe would go the way of the *wasicu*," Willie added. "Sell Moses Ten Bears dolls. Maps where he walked and where they think he fell from the cliff. They'd make a mockery of prints of the few known paintings still in existence. Like the one hanging in Lt. Looks Twice's office. Marshal just wants to be left alone to guide and collect his herbs."

"Bullshit!" Janet threw up her hands. "He's just stubborn and mean. I've known people who hiked all the way to the bottom of the Badlands just to see where Moses lived. To find out where he got his visions from, only to have Marshal put the gun on them and run them off."

"He's just protecting them."

"From what?" Janet laughed. "Some crotchety old man that might put a hex on them?"

"How should I know?" Willie said, turning to Manny. "What could harm them there, except the blistering heat, sharp drop-offs, and occasional mountain lion."

"He's protecting them from the bad rocks."

"What bad rocks?"

Manny faced Willie. "What, the holy-man-in-training doesn't know everything about the reservation?"

"Give me a break, I'm from Crow Creek. Just tell me about these bad rocks."

Manny fought to recall what Unc had told him about where the bad rocks live, one night over a small campfire in the Stronghold. "There's an area of the Stronghold District— not far from Marshal's cabin—where Big Foot led his band fleeing the 7th Cavalry."

"In 1890," Janet added. "Just before the Wounded Knee Massacre."

Manny nodded. "A place so inaccessible and spooky, even the army wouldn't follow them. The Old Ones said that was where the bad rocks live. The rocks that kill people."

"What, loose rocks or something?" Willie leaned closer,

much as Manny had done as he sat enthralled by Unc's tale that night, oblivious to the pitch pine sparks that crackled and flickered off his shirtfront. "How can rocks kill anyone?"

"They didn't." Janet patted Willie's hand. "It's just an old legend."

"Don't discount the Old Ones." Manny grabbed his half-empty drink cup and walked to the soda machine.

Tinkling over the door announced customers, and Manny glanced over his shoulder. Doreen Big Eagle walked ahead of another woman, and she froze when she spotted Willie, still with Janet's hand covering his, inches from his face, talking. The other woman bumped into Doreen, but she stood staring, her face reddening as she whispered. The other woman took a booth by the door and waited.

Manny grabbed his cup and hustled back to the booth in an effort to get between Doreen and Willie. But it was too late. Doreen stood cross-armed looking down at them. Willie looked up and the color drained from his face. Or rather, dripped in huge puddles. As did his ability to speak. He jerked his hand back from Janet's, but not before Doreen nodded to it. Her tirade was in full swing as Manny rushed across the room.

He tried to squeeze between the booth and Doreen as spittle flew inches from Janet's face. A trucker just entering Big Bat's stopped and gave curious examination to the one-sided verbal fight before he turned and promptly left.

Philbilly emerged from around the counter to break things up. Doreen saw him and gave him an I'll-kick-your-ass look and he wilted back into the kitchen. *No one could ever accuse Philbilly of being brave.*

"Willie's here with Janet and me." Manny wormed his way between Doreen and the booth. "We're discussing business."

"You mean you're all together? That's sick."

"Not that together."

She turned to Willie. "After last night, I almost believed you."

"But Doreen . . ."

Willie's pleas fell on red, dampened ears as Doreen turned on her heels and stomped out the door, the other woman she'd come in with close behind.

"She's pretty sore about nothing." Janet smiled.

Willie slumped back in the booth. "Can't blame her any." He leaned across the table, his face red, inches from Janet's. She backed as far away from Willie as the booth would allow as her eyes looked around for an escape route. Manny predicted bad things coming, like one of those visions Moses was said to have had. Except it didn't take a holy man to see this train wreck about to happen.

Manny set the cups on the table. "Maybe I can patch things up."

Willie shot a glance at Manny as if to tell him to keep quiet while he gave Janet the what-for, when Manny's cell phone rang. He held up his hand and Willie quieted for the moment.

"That was the Lawrence County Sheriff's Office. They found the judge's Suburban at his Spearfish cabin. They're going to hold off making entry until we get there with a search warrant."

Willie left his soda on the table as he followed Manny out the door. "Good luck getting a warrant for the judge's cabin."

CHAPTER 19

"Took you long enough," Willie whispered from behind a tree as Manny moved to him, hunched over. "We thought about having pizza delivered as gaunt as we were getting."

Manny reached inside his shirt and retrieved the no-knock warrant. "I'd like to see you convince Judge Ames to sign off on a search warrant of a federal judge's house." Manny had found Circuit Judge Henry Ames fly-fishing in Spearfish Creek. The old man hadn't had luck all day, and was as surly as Lawrence County deputies warned him he'd be.

Ames started to read the probable cause statement Manny handed him. "How the hell you expect me to issue a warrant based on his vehicle matching the one you're searching for? You know how many black Chevy Suburbans there are running around?"

"There's more, Judge." Manny flipped the statement form and ran his finger over additional information. "First, there's not many Suburbans—regardless of color—with feathers painted on the fenders. I'm convinced Joe Dozi drove the Suburban that ambushed me on the road and shot at me.

"And when I went into his shop, I saw enough to convince me he posed as Secret Service to seize files from the Spearfish PD."

"So you don't suspect Judge High Elk?"

Manny wanted to tell him he hadn't crossed Judge High Elk off the list, but didn't. "Our target is Joe Dozi."

In the end, Judge Ames had agreed that, more likely than not, Dozi was the driver and shooter on the road going to Pine Ridge, and had signed off on the no-knock before he went back to drowning flies in Spearfish Creek.

><><><><

"That front door's about half a foot thick," a deputy said. He had run over to Manny and squatted next to him. Willie had joined Janet and two other Lawrence County deputies hidden on the other side of the door by a stand of pine. Manny cramped up as he squatted watching the cabin from a different vantage point than Willie and Janet.

"It's going to be a bear to get inside." The deputy's voice had a happy tone to it, as if he relished taking doors off at their hinges.

Manny stood, his knees popping so loudly he feared someone inside might hear him. *A few more pounds less and that popping will stop. Hopefully.*

The deputy sporting a name tag reading BONER peeked from around Black Hills spruce, and Manny was uncertain if the name tag referred to the deputy's name or what he was experiencing as he anticipated breaking the door down. He clung to a heavy round battering ram that, like the man's knuckles, hung nearly to the ground, and Manny was certain there was nothing under his hat but hair. "Not much I can't bust through with this baby, but this is going to take some thinking."

"Let's hope we don't need it." *And hope you won't need to think.*

Janet squeezed herself thin, hiding behind Willie peeking around a stand of spruce. Even twenty yards from where Manny and Boner squatted, Manny could see her tremble at her first no-knock warrant.

"Sturgis PD said it looked like Dozi's shop had been locked up," Boner said, as if explaining the reason they'd called Manny here. "This was the next logical place."

Manny nodded. He took a final deep breath and wiped his sweaty palms on his trousers. He got a death grip on his Glock before giving the others the thumbs-up. Willie, Janet, and the other two deputies reached their side of the door a split second after Manny and Boner did. Willie flattened himself against the side of the door, no mean feat for such a big man, and Janet followed suit. She held her gun in the TV Ready Position, like fools on television or movies did, barrel beside her ear, just waiting for a sharp sound or movement to frighten her and put a Hydra-Shok hollow point through her temple. Manny prayed she wouldn't shoot herself in the head when the action started. *Lumpy would be pissed if his niece accidentally shot and killed herself.*

Boner stepped around Manny and adjusted his grip on the battering ram. And began singing. Although Boner's fine baritone voice bounced off the cabin porch, Manny stopped him. "What *are* you doing?"

Boner looked at him as if he were daft. "We do singing search warrants here."

Manny expected someone being alerted inside to start shooting at any moment. "What the hell's that?"

"Like a singing telegram. Only better. It's our little touch

of irony we like to inject just before we take a door down."
Boner reared the battering ram while his voice belted out "The
Yellow Rose of Texas," but Manny stopped him and tried the
knob. The door swung open and hit the back of the inside
wall as loudly as if a shot had been fired. Janet jumped, and
Manny expected to see another hole in her head she didn't
need.

Manny took in deep, calming breaths, listening. How
many of these had he been on where the short pause before
entering had saved a life, had told him someone dangerous
waited just around the corner of a wall or under a table. He
detected nothing, and motioned for the others. They quickly
button-hooked around the door. Boner dropped his battering
ram and followed, with Willie and the other two deputies
close behind as they took up a covering position on either side
of the massive door. Janet stood on the porch, shaking. *Watching our six, no doubt. Comforting.*

Willie bounded up the stairs to the loft faster than his
cover officer could follow, and stood looking over the railing
at the others below as he holstered his gun. "Clear up here."

Manny holstered his own Glock. "Looks like they cleared
out quick. Food still in the skillet. Dirty dishes in the sink. I
wouldn't figure the judge to be a sloppy man."

"Unless he was on the run," Boner said. "A shame."

Unlike Boner, Manny was grateful they didn't have to use
the battering ram. Or their guns. And a small part of Manny
was glad they didn't find the judge home, either. He'd just
started warming to the man.

Manny nudged Willie and nodded to the porch. "Better go
calm your trainee or she'll mess her pants. Last thing I want to
do is drive all the way back to Pine Ridge with the windows
open." Willie rolled his eyes and disappeared outside.

Manny began systematically searching the one huge room
for anything that might tell him where Ham might have fled.

Manny walked into the tiny alcove that Ham used as an office, different than the main rooms in disarray and chaos. Not dirty, just messy as if the Ham had other things on his mind besides business. Like Senate hearings.

Manny picked up one of the sticky notes that Ham had pasted across the top of the roll top. Cheat sheets. Questions anticipated. Rehearsal cues that Ham would need to practice.

On Ham's I-love-me-wall hung his South Dakota Bar license, just above his master's diploma from the University of South Dakota, and below that a copy of the *Argus Leader* article that proclaimed Alexander Hamilton High Elk had just performed a jurisprudence miracle by gaining an acquittal for Cal Wolf Guts. The paper had yellowed with age. But then who hadn't.

Manny walked into the main room and dropped onto the sofa. He propped his feet on the footstool just as Willie led Janet inside. She stopped just inside the door, looking around, still shaking.

Deputy Boner's eyes roamed over Janet's tight uniform, and he nodded to Willie. "Your squeeze?"

"Hardly," Willie answered and turned to Manny. "No sign of the judge or Joe Dozi out back, either. And like the deputies said, there's recent damage and white paint transfer."

"Malibu white?"

"You got it."

Manny stood and followed Willie, while Janet fell in step as they walked to Ham's Suburban. The front bumper was caved in, and the headlight on the driver's side was missing. White paint transfer was smeared along the driver's side fender and obliterated one of the painted eagle feathers. The tire had rubbed against the wheel, pieces of shredded tire sticking to the inside of the fender well. "Standard white."

"Got chip samples to send in."

"And compare them with what?" Manny asked. "That

charcoal barbequed car that used to be my government ride? Any other vehicles out back? In the shed?"

Willie shook his head. "Nothing."

"Bikes?"

He shook his head again and pointed to the two outbuildings. "We checked those sheds. All that was in there was fishing gear, a couple deer mounts, and a lot of pigeon shit."

"Then put out a BOLO for that red Indian Chief the judge rides. And see if Sturgis PD can figure out what Dozi might be driving."

"You figure they're on the run?" Janet whispered, as if she didn't trust the other law officers there. More likely, Manny figured, she stammered because she was still too frightened to speak loudly.

"Only explanation that makes sense." Manny sat in one of the Adirondack chairs on Ham's porch. Boner and the other two deputies were rooting through things inside the cabin. *At least it'll keep them busy.*

"My guess is we'll find them farther away from here rather than closer. If the judge has to establish an alibi for last night when his 'Burb ran me over, he'll need to make contact with folks far from here that will vouch for him."

Boner and the other deputies emerged from the house. They stared at Janet, and she moved behind Willie. "You think Judge High Elk needs an alibi?"

"Let's say I have some questions for him."

Janet laughed. "A sitting federal judge? I don't think he'd stoop to trying to kill you."

"Wouldn't he?" Willie looked down on Janet, talking slowly as a teacher talks to a student. "Put yourself in his shoes, and tell me that anything would stand in your way if you had a chance to be the first Indian anything. Judge High Elk has an opportunity to make history, and by God he'll do it."

"But we don't have a clue where he might have run."

"Maybe we don't," Manny said. "But Micah Crowder might."

"What's he got to do with this?" Willie moved away from Janet, and all three Lawrence County Deputies' eyes gave her the twice over.

"Micah searched Gunnar's room when he went missing back in '69. He went to the Badlands in search of Gunnar when he went missing. He might remember where Ham and Joe searched for him in the Badlands back then. There's people still missing in the Stronghold that don't want to be found. Maybe the judge wants to add himself to that list until the confirmation hearings." Manny stood and started for the car. "You two stay here. Sort of like an advance honeymoon."

"No way." Willie ran after him.

Janet ran after Willie. "Wait. If I'm ever going to learn this stuff, I got to stick to you like glue."

"That's what I'm afraid of," Willie said and held the back door for her.

CHAPTER 20

"Have you seen Micah Crowder?"

Joey smiled at Manny from behind her desk and laid her Harlequin romance on her lap. The book jacket showed a swarthy Fabio-type hunk holding a blond vixen by her thin waist. Willie nudged Manny and nodded to the book jacket.

"Maybe your admirer Joey will be working today," Willie had chided Manny as they pulled into the Parkside Manor parking lot. "As I recall, she had the eye for you."

"She was hot for you."

"Not so," Janet added and nudged Manny. "Willie said the last time she practically hauled you into her room and did the wild thing right then."

"Maybe you should take one for the team," Willie had prodded as they walked the parking lot to the office of the Parkside past Richard Head's empty parking space. "Get close to Joey for the sake of information."

"He's not answering his door," Joey said. She stood and came around the counter, standing a little closer than Manny wanted. He remained motionless. This was as close as he'd get to taking one for the team.

"Have you tried him lately?" Manny asked.

" 'Bout this time yesterday. Nice, isn't it?"

"Pardon?

"Micah. The pain in the ass hasn't been here for the past two days and it's been nice and quiet. And boring, until now." She winked with sixty-something-year-old eyes that had started to cloud with cataracts.

"Where did he go?"

Joey looked over her half-glasses at Janet and shrugged. "How should I know, I just live here. I didn't adopt the damned fool."

"Maybe something's happened to him." Willie put on his best concerned look. "Maybe he's dead in his apartment."

Joey shook her head. "Didn't see a cloud of flies hovering around his door. He's gone, all right."

"Maybe we could take a little peek inside."

"Can't. Regulations. People might take something once they got inside." Joey looked over her glasses at Janet.

"Just this once." Manny delved into his memory to put on his best Bogart charm. It worked. Joey snatched a ring of keys from an eye hook above the counter. "Just for you. But you got to promise if we find him you got to throw him back."

Joey led them to Micah's apartment and started to insert the key into the lock when Willie stopped her. "Aren't you going to knock first? Just in case?"

"The old bastard's gone, I told you."

"How can you be so sure?"

"Agent Tanno." Manny's name rolled off her tongue like she was enthralled by the sound. "Call it women's intuition. Besides, that beater blue Pontiac of his has been gone from the parking lot for two days. He wouldn't have sold it. No one would buy that piece of crap metal. You know that nut brush paints his car a different color every spring. Right there in the parking lot."

"He's just enjoying the fine amenities of the Parkside."

Joey rolled her eyes as she unlocked the door and stuck her head inside. "See. He's flown the coop."

"We'll just look around for a moment," Manny said. "If that's all right with you, Joey."

She smiled and batted eyelashes hovering over rummy gray eyes. As during their previous visit, she'd forgotten her dentures this afternoon. "Just shut the door when you're done. I'd hate for someone to wander in here and accidentally clean up this dump."

They waited until Joey left before entering Micah's apartment, typical of other low rent, low upkeep retirement homes: one main room half the size it should be, tiny kitchen barely big enough to accommodate the two-burner stove and micro icebox, and a bathroom too small to allow a man to sit without his knees scraping the wall. Manny hoped Micah was not overly regular.

"If he planned on leaving he didn't take much." Janet stood in front of an armoire missing one door. Slacks and shirts were matched and hung together, and the single drawer below had been left open. Underwear and socks packed the drawer so that it was impossible to tell if any were missing. "Looks like he left most of his clothes."

A recent copy of the *Lakota County Times* lay open on the table beside *Indian County Today*. The newspapers had been carved up, with old clippings glued to notebook pages and arranged in a binder. Manny flipped the pages, all pertaining to mining in the Badlands.

Under the clippings a hand-drawn map of the Badlands lay beside a National Park Service trail map. Manny put on his reading glasses and opened the curtain in the single room window. He turned the Park Service map around to look at different angles until he recognized the area: the Stronghold District. He picked up the hand-drawn map, yellowed and aged and drawn on the back of a 1969 Publishers Clearing House come-on ad. The ad was addressed to Gunnar Janssen.

"Looks like Micah went camping, back in the day."

"How'd he get Gunnar's mail?" Willie asked, than answered his own question. "I guess he took it from Gunnar's apartment after the judge reported Gunnar missing in college. Micah mentioned he went into Gunnar's apartment looking for anything that might tell him where he'd gone. Some obsession to have kept it all these years. Wonder if he found Gunnar?"

"You wonder if he found him and killed him back in 1969?" Manny held the map to the light. Damned desolate area.

"These maps put Micah in the area where that ordnance crew found Gunnar's skeleton." Willie handed Manny a crumpled letter addressed to the U.S. Senate, dated two days ago, written—or scratched—longhand. "And this looks like Micah had other things besides camping on his mind." Micah had outlined the reasons he felt Alexander Hamilton High Elk shouldn't be confirmed for the Supreme Court, but the letter had several words crossed out and written over as if Micah perfected it before he sent the final copy.

"So he sent the final copy?" Janet asked.

"Or maybe someone interrupted him before he was able to send it," Willie added. "Someone not wanting this kind of rhetoric hitting the newspapers right before the hearings."

Manny kicked those arguments around in his head. Micah—though getting on in years—appeared pretty sharp the time Manny had spoken with him. His guess was that Micah would be one step ahead of the one or both of the only men who could figure out where he'd fled; men who had gone into the Badlands a time or two with Gunnar back in the day, both men who would benefit the most if Ham was confirmed. One man that could make anyone disappear, the other with the most to gain by such a disappearance: Joe Dozi and Judge Alexander Hamilton High Elk.

CHAPTER 21

FALL 1939

Moses pulled Clayton behind a rock. Dirt clung to his sweaty cheek as he chanced a peek over the hill. "That's a nice buck, hoss."

"Wait until he walks away from those doe," Moses said. "We do not want to shoot one of them by accident."

Clayton chuckled. "There's enough to spare in that herd if we shot one by mistake."

"We do not shoot what we do not need."

Clayton looked sideways at Moses and grabbed the binoculars from the case. "Of course, the Lakota way."

"You say that with some sarcasm. Like it is a bad thing to want to preserve life."

Clayton let the binos drop by the leather thong and dangle at his chest. He abruptly stood and whistled. The nearest deer barked a warning to the rest of the herd and bolted over the canyon rim, flickering tails waving good-bye.

"Why?"

"I got a bigger one last year. I want a nice one, with at least a thirty-inch spread to hang in my Senate office."

Moses shook his head. "You get to be a bigger pain in the rear every year."

Clayton smiled. "But I'm your pain in the rear. Where can we find a bigger buck?"

Moses stood and brushed the dust from his trousers. He pointed toward V-Tail Draw. "Through that narrow pass we can get to Cottonwood Creek. There is a watering hole there that never dries up. Deer know that, too."

"How about there?" Clayton pointed to two large buttes on either side of a deep saddle of sandstone and dirt and fine alkaline dust. "We saw some big ones hightail it thataway yesterday."

"We have been over this before. That is where the bad rocks live."

"Not that cock-and-bull story again." Clayton sat in the shade of a shale outcrop and grabbed a bottle of whiskey from his backpack. He started to hand it to Moses, who reached for it a second before Clayton jerked it away. "I know what you'd do with it."

"What I should have done years ago."

"Not again. What bug crawled up your ass this morning? You know I need a nip now and again."

"That is not what I am upset about and you know it."

"Will you let it lie for a couple hours at least?"

"How can I?" The morning sun bounced off Moses as he paced in front of Clayton. "Samuel needs you. Needs your influence right now. You could talk to the prosecutor. See if they could go easy on the boy. Cut a deal."

Clayton propped his pack against the overhang and leaned back against it while he supported his head with his hands. "If it were just another drunk and disorderly charge, there'd be no problem. But Samuel got himself hoary-eyed drunk and knifed that man. I'd play hell getting him out of that charge, U.S. senator or not. He shouldn't have been liquored up at that barn dance."

"I remember someone else getting himself drunk and on the fight at a dance some years ago. Someone that was lucky that the man he fought with did not kill him for what he did to two Indian boys."

"That was different."

"Was it?"

Clayton looked away. "Samuel got himself into that mess; no one twisted his arm. He went to that dance knowing he'd be the only Indian there. He went looking for trouble."

"What else did the kid have to do with his time?" Moses sipped water from his deerskin bladder, the same water bladder he'd offered to Clayton that first wagon ride to the Charles Town Ranch. They'd come a long way together, yet they hadn't even taken the first step as brothers should, and Moses had long ago thought of Clayton as his brother. Moses stooped to get under the overhang and dropped beside Clayton. "Your people took our land and treated us like pets. Except your people treated your dogs better than you did my people. And you have never treated Samuel properly."

"Properly! Like you treat those scrub cows of yours?"

Moses looked to the saddle where he knew the cows wandered on the other side, looking for food and some semblance of water. "I have done what I could for those cows, but nothing helps. Think I want to ever see a living thing suffer as those critters have?"

"I might be able to help."

"How?"

"Supplements. Cake. Hay and alfalfa. Those cattle need nourishment they're not getting here in this damned desert."

"Okay, then have it delivered."

"Can't." Clayton shook out a cigarette. He waited until the smoke had dissipated inside the overhang to continue. "How would it look if the chairman of the Senate Indian Commission gave preferential treatment to his friend? Even if I could arrange it, it'd look like I'm buying you off. But I know a man who could do so legally."

"Not that fat Frenchman again?"

"What's wrong with Renaud?"

Moses kicked the dirt, and a scorpion crawled from under the dust cloud. Moses held out his hand and the creature crawled into his palm. Moses rested his hand on the rock outcropping and it scampered into a crevice. "Renaud LaJaneuse wants to get his hands on my paintings. I told him a dozen times they are not mine to give."

"I've heard your argument a dozen times." Clayton stood and flicked his butt into a clump of sagebrush. Embers shot skyward then as quickly died. He stood and dusted off his chinos. "You always say you can't destroy them, even if the people you paint them for don't want them. He understands that and respects your decision. The only thing he wants is for you to bring some of your paintings to New York."

Moses chuckled. "A Lakota Picasso I think is what he called me."

"The world deserves to know how the Lakota think of their world. There's no better way than to let them experience the Lakota vision through your work. And your cattle might live because of it."

Moses stood and scraped his head on the outcropping. He put his Stetson back on. "You think I would come to New York in trade for supplements for cows that will be dead by winter anyway?"

"No, I don't." Clayton stood and draped his arm around

Moses's shoulder. "But you would for your own people. Ren-aud's already promised food for the Oglala."

"Let me think it over."

"Sure, hoss. And think over another thing—the place where the bad rocks live."

"What is to think over? We have been there . . ."

"I talked to this geologist friend at the School of Mines, Ellis Lawler. He's got a notion what those rocks are."

"Already told you they are bad. Nothing good will come out of them."

"If what my friend says is right, good things will come out of them. For the Oglala."

Moses looked sideways at Clayton. "What good can come out of them?"

"Jobs. Prosperity. Independence you have so long sought."

Moses looked to the west, to the saddle that protected the rocks on the other side, as if seeing the rocks through those huge pieces of earth. There was so much to think about, with his critters fighting to survive, the sour thought of having to travel to New York with his paintings, and now, Clayton piling it on demanding to be shown the rocks. And one very pressing matter. "I will show you the place where the bad rocks live, but I cannot show you them alone."

Clayton stepped back and looked up at Moses. "What the hell you mean, you can't show me alone?"

"I need help guiding you."

"Okay, get your help."

"Not just any help. I need Samuel. Out of jail with nothing hanging over his head."

Clayton's jaw tightened and his lip began to quiver. "That's bullshit! That's blackmail. You'd blackmail a U.S. senator?"

"Absolutely."

"Damn it." Clayton dug a furrow into the dirt with his

boot tip. "All right. I'll get Samuel out of that Pennington County lockup. But you have to promise to show me those rocks."

"You sound as if you think I would go back on an agreement."

"Just promise me you'll show me as soon as I spring Samuel."

Moses smiled. "We will show you. Trust me."

CHAPTER 22

"We're headed to Cuny Table to meet up with Benny Black Fox." The sound of the police dispatcher in the background echoed in Willie's phone.

"We?"

"We. As in me and Janet." Willie sounded as if he expected Doreen Big Eagle to ride up and deliver another verbal whipping.

"But Marshal Ten Bears has agreed to take us right where he found Micah's body," Manny said. Marshal had found Micah Crowder's body within walking distance from his cabin this morning.

"Don't think I'm not pissed over this. I planned to go with you, but these are orders from Acting Frigging Chief Looks Twice—orders that I take his niece along."

"Can't talk him out of it?"

"Not today. He's upset that someone outbid him on that pair of Elvis boots on eBay and needs to take it out on someone. Who better than the man training his niece to be the next tribal investigator. Shit, here she comes. Wouldn't do to get caught talking about Uncle Leon."

"Keep me posted."

The line went dead, and Manny called Pee Pee. He'd meet him at the justice building and go to the scene in the evidence van. Manny knew his limitations, and his ineptness behind the wheel. He'd trade Pee Pee's sick graveside humor for a safe ride any day.

>◇◇◇<

"Come in here while Pee Pee's warming the evidence van up." Lumpy held his office door for Manny.

"It's one hundred degrees. What's to warm up?"

"Humor me."

Lumpy shut the door and dropped into his Elvis chair. The King wrapped his vinyl arms around Lumpy, who reached over and turned off his stereo. "Love Me Tender" faded into silence.

Many waited while Lumpy fiddled with a pencil, making increasingly smaller circles on his desktop planner. The tip of the pencil broke and flew across the desk. "Willie. I just don't know what to do with him."

"You got him meeting up with Benny Black Fox this morning."

"Not that. He's not the same Willie that hired on."

"People change." Manny stood and poured a cup of coffee. Lumpy waived it away.

"People change, but not everyone changes for the worse. Have you seen how he wears his uniform these last months?"

"So he hasn't time to stop at the Laundromat."

"Laundromat? I can tell what the hell he's had to eat for the last week by looking at his uniform shirt. And he's got more bags under his eyes than Hillary Clinton."

"He mentioned he's been having a hard time sleeping."

"You know what's going on with him?"

Manny shrugged. He wanted to tell Lumpy that Willie was having some prostate problems, but thought better. Young Lakota men didn't want their private lives bandied around their bosses' offices. And he sure didn't want to mention Willie had taken up drinking lately. "Maybe it's the stress of training his replacement."

Lumpy slammed the pencil on the table. "He better be able to handle stress like that or he won't make it in law enforcement. There's something else bothering him. I'm thinking he's been having a hard time after his aunt Lizzy wound up in the state hospital."

"It didn't help any that you kept reminding him she'll never get out of there."

"He feels responsible."

"And what responsibility do you have? You pushed him . . ."

"I didn't force him into anything." Manny stood and walked across the room. "He was an officer doing his job."

"He looked up to the legendary Manny Tanno. That was enough. Then to heap insult on top, you talk down to him like he's a rookie."

"I don't talk down to . . ."

"You talk down to everyone, mister hotshot agent." Lumpy turned to the wall, and Manny couldn't tell if he was smiling at his victory or angry. "Guess you have to do that when you abandon your people and go to D.C."

"That's about enough!"

"Or what?" Lumpy turned and stepped closer. Even though Manny had trounced Lumpy every time they'd wrestled as schoolboys, Lumpy showed no fear now. "You going to beat me again? How about you try talking down to me?"

Manny stood and walked around the desk, his knuckles whitening with each step. He took deep breaths and shoved his hands in his pockets. The hand with the cat bite shot pain through his entire arm. "Maybe I got into the habit of talking down to my students."

"That's not right, either. You didn't use to be such a condescending bastard."

"At least you don't mince words."

"Did I ever?"

Lumpy had always told Manny just what he thought. It had remained the one thing Manny could count on—even though it was often painful. "I thought you wanted to talk about Willie."

Lumpy nodded and dropped in his chair. He scooted it close to the desk so his short arms could reach across and shoved a notebook at Manny. "That lists the times Willie's been late. And sick. And just plain not calling in when he's supposed to be working."

Manny looked over the list. "What explanation did he give?"

"He just shrugged. Said 'like whatever,' or something as vague. Even the threat of Janet replacing him for the investigator position—and I can tell you he wanted that job badly—can't seem to snap him out of his rut."

"How about ordering Willie to talk with a counselor?"

Lumpy shook his head. "I can't mandate that."

"If he worked for the bureau, we could mandate it."

"Is that how you handle everything? Force people into it?"

›‹›‹›‹

One fender of Micah Crowder's blue Catalina jutted from one side of a short hill as if drawing attention to the car's final resting spot. "I saw it when I was out this way gathering herbs." Marshal Ten Bears pointed to a trail adjacent to Cottonwood Creek. "You can get there along that two-track."

"Hop in."

Manny climbed in back of the evidence van as Pee Pee put

it in four-wheel drive. Marshal crawled in the front and directed Pee Pee along a shallow arroyo between two shifting sandstone spires. The van crawled over a rise and Pee Pee stopped beside the Pontiac. The driver's door was open and a dark trail in the dust showed where Micah had crawled into some sagebrush and died. Flies seemed to hover over Micah's body, their buzzing getting louder as the three walked toward the corpse.

Pee Pee led the way with his camera in hand. He breathed in and held it for long moments before exhaling and smiling at Manny. "Don't you just love the smell of maggots in the morning."

Manny waited until Pee Pee had photographed the scene before he walked to the body. Manny squatted on his heels. Generations of flies had already laid their eggs, and the back of Micah's head crawled. Pee Pee fished into his evidence bag and grabbed small vials and tweezers and began plucking the larvae from the body. "Collecting creepy crawlies. Want to help?"

"I'll pass." Manny stood and moved upwind. "Looks like he got popped near his car and crawled the twenty yards."

"Pretty cool, huh?" Pee Pee said, continuing picking larvae.

"Know what he was doing out here?"

"Haven't the slightest," Marshal said between a bandanna that he had covering his nose. "I haven't been to my cabin in a couple days so I don't know when he showed up. And he would have had to come past my cabin to get here."

"Get many people down this way?"

"Hell no." Marshal joined Manny upwind, while Pee Pee whistled as he collected bugs. "I get some hikers down this way now and again. Usually some damned granola-head from Colorado or some Californicator hiking this way to live the adventure only to get in trouble. They get this far before they realize this land is no joke. We get a few every year that end up like that poor stiff. But I never see someone trying to make it through here in a car."

"Wasn't the land that killed this dude," Pee Pee called cheerily over his shoulder. Manny stepped to the body and looked over Pee Pee's shoulder as he attached a macro lens to his camera for a close-up shot. "Pretty good-sized hole in the back of his head. You want to see the exit wound, step around and take a look-see at his left eye."

Manny walked around and squatted on his heels. Except for the eye socket being disintegrated, the insects that had invaded the body as it cooled, and the blackened condition of the corpse, Micah looked just like Manny remembered him.

"Ever see this car around here before?"

Pee Pee whistled as he shook his head. "Never. But then I don't get to the northern fringes of the frontier, as Elvis would have put it."

Manny turned to Marshal, still with the bandanna covering his nose. "Ever see this man before?"

Marshal shook his head.

"Micah Crowder?"

Marshal shook his head again. Either he was telling the truth or, together with Joe Dozi, he was one of the best liars he'd had the misfortune to meet. "Should I know him?"

"He used to be a policeman in Spearfish in the late sixties, early seventies."

"Don't recognize the man."

Manny let it drop for the moment. "How long you going to be?"

Pee Pee smiled. "At least until the sun is so hot overhead a new batch of larvae hatch."

"Pee Pee . . ."

"All right. At least two hours."

Manny turned to Marshal. "Mind if we wait in the shade of your cabin?"

Marshal grinned. "Sure, if you're up to the half-mile walk back."

"I'll pace myself." He called over his shoulder to Pee Pee, "Pick me up when you're through with your orgasms."

"Sure thing," Pee Pee answered, whistling and rummaging through his evidence kit. Then Pee Pee always was a multi-tasker.

>()()()<

They arrived at Marshal's cabin fifteen minutes later. Marshal tossed his sweaty ball cap on an antler coat hook before he turned to the water jug and began making coffee.

Manny dropped into a chair at the table and wiped his head with his handkerchief. Marshal's one-room shack was neater than Manny had expected for being a seasonal dwelling. Two cots were suspended by a length of chain anchored to one log wall, handwoven blankets resting on the bottom bunk, mountain lion rug on the top bunk that served as storage for a sleeping bag, rifle, and camping gear. The north and west walls where the bunks were anchored had wood nailed over the exposed logs.

"Keeps the wind out." Marshal chin-pointed to the wood. "I don't think grandfather ever had much mud chinking between these old logs. I don't know how he survived winters here." Marshal tossed a match into the Franklin stove in the middle of the room. The door clanged shut and the loud sound was lost somewhere inside the cabin, much like things—and people—were often lost to the Stronghold. "This and a few scrub cows were all my father left me." Marshal waved his hand around the room. " 'Cause that's all Grandfather Moses left him."

"Moses Ten Bears must have been a busy man, what with running cows and tending to the spiritual needs of the Oglala."

"Don't forget those visions he painted that made him exactly zero."

Manny ran his hand over the Pendleton blankets on the bunk. "You don't sound too enthused with your lot in life."

"Not too enthused?" Marshal grabbed two metal cups from a cup rack on the table. "Why would you think that? Grandfather left my father, and now me, with this splendid Badlands getaway. Kind of a Shangri-la in the Stronghold." Marshal kicked the wall beside the cots and mud chinking fell from the cracks between the logs.

"I understand the Cultural Committee wants you to move this into Pine Ridge, in that lot by Billy Mills Hall so everyone can see how Moses Ten Bears lived."

Marshal chuckled and opened the door. He gestured outside. "That's where my grandfather lived, out there in the elements. That's where he gathered strength for his visions. Where he laid his head most nights."

"Then that's what people would experience."

"They're willing to give nothing for it. If it was that important to the Lakota, the tribe would pony up some bucks for it."

"Thought you wouldn't sell it for any amount?"

"I wouldn't." Marshal opened a tiny cupboard and grabbed two more "I'd turn down whatever the tribe offered. But they got to want it bad enough. Haven't you ever heard that what you get for nothing is worth exactly what you paid for it? I might have donated it to the tribe if they'd offered a chunk of change. No, I think I'll leave it here and enjoy the looks on people's faces as they finally make it down here to see this shack where Moses lived."

"And near where he died? You think that was him in that car on the bombing range, don't you?"

Marshal turned away. "Possible."

"You believed it enough that you gave a DNA sample."

Marshal handed Manny a cup of coffee and motioned to a chair at the tiny table. He examined his own cup and the FREE ICE AT WALL DRUG all but faded beneath the broken handle. "One of those skeletons was large. Very large. It's almost a certainty it was Grandfather. Not that you'll be able to make anything of it."

"You don't much like law enforcement, do you?"

Marshal stood in the doorway and spread his arms across the frame, standing immobile long enough that Manny was uncertain if he'd heard him. When he turned back, Marshal's jaw tightened, working muscles beneath into an angry mood. "Cops arrested my old man. Often. Tribal cops and those bigots in Rapid City."

"I wouldn't say they're racist. That might be back in your father's day . . ."

"It still exists. Point is, my old man went the way of so many of our people with the booze."

Manny sat at the table, moving aside last month's *Rapid City Journal*. The corner of a crude map jutted out of the Sports section. A crude map with handwriting Manny recognized as Micah's. While Marshal turned to the stove and refilled his coffee cup, Manny palmed the map. "Maybe your father needed arresting."

Marshal laughed, but his face remained taut. "I almost forgot—you were once tribal police. Dad might have been a mean drunk later in life, but he wasn't when I was growing up. He was just a rummy that needed his hooch every day. There was no one to help him."

"Even back then there was AA. People he could talk to. If he wanted to get clean . . ."

Marshal laughed again, this time his face softening as he remembered Eldon Ten Bears. "Dad knew about AA. He was proud he was just a drunk. Said if he was an alcoholic he'd need to attend all those meetings."

"And you blame the law for his addiction?"

Marshal spit tobacco juice outside the door. He wiped his mouth with his shirtsleeve. "Dad died in the lockup in Pine Ridge. I didn't even have a chance to say my good-byes. He died while I was stationed in Germany."

"I was stationed in Germany."

Marshal glanced over his shoulder. "That the strategy— establish some solidarity with the one you want information from. That it, Agent Tanno?"

"Just making conversation until Pee Pee finishes processing the scene."

"Then let's cut the games." Marshal closed the door and refilled his coffee cup. "You want to find out if I killed Gunnar Janssen?"

"Then you do remember him?"

"I guided him on a couple hunts when I was home on leave. At the time he went missing, I was a Spec Four drinking warm beer in Bonn."

Manny grabbed his notebook, his prop, from his pocket while he slipped the parchment map into his back trouser pocket. "Right now, I'm here to investigate Micah Crowder's murder, but now that you mentioned him, let's talk about Gunnar. Your army records show you were home on leave during the time he went missing."

Marshal laughed "So you think I lied?" Manny had interviewed enough people to detect nervousness in Marshal's question.

Manny shrugged. "Apparently. What other explanation is there?"

"So now I'm a suspect? People make honest mistakes. I thought I was back in Germany when Gunnar went missing."

Manny flipped pages that had no writing on them. "You

could have had the opportunity to kill Gunnar. Either lure him here to your cabin, or lead him off into the Badlands and shoot him. With something like that .22 hanging on your wall."

Marshal snatched the rifle from the deer antlers and turned toward Manny. The muzzle crossed his midsection for a brief moment before Marshal unscrewed the magazine tube in the butt. He tipped the rifle up and shells fell into his hand. He handed both the rifle and ammunition to Manny. "Lot of people here have .22s. Great hunting gun."

"And poaching?"

Marshal smiled. "Just take the gun and ammo and do whatever ballistic test you need. I got nothing to hide. I didn't kill Gunnar."

"Not him I'm thinking of." Manny set the gun on the bunk and pocketed the bullets. "It's Micah Crowder."

"Told you already, I never met the man."

"Then what's this?" Manny retrieved the parchment map from his pocket and handed it to Marshal. "Found this on your table just now. It's Micah's handwriting."

Marshal grabbed the map and tossed it back onto the table. "I was wondering myself how it got here. I saw it earlier when I got here."

"How did it come to be on your table?"

"Look, I leave the cabin unlocked, in case some fool hiking out here gets in trouble and needs a place to rest up."

Manny smiled. "You don't strike me as the Good Samaritan type."

"Ain't. It's just the right thing to do. There isn't anything worth stealing so I keep the cabin unlocked. Micah Crowder must have come in here. Left the map on the table."

"Perhaps you're right. We'll leave it for now."

Manny grabbed the map and opened the door, orienting the map to the landscape. Twin buttes guarded a deep arroyo that had been circled on the parchment. "What's down that gully?" Manny pointed out the door.

Marshal glanced at the paper for the first time and frowned as he turned the paper to the light. "That's the place where the bad rocks live."

"Tell me about them."

Marshal chin-pointed to the west. "Just an old legend Dad told me about that my grandfather told him once."

"You don't sound convinced."

Marshal's face softened. He pinched tobacco in his lower lip and offered Manny a pinch, but he waved it away. "Grandfather Moses had disappeared by the time I was born, but Dad told me stories. When he could remember them between drinking bouts. Grandfather claimed bad rocks lived there. Guess it was just like his visions—something his imagination came up with."

Manny's stomach growled and he reached in his jacket pocket for a Tanka Bar. He offered to share with Marshal, but he shook his head as he pointed to his lip swollen with Copenhagen. "That's too healthy. I'm too busy helping myself into an early grave."

"Been there. But you got to be proud of your grandfather. He was a wonderful role model for traditional Lakota ways."

Marshal spit tobacco on top of a lizard crawling inside the cabin to escape the heat then ground it with his boot. "Grandpa Moses fought to keep traditions alive when everyone around him was conforming to the ways of the *wasicu*."

"Assimilation. My uncle Marion told me horror stories of the boarding school he was forced to attend until he ran away once too many times. After that they told him good riddance." *Unc, you clung to the traditional ways until you died from the White man's disease, until you succumbed to diabetes.* Manny turned away from Marshal when tears began forming in his eyes.

"Grandfather Moses was Mata Ihanblapi. Bear Dreamer. He cured many people in his day. But his greatest gift was his ability to heal people spiritually." He faced Manny. "To answer your earlier question, I do think Grandfather Moses is that other man in the car. He was just at the wrong place during bombing practice. Why they were there is the mystery."

"So you don't buy the possibility that Moses was there with the White guy, drinking where they shouldn't have been?"

Marshal shook his head. "Unlike my dad, Grandfather never drank. Ever. Ellis Lawler might have been shitfaced when those bombs dropped, but not Grandfather."

"How'd you find out the name of the other man in the car?"

Marshal grinned wide. "I got my sources."

"Janet Grass?"

Marshal shrugged and sipped his coffee.

"Guess I'll have to plug a leak when I find it. But tell me about these bad rocks."

Marshal topped off his cup and set the pot back on the stove as he pulled a chair away from the table and sat. "I will tell you, not because you'll use the information wisely, but because I have no desire for anything bad to happen to you."

"Then there is truth to the legend?"

"Every legend had some truth to it." He pointed out the doorway framing the twin buttes drawn on the map. "Grandfather claimed the bad rocks kept people from leaving the Stronghold. He said only the *Wanbli Oyate* thrives there. Only the eagle soaring overhead does not feel the wrath of the bad rocks."

"So the Eagle Nation navigates around that region in safety?"

Marshal nodded. "To soar above the evil. Never touching the rocks. The place is cursed. Or so Grandfather claimed."

"Can't be too cursed if the Air Corps used the area for bombing practice, dragging cars out there for practice targets."

"All I know is those scrub cows I've tried raising all die prematurely. Some cows abort spontaneously. Just like those critters Grandfather raised, and like those Dad had."

"Did you ever think they died because you were a poor rancher, like your father and his father?"

"Got nothing to do with that." Marshal reached inside his lip. He scrapped Copenhagen away and tossed it out the door. "I've fed them every supplement, supplied them every mineral cake I could to nurse them back to health. I've had three two-headed calves the last five years. Three from a herd of forty heifers. What's the odds in that?"

"But you've gone to where the rocks live and came back to tell me about it."

"I go there every spring and every fall to pray. Offer tobacco to the four winds. Make a sweat and purify myself. Still, the curse that's lingered so long won't go away."

"Could you show me the rocks?"

Marshal stood and pointed to the buttes. "There somewhere. I've never found them, but I feel them. They're there, watching me when I pass. Go. Hike to your heart's content. But I won't be responsible for you not making it out alive."

Manny thought of the prayers he would need to offer, of the purity he would need. He'd need the guidance of a sacred man to show him the proper rituals to survive the rocks. Not that he was superstitious, but because a smart Oglala needed to hedge his bet against all enemies. Even bad rocks.

A horn honked outside. Pee Pee sat in his OST evidence van and stuck his head out the window, the wind whipping his long, gray braids across his face. "Train's leaving. You want to be on it?"

Manny turned to Marshal. "I'm here to clear the three cold cases, and this fresh homicide. If you're innocent, I'll clear you. If you're connected, I'll hunt you down like you hunt deer and antelope."

"Same as all cops—up against the wall and spread 'em?"

CHAPTER 23

Lumpy glared at Pee Pee's boots propped on the conference room table. He turned then so the rhinestones glinted in contrast to the pink leather uppers. With a wide smile, Pee Pee flicked away imaginary dust that had settled on Elvis Presley's signature on the outside of one boot. "Why didn't you tell me you were bidding on these, Chief? I feel bad now that I know I was bidding against you."

"How the hell should I know who was running me up?" Lumpy paced in front of the table. "What would you take for them?"

"Yes, what's your price?" Janet looked up at Lumpy. "I'll buy them for Uncle Leon."

Pee Pee held up both hands. "I just got them. I got to see if I want to keep them for my collection. They're a mite small for you, anyway."

"Don't matter. Name your price."

Pee Pee played with a gray braid and seemed to be mulling

the idea over. "I'll sleep on it. Or should I say, I'll walk on it." Pee Pee laughed, and Lumpy turned to Manny.

"Where's Willie?"

"Here, Chief." Willie burst through the door, one side of his shirttail hanging out of his trousers, and the cuff of one uniform shirt had caught on something and ripped. He rubbed morning stubble, and his eyes were so red it looked as if he would bleed to death if he didn't close them. "Just couldn't get up today."

"You wanted to know about Micah Crowder," Manny said, diverting Lumpy's attention from Willie.

Lumpy dropped into his Elvis chair. "I got to have something on Crowder. Sonja Myers is breathing down my neck wanting information. She's hinting at a cover-up."

Manny winked at Lumpy. "Thought that's what you always wanted—Sonja breathing down your neck."

Lumpy scowled and pointed a finger at Manny. "You sicced her on me in the first place."

"Not like you resisted much." When Sonja Myers got assigned to cover the Red Cloud murder case for the *Rapid City Journal* two months ago, she'd played Lumpy like a fine Stradivarius, or more like a pawnshop fiddle missing strings, and Lumpy had become one more victim of Sonja's beauty and charm, giving out information he didn't intend. Lumpy knew how biting her reports could be, and Manny was certain he wanted no more of that. But Manny wouldn't let Lumpy off the hook that easily. "Maybe you still got a chance with Sonja."

"Not likely. She's been spending time with Judge High Elk as of late."

"That's a serious conflict of interest, both for him as an object of her investigation, and for the *Journal* for allowing her to." On the Red Cloud murder, Sonja had played Manny against Lumpy, working each in order to gain inside informa-tion for her articles. Apparently, she was still working hard to gain attention of the big newspapers and fly out of Rapid for the Big Time. Had Ham put her up to snooping?

"Relax, Chief," Willie said. "She didn't get any inside info the last time she called."

Lumpy glared at Willie. "Maybe not, but this time she bent Hazel Horse's ear."

Hazel was the chairperson on the Committee to Appoint a Permanent Tribal Police Chief. "That explains why you're so upset." Manny said.

"Hazel's pushy," Janet volunteered. She scooted closer to Lumpy and draped her arm around his shoulders. "She calls up here three, four times a day wanting an update, so Sonja Myers will stop bugging her."

"Well, watch what you say to Sonja."

"I've been doing this longer than you have, Mister Agent Man." Red-faced, Lumpy turned to Pee Pee still twirling his long braid. "Take your damned feet off my table and tell me something about this Micah Crowder I don't already know."

Pee Pee feigned hurt feelings as he dabbed at the corners of his eyes with an imaginary handkerchief. He opened his brief-case on the table and slid the autopsy report toward Lumpy. "Contact wound to the back of the head, .38 caliber."

"Sure about the caliber?" Manny reached for the report, but Lumpy jerked it back.

"Not many people shoot .38s anymore," Lumpy added.

Pee Pee motioned to the report as he straightened his Elvis vest. The King seemed to be smiling at Lumpy as Pee Pee turned to show off both lapels. "The recovered slug was a hol-low point, nonbonded, and it fragmented. There was enough to measure—.356—and weigh, ninety grains of soft lead, plus whatever jacket material was floating around in Crowder's skull."

"With that diameter, it could be a .357." Lumpy relinquished the report, and Manny studied the file. "Could even be a 9mm, which is more common."

"Could be." Pee Pee brushed dirt from his boots. "But I'm making a best guess with what Doc Gruesome found."

"So we have an idea of the murder weapon." Lumpy's eyes kept darting back to Pee Pee's Elvis boots. He turned to Willie. "What did Benny Black Fox have to say?"

Willie began to speak but Janet interrupted him. "Benny remembers Crowder's blue Pontiac like it was yesterday."

Lumpy laughed. "That rummy can't remember what he did an hour ago let alone yesterday."

"How does he remember?" Manny leaned closer and cocked his ear toward her as he took off his reading glasses and set them beside the autopsy report.

"Because of Crowder's driving," Willie cut in. Janet threw him a shut-the-hell-up look, but he forced a smile and continued. "Benny saw the car when he was changing a lightbulb at the KILI booster tower by Cuny Table."

"He still doing that?" Pee Pee popped another Elvis PEZ and let the dispenser linger in front of Lumpy for a few moments before pocketing it. "Didn't we arrest him last year for shooting out those bulbs with his .22?"

Willie nodded. "We did but the station manager dropped charges. Said they couldn't get anyone else to change the bulbs."

"What's with the bulbs?" Manny asked.

Willie nodded to the ceiling. "KILI pays Benny ten bucks for every lightbulb he changes, because no one else is crazy enough to crawl all the way up their tower and do it."

Pee Pee laughed. "And last spring a KILI maintenance crew caught Benny shooting out the bulbs and running home to wait for the call to come back and change them. At the ten-dollar-a-bulb fee."

"The Pontiac already!" Lumpy leaned on the table with his pudgy arms. "How the hell does he remember Crowder's car?"

"He didn't see the car at first," Janet blurted out, wanting to be the bearer of news to Uncle Leon. "Benny said it looked like every other rez rod. He remembered the car because it kicked up so much dust, the Indian following him was having a hard time keeping up."

"That's it? That's Benny's pearl of wisdom?" Lumpy threw up his hands. "I could have told you an Indian was following Crowder and I wasn't even there. Could have been any one of us twenty thousand Indians hereabouts."

"Janet means an Indian motorcycle was chasing Crowder," Willie said. "A crimson Indian Chief. Benny was certain of that."

"Just like the one Judge High Elk drives," Janet added.

"Doesn't mean the judge was driving." Lumpy rubbed his forehead. "When did Benny see this motorcycle chasing Crowder?"

"Yesterday."

"And he didn't tell anyone?"

Willie shrugged. "Benny had a fresh ten-spot waiting for him and a big thirst. He had other priorities. Went down to White Clay to spend it and forgot to tell anyone when he got back."

Lumpy stood and his chair rolled back and hit the wall. He turned as if to apologize to the King. "If you're saying Judge High Elk's our shooter, you'd better have your ducks in a row before you even interview him."

"Can't do that just yet."

"And why the hell not?" Lumpy turned to Willie. "I don't relish this agency getting tied up talking with a sitting federal judge, but it looks like it has to be done."

"He's missing."

"Missing? What kind of police work is that when you can't even keep tabs on someone as high profile as the judge?"

Willie filled Lumpy in on the search warrant they had served with the Lawrence County Sheriff's Department, leaving out Janet puking twice from fear. "After we found him missing from his cabin, we put out a BOLO on him. We figure he and Joe Dozi went somewhere to establish an alibi for the judge."

"Oh, he's got an alibi, all right, doesn't he?" Lumpy nodded to Janet.

"I found out the judge has been at his mother's house since yesterday." She winked at Willie. "Just good police work."

Pee Pee laughed. "Just rookie luck, from what I hear." He turned to Willie. "Don't feel too bad, kid. Dirty Harriet over there happened onto the judge's outfit sitting at Sophie's house when she passed it on another investigation."

"That so?" Manny leaned across the table and met Lumpy's stare. "The judge's been there for a day and you didn't tell us?"

Lumpy scooted his chair back as if to escape. "Janet passed Sophie's place in Oglala on her way to interviewing a suspect on the damages to Willie's Durango."

"And the judge was just sitting there with his mother, in front of her house."

"Why didn't you tell anyone?"

"I did." Janet smiled at Manny, then turned to Willie and winked. "I told Uncle Leon."

>‹›‹›‹

"Now what the hell you want? To rub it in that one of your officers found the judge when the FBI couldn't?"

Lumpy eased himself into his chair. "Sit for a moment. Please."

Manny couldn't recall the last time Lumpy had said *please* to him, and he sat out of curiosity.

Lumpy made a tiny tent with his stubby fingers, started to speak, then stopped.

I guess he stopped to think and forgot to start again. "Spit it out and get it over with."

"I'm concerned about Willie," he said at last. "There's something going on that I can't fix."

"How the hell do you think he feels? How would you feel if the rookie you're training is slated to replace you at the first excuse?"

"He needs to push his envelope, which he didn't do on that last homicide case."

"Why, just because we didn't solve it? It's not like Willie didn't put his heart into the case. And it's not like I didn't try to bring him along."

"For once get off your high horse and come down here were we mortals live. It's not because he—and you, Hotshot—couldn't find Jason Red Cloud's murderer. Some crimes are unsolvable, even for the legendary Manny Tanno."

"Then why are you on his ass? Why did you oppose his promotion to criminal investigator?"

"He's too green."

"We were all too green once. We all had to learn on the job. But Janet is even greener than he is, and you want to replace him with her."

"Because she has the requisite degree."

"That's bull, Lumpy, and you know it."

Lumpy's face reddened and he leaned across the table. "I wanted to put pressure on Willie to perform. Wanted him to use his intellect. And all I get from him is coming in late, if he comes in at all. And when he does, he looks like he's been on a weeklong bender down in White Clay."

"Willie doesn't drink."

"He does now. He needs to get his head out of his ass."

"I bet you told him that."

Lumpy nodded. "Yesterday."

"Well, why don't you be a little more direct? Tell Willie he's shit for an officer. I'm sure that will improve his performance."

"I think someone else could use more direct criticism."

"Meaning?"

"One Hotshot Agent Man needs to be told maybe he's not the star attraction in the investigative world anymore. Maybe he was exiled here to the Rapid City Field Office because he's lost his edge. Lost his ability to put things together."

"And that's bull, too."

"Is it? The one case you failed to solve—perhaps your biggest one—and suddenly you're a common man." Lumpy laughed, but it was a forced laugh and he settled back in his chair. "Just accept that happens to everyone. Even the Manny Tannos of the world."

"All right, we've analyzed my deep emotional problems with the Red Cloud case, now let's get down to what you brought me in here for."

Lumpy frowned. "Willie needs help, and I'm fishing for advice. What would the FBI do if an agent exhibited the problems Willie has?"

Manny stood and reached for the coffeepot, pouring each one a cup before sitting. The coffee was stale and bitter, but not as stale and bitter as this conversation with Manny's childhood nemesis had grown. "EAP."

Lumpy chuckled. "Employee Assistance Program? What do you think we have here, bottomless coffers? We don't have the funds the federal government has."

"Find the funds. Somewhere. Because if you don't, you'll lose a good officer to depression."

Lumpy took a sip of his coffee, wrinkled his nose, and

tossed the rest into the wastebasket beside the table. "Think that's what it is?"

Manny nodded. "Oh, he's depressed all right. How would you feel if the woman who raised you goes to bed every night wondering if some other loony's going to slit her throat. And you may be right—he may have gone to the bottle to forget."

Lumpy dropped his eyes. "Understood. Go on."

"Elizabeth was his family, and now that family resides in Ordway section in Yankton with other members of the criminally insane of this state. And he's not handling it well."

"Tell me about it. Janet says even his girlfriend makes life miserable for him."

"Could be it's because your niece is pushing *her* envelope? Purposely getting between Willie and Doreen Big Eagle."

Lumpy's fists clenched, then he relaxed. "I'll talk to Janet about that."

"And talk to your finance officer. The tribe has to find the money to help one of their officers soon, or he won't be an officer. He'll just be another drunk staggering on the road to White Clay every morning to drink his breakfast."

CHAPTER 24

Ham dropped the legs of his chair onto the porch and set his book on the pine log table in front of him just as Sonja Myers emerged from Sophie's house with a glass of tea. "Would you like a glass?" She rimmed the glass with her tongue and smiled demurely at Manny. He was transported back two months ago to a Rapid City bistro. He had sat close to Sonja, taking in her beauty, enjoying her womanly smells. He had disregarded the conniving reporter scamming for a feature piece in the front page of the *Journal* while telling himself she was attracted to him. His trust in her had accounted for another chunk of his ass being ripped away by his supervisor, Ben Niles, and had contributed to his transfer from the FBI Academy in Quantico to Rapid City.

"Tea does such wonders for the complexion." She held up a pitcher.

"Just had coffee. Thanks." Manny wanted to tell her his sore ribs prevented him from drinking anything right now, but he wouldn't give her the satisfaction. He turned to Ham. "I would have called, but your mother doesn't have a phone."

Ham smiled and sipped. "Sometimes not having a phone is an advantage. Like now, when friends just drop in."

Phony bastard's rehearsing for the confirmation hearings. "I understand you've been here since yesterday."

"I have."

"Anyone vouch for that?"

"Do I need vouching?"

"Micah Crowder was found murdered in the Badlands yesterday."

"Micah Crowder." Ham looked at his feet. He slapped his forehead. "Sure, that whacko cop that's been writing those libelous letters about me."

Manny nodded and retrieved his notebook from his jacket pocket, watching Ham as he flipped blank pages. "A KILI maintenance man saw your motorcycle chasing—or following—Crowder into the Stronghold yesterday afternoon."

Ham walked to the edge of the porch. Stalling. "I've been here at Mother's since yesterday morning."

"All that does is get you closer to the murder scene than if you were in Spearfish."

Ham turned, his jaw muscles tight. He flexed his hands, the muscles on his forearms dancing under his thin, silk shirt. "That's not the first time you've accused me of murder." He stepped closer to Manny. "I'm a prolaw guy, but this is getting old." Even angry, Ham's ice blue eyes projected warmth. Disarming. For a moment Manny forgot Ham was on his suspect list. And potentially dangerous.

"I can vouch for him." Sonja moved behind Ham and wrapped her arm around his waist, bending and whispering into his ear. They both laughed and she winked at Manny. "We were both here yesterday. And all night."

Ham drew Sonja closer and nestled his chin in the crook of her neck. "You don't approve?"

"I'd think the last thing you'd want now is a rumor of impropriety."

"How so?"

"She's a reporter. One that will stop at nothing to get that big story that'll be her ticket out of Smallville. How would it look if the reporter covering the murders had relations with one of the suspects?"

Ham tilted his back and laughed. Disarming. "And I thought you disapproved because of our age difference. You know a man is only as old as the woman he feels."

"*That's* none of my business."

"Then relax, Agent Tanno. I got no reason to read conflict of interest in Sonja. She knows I won't give her an exclusive until after the Senate hearings."

"That's right." Sonja held the tea glass sweating moisture against the side of her head. "I got no interest in a story right now. My interest is in Hamilton."

"And I can vouch they were here all night." Sophie slammed the screen door. "And noisy." It bounced against the side of the house and stayed open as if it didn't want any more abuse. "Hamilton and his lady came here yesterday. He was gone just long enough to be by himself. Praying in the Oonagazhee."

"Why would you go to the Stronghold?"

"If you'd have stuck around the reservation you'd know the importance," Sophie said, stepping between Ham and Manny. "Rather than going off to the White man's city."

"Mother . . ."

"It's the truth. He abandoned his own people to pursue the almighty—"

"Mother!"

Ham took her by the shoulders and looked into her eyes. "It's all right. Just let Agent Tanno do his job."

She peeked around Ham and glared at Manny before turning on her heels and stomping over to her chair. She set the bowl of quills in her lap and began softening them for her hoop project.

Ham turned back to Manny and lowered his voice. "The Old Ones are still set in their ways."

"So I see."

"But to answer your question, I went to the Sheltering Place to prepare myself, make myself right with *Wakan Tanka*. I have the hearings in a few days and I'm just a little overwhelmed by the nomination."

"Did you ride your bike there?"

"He took my car," Sonja answered, pointing to her silver BMW, shiny and bright and appearing as if it hadn't stepped a tire into the Badlands. "I picked the judge up at his Spearfish cabin."

"Out of the goodness of your big heart?"

Sonja scowled. "You know better than that. I wanted to talk with the judge, and he needed a ride here."

Manny looked over Ham's shoulder at Sonja. Except for having a recorder handy where she could tape their conversation, she looked the part of a predator reporter salivating to land the next big scoop. Manny motioned Ham off the porch and away from Sonja. "I saw your Suburban got damaged."

"Joe. Got tuned up in Spearfish again and had a fender bender."

"Where?"

"Don't know."

"Did he report it?"

Ham shrugged. "Doubt it, knowing him."

"You in the habit of covering for him?"

Ham's eyebrows came together in a stiff glare that Manny had not seen before. After a moment he relaxed and the smile reappeared. "Look, all I know is Joe was doing a brake job on my Suburban. When he brought it back, he was a little tipsy and the 'Burb was damaged. Tire shredded where the fender had caved in. He wanted to take my bike so I let him."

"Even though he was drunk?"

"Joe is a better rider drunk than most people are sober. He needed to tune it up anyway. We planned a run to Devils Tower, swinging by Bear Butte to pray before I went to Washington for the hearings."

"Where is Joe now?"

Ham shrugged. "Let's see." He flipped his cell phone out and pocketed it again. "Damned rez. No service. But he's probably at his shop. Like I said, he needed to do a tune-up and adjust the valves on the Indian before we took our road trip."

"And you never saw Micah Crowder in the last couple days?"

Ham's response was slow, measured, as if he were convincing a jury. "I haven't set eyes on Micah Crowder since he was a Spearfish cop in my college days. I've heard from him—in the form of those cockamamie letters he writes about me—but I haven't seen him since I graduated college."

"Why do you think Joe Dozi would be in the Badlands, riding your collector bike on those terrible trails?"

Ham shrugged. "Testing it."

"Don't you think he'd test it closer to his shop?"

"How should I know?"

Sophie got up from her chair when Ham raised his voice. He gestured to her that he was all right and she sat back down. Sophie looked after her son, even now that that he was grown, like she'd always done. A traditional Oglala mother.

Ham sipped the rest of his tea and tossed the ice cubes into the dirt in front of the porch. "Joe must have had a reason to take it in the backcountry."

"You don't sound too concerned. If it were me, I'd be mad

as the dickens that someone rode my collector bike into the Badlands."

"If Joe bangs it up, he'll fix it. Believe me, the Indian's in good hands."

"And so are you." Sonja walked up behind Ham and draped her arm over his shoulder and kissed his neck. She smiled at Manny. "The judge needs to prep for his hearing."

Ham nodded. "She right. Sonja's giving me a different perspective, a different line of questioning to prepare for. Now if you'll excuse us." Ham turned back to Sophie's porch. "Let me know when you find Joe, Agent Tanno."

Manny nodded. "Even if we find him in that sacred place?"

CHAPTER 25

SPRING 1940

Moses led the way down the precarious path that wound between the two buttes. Popcorn gravel gave way underneath the huge man, and he grabbed onto a scrub juniper jutting from the hillside.

"You didn't say it was going to be this hard getting there." Ellis Lawler fell, picked himself up, then slid down the last twenty feet on his butt. He screamed just before he hit a boulder on the bottom that stopped him from falling over the edge and into the chasm a hundred feet down. "What the hell you guys laughing at?"

Moses shook his head as he looked down at Ellis slapping dirt from his trousers, and he turned to Clayton. "I cannot understand why you brought that pissy little man along."

Clayton finally stopped laughing. "Let's say he's entertainment."

"Be real entertainment if he would have sailed off over the side."

"That any way for a holy man to talk? Besides, Ellis knows minerals better than anyone I know. And, he'll keep his mouth shut."

"Will it need shutting?"

"Depends on what those bad rocks of yours tell us."

"I just wished you would have brought somebody quieter."

"He is what he is." Clayton laughed again as Ellis scrambled up the hillside. "He'll be all right once we bed for the night. Trust me."

"Seems like I trusted you once before." Moses handed Clayton a water bladder and he took shallow sips. He took off his hat and dribbled water inside the brim.

"You're not going to get on me about Renaud LaJeneuse again."

"I would if it would do any good. You promised me that man was honorable."

Clayton uncoiled his rope from his shoulder and fashioned a loop for Ellis. "How was I to know Renaud intended keeping those paintings you took to New York."

"I should have hired an attorney."

"You signed the papers, hoss."

Moses's voice became low, hostile, as he vented his anger on Clayton. "So you said. I thought I was signing a paper allowing him to show the paintings for an extra month in exchange for more food delivered to Pine Ridge."

"Don't forget the mineral supplements for your cattle."

"That just prolonged their deaths by a couple months."

"And the donation in your name he made to the tribe."

"That donation he made will just about cover the price of vegetable seeds for one season. I should still hire a lawyer."

Clayton tossed Ellis the rope. "Slip it around your waist."

"Make it your neck," Moses yelled down, but Ellis was too busy wiggling into the loop.

"Renaud is a lawyer and he set the agreement in stone. Couldn't be broke. Guess it isn't his fault you can't read English. Now if it had been in Lakota . . ."

Clayton braced his feet against the side of the hill while Ellis took up slack on the rope and pulled himself up hand over hand. Ellis glared at Moses as he made the top and dropped into the dirt.

"What you grinning at? I could have been killed."

"Have you not heard—only the good die young. You are in for a very long life."

Ellis undid the loop and walked to where the water bladder was propped against a rock.

"It is not the same out here without Samuel." Moses looked after Ellis pouring water over his sweaty face.

"Couldn't be helped," Clayton said. "He's lucky they plea-bargained the aggravated assault down to a high grade misdemeanor. Best I could do."

"Still, a year in the Pennington County lockup for stabbing a ranch hand that picked the fight with him is pretty stiff. Guess you *wasicu* will always treat Indians differently than you do Whites."

Clayton coiled his rope and slipped it over his shoulder. "What more could I have done for Samuel—I sent my aide to talk with the prosecutor."

"You could have been a father to him."

Clayton shook his head. "Little late for that, isn't it? What do you want me to do, bust him out of jail and drag him back to D.C. with me?"

"If that is what it takes to be the father you should have been all along." Moses grabbed the water bladder and walked along the path with Clayton close behind. Ellis brought up the rear, yelling and cursing as he slipped and nearly fell again.

Clayton scrambled to catch up. "I'm not like you. I don't have the time to spend with Samuel like you do with Eldon. You show him the old ways, and that's a good thing. Never let him forget his heritage. But Samuel's a half-breed . . ."

Moses turned and grabbed Clayton's shirtfront. He lifted him off the ground and debated if he should toss his friend over the cliff. Clayton, wide eyes darting to the hundred-foot drop, tried speaking, but couldn't. Moses took deep, calming breaths and gently lowered Clayton to the ground. "In the old days, Samuel would have been called *atkuku*. Bastard. But your son is much more than *atkuku*. He deserves more respect than to be called a half-breed."

Clayton stepped away and straightened his shirt. Somewhere behind him Ellis yelled about cactus sticking to his butt. "You're right, hoss. But my point was that I wouldn't have known what to teach him. We're from different worlds."

"You could have taught him the White man's ways. Leave the old ways to me. At least he would have had a chance."

"More of a chance than we'll have in finding these legendary rocks you've been telling me about. How much farther?"

"Don't be too anxious to get there. They are evil *wakan*."

Ellis stumbled on the shifting dirt of the Badlands and yelled when he hit his shin against a rock. Moses jerked his thumb behind him. "I am having second thoughts about showing you the place with that bonehead along. I got half a notion to leave him and let him make it on his own."

"That'd be like killing him."

"Don't tempt me." Moses sneered and started back along the trail.

"Look at the bright side." Clayton scrambled to keep up. "If these rocks pan out, it'll be good for the tribe."

"Sure. Trust you?"

>‹›‹›‹‹

Moses turned the venison backstraps crackling just above the embers and checked the wild onions and turnips roasting under the venison to catch the drippings. Embers sizzled and popped and landed in the dirt in front of Moses. "What is Ellis doing in there?" He nodded to his cabin. "Sounds like he is giving a speech, but there is no one in there with him. Like, if some *wasicu* rambles in the Badlands and there is no one to hear him, is he still crazy? And still a pain in the butt?"

Clayton shrugged. "Ellis talks to himself when he's in the throes of discovery, as he puts it. He's making some calculations based on what he measured today."

"All the same, if I would have left him where you shot that deer, I would not have had to listen to his drivel."

Clayton prodded the venison with his knife and licked the blade. "Look, he's been a professor at the School of Mines all his life. Geology is all he has. His wife won't even talk to him."

"From what the moccasin telegraph tells me, Ellis has other, younger women he talks to. His students, from what I hear."

"I don't know about that. I just know he's never at home long enough to be very intimate with his wife."

"That is a blessing. Thank *Wakan Tanka* he won't have any offspring. But if he says one more thing about my cooking, I will sacrifice him to the Gods of Night."

Clayton slid his knife in the belt sheath. "Never heard you mention those gods before."

"Just made it up. I did not want to offend any real gods."

The cabin door burst open and Ellis ran to the campfire. "I got it!" he yelled, and stumbled in the soft dirt. He plopped onto a log beside Clayton. "I got it."

"What you got?" Moses winked at Clayton. "VD? Some other White man's disease?"

"What?"

"By the way you're jerking around, you would think you had the itch."

Ellis ignored him and turned to Clayton, shoving a paper at him, but Clayton waved it away. "Just tell me what it says."

Ellis folded his legs under him and turned the paper so that it caught the light of the campfire. "By my calculations, it's here. I'm positive we can make a go of it if we get the mining permits."

Clayton twirled his handlebar mustache while his eyes roamed over Ellis's paper. "Guess that's where you come in."

Moses turned the turnips with a cottonwood stick. "How is that?"

"We need you to grease the wheels for us. Talk the tribe into issuing mining permits."

"The tribe has never issued any permits for the Stronghold before."

Clayton put his hand on Moses's arm. "They will if Moses Ten Bears says it's all right."

Moses sliced into the deer meat and rotated it just above the fire. *A few more minutes.* "This Moses Ten Bears is not convinced you will do right by the tribe."

"What the hell's that supposed to mean? I've done more in Washington for the Sioux than any other senator."

"That's right. Senator Clayton's done more for Indians . . ."

Moses's glare cut Ellis short. "Like bootlegging whiskey helped us so much?"

"What about bootleg whiskey?"

Moses sat cross-legged in front of the fire, warming his palms against the heat. "You forget so soon what your booze operation has done to so many of my people?"

Clayton slid his knife from the sheath and once more sampled the venison. "I'll tell you what it's done—it's helped finance my run for Senate, which in turn allowed me to help the Sioux where I couldn't before."

"Drive around Pine Ridge at any time and see the men passed out in the afternoon from drinking their breakfasts, then tell me how your Senate position has helped us. Given the choice of drinking or going another day without jobs, my people drink to forget. The Lakota have never had to rely on the *wasicu* for food like we have in the last hundred years."

"We give food rations once a month."

Moses shook his head. "Sure, you dole out rations and make us feel like beggars. Look at the people lining up in the food line—you will not find an able man among the bunch of women there. All the men are passed out. Or dead."

"That's just my point." Clayton scooted closer to Moses. "This is the chance we've been waiting for. If we get issued these mining permits, we'll employ all local men. We'll pay the tribe a royalty. Things will look up for the Lakota at last. Think what you can do for your people if you convince them to mine the Stronghold."

"I do not know." Moses stood as if to get away from Clayton. "I will have to pray on it."

"Okay. Praying's okay. But just remember the words of a famous Oglala sacred man: trust me."

CHAPTER 26

"Thought you didn't drive?"

Reuben held the door for Manny. "Never said I didn't. Just said I didn't like to."

"What do you do for a driver's license?"

Reuben put his finger to his lips. "Don't tell the OST cops. But as little driving as I do, the rez is a lot safer with me behind the wheel than you."

"Can't argue there. But at least you're familiar with this heap."

Reuben scowled as he started toward the Pine Ridge Hospital. "Crazy George He Crow lets me use the Buick now and again, and I let him ride the paint when he feels tradition pulling on his skirt."

Manny smiled, remembering Crazy George, the *berdache* wannabe, the cross-dresser, parading in front of his house in the latest seventies ladies fashion. "I'd just give a month's pay to see him ride that damned junkyard horse he keeps penned up by his house."

"That's not a riding horse." Reuben grinned. "That's a watch horse. Even he can't sit it. Besides, he's raising goats now, too."

Manny chuckled. "Great. Now he'll be complaining someone took his goats. Or fed them the wrong treat. Or any one of a number of nutty stuff to complain about. What prompted him to want to raise goats?"

Reuben adjusted the volume on the radio so that KILI's music bounced around the car. "He says he was at an auction north of Kyle last week and just fell in love with her. He just had to have Josey—that's what he named her."

"That would account for the smell." Manny wrinkled his nose and Reuben jerked his thumb toward the backseat.

"You got it. He brought her home seat belted in the back like a cheap date he didn't want his mom to see."

"Where else to put the one you love."

They pulled away from Willie's apartment. He had stayed at Willie's last night and felt more like a big brother worrying about his kid brother. Manny looked around but didn't see Willie's pickup.

"He'll be home."

"Not like Willie to take off and not tell me."

"It's not like you adopted him." Reuben moved the seat back, his bulk scrunched behind the wheel making him look like a monkey screwing a football. "Maybe he and Doreen Big Eagle went someplace for the night. Maybe he's getting his ashes hauled right now."

Manny shook his head and patted his shirt pocket. What he wouldn't give for a Camel at this moment of stress. "He knows we got to move on this investigation. And I *told* him I needed a ride for my checkup today so Clara will let me back home."

"You should have made the appointment sooner like you promised. I don't feel sorry for you getting kicked out."

"But stay with Willie? I need to get back in Clara's good graces so I can go home."

"Ah, that's love, *kola*."

Reuben slowed and allowed a mangy black cur to cross the road. The dog stopped for a moment as if daring Reuben to run him down. *Damned suicidal dog.* "You know both of the folks had diabetes. I read some letters they wrote when Dad was away on that road project in Interior. He was worried they might not be able to afford the insulin. If they hadn't gotten into that car wreck they would have suffered because they couldn't afford proper care."

"Indian Public Health wasn't worth a shit back then, either."

"No, it wasn't. Been better since the seventies though."

"Back when AIM protested?"

Reuben pulled into the parking lot of Pine Ridge Hospital. "You bust on AIM, but the public health wouldn't be as advanced as it is today if we hadn't raised hell about Red Rights."

Manny laughed. "Oh it's advanced all right. Pity the poor slob that gets sick after midyear when Health Services runs out of money. People on the reservation would be better off going to a medicine man."

Reuben extracted himself from the Buick with much difficulty and stretched against the car. "There's so few *pejuta wicasa* hereabouts anymore, they'd all be up to their asses in alligators treating folks."

"Well, besides having diabetes, I got my belly full of that damned alligator with hair camped out in Clara's garage." Manny rubbed his leg, still throbbing from the cat attack.

"Didn't you hear"—Reuben smiled—"we Lakota have a way with animals."

Reuben held the door, and they entered the waiting room. Even though it was eight o'clock, the ER was packed with patients. Reuben led them to the last two empty chairs on the far side of the waiting room.

"She was here the other day." Manny chin-pointed to Adelle Friend of All, who huddled with Morissa. She hugged her mother close as she coughed constantly into Adelle's arm. "Looks like she's gotten worse."

"Red Shirt Table?"

"What?"

"Red Shirt Table. She lives around Red Shirt Table?"

Manny nodded. "Cuny Table, but Adelle's sister babysits for her every day and she lives around Red Shirt Table. Know her?"

Reuben shook his head. "No, but lot of folks that live there get sick a little too often. Especially those that spend time around the Cheyenne River."

Adelle stroked Morissa's hair. Wispy strands came away in her hand. Adelle looked around before she stuffed the hair into her pocket as if she could glue them to Morissa's head later. "I know some people living in Red Shirt Table. None of them get sick any more than I do."

"Okay, *misun*. But remember what I said about that area when you go traipsing in that part of the country around where the bad rocks live."

"Right now I got more than that old legend to worry about. I got to survive this checkup so I can get back in the house again."

"Maybe you should worry about the checkup because we Lakota have a history of diabetes, our family included."

"How about you? When are you getting checked out?"

Reuben smiled and puffed his chest out even farther. "You're looking at the picture of health. At least that's what the VA docs in Fort Meade say. 'For a man pushing sixty, you have the physique of a thirty-year-old,' the doc said. Blood sugar is that of a twenty-year-old. Blood pressure like I could run a marathon. That's 'cause of my clean living."

"That's 'cause you lived the last twenty-five years of your life eating bland, restricted meals in that gated community."

Reuben shook his head. "That an obligation of you FBI agents—keep reminding people when they've spent time in prison?"

Manny fought for a quick comeback, but had none, and he stood, stretching his cramping leg. "Let me know when they call my name," he called over his shoulder and walked past the chairs, rubbing the bandage covering the cat scratches, and through the door outside. A light breeze from the west cooled his face and he took his hat off to let it dry the sweat in his thinning hair. He hobbled to the wino bench in front of a flower garden someone had forgotten to water. The petunias wilted against one another as if finding comfort in their drought that they shared with daffodils.

The door creaked and Manny half turned in his seat. Morissa peeked her head out and stared at Manny for a moment before letting the door shut behind her. She stood with her back leaned against the door before she braved a step closer. Manny produced a pack of Juicy Fruit from his pocket and held a piece to her. She smiled and inched close, sitting on the bench beside Manny, and popped the gum in her mouth.

She started coughing and Manny was certain she was choking on the gum when she stopped. She looked up at Manny, the whites in her eyes red, the controlled pain etched in her face. She slid closer to him. "Momma tells me you're one of the good guys."

Manny smiled. "I try to be."

Morissa forced a smile in return, looking up at the clouds lazily drifting by, and pointed to them. "I'll be up there soon, won't I?"

"What do you mean?"

"I'm going to die like my cousin Julie, aren't I?"

Manny wasn't sure how to answer her. Being one of the Good Guys, the last thing he wanted to do was hurt this little child. But she was just sharp enough to know if he was lying.

"You ever just lie on your back outside at night and look up at the Milky Way?"

Morissa nodded. "In the summer when it's so clear, I lay on a blanket outside. It's just wonderful. Momma said she can't afford a yard light, but that's okay. It brings out the stars better, don't you think?" She scooted closer to Manny, now touching him, and he forgot all about his itching and cramping in his leg. He draped his arm around her shoulders, and she leaned against him.

"Those stars you see up there—they're the Wanagi Oyate, the Spirit Nation." It surprised Manny how naturally Unc's lessons returned to him. "When one dies, your *sicun* guides you south along the *Wanagi Tacanku*."

"The Ghost Road?"

Manny nodded. Adelle was teaching her children the old ways as Unc had taught Manny. "So those stars twinkling and winking down at us"—Manny brushed at the corners of his eyes with the back of his hand—"are those that have gone before."

Morissa patted Manny's hand. "It'll be okay, Mr. Tanno. I'll be up there winking at you soon."

Before Manny could convince Morissa she had a long life ahead of her, Adelle burst through the door. "Morissa, it's our turn."

Morissa, coughing and doubling over, stood and started for the door when she turned back. She kissed Manny's hand and nodded upward as if they shared a secret before taking her mother's hand and disappearing through the door.

Before the door closed, Reuben moved out into the foyer and sat beside Manny. He bent around and looked at him as he reached into his back pocket and grabbed a bandanna. Manny started to object, but Reuben shoved it in his hand. "Dry your eyes, *misun*, or everyone will think all you agent types are bawling wimps. Little kid got to you, huh?"

Manny dried his eyes with the cleanest portion of Reuben's snot-rag. "What the hell can I tell a little girl like that? She knows she's dying, and yet she's braver than anyone I know. What do I tell her when she knows she'll die soon?"

Reuben leaned his elbows on his knees. "I think we owe it to tell them the truth. And to fight what's killing them."

"I'm trying my damndest. Doctors told Adelle that Morissa was malnourished. Hinted of child abuse. I'm trying to get to the bottom of what's been happening there in the Stronghold, but the doctors are too worried about HIPAA. Too worried about their damned licenses to give a hint of what they really think."

"I wish I had an answer for you." Reuben accepted the bandanna, blew his nose, offered it to Manny again. Manny shook his head and Reuben stuffed it back in his pocket. "Maybe talking about something else will get the little girl off your mind. Like just why did Clara give you the boot?"

"Because I didn't get a checkup soon enough." Manny's quickness with an answer surprised him.

"Bullshit. Clara wouldn't have kicked you out just for that. From what you tell me about your woman, she wouldn't toss you out for that."

Manny looked around and lowered his voice as if those in the waiting room could hear through solid glass. "I've been, well, less than stellar in the bedroom lately."

"No lead left in the pencil, huh?"

"Just say the lead's been worked to a frazzle and it's duller than hell."

"How about the little blue pill?"

Manny shook his head. "I took it once but it didn't do any good. Guess all those warnings about having a four-hour erection scared me or something."

Reuben laughed. "Hell, if I got an erection lasting four hours I'd have thought I'd died and went to Heaven." He stopped laughing and leaned closer. "What else is going on, *misun*? Clara's a good woman. I don't want to see you lose her."

"We've had arguments lately. Things besides my bedroom problems."

"What, like you talk down to her?"

"You and she been comparing notes?"

Reuben shifted on the wino bench trying to get comfortable. Like Willie, seats never seemed to fit Reuben. "You do that to everyone."

"Do what?"

"Just like now with that tone. You're damned condescending to most folks I talk with about you."

"So now you're going behind my back?"

Reuben shook his head and nudged Manny's arm. "I'm your big brother. Of course I don't go behind your back. The moccasin telegraph has it you treat most folks that way. Whenever I hear it, I chalk it up to you living in a White man's world—away from the rez—for so many years. I tell folks you'll come back to the blanket, that you'll find your Lakota voice, once you get used to the idea that you're back home permanently."

Manny turned and looked through the window at the people in the waiting room. Many were his age, younger even, looking as if they had one foot on the banana peel, waiting to slip on that peel and travel along the Spirit Road early. People just waiting to die.

"I just don't want you to blow it with Clara."

Manny scratched his leg. "As soon as this doctor sets the record straight that I don't have the disease, Clara and I will have our talk we should have had long before now."

"Manny Tanno." The receptionist scowled at Manny as she held the door leading back into the waiting room for him. Manny recognized her from before, and she knew he was federal law enforcement, her tone hostile. He stood and started for the door, turning back to Reuben amid the scowl of the receptionist. "Maybe we'll get together this week and sweat. Maybe I'll find some courage when I cleanse myself to talk with Clara."

"You asking me to sweat with you? That's a change. Maybe you're coming along after all."

Manny shrugged. "Nothing else I've done has worked. Maybe a hint of the old ways . . ."

"Better hope so, *kola*. You're not getting any younger. And you won't get much older if you ignore what the doc's gonna tell you about your diabetes."

CHAPTER 27

"Pine Ridge has become a damned dumping ground like it was when we were kids." Lumpy sat behind the wheel and toyed with his newest acquisition—a reproduction of the patent leather belt Elvis wore on his tours. Lumpy insisted it was an original until Pee Pee was gracious enough to point out the MADE IN HONG KONG sticker under the buckle. "First those three ancient homicides in that car. Then that old Spearfish cop. Now Judge High Elk's personal friend." Marshal had called in to the dispatcher, surprisingly calm. He'd found a man dead in the Stronghold, and Marshal had lifted the man's driver's license before he called: Joe Dozi. "Feces will hit the wind rotating device when the judge finds out."

"He already has."

Lumpy pulled to the side of the road and half turned in his seat. "Who the hell called him already? You?"

Manny shook his head. "Someone from your office. Seems like your dike's got a nasty little leak you need to plug."

Lumpy watched the rearview mirror for Willie and Janet

following in Willie's Durango. "I'll handle this problem personally. Somebody's gonna get reassigned to animal control— or worse— when I find out who shot their mouth off."

Willie came up fast and passed them, with Pee Pee following in the evidence van close on their tail. Lumpy pulled the Suburban behind them, following until they went off-road along an old game trail. Manny chanced a look out the side window and turned away. Lumpy laughed.

"You always were the squeamish one as I recall." Lumpy laughed again and jerked the wheel to the right, nearly dropping a wheel off the edge. He snapped the wheel and the 'Burb came back on trail. "Still can't take it, Hotshot."

"Let's just say I've come to grips with my mortality in my old age. I'd rather be living on a meager retirement check than go out in a blaze of glory. In other words, keep the damned outfit on the road or you'll have my breakfast all over your dashboard."

"You wouldn't."

"I would . . ." Manny retched and clutched his throat as if he were going to puke in the dashboard vents. Lumpy slowed and turned his full attention to traversing the narrow path, while Manny sat back in the seat and grabbed the oh-shit handle above the door.

It took the procession the better part of an hour to pick their way down the game trail. Just before hitting the floor of the Badlands they drove around a boulder and something caught Manny's eye. He squinted against the bright light. Handlebars jutted from the dirt a hundred yards distant. Beside the handlebars a hand seemed to cling to a patch of sagebrush growing beside the bike.

Pee Pee stopped the evidence van well away from the scene so as not to contaminate it, and leapt from the van. He exaggerated taking a deep breath and let it out slowly. "One more croaker in the summer heat and I'll think I died and went to heaven."

"Just get on with it." Lumpy covered his nose as he opened the Durango door for Janet. She stepped out into the wind and ran to her own piece of sagebrush. Sounds of Janet heaving brought a wider smile to Pee Pee's face.

Willie stood beside Manny and shook his head. "I guess *CSI: Miami* can't replicate that smell."

"Or the sounds of larvae feeding on fresh flesh." Pee Pee smiled one-toothed while he pulled on white coveralls.

"Enough!" Lumpy looked over his shoulder as he rubbed Janet's back. "You don't need to add to her problems."

"She's got to get used to it sometime," Willie said. "If she's going to replace me."

Janet stood and Lumpy handed her a bandanna to wipe her mouth. Pee Pee retrieved his own snotty bandanna from his back pocket and made a production of wiping the dust from his boots. "The King would never forgive me if I got these dusty."

"Get on with it." Lumpy led Janet upwind from the body.

"She's a lot more ornamental than she is useful." Willie looked after Janet and Lumpy as they walked upwind from the body. "Scary to think she's going to be my replacement."

Manny nodded. "She will be sooner than you want if you don't show up for work. Where the hell were you yesterday morning? Last I talked with you, you were going to give me a lift to the hospital and we were going to conduct some follow-up interviews afterward."

"Doctor."

"What he say? Your prostate growing again?"

"I don't want to talk about it."

"It's not like you're the first one that has that problem."

"And what did you doctor say about your diabetes?"

"I don't want to talk about it."

"It's not like you're the first person with that problem."

Manny changed the subject and snapped on a pair of gloves. "Might as well help Pee Pee while we're here." He handed Willie a pair. "You'll learn more digging than watching."

Willie somehow got his huge hands into gloves that were Manny's size and stood beside Manny. "Now what?"

"Whatever Precious wants us to do."

Pee Pee walked around the motorcycle, photographing it at every possible angle. The bike lay on its side, as if Joe Dozi had ridden it into the Badlands and gotten bogged down by the dirt and fine volcanic ash that had settled here a million years ago. Except he hadn't gotten bogged down by the dirt. Joe Dozi had gotten bogged down by a bullet to the forehead, and he lay faceup with that stare reserved for the dead, one arm clutching, black and bloated sagebrush, the other hidden inside his vest.

"Any guesses on when?" Willie squatted to get a closer look at Dozi.

"Tough unless the victim's fresh." Manny squatted beside Dozi. "A body cools at a predetermined rate unless affected by temperature. I'd give Dozi here a day. Two at the most. What you think, Pee Pee?"

Pee Pee popped a PEZ and tucked Elvis back into his pocket. "Two days, give or take, by the larvae."

Manny walked around to examine Dozi from the front. Insects had long before begun their scavenging, and Dozi's bald head moved as if he'd been reanimated. He squatted beside the body and motioned for Willie to join him while he pointed out the different stages of insects feeding on flesh. "Think we're right. Day and a half at the least."

"What would he have been doing here anyway?" Janet had regained her composure and gotten back into the conversation. "Not like that was a dirt bike he was riding."

Manny couldn't argue with that. For all the love and attention that Dozi had put into Ham's collectable Indian, he knew there had to be a compelling reason Dozi had ridden the bike out here. He recalled Benny Black Fox seeing a red Indian chasing Micah Crowder's blue Pontiac.

"Grab some vials and tweezers in back of the van." Pee Pee placed a fresh memory card in the camera.

Willie and Manny walked to the back of the van, and Willie peeked around the open door. "I got a theory."

"Let's hear it."

Willie cleared his throat, looking around at Janet and Lumpy out of earshot. "I got some suspicions, but I'd risk being replaced by that female land shark if I even whispered them to the chief."

Manny nodded. "I know, been thinking the same. Judge High Elk floats to the top of my suspect heap. He's been on the reservation for at least the past twenty-four hours and he knows this area well."

Willie grabbed a box containing vials to collect insects and closed the door. "Joe Dozi didn't strike me as an easy man to kill. It would make sense that his best friend could lure him out here. Get the drop on him without even trying. Dozi wouldn't have thought a thing about it."

Manny agreed. He recalled Dozi somehow knowing Manny had entered his shop despite the loud motorcycle revving up. He wouldn't have been an easy man to put the sneak on. "But why his best friend? Don't make any sense."

"Need a hand over here, Chief." Pee Pee put the camera back into the case and set it on the ground. "We got to roll our customer over."

"Willie." Lumpy nodded but stayed upwind with Janet, wide-eyed even as she forced herself to look at the body.

Willie and Manny helped Pee Pee ease the body away from the bike. Maggots dropped off when the corpse was rolled over, and Pee Pee took the vial case and tweezers from Willie. He began picking larvae from the body. He looked up at Janet staring down at him, and he held up a wiggling maggot with the tweezers. He opened his mouth in a gesture of a midmorning snack. Lumpy retched and turned away, while Janet retreated to another patch of sagebrush, the sound of dry heaves echoing off the sandstone spires surrounding the crime scene. She stood and walked back, wiping her mouth with the back of her shirtsleeve, a disgusted look on her face.

"Welcome to police work." Willie smiled.

She glared at him and turned away from the corpse.

"Any preliminary guesses?" Lumpy had moved closer, wiping his mouth with the back of his hand, but not so close that flies might land on him.

Pee Pee began capping vials with specimens and spoke as he labeled them. "One tiny hole to the forehead. Close range. Powder stripling."

"Caliber?"

Pee Pee popped an Elvis PEZ and offered Lumpy one. He shook his head. "Small caliber .25 auto. Maybe .22."

"Long rifle .22?" Janet puffed her chest out, either to distract Willie or to show she knew some slight thing about firearms. "Lot of people use .22 long rifle ammunition for hunting everything from rabbits to deer on the rez."

Pee Pee shrugged. "Can't tell just yet. As you can see, our customer is just a little bloated. Skin's swollen around the entry wound." Pee Pee grabbed Dozi's blackened head and turned it toward Janet. "We'll have to wait for my autopsy." Pee Pee gave his best ventriloquist impression as he moved Dozi's head up and down as if he were speaking.

"You're sick." She turned to Manny. "Can't you get your own evidence team to do this? Be a lot more palatable than toothless Precious there."

"I'm hurt," Pee Pee said. "This isn't *CSI* that you watch

every week. We don't solve crimes within forty-eight minutes. And the FBI's evidence techs are perpetually swamped. So you got me. Sorry, kiddo." Pee Pee brought the tweezers to his mouth again, and Janet turned and stomped toward the Durango. Precious smiled after her. "Teach her to forget I got one tooth left."

Manny squatted beside the body when he spotted a bulge under Dozi's vest. He pulled the leather vest away to reveal Dozi's hand clutching a snubbie revolver in a shoulder holster. He had grabbed the gun as he was shot and the cadaveric spasm had melded his hand to the gun.

"Make sure his gun gets to ballistics, along with that slug Doc Gruesome dug out of Micah Crowder. Nothing with Dozi's death makes sense, but I think we may have found Micah's killer. And let me know if you find any shell casings around here when you dig the bike out."

"What are you going to do?"

Manny stood, and his leg ached from the cat scratches, his breathing restricted by the bandages encircling his ribs. "We got our own digging we need to do."

CHAPTER 28

Manny parked the car beside the porch and walked up to the old woman sitting in a rocker. "Hamilton's not here." Sophie didn't look up from the cradleboard she worked on. Porcupine quills softened in her mouth, sticking out like so many needles. She bit down on one, flattening it as she pulled it hard between clenched teeth. Her too-white teeth that Ham had paid for. "He took Sonja Myers home."

"Where can I find him?"

"He was going to drive to Marshal Ten Bears's cabin after he dropped her off," she mumbled as she pulled another softened quill between her teeth.

"I wasn't aware Marshal and the judge were friends."

Sophie spit the quills into the bowl on her lap and met Manny's stare. "There's bad blood between the Ten Bears clan and the relatives of Clayton Charles. Hamilton wanted to patch things up before the confirmation hearings. Thought if he cleared things up with the sole surviving relative of Moses Ten Bears that he would go into the hearings with a pure soul."

"Does he need a pure soul?"

She studied her project. "Everyone could use a pure soul. It didn't help Hamilton that his best friend was found dead, even though Joe Dozi was a no account of the highest order."

"So he went to Marshal's to bury the hatchet?"

"Or the tomahawk." Sophie smiled. At least Manny thought she smiled, right before she pushed on her uppers before they dropped out.

Sophie rocked in her chair as she turned the cradleboard to the light, ignoring Manny. He'd get no more information from her today and started for his car. He turned back and rested one foot on the porch. "One more thing—when was the last time your son rode his motorcycle?"

Sophie put some quills in her mouth and turned the cradleboard over, matching colored quills to what was already on the board. Manny thought she hadn't heard him when she looked up and squinted at him. "Don't know, but you're not going to pin Joe Dozi's murder on Hamilton."

"How did you hear about Dozi's murder so soon?"

"Got a call a while ago. Said Dozi was found shot in the head sometime yesterday."

"Who called you? Sonja Myers?"

Sophie smiled, the sun glinting off white pearlies. "Now why would I want to ruin the best source of information I got on the rez?"

><><><><

Manny tried his cell one last time before he dropped over the hill toward the floor of the Badlands. He got no bars and pocketed his phone. No big issue. He'd be back in Rapid City before the sun went down in a couple of hours. More than enough time to take Clara out for her birthday. He set Clara's present, a star quilt he'd bought from Mazy White Antelope, on the seat beside him. The quilt, made perhaps fifty years ago, contrasted blue and white and yellow colors that showed the less-than-perfect star that proved it had been hand sewn, not machine-made as so many nowadays were.

Manny herded the government Malibu, a carbon copy of the white one that had crashed and burned, around large boulders, keeping on top of the deep ruts, finally clearing the first large pinnacle of million-year-old sandstone. Marshal Ten Bears's cabin sat huddled between hills older than even the Lakota could ever record. Manny stopped the car and grabbed his binoculars. Marshal's truck was parked beside Ham's Suburban, the crumpled front fender glinting fresh exposed metal, the bumper listing to one side like a drunken politician. Manny imagined two cowpokes who had ridden up to the hitching rail in front of the cabin, tied their mustangs off, and sat inside visiting over a whiskey.

Manny eyed the deep ruts cut by flash floods. He put the car in low gear and kept on top of the ruts, stopping beside Marshal's truck.

Manny left the car where it was as he made his way around sage and cactus higher than his waist. Alkaline dust quickly erased whatever shine he'd put on his wing tips this morning, and he beat dust from his pant leg. The wooden porch showed dust undisturbed, thick, the faint trail of a lizard having crossed it the dust's only disturbance. He bent and brushed his hand across the wood: no one had disturbed the dirt today. Perhaps not since yesterday.

Manny grabbed onto the horseshoe knocker and banged hard, even though he didn't expect an answer. A meadowlark screeched overhead and Manny jumped. The meadowlark speaks Lakota; was it warning Manny not to enter the cabin? But the bird swooped down, preoccupied with a bull snake slithering across the road. The snake had nearly made it to the safety of a clump of sagebrush when the dive-bombing bird sank its talons into the head of the snake. "Have a good feast little brother," Manny called after the meadowlark as it rose in the air, the writhing snake whipping the air as snake and predator flew out of Manny's sight.

He rapped again, and turned away from the door, resting his hands on the hitching rail scarred from countless horses tied there. A dust devil twirled choking dust, air-dancing across the rough hills, and disappeared in the direction the meadowlark had gone.

Manny turned back to the door and opened it. He stepped inside as the fierce wind cut through the gaps in the log structure, whistling past the wood that Moses had nailed onto the west side.

Manny took a moment to allow his eyes to adjust to the faint light filtering in through the single window. He flipped his cell phone open to call Clara. It showed no more bars than it had before and he pocketed it.

He plopped into a chair to wait. It had been two hours since he'd left Sophie's, and he'd hoped Marshal would be here so he could ask his questions and get home in time to take Clara to the Olive Garden for her birthday.

The wind rose, blowing dust through gaps in the logs. The wind. Always the wind here in the Badlands, wind that had eroded the landscape since before the Lakota claimed this as a sacred place. Manny closed his eyes to a rising headache, imagining the first man that had inhabited this cabin, imagining Moses Ten Bears. The sacred man lived a life of simplicity, one of sacrifice, praying to the four winds every morning before starting to paint for the day, paintings that could have brought him riches. If he'd had any desire for the White man's money. Moses's existence reminded Manny of that of religious monastics who lived a sacrificial life when they could have lived like kings.

A screech owl woke him. How long he'd been asleep, he didn't know, except the sunlight through the tiny window had turned to moonlight. The harbinger of death—the owl—warned him of some grave danger that awaited him. He stood, and the hairs on the back of his neck stood with him. Still, no Marshal or Ham.

He willed his breathing to slow, assuring himself that not all owls were messengers of death, when he heard a faint voice call out. He cracked the door and stuck his head outside. A voice trailed on the wind, rising and falling, coming from a saddle between two buttes.

He cocked an ear. *Crying.* Or was it merely the wind, fear from the screech owl earlier putting voices in his head, the moans of ancestors forever lost to this place. This Sheltering Place.

The voice again, a human voice, as intelligence rose and fell with the cries. The voice grew stronger, more intense. He stepped onto the porch and cocked his head, aiming his ear like a living homing antenna. "Who's there?"

No answer, save for the wailing that sounded human. He stepped off the porch in the direction of the sound. "Who's there? Tell me where you are so I can help you."

The voice stopped as abruptly as it had begun. A meadowlark flew overhead, talking to him, in time with the distant rumble of thunder miles to the west, to the storm that approached.

But no crying. Perhaps it had been his imagination, and he turned back to the cabin.

A shot erupted, muzzle flash like tiny lightning bolts. A bullet whizzed close enough to his head it sounded as if a yellow jacket had strafed him. Manny dropped to the ground. Another bullet hit the sagebrush he'd stood beside a heartbeat before. Another shot, kicking up dirt an inch from Manny's face. The shooter had his location bracketed.

Manny scrambled on all fours to a tall clump of purple sagebrush, unholstering his auto as he dropped behind the bush. He peered around the sage and squinted against the fading light, grateful for the flashes of lightning that gave him some illumination. Whoever had shot at him had lured Manny out of the cabin and within gunshot range with the expertise of a seasoned hunter that lures the coyote with a predator call, knowing Manny would respond to wails of help. But the prey shot back. Manny ripped two quick shots in the direction of where the muzzle flash had been, dropping down low to the ground.

Lightning flashed, closer this time, illuminating for a brief moment another vehicle parked behind his Malibu, a vehicle that had not been parked with Ham's 'Burb or Marshal's truck. The vehicle's driver door stood open: the shooter had not risked shutting it.

He strained to hear above the thunder. Quiet. He gathered his legs beneath him and duckwalked toward cactus closer to the cabin when two shots in quick succession came his way, and he dropped as much from surprise as from the throbbing pain from one slug that hit his shoulder. He rolled to one side, avoiding another bullet that kicked dirt where he had lain a foot away. Whoever the shooter was, he knew how to target prey.

Manny lay on his side, concentrating on where he thought the shots had originated, watching the area between him and the cabin as he slipped his bandanna from his pocket and stuffed it under his shirt to stop the bleeding in his shoulder. He chanced moving his arm in a tight circle, wounded but not broken.

Finished with his field dressing, Manny rolled back on his stomach, holding his pistol like a divining rod in front of him, a divining rod that would do him no good if he couldn't even spot his attacker. And if he couldn't get within pistol range of the shooter.

A bullet tore into the sagebrush and drove a piece of

branch into Manny's cheek. The shooter was working around one side of the cactus for a clean shot.

Manny gritted his teeth against the burning in his shoulder and waited until lightning flashed between black, roiling storm clouds. Just as the lightning died, Manny low crawled to a piece of sage ten feet away. He paused, timing the lightning again, and scrambled for a dead cottonwood ten feet past that. He hugged the ground and dropped behind the tree. He chanced a look around the trunk. Nothing stirred, yet he knew his attacker lay in wait for him to make a sound, cause movement that would betray his position. If I can hold out for another half hour, he thought. *If I can hold off until the sun sets fully, darkness will be my ally.*

He reached inside his shirt and grabbed his beaded turtle containing his medicine hanging from a leather thong. How many times had his *wopiye* helped him through some crises? Wakan Tanka *unsimalye. Wakan Tanka* pity me, he whispered, then laughed to himself. Reuben would be proud of his little brother intoning the Great Mysterious in such a time of need. *Give me strength, and a whole lot of old-fashioned Lakota luck right about now.*

Manny rolled onto his back and dabbed at the bandanna, which was soaking up blood. He peeled off his polo shirt and gathered his leg under him as he sat poised to time his move between lightning flashes. Thunder close enough to reverberate inside his aching head accompanied a mighty flash. When it died, he draped his shirt over the cactus and backed into an arroyo thirty feet away, dropping down below a dirt bank just as two quick shots accompanied more thunder, as if the Thunder Beings themselves were angered at the desecration of their sacred ground.

Manny didn't wait to see what damage his shirt sustained or how close the shooter had gotten. He ran hunched over along the arroyo bottom, deep and offering him the protection he needed. When he'd gone fifty yards, he dropped onto his stomach and crawled to the top of the bank. A figure, indistinct in the darkness and lit by lightning flashes, hunched over studying the tracks, looking toward where Manny had scurried after he'd tossed his shirt over the cactus. The figure seemed to be studying the terrain, deciding whether to follow an armed man into the brush, then turned toward the cabin and was lost to the night.

Manny strained, eyes adjusting to the darkness. The lightning played tricks on his eyes, illuminating a dark figure that shadowed his shooter. Was the attacker nearing where Manny hid? Was the shooter out there still, waiting for Manny to move, to reveal himself for another ambush? Manny rubbed his eyes. The shadow had disappeared.

Manny's questions were answered as a car door slammed moments later and an engine started. Headlights burst the darkness and ruined his night vision. Manny turned his head, knowing the receptors at the sides of the eyes were much more sensitive, better able to cut through the lack of light looking sideways. The car crept up the slope on that trail leading from the cabin to the rim of the Badlands, light and sound fading, staying in the Stronghold. Nothing leaves the Stronghold, including the noise of the shooter leaving.

Manny checked his watch when the lightning flashes were bright overhead. The storm approached rapidly as did all summer thunderstorms in the Badlands, swooping down as if to catch Manny in a flash flood and drown him.

He felt foolish, cowering in the arroyo rather than working his way around to get the advantage on his attacker. But Manny had been afraid. He'd frozen in fear, as much from the persistence of the shooter as from not knowing who it had been. Or where the next shot would come from. A man should at least know his executioner.

Manny breathed deep, his racing heart slowing. He breathed

again of the air heavy with moisture, heavy with a different kind of assault: thunderstorm approaching fast, as if the Thunder Beings themselves were animating the clouds and the wind and the lightning.

He gathered his legs beneath him and crawled out of the gully as occasional drops of rain, cold on his bare back, harbingers of something more violent coming his way, stung his cheeks. He hunched over and scrambled to his car, as much as to try to pick up tracks of his attacker as to make himself as small a target as possible. The shooter's car had driven away, but had there been more than one person? Was the shooter still lying close to the cabin, waiting for Manny to show himself?

Marshal's truck and Ham's Suburban were still parked by his Malibu. When Manny opened the car door to climb in, the dome light failed to come on. He grabbed the key hidden in the ashtray. The starter was as dead as the lights.

He fumbled in the glove box and his hand fell on his flashlight. He looked the way the shooter had driven off while he popped the hood and shone the light around. He was no mechanic, but battery cables had been cut. *In law enforcement, we call that a clue.*

He squatted and opened Ham's Suburban's door. The dome light weakly illuminated the inside, and he slammed the door. He felt under the floor mat, above the visor. The key dropped down and he jammed it into the ignition. The Suburban burped once, then died as the dome light went out.

He crept hunched over to Marshal's truck, expecting a shot. He reached for the door handle; sticky blood dripped onto his hand and made it slip off the handle. He wiped his hand on his Dockers and eased the door open. The hinges creaked loud enough he thought someone nearby could have heard it over the noise of the thunder. Manny checked the usual places, but no keys.

He slammed the hood of his Malibu as the rain started in earnest. He hopped inside to get out of the rain and lay down in the seat before he realized how dumb that move was. If the shooter returned, he'd have nowhere to go. He'd be a captive audience to his own execution.

He stuffed the flashlight into his trouser pocket and double-checked the snap on his holster before running for the cabin. His feet slipped on gumbo and he fell on the slippery wooden walkway in front of the shack. Pain shot up his shoulder as he fell against the door. He rolled onto the floor and kicked it shut. He scooted on the floor, backed against one wall as the rain came in great torrents, the Wakinya Oyate, the Thunder Nation, yelling in unison, shaking the cabin with their noise as they threw fierce lightning that flickered through the chinks in the logs.

Manny reached for an oil lamp on the table and fumbled for a match. He sat back down in the darkness, the adrenaline dump catching up with him, causing him to feel more exhausted than he ever remembered. He knew as he jumped with each thunder clash that his diabetes had stolen his strength, and he cursed himself for not getting it under control before. *If I ever get out of this, Clara, I'll go to the doctor. Promise.*

He grabbed his Glock and placed it on the floor beside him, expecting the storm to announce his attacker coming through the door to finish him off. *Well, bring it on. I'm not the best shot but I can shoot across the room accurately enough. Come through the door.* And sometime during the night, the Thunder Beings lulled him to sleep.

CHAPTER 29

The cabin door burst open and Manny awoke, aiming his Glock at the man filling the doorway.

"Whoa," Willie said, his hands raised to shoulder level. "You been here all night?"

Manny set the gun back on the floor beside him and rubbed the sleepers from his eyes. He looked past Willie to the open doorway. Light, bright and devoid of any thunderstorms. Manny squinted. He offered his good hand and Willie grabbed on, hoisting him up. "How'd you know where to find me?"

"Clara. Sort of." Willie frowned as he eyed the blood-crusted bandanna stuck on Manny's shoulder. "She called me last night when you didn't come home. She knew you'd be there for her birthday and she was worried sick. So Janet and I split up and started making the rounds of the most likely places."

"Where is your sidekick?" Manny asked between clenched teeth. Willie pulled the bandanna away from the bullet wound. Stuck to dried blood, the cloth ripped away with a sickening sound.

"She went with her Uncle Leon to look some other places. Better let me attend to that before we get you to the ER."

"I don't need . . ."

"Don't even argue with me about this." He dipped the ladle in the water bucket hanging beside the bunks and dribbled it over the bullet wound. Dried blood started to dissolve. He returned the ladle to the bucket and began looking around the cabin.

"Under the washbasin. A first-aid kit, if that's what you're looking for."

Willie bent and moved some rags aside and came away with a Johnson & Johnson, the plastic so old it had begun fading to yellow, like an old meerschaum pipe that's been smoked for too many years. He doubled over a gauze pad and slapped white tape over it to hold it to Manny's shoulder. "Now we get to the ER."

Manny brushed past Willie. "I got to see something first," he called over his shoulder and stumbled toward the first small hill that had hidden him from his attacker last night. A pale yellow shirt, embossed with the FBI logo, flapped like a distorted, miniature scarecrow held up by the cactus barbs. A scarecrow that had given Manny just enough time to distract the shooter and slip away. He snatched the shirt. Light shone through four tiny holes. "Couldn't tell last night for all the thunder."

"Couldn't tell what?"

"If I was being shot at with a large or small caliber weapon. Now I know. I'll fill you in on the way to the ER."

><><><><

"You'd think they'd give a man with a gunshot wound some priority. Even Doc Gruesome would be a welcome sight about now. Whatever happened to triage?"

Willie smiled. "You want quick, you go to the doctor in

Gordon or Hot Springs or Rapid. Pine Ridge has only so many ER docs."

A pregnant woman sat huddled across from them, a toddler clinging to her as she rocked him. He groaned and held his stomach, while an older couple sat next to her, eying Manny with suspicion. He appeared to be slouching, wearing one of Willie's T-shirts that was three sizes too big.

"Where's your girlfriend?"

"Doreen?"

"Janet."

Willie looked sideways at him. "Funny man. She's hot on the trail of the dude that broke into my outfit and stole my flashlight."

"That happened in Rapid . . . little out of her jurisdiction."

"She says it connects with the broken window from the week before, that the same man did both. And her suspect is right here on the rez."

"Does she know who did it?"

Willie nodded and pinched a lip full of Copenhagen. The old couple across from them glared but remained silent. "Henry Lone Wolf."

"Henry? That's not like him. What would he have against you?"

Willie shrugged. "He must be pissed at me because I've arrested him for public intox so many times."

"If that were the case, he'd break into every officer's car working the rez. Besides, most of the time Henry wants to get arrested. At least he gets a warm place to stay and three squares when he's in the hoosegow. Why does Janet think he's your man?"

"She found my flashlight next to Henry when he was passed out under the bleachers at the powwow grounds. And she says she can place Henry in Rapid City the day my Durango got keyed in front of the Alex Johnson."

"But how would Henry get to Rapid? He hasn't driven since I was a tribal cop."

"He caught a ride. Both ways. Janet dug up records that show Henry was at Mother Butler's the day the Durango got keyed at the Alex Johnson and the day my truck got broken into. She speculates he might have heard that Doreen and I were going to Rapid and decided to extract some revenge. Doesn't make a lot of sense, but it'll keep her busy and out of my hair."

"Agent Tanno," the receptionist called out.

Manny stood, eyes in the waiting room following him as he made his way to the door. Willie stood with him and held the gauze on his shoulder, though he needn't as the bleeding had stopped hours ago.

"Want me to go in there with you?"

"And do what, hold my hand?"

"I'd offer to hold something else, but you probably still don't have feeling down there."

"Smart ass."

Manny followed the ER nurse through the receiving doors and into an examination room. She tossed him an undersized gown and motioned to a stainless steel table. "Put this on." She made no attempt to leave the room.

"Can't you leave?"

"I'd just have to come back in."

"But it's not my butt that's been shot. It's my shoulder. I shouldn't need to put this on . . ."

"The gown."

She stood with hands perched on meaty hips, and Manny calculated the chances of bucking her. She had him by forty pounds and, by the looks of her, a whole lot of mean. Even on a good day he doubted if he could take her. He unzipped his trousers and draped them over a chair.

She nodded to the boxers. "Hearts. That's kind of sweet."

He stuck his arms in the gown while keeping his butt to the wall. "I was going to my lady's birthday party. Except I got a little sidetracked."

"So you were hoping to get lucky?"

"Isn't there some place you have to be?"

"Not right now." She grinned.

Manny finished putting on the gown and tried securing the back. Like all hospital gowns in the western world, it lacked sufficient material to cover him. You had to be an Eagle Scout to tie the strings, so he held the back closed. He speculated the nurse had given him a gown two sizes too small for entertainment purposes.

The blond Doctor Kildare entered the examination room, the same one that had treated him for the cat scratches. "Wish I got a commission on you. I could retire today."

Manny forced a smile. "If you see me naked once more I'm going to have start charging you."

The physician donned latex gloves and began peeling away the gauze stuck to Manny's shoulder. "I'm not even going to ask."

"Thanks."

Doctor Kildare lowered his glasses from the perch atop his blond locks and bent close to the wound. "Irrigate it," he told the nurse. "And give Agent Tanno a tetanus."

The doctor left the room, and the nurse went to work. She wheeled a cart close to the table and opened a bottle of sterile water. Manny gritted his teeth as she ran water over the bullet wound. When she was done she turned to a cabinet and came away with a nasty-looking needle. "Now you see why your butt's exposed. Bend over."

The thought crossed Manny's mind that he should resist, realized he couldn't, and he pointed his butt at the smiling woman with the needle poised in her hand. She'd just withdrawn the needle from his butt when the ER doctor reentered the room.

"He'll survive," the nurse called over her shoulder, still grinning.

"We'll see." The glasses dropped over the doctor's nose again. He opened a surgical kit. After working a lidocaine-filled needle around the wound to deaden it, he pinched a vein with a hemostat and grabbed a forceps. He spread torn skin and muscle apart and came away with a bullet fragmentation. He started to drop it into the bedpan when Manny stopped him.

"Won't do you any good," the physician said, handing Manny the piece of lead. "It's too broken up to tell you much of anything. I watch *CSI* religiously."

"I should have known." Manny held the bullet to the light. The doctor was right: The bullet had fragmented when it nicked his bone and no rifling remained to compare it with a suspect gun, if he had one. But there was something: the bullet was pure, soft lead. And a small caliber, judging by its base. He'd have Pee Pee look at it.

The doctor had just closed the wound with three staples and dressed Manny's shoulder with gauze when the nurse came into the room. "Officer With Horn brought you a clean shirt." She looked at the shirt and smirked. "One that fits."

Manny unfolded the double-breasted Western shirt that he was certain was too big for Willie. It was clean, pressed, and unspotted unlike those Willie had been wearing. Manny buttoned the shirt as the physician started out the door. He stopped and motioned for the nurse to leave the room before turning back to Manny.

"I checked Frederick's symptoms . . ."

"The old man in my room the other day that looked like he was knocking on death's door?"

The doctor nodded. "His symptoms were the same as that girl of Adelle Friend of All's. I had to double-check, but they suffer from the same thing."

"Radiation poisoning."

"How'd you know?"

"SWAG," Manny answered. "Scientific wild-ass guess. The bombing range used depleted uranium in the sixties. Some could have gotten into the aquifer."

"More likely from the Cheyenne River. There's been some rumor that radiation from uranium mining in the Edgemont area may have contaminated the water."

"Then I got my work cut out for me," Manny said, tucking the shirt that was three full sizes too big into his Dockers with the bloody handprint. "No one will believe it." As Manny left the examination room, he knew how difficult his task would be to prove radiation poisoning. And find the source.

CHAPTER 30

Manny and Willie duckwalked, using the prairie grass for cover as they approached the van. Janet sat behind the wheel with binoculars glued to her face. She jumped when they opened the door and slid in. "What you got?"

She scowled at Manny and smiled at Willie. "Nada. Sophie's been quilling on her porch for the last three hours. Hasn't even gotten up once to go to the bathroom. Sonja's a different story. She's more nervous than a lizard on a hot rock, getting up every ten minutes to go inside." Janet laughed.

"That funny?"

Janet frowned and turned her back on Manny. Her arm brushed Willie's leg as she leaned over the seat. "Every time she comes out of the house she's got a glass of ice tea or water or whatever she's drinking. I can just imagine her using Sophie's outhouse in back. I think I heard her scream once."

"Probably had a spider bite her behind. I envy the spider," Manny said, even though Sonja would be a black widow if she was any species of spider. Manny thought he detected the odor of her cologne drifting past his nose, amazed at how memories can bring good things to the present.

Willie took the binos from Janet and adjusted the focus ring. Janet had had them pressed to her face so long she looked like a raccoon, the binoculars making perfect circular indents around her eyes. "I thought for sure he'd show up here."

"I got the feeling that Judge High Elk's been a step ahead of us all along." Manny scanned Sophie's porch, shimmering heat sending rippling waves over the old woman, accentuated by the magnification of the field glasses. Sophie held a dozen quills soaking in her mouth, while Sonja looked bored and dabbed at the sweat along her neck with a handkerchief. Manny even envied the handkerchief. "I'm still not convinced the judge is my shooter. Or Joe Dozi's shooter."

Willie spit Copenhagen out the open window of the van. He didn't bother wiping the drips from the three-day stubble forming on his ragged face. "No one's got more to lose than Judge High Elk."

"I have to agree with Willie," Janet said. "I'd put money that the good judge would do most anything not to blow this chance at the Supreme Court. I know I would."

"That's assuming Judge High Elk knew that Dozi killed Micah Crowder." Willie opened a MoonPie and took a bite. Crumbs fell onto his shirtfront but he ignored it. "If it got out that Dozi killed Micah Crowder, there would be no worse publicity for the judge."

"Unless he asked Dozi to kill Micah," Janet pressed home her point.

Willie turned in the seat and faced Manny. "Or if he killed Micah himself."

It was out, that scenario Manny didn't want to consider, that Judge High Elk, appellate court jurist, had killed a man because he wanted the Supreme Court nomination so badly.

"Why would the judge want Micah Crowder dead?" Janet dabbed at the corners of her mouth as she finished her soda. "Just because Micah sent all those nasty letters to the newspapers?"

"No." Manny paused, gathering thoughts that had been brewing since seeing Micah dead soaking up Badlands dirt. "If the judge killed Gunnar in '69—and if Micah knew more than he ever told anyone—he'd have to die. If Micah felt so compelled to prevent Judge High Elk from gaining the Supreme Court appointment that he had plans to go public with what he knows, that would be motive enough."

"Or if Micah was blackmailing the judge."

"Or blackmailing Dozi." Manny considered the possibility that Dozi had somehow found Gunnar when he fled to the Badlands during their college days, killing him. Dozi had admitted he and Gunnar had had differences with regards to the war. Had Dozi done just that, and had Micah found out somehow?

"Either way—Dozi or the judge killing Micah," Willie said—"the judge would have to silence Dozi. The man just knew too much dirt about him."

Manny gave the binos back to Janet when Sonja left to go to the outhouse. "I just don't see Ham killing his friend."

Willie shook his head. "But who else would have been able to walk up on Dozi without raising any alarm bells? He'd have been a hard man to sneak up on and kill unless he dropped his guard."

Janet set the binos on the seat and rubbed her eyes. "What's the chance the judge fled the rez?"

Sophie continued pulling, flattening the quills between her teeth, oblivious to their surveillance on the hill three hundred yards from her house. "He'd stay in Pine Ridge," Manny said at last.

Willie agreed. "He's comfortable here. Knows the area since his childhood days."

"He might run to his Spearfish cabin. Somebody's got to take a drive there."

"How about asking the Lawrence County SO to send a deputy over there?"

"And risk Deputy Boner busting in on the judge and doing something rash? The judge is only a person of interest—I don't want Boner getting a boner hurting our witness."

Willie sighed. "Guess you're right. I'll check out his cabin. See if he's there. If not, there might be something in that cabin we missed."

"I'll go with you." Janet smiled, and in one motion she'd unbuttoned another button on her uniform shirt. She dabbed the sweat from her neck like Sonja was doing on Sophie's porch. "You can thank me for finding out who stole your flashlight and broke your windows. It'll give us time to be alone."

"That's what I'm afraid of," Willie said and led the way to his truck hidden by the hillside.

><><><><

Manny chased his crackers down with the rest of his root beer and stuffed the empty can in the litter bag before taking up the binoculars once again. The sun inched low over Sophie's house and still no sign of Ham, or of Sophie or Sonja since they'd gone inside an hour ago. And no word from Willie. He and Janet should have been at Ham's cabin by now, and Manny closed his cell phone.

He put the binos on the seat and set the van in neutral, coasting down the hill toward Sophie's house, listening. Nothing, as if the crickets and the larks and the chirping ground squirrels had been alerted to his presence and quieted. Manny could hear no sound coming from inside to indicate that Sophie was cleaning or cooking or stirring about.

Was Ham here, inside the house, waiting? Had Janet parked the van where it could be spotted from Sophie's house? Manny looked where the van had been parked on the hill, doubting he would have been spotted up there.

His arm brushed the pistol under his coat as he eased the van door shut, expecting the worst as he stepped onto the porch. A loose board creaked under his weight, loud and accusing, and Manny was certain it could have been heard all the way back to town. He held his breath. Silence.

He peeked around the door. Darkness inside. Perhaps Sophie and Sonja were napping, a vain attempt to escape the intense evening heat. Manny took a breath to slow his heart and eased the screen door open. He felt the rough stucco walls as he inched his way along the kitchen, trying to recall the layout of the room. He bumped against the tiny kitchen table. It shoved against the wall and made a faint thud, a moment before a rifle barrel was thrust into his face.

A person gets tunnel vision when confronted by danger, focusing on odd things. Like the spaghetti stain on Sophie's apron. Or the sprig of purple sage stuck to her shoe. Or the .22 rifle leveled with his head, which appeared much larger at this moment.

"People have been shot for breaking into a house." Sophie flicked on lights, and her finger grew progressively whiter as it increased pressure on the trigger. "Give me a good reason not to."

"It would hurt."

For the first time, Sophie broke into a toothy grin, and she laughed, her dentures clacking against one another, sounding like a pair of castanets as she held them in her mouth. She dropped the muzzle to the floor. "I got to hand it to you, you got guts. But this better be good."

"I need to talk to Hamilton." Manny wished he'd had an extra moment to check his pants. As he'd once told Willie, even hotshot federal agents don't get shot at every day. Or have guns stuck in their faces. "It's important."

"He's not here." Sonja appeared from the bedroom, her hair matted with sweat as she dabbed at her chest with a wet towel draped around her neck. She looked hot in more ways than Manny could imagine. "He got back late from Marshal Ten Bears's cabin."

Sophie glared at Sonja.

"His Suburban was there last night. I was shot at by Marshal's cabin."

"What's that got to do with Hamilton?" Sophie still cradled the .22 in the crook of her arm.

"His 'Burb was still there in the morning when I awoke."

"He had trouble with it." Sonja undid another button on her top as if to distract Manny. It worked. "His Suburban wouldn't start. He said some cells in the battery were dead. Not enough juice to start it. And Marshal wasn't at his cabin so he walked to the Cuny Café last night and called. I drove up there to pick him up."

"What time was that?"

Sonja averted her eyes from Sophie's hard glare. "He said he started walking to the café in the afternoon, but he didn't make it until dark."

"That's a long walk."

"He's in shape." Sonja winked. "Great shape."

"And where did you drop him off?"

"Here." Sophie propped her rifle in a corner of the room. "Hamilton stayed here last night. With her." She jerked her thumb over her shoulder, and it was Sonja's turn to glare at the old woman.

"And where's he now?"

Sonja shrugged. "Somewhere in my new BMW. He drove Sophie's car to Gordon this morning."

"Problems?"

"Hamilton said tie rods were bent." Sophie glared at Sonja as if she were angry that Sonja was cooperating with a federal lawman. Which she was. "I followed him to a repair shop there and picked him up."

"Still doesn't answer where he is now."

Sonja shrugged. "When he came back he dropped me off and left. Said he'd be back. But I didn't think he'd leave me stranded like this."

"He went back up to find Marshal." Sophie grinned.

"In my Beamer!" Sonja walked around and stood chest to nose with Sophie. "That's not some rez rod he can ride the ruts down to that cabin. I don't care how important he thinks he is."

"Why don't you wait out on the porch while I talk with Agent Tanno."

Sonja began to argue, but Sophie stepped closer and the *Journal* reporter turned on her heels and slammed the screen door behind her.

"Guess she's not used to being ordered around." Sophie motioned for the couch and Manny sat opposite her. "Last thing Hamilton needs is a damned reporter blowing things out of proportion right before the Senate hearings."

"Is there something that might blow up?"

Sophie eased herself into her overstuffed chair. Tufts of batting fell onto the floor from a ripped arm. "Hamilton said the bad blood between the Ten Bears clan and that of that good-for-nothing Clayton Charles needed to be buried for good."

"The way you talk, there's more than just a little bad feelings between the two."

Sophie nodded and took out a pipe, filling it with loose tobacco from a tan Bull Durham pouch. She tied the thick green string to seal the bag and dropped it into her apron pocket before lighting up. Stalling. "Clayton Charles—that fine U. S. senator and friend of the Lakota—did nothing for us Oglala. And even less for his son—my husband, Samuel. Didn't bother Clayton none to abandon him."

"I don't see the connection."

Sophie blew a smoke ring and leaned closer. "Clayton used Moses Ten Bears to get a foothold on Pine Ridge. He made a lot of money selling illegal booze to Indians here. He hung around just enough to get involved with Hannah High Elk—Hamilton's grandmother—and left Samuel to his own devices. He went to an early grave. Like Moses."

"You're not saying Senator Charles killed Moses Ten Bears?"

Sophie shook her head and tamped the embers from her pipe in a Crisco can. "All I'm saying is that Moses spent so much time praying to *Wakan Tanka* for forgiveness for allowing the *wasicu* into the reservation, he fell to his death somewhere in the Stronghold. It's that bad blood that Hamilton went to clear up with Marshal."

By now, Sophie would have heard the stories about Moses being found dead in that car with Ellis Lawler. Like so many others on Pine Ridge, she had lived with the story of Moses falling to his death while praying for so long that she was in denial. Something Manny had no intention of arguing over right now. "That brings us back to where I was shot. Within walking distance of Hamilton's 'Burb."

"You saying I'm lying to cover for my son?" Sophie's lip tightened, pursing her dentures out. She clutched the arms of the chair and leaned closer. "Hamilton and his lady was here all night. I should know, those noisy bedsprings kept me awake from the time she brought him back from Marshal's cabin to when he limped my car to the mechanic in Gordon."

"Just the same, I'd like to ask him myself."

Sophie used the arms of her chair to stand. "Good day, Agent Tanno."

Their conversation ended, Manny knew he'd get nothing else from the old woman today. He'd have to gather his information another way.

CHAPTER 31

Manny leaned over and whispered to Willie, "You never did tell me where the hell you were yesterday. I waited at your apartment for two hours. That's two hours Janet could have been spotted above Sophie's."

"Out."

"I know you were out, but out where?"

Willie glanced across the conference table at Janet smiling at him. He leaned close and covered his mouth with his hand. "I was late getting back from Rapid."

"What were you doing there?"

"Buying clothes."

Manny backed away and nodded to Willie's shirt. It was the first clean uniform shirt he'd worn in months, and his T-shirt still had the crinkling going on when Willie fidgeted in his seat. Willie had shaved this morning, and the pungent odor of Old Spice was strong.

Lumpy burst into the room and slammed the door. He dropped a teletype on the table and scowled at Manny. "I don't like the idea of putting a BOLO out on a federal judge."

"I told him it was a bad idea." Janet scooted her chair closer to her uncle Leon.

"We had no choice," Willie blurted out before Manny could defend his decision. "When I found Manny in Marshal's cabin . . ."

"That's right," Lumpy chuckled. "The brave FBI agent cowering, waiting for the bad guys to return."

"When I found Manny," Willie continued, "I checked the judge's Suburban. There were boxes of MREs. Tanka Bars. Things a person takes when they're going into the Badlands for some length of time. All they left behind were the wrappers. I'm guessing they stocked up before disappearing."

Janet shook her head. "Just how long do you think they can last in the Badlands with just those snacks?"

Lumpy dropped into Elvis and looked sideways at her. "They could last quite a while. Marshal's lived there all his life, hunted and guided throughout that Stronghold region."

"And by what Sophie says," Manny added, "the judge goes down there often to pray. And he went there often when he was in college. They're both familiar with the Stronghold. And both in good enough shape to last."

"Maybe they just left their trucks there to throw us off. Got another ride from someone, like Sonja Myers."

Willie grinned at Janet. "Got it all figured out, don't you. Guess you forgot all about Benny Black Fox seeing two men hoofin' it west of Marshal's cabin yesterday."

"Thank the stars for burnt-out antenna bulbs," Manny said.

"Or shot-out ones," Lumpy added. "We're back to not knowing where the judge is exactly."

"Not entirely. I asked one of the field agents to reinterview Sonja Myers at the *Journal* offices yesterday."

At the mention of Sonja's name, Lumpy winced. Lumpy had developed a relationship with the reporter two months ago. At least in Lumpy's mind he was getting close to Sonja. But not in her mind, and she'd broke Lumpy's heart. "And what pearls of information did your agent unearth?"

"Sonja's angry that the judge took off without telling her when he'd return. Especially with her baby."

"Baby?"

"Her new BMW. She's pissed." Manny recalled how red Sonja had become when she realized Ham took her new car for a cross-country ride and left her stranded at Sophie's shack. "She has plans for that man. Long lasting plans."

"Her anger doesn't interest me. Does she know where he is?" Lumpy grabbed the teletype. "So we can cancel this BOLO."

Manny shook his head. He stood and passed the coffeepot around the table. Janet waved him away as she dunked her tea bag in her Sioux Nation coffee cup. "All Sonja knows is she's pissed. The judge paid Joey Antelope fifty bucks to drive her BMW back from the Cuny Café today and drop it off."

"Did he wreck it or something?"

"Joey didn't," Manny laughed. "But giving Sophie a ride did it no good. The old lady called Sonja. Said she needed a lift to pick up the judge's Suburban at Marshal's cabin 'cause her car's still at the repair shop in Gordon. Like I said, Sonja will do most anything to get in tight with the judge."

Lumpy broke open a cream puff and had half of it eaten before filling dripped down his hand. *Guess Lumpy doesn't have Clara to contend with if he gains an ounce.* "Just tell me what's up with Judge High Elk's mother."

Manny waited until he was sure Lumpy would bust a gut from waiting for an explanation before continuing. "Sonja drove all the way from Rapid City to pick up Sophie at her house and drove to the Pronto Auto Parts for a new battery.

Sophie conned Sonja into driving her nice, shiny, previously unblemished BMW to Marshal's cabin with Sophie and the battery to stick the new battery in and pick up the Suburban. Her Beamer's at the dealer in Rapid getting the undercarriage looked at. Guess it wasn't designed for the Badlands. She screwed the struts up hitting all those ruts and rocks."

Lumpy smiled as if he'd just solved Rubik's Cube. "Then Sophie knows the judge will be gone for some time and won't need his outfit." He turned to Willie. "Get hold of Robert Hollow Thunder and tell him to find the judge's outfit and follow it. But for heaven's sake, don't get burned. Sophie's driving it and we don't want to lose her. My guess is she knows where the judge is going and plans to pick him up where we won't be expecting it."

"You're saying Sophie's helping the judge hide out?" Manny asked.

"What would you call it?" He turned to Willie. "Call Robert. He's driving the Medicine Root today and not doing much of anything except looking ugly."

Willie checked his watch. "I got an appointment."

"With who?" Lumpy demanded.

"Just an appointment. Maybe Janet can look up Robert and give him the assignment."

Lumpy shook his head. "All right, then get on it. We need to find that Suburban."

Willie left the room with Janet on his heels. Lumpy looked after her. "She can't get it through her head that she's bound for greater things than being with a tribal cop."

"You're a tribal cop."

Lumpy's face reddened. "That's different. I got rank."

"You're rank, all right."

"Point is, with her looks and education, Janet could land anyone she wanted. She should be hanging around the ER where those visiting doctors work. What she'll end up with is like the difference between Pee Pee's original Elvis vest and this imitation."

"Then you knew Pee Pee's was original?"

Lumpy watched the open door. "Don't breathe a word to Precious. How do you think the bid got up so high on that vest of his? But enough of Pee Pee. We got to solve these murders pronto."

"We're going as fast as our resources . . ."

"Look, I got the tribal chairman and the fifth member of the tribal commission climbing my sphincter." Lumpy refilled both coffee cups, leaving the dregs for Manny. "They're equating these deaths with what happened in the seventies. They don't want a bunch of bodies littering the countryside."

"I hardly think three cold cases and Micah's and Joe Dozi's deaths make it like the seventies were here." Manny and Lumpy had lived through the turbulent times when the American Indian Movement and the forces of Dick Wilson were at each other's throats. And bodies did litter the streets and back roads back then. "I'll need more help if you want quick."

"What more?"

Manny walked to the copy of the Moses Ten Bears painting hanging on the wall, tracing the ribs of the cows with his finger, ribs showing through too-white bodies. "I need Willie for a couple days. All your tribal cops can drive around the reservation for days and never spot them. We need to go after them on foot."

"Into the Stronghold?"

Manny nodded. He'd plotted out the way he thought Ham and Marshal would have gone, recalling the way Reuben suggested. But he had no desire to go it alone. "I need Willie."

Lumpy stood and smoothed Elvis. The chair forgave him. "I assign Willie to help you when I can."

"Like yesterday? I needed someone a bit more sophisticated than Janet to watch Sophie's house."

"He was tied up."

"What was so important that you couldn't spare him?"

"Tribal business."

"Well, I'll need him for this."

Lumpy shook his head. "You know how big and remote that part of the Badlands is. You'll be shooting arrows in the dark."

"Maybe just a few flaming arrows to light the way."

"How's that?"

"I figure they've gone to where the bad rocks live."

Lumpy threw up his hands and leaned back in his chair so far Elvis protested with creaks and threatened to break his back. "That old legend? You have no idea where that is."

"Sure I do." Manny turned and faced Lumpy. "I got Micah Crowder's maps from his apartment, and one I found in Marshal's cabin when I talked with him. I'll find it."

"Hate to toss water on those flaming arrows, but Willie tells me no one can decipher those maps. How do you figure you'll be able to?"

"I guess I'll just have to get religion."

CHAPTER 32

Manny paused at the long driveway leading to the single-wide trailer, the windows sporting enough duct tape to weigh down a grown buffalo. A thin tendril of smoke rose from somewhere behind Reuben's trailer, and Manny closed his eyes, envisioning his brother just emerging from the *initipi*. Or about ready to enter the sweat lodge.

Manny drove the rest of the way down the drive and parked by the front door. He didn't bother to knock, knowing Reuben never used that entrance, which was fortified with railroad ties on the other side. Leftover attitude from Reuben's AIM days.

The odor of burning cedar and sacred sage met him before Manny even cleared the corner of the trailer out back. He walked to the bank overlooking the tiny creek that ran in back of Reuben's property, and where Reuben had erected his permanent sweat lodge just down the bank along the creek.

"*Kola*!" Reuben shouted, stumbling out of the *initipi*, towel draped over his gray hair and around his glistening neck, his smile consuming his face. He started up the bank, and Manny held out his hand to help him up. Reuben hauled him up and they collapsed on the bank. Reuben embraced Manny and rocked him gently, like the gentle breeze whisking the sweat away. "You need to come around more often, *misun*. Sit and we'll jaw a little."

Manny knew it was pointless to ask Reuben anything until the formalities were met. Although they were brothers, Reuben was fifteen years his senior and more attuned to traditional ways. As a traditionalist, Reuben had found the Good Red Road in prison, incarcerated for a crime he didn't commit but which, oddly, hadn't left him bitter as he should be. Perhaps it was receiving his own vision *Wakan Tanka* had for him, the vision of a sacred man helping the people. "Sit, little brother."

Reuben took his rightful place in a dilapidated lawn chair missing half the slats so that his butt poked through the bottom. They chatted about upcoming tribal elections and which of the eight districts were up for grabs. They talked about how the trial of Richard Marshal and John Graham for the murder of Anna Mae Aquash in the seventies had been remanded back to state courts. Finally, Manny broached the subject of Reuben's wife, incarcerated in Yankton State Hospital.

Reuben's mouth downturned and he looked out across the prairie as if she'd materialize there. "The shrinks tell me she'll never see the light of day."

"But you got to admit she's better off there than in prison."

Reuben nodded. "Doesn't make it any easier."

Reuben reached into an ice-filled cooler and grabbed a Diet Coke and tossed it to Manny. "I got the feeling you didn't come out here for a brother-to-brother visit."

Manny flushed. Since being assigned to the Rapid City Field Office, he'd promised himself that he would spend more time with Reuben, develop that relationship he'd always wanted growing up in the shadow of his big brother, a relationship he thought would last until they both went south along the Spirit Road. He had failed himself in that promise. "I got to find a man."

"Or men?"

"How'd you know?"

Reuben smiled. His teeth were as straight and white as Sophie's. Except Reuben's weren't store bought. "Moccasin telegraph tells me that you're looking for that federal judge and Marshal Ten Bears."

Manny nodded and took out the maps he'd found in Micah Crowder's apartment, and the Park Service map. He unfolded them and placed rocks on each corner to defeat the wind. "As I recall, you know the Stronghold better than most."

Reuben frowned but said nothing as he grabbed reading glasses from beside a tree stump where it held down this week's edition of the *Lakota Country Times*. He caught Manny looking at the glasses perched on the end of his nose. "They were given to me."

"Suit yourself," Manny said as Reuben adjusted the tortoiseshell glasses in the shape of a butterfly. "But they look like something Crazy George He Crow would wear."

"I got to go a long ways to be a cross-dresser like Crazy George." Reuben bent to the map and ran his hand over the paper. "Where'd they start out?"

"Marshal's cabin."

"Here," Reuben tapped the map. "I go to that part of the Stronghold four times a year to pray and cleanse. A sacred man's got to do that often. Wouldn't hurt you none, either."

"It wouldn't, but that doesn't help me now. They lit out from the cabin, and I got the feeling they're holed up somewhere. I just have no idea which of all those trails they might have taken. Could be any one of a hundred."

Reuben remained silent, murmuring to himself as if seeking guidance. "Here. They took this trail." Reuben traced the trail winding along the floor of the Badlands with his finger.

"You sure?"

Reuben shrugged. "As sure as I can be with maps this old. You said they went into the Stronghold to find the place where the bad rocks live. Legend has it the bad rocks live in this area." Reuben tapped Micah Crowder's map. "Maybe they didn't go there to find the rocks. Maybe they just went in there to pray. Like good Lakota do."

Manny blushed. "Your point?"

"A man takes the hardest trail when he wants to lose someone. You figure they're trying to stay lost?"

Manny nodded.

"I don't. My intuition is their trek into the Stronghold has nothing to do with you hunting them. I figure they took the easy trail. A man doesn't go into that country and make it any harder for himself than he has to. Not if he wants to survive."

"But these maps are so old. Trails change almost daily. How will I know which trail is the right one?"

Reuben set the glasses on the map and sipped his soda. "Pray, *kola*. Pray to *Wakan Tanka*. When you have your doubts, draw upon your own intuitions. Remember the vision you had of Jason Red Cloud's *wanagi*? It was no accident that his spirit sought you out. You've always had the gift. You've just always denied it."

"How will that help me?"

"When you pray, the Spirit Helpers will show you the way."

"I deal in realities."

Reuben laughed. "See. You're still denying it. You want me to go with you?"

Manny thought about that. Having his brother along, former Marine and AIM enforcer, would have assured his safety.

But he couldn't take a felon along, *kola* or not. "Willie and I will have to go it alone. Thanks for the offer."

Reuben nodded. "Understood. But when you find this trail, you'll know it. It has been used for generations by Lakota hunters seeking elk and deer. And primitive men used it before that, driving buffalo herds over the side of these steep cliffs. But take care, *misun*. Marshal knows that country better than anyone, and I understand Alex High Elk is no slouch either. Watch your back trail if you think they pose a danger for you. And game is scarce there. And water. Pack well."

Manny smiled. "We'll pack like we're there for the duration."

"You do that. And you be careful when you get close to where the bad rocks live. I want you to come back to me."

Manny laughed. "Sure, I'll be careful of the legend."

Reuben took off his glasses and leaned closer, a stern look on his face, as if he were a schoolteacher educating a child. "Men have been stumbling into that place and never coming out again for so long it goes beyond just legend. Since before the time of our winter counts, oral history tells us of men dying by the rocks and never returning."

Manny forced a smile. "I deal in realities, remember? Not the stuff of campfire tales."

Reuben scooted his chair close enough that Manny smelled the jerky on his breath. "If you do nothing else I tell you, take care of where the bad rocks live. I want my brother back, even if he is a lawman."

"Oh I intend on coming back."

"It'll be even harder with that bum shoulder. You'll need to change that dressing every day."

Manny's hand shot up instinctively to the shoulder with the oversized bandage.

"I want you to have the strength, the wisdom to make it there. And back. I want you to be pure."

"Hard to be pure when I'm so pissed someone shot me."

"And you have no idea who?"

"Too dark. But I'm putting my money on one of those two men hiking somewhere in the Stronghold."

Reuben stood and stretched and jerked his thumb toward the bank. "Just to make sure you come back, we'll sweat, you and me, there in the *initipi*. And when you come out, your heart will be pure."

Reuben tossed Manny a towel and led the way down the creek bank to where rocks heated on a fire. He knew it would do no good to argue with Reuben about entering the sacred sweat lodge. Nor was he certain he wanted to argue. He would need purity to go where the bad rocks live.

CHAPTER 33

FALL 1941

Clayton put his hand on Moses's arm and pointed to cows at a watering hole nestled in a deep valley between two towering sandstone spires. "Those your cows? The ones Renaud bought the mineral blocks for?"

Moses nodded. "What's left of them. They just keep getting sicker. But don't go near them—they're wild and mean as hell." Moses shook his head as Clayton eyed the cows, amazed that Clayton never saw the obvious things in life. Growing up on a cattle ranch should have taught Clayton how dangerous wild range cows could be. Even cows weakened by sickness.

"When do we get to where the bad rocks live?"

"Don't be so anxious." Moses led the pack mule through a narrow passage that opened up into a vast valley of million-year-old rock and shifting shapes. "Men have never been heard from again after seeing the rocks."

Clayton laughed. "I'll take my chances with that old legend, as long as we can find a suitable route to build a road into them."

"How much room will the drivers need?"

Clayton reined his horse and turned in the saddle. He pointed to where they had just ridden. "That's about as narrow as the trucks can take. Any narrower and they won't be able to get the mining equipment through. The last thing I want is to bankroll an operation that depends on just mules to get the rock out."

They resumed riding down the winding, steep slope toward the floor of the Badlands. The sun dipped low over the two tall buttes on either side of the giant sandstone saddle. Moses pointed to a clearing large enough to picket their horses and mule, with their backs to a wall of rock two hundred feet high.

While Clayton disappeared over the next hill with Moses's rifle, Moses unsaddled their horses and mule, and began rubbing them down with clumps of gama grass he's pulled from beside a fallen cottonwood. The horses jumped when Clayton's shot echoed off canyon walls, but the mule remained with head bent nibbling grass at the outside edge of the clearing.

Moses had just finished rubbing Clayton's horse down when he tramped over the hill toward their camp, a rabbit slung over his shoulder. "That all you found to shoot?" Moses taunted him.

"Hell, all you gave me is this little .22. What the hell am I supposed to kill with it—elk?" Clayton answered.

"Been done before. But we'll make do."

Within minutes, Moses had both skinned the rabbit and tossed the innards into the brush, saying a silent prayer that brother coyote would find the morsels and not go hungry tonight.

><><><><

Clayton rubbed sand on their metal dishes to clean them while Moses put the pan aside for their breakfast in the morning. He grabbed his pipe and tobacco pouch from his knapsack and began filling it while he settled back against a boulder. With the sun down, the temperature had dropped thirty degrees in the last two hours, and Moses pulled his collar around his neck.

Clayton squinted into the darkness as he tossed more cottonwood logs into the fire. He started to sit back down, squinted again, and retrieved the whiskey flask from his back pocket.

"You expecting company?"

Clayton shook his head as he took a long pull of the whiskey, squinting into the darkness just beyond the periphery of the campfire.

"Then why such a big fire? You expect some bogeyman to come sneaking up on us tonight?" To punctuate his question, Moses tossed a pebble and hit Clayton on the foot. Clayton jumped and spilled liquid down his chin.

"Damn it," he sputtered, wiping his face with the back of his hand. "You got me spooked with talk of some damned rocks killing people. About how folks come into this part of the Stronghold and never come out."

Moses chuckled. "You're pretty brave for a war vet."

"Cut it out." Clayton capped the flask, his attention still somewhere past the cracking campfire flames.

"All right. But I never said the rocks kill people. I said men don't come back from here once they see them. Maybe they come to the place where the bad rocks live and just decide to stay. Maybe it's the paradise you *wasicu* always seek."

"Well, I got other places I want to live my life out, and it doesn't include a damned desert full of rocks that kill and crawly things that bite the hell out of me."

"Don't forget the mountain lion that might sneak into

camp and take a chunk out of your White butt. Besides, this desert will make you rich, if what Ellis says is true."

"It'll make us both rich."

Moses spat in the dirt. "Told you before, I don't want any of your money."

"All right then. It'll make the tribe rich."

"If things go as you plan."

"If? What makes you think they won't? You got the mining permits approved, didn't you?"

Moses nodded and tamped the faint embers of his pipe on the bottom of his boots. "But I'm not so sure it was the right thing to do."

Clayton tossed another log onto the fire. It crackled and spit, tiny embers shooting upward into the dark, cold night like miniature meteors. He dropped in the dirt beside Moses, staring into the darkness, flames reflecting off his cold blue eyes. "Now what's changed your mind?"

Moses looked sideways at him, and went back to studying the flames licking the logs. "I had a vision that you treated the tribe on this mining deal like you've treated the people you sell whiskey to."

"We've been through this for the eleventy-eighth time—I had to raise money somewhere to get elected. And haven't I done more for the Oglala than any other senator? And suddenly you don't trust me?"

Moses frowned. "That's my problem—I do trust you. Despite what my vision tells me will happen, I trust you to do right by the tribe."

"That's the spirit." Clayton slapped Moses on the back and took a last pull from the whiskey flask for the night. "Things will be all right for all of us. Trust me."

CHAPTER 34

Willie parked the Durango off the trail running along the hill overlooking Marshal's cabin. Manny unloaded their supplies one arm at a time, the shot shoulder throbbing with the effort. Each had thrown in an ALICE pack with enough MREs and freeze-dried entrees and water to last a week, even if they didn't kill any game for meat.

"Sure the outfit will be all right here? They might see it."

Manny adjusted the hip strap on his pack and tested the weight on his shoulders. "They're both gone over more hills, farther than I'd like to think about. Only way they'll see your Durango is if they come back here. Marshal might, but we can live with that. He's not a . . ."

"Suspect?" Willie finished. "Hard to think of a federal judge as a murder suspect, enit?"

Manny adjusted his holster so the pack's hip straps rode lower. "I still don't think he's our man. But it is suspicious he disappeared at the moment we needed to talk with him. And

Sophie driving his Suburban somewhere out here to pick him up, I'm thinking."

Willie let out the hip strap on his pack, as if he had gained some of the weight back he'd lost since he started falling into whatever mental abyss guilt falls into.

They dug their heels into the loose gravel and alkaline dirt leading to Marshal's cabin, top heavy with their packs. When they reached the shack, they took a breather and walked to the porch and bent down. He studied the tracks on the wooden planks of the porch floor. Nothing had disturbed the dust today.

He opened the door, not expecting to find anyone. He relived that night when he'd cowered against the wall, gun on the floor beside his leg, waiting for his attacker to burst through the door for an old-fashioned western shoot-out that never happened. He vowed not to back away from such danger again on this trip.

Two coffee cups sat on the table, dark rings crusted to the rims, and Manny grabbed the percolator atop the woodstove. He opened the lid and sniffed: old, perhaps a day, maybe more, coffee burnt, acrid. Ham and Marshal had a good head start on them.

Willie yelled and Manny ran from the cabin as a beat-to-hell Studebaker pickup pulled up, gas can and spare tire and odd tools jostling around and bouncing off the bed as the truck bounced between ruts on its way down the hill. Janet sat behind the wheel, a terrified look etched on her face as she skidded the pickup to a stop beside the OST Dodge. Dust pelted the clean, white finish of Willie's Durango.

Janet flung the door open and caught herself climbing out. She used the fender to stand as she batted dust from her hiking shorts, and grabbed a small, multicolored day pack that looked like she'd bought it at Macy's rather than Cabela's.

"What do you think you're doing?" Willie nodded to her ensemble. Khaki shorts that stopped just above her knees color coordinated with her too-tight pink and lavender tank top. Her Nikes looked more suited for a day trip at a tourist site than a week in the most unforgiving country in the west.

"I'm coming along."

"Bullshit!" Willie motioned for Manny to adjust the straps on his ALICE pack.

"Uncle Leon will not like that. You're ordered to take me."

Willie, a resigned look on his face, looked to Manny for help. Manny shrugged. "I don't work for your Uncle Leon, and I can't stop you from coming. But if you hang back and can't cut it, I'll leave you to the coyotes. Or to that mountain lion that I heard the other night. This is no mall outing."

Janet's face reddened and her lips pursed. She drew in a long breath before she spoke. "I won't get in the way."

"Suit yourself."

Manny unfolded the map and oriented his compass to the trail leading from Marshal's cabin. Without another word, he started along the path Reuben felt Marshal and Ham would have taken. As they crossed the streambed, Janet yelled. She'd fallen into tall sage, the thick roots gouging her legs, blood dripping onto the ashen dirt. Willie squatted beside her, hefting her erect while her dimples showed through a broad grin. *This is going to be one great little adventure.*

>◇◇◇◇<

They unrolled their bedrolls that night under a sandstone overhang. Lightning, faint in the west but growing more intense, illuminated fingers of stone jutting skyward. But it wasn't the lightning that brought rain, rain that would threaten to fill deep gullies in minutes and drown a man in moments. This was what Unc had called heat lightning. *"When you see heat lightning,"* Unc would say, *"the Thunder*

Beings aren't so angry. They just want us two-leggeds to re-member they exist and can harm us at any moment. They won't bring us a lot of rain, just enough that we don't forget them."

Unc's teachings were forever stored at the fringes of Manny's mind, waiting for the chance to surface when Manny needed Unc's help. Like now. Manny scooped out depressions in the dirt, like Unc had taught him to do, so that his head and shoulders were more comfortable when he slept.

Unc's Good Red Road had always been an example for Manny, yet he'd fought so hard to suppress Uncle Marion's traditional teachings. The man had died penniless, in a shanty he didn't even own on the outskirts of Pine Ridge, both legs amputated, body racked by diabetes. But Unc had been the richest man Manny had ever known, rich in the warrior spirit that lived in all Lakota, just waiting to be brought to the surface by prayer or ritual.

"Never thought about doing that." Willie watched as Manny finished scooping out dirt with the small folding shovel he'd strapped to his ALICE pack.

Manny handed Willie the shovel. "I'll let Janet in on this little trick when she gets back."

"Back from where?" For the first time, Manny realized she was gone. "She was just sitting around the fire a moment ago."

"She took her Glock and went to get supper. I told her she didn't have to but she insisted. Said she wanted to pull her weight. She took off south with my GPS unit, so I know she can make it back."

"Shit! The last thing we need is for her to go blasting away and alert Marshal and the judge we're on their back trail."

As if to punctuate his concern, a single shot bounced off canyon walls somewhere to the south, or the west, it was difficult to tell in the still night air, the sound bouncing off cliffs and spires, fading as if the Stronghold wouldn't allow the sound to go farther. Manny struggled to hear another shot, but all that was left was silence.

Willie grabbed his own Glock and strapped it on.

"Where are you going?"

"After her."

"She could be anywhere," Manny reasoned. "All you'd do is manage to get yourself lost at night."

"Well, we got to do something."

"We will." Manny tossed another branch into the fire. "As soon as our MREs heat, we'll have supper. Hope she knows how to use that GPS unit."

><><><><

The rain came gentle, dripping on Manny's exposed neck. He pulled his poncho hood over his head while he retreated to the sanctuary of the overhang just as Janet yelled from over the small hill fifty yards distant. Manny thought for a moment about leaving the dry sandstone enclosure. But just for a moment, and sat dry, his hands wrapped around the warm coffee cup.

Janet burst through sagebrush and stumbled, falling onto the wet sand. Willie ran to her and helped her up, but she threw his arm away and fell again. Willie shrugged and returned to join Manny under the overhang.

"What you two looking at?"

Manny warmed his hands by the fire just outside his reach. "The great hunter. Where's supper?"

"Missed the damned deer."

"Good." Willie took off his raincoat and slipped on a hooded sweatshirt against the cool, damp air. " 'Cause they're not in season. I would have had to sign out a warrant for poaching."

"You wouldn't."

"He'd have to. I'm a witness."

Janet stood openmouthed until Willie snapped her trance. "Get in out of the rain or you'll get soaked."

She snatched her sleeping bag and day pack and scurried under the overhang. She dropped on the ground between Manny and Willie and ran her hand through her wet hair. "I'm starving. What's for supper?"

"What did you bring?"

"Bring?" She looked at Manny like a cow looking at a new gate. "All I got is some Tanka Bars for energy. I figured you'd at least take us someplace where we could kill our supper."

Manny shook his head. "This is no slumber party with the girls." He reached around his pack and came up with a can of Spam and a fork. "Heat it over the fire."

"Spam? Ugh."

"Squirrel, Possum, and Mice. If it was good enough for our combat troops, it'll get you by. Heat it over the fire."

"And chew this when you're done." Willie reached into an open bag of MREs and tossed Janet a packet of gum. "It'll keep you moving."

"I hate gum. Besides, I got enough energy to keep me moving."

"That's not the moving I'm talking about." Willie grinned. "It'll keep your plumbing moving so you can at least make an effort to keep up tomorrow."

Janet jumped at a thunderclap that bounced off the inside of the overhang, and she looked at the rain pelting the fire outside the safety of their enclosure. "Maybe it'll rain too much and we'll have to go back in the morning."

Manny arranged his bedroll over the scoops in the sand. "Not likely. In an hour, it'll be all soaked in and you won't even know it had rained here at all. Tomorrow you get lesson two of police work—come a little more prepared."

><><><><

"What's he doing out there?" Janet, hungrier this morning, devoured the can of Spam she was too good to eat last night. Cold. She wiped the jelly packing off one cheek and motioned to Willie standing, face to the sky, thirty yards from the overhang, his trilling voice rising and falling with the motion of his arms. "Rather than wasting time, we could be looking for the judge and Marshal. The sooner we find them the sooner we can crawl back to civilization."

"For an Oglala, you don't know much about your culture."

"I'm Sincangu," she corrected. "And it still doesn't answer my question."

Manny nodded to Willie in the clearing between two boulders. Dust swirled around him as he turned to the south and tossed a pinch of tobacco into the air. The wind took it somewhere the spirits could use it. "He's praying to the four winds. Offering tobacco." *Always sanctify the west wind first*, he heard Unc's voice whisper from the Spirit Road. Still teaching Manny the ways. He repeated the advice for Janet.

"Well, the west wind can stop blowing anytime. I'm sick of it. Besides, I had other things in school to worry about than my culture."

"Like how to get in trouble?"

Janet grinned and dabbed at the corner of her mouth with her shirttail. "Not me. I was too smart to get caught."

"Like that shoplifting charge in Hot Springs? Or selling pot to that state DCI agent in Rapid City?"

Janet tossed the can aside, but picked it up when Manny glared at her and held his hand out. She gave it to him, and he set it beside their trash from the night before. "So I got caught a few times. Ever heard practice makes perfect?"

"So you perfected being a criminal?" Manny grabbed his folding shovel to dig a hole to bury their trash. "Hardly the makings of a good law officer."

"Let's just say I was on my own during those school years. Uncle Leon convinced me that former bad people make the best police officers. That they know best how the criminal mind works. They think like their adversary and catch them."

"Like catching Henry Lone Wolf after he busted Willie's truck and stole his flashlight?"

"Just like that."

"Even though Henry wasn't available to do the dirty deed?"

"What you talking about? I caught him with Willie's Sure-Fire."

Manny shoved dirt over the dirt and patted the sand with his shovel. "I called a lieutenant I know at the Rapid City PD. I had some issues with the way they treated Henry after an arrest." Manny left out the ass cleaning Henry had received. "And I told him Henry had broken into Willie's truck, and about the Durango getting keyed."

"Is there a point to this?"

"Henry had a previous engagement during both those times. Henry was sitting in the Pennington County hoosegow on a pissing-in-public charge. He couldn't have been the one."

"All I know is that I got Henry dead to rights with the flashlight."

"And credit for the collar?"

"You got it." Janet watched Willie tuck his medicine pouch inside his shirtfront as she grabbed a roll of toilet paper and slung her canteen over her shoulder. She started for some dead cottonwood in a dry creek bed. She disappeared over the dirt bank as Willie walked back to the campfire.

"She give up and go home on her own?"

"You don't want to know. Let's take a look where we are."

Manny spread Micah's wrinkled map out beside the Park Service map and weighted the edges with pebbles. "We're close to where Reuben—and everyone else until now—thought that

Moses fell to his death. No one knew for certain, it's such a vast area. But this is where Moses often went to pray. This is where it was rumored he went missing, a mile along this trail. Maybe less."

"Then we better keep sharp. Last thing I want is for the next generations to think this holy-man-in-training fell to his death instead of getting shot. If Marshal or the judge is our shooter . . . hear that?"

"Hear what? There's nothing except the wind."

"That's 'cause you're getting old. Listen."

The shifting wind brought a woman's wail with it. "Janet," Willie said, and turned his head into the wind. "There." He pointed to a spot over the hill where she had disappeared with her roll of TP. Willie started down the trail and Manny had to run to keep up. Willie paused for a moment, cocking his ear, altering his direction as Janet's cries grew louder.

Willie scrambled up a popcorn-gravel hillside and lost his balance and slid down, and Manny grabbed his arm and helped him up. They crested the hill above Janet. She sat on the ground, her arms wrapped around her bent knees, face buried in her arms crying and eying a body ten yards in front of her.

They half slid down the other side, and Willie dropped on his knees beside her. He wrapped his arms around her as he glanced at the man with his legs sticking from beneath a gnarled, dead cedar log. "What happened?"

"Dead," Janet cried into Willie's shoulder. "I came over the hill to do my morning thing. I didn't see him at first until I finished and got around that bunch of downed cedar. Terrible. Man must have died a slow death out here all alone."

"He's not dead." Manny squatted beside the man and rolled him onto his back.

Janet chanced a peek around Willie. "He's got to be dead. Look at all that blood."

Manny brushed the dirt and flies away from Marshal Ten Bears's face. His breathing came slow, shallow. Manny checked his pupils: even and reactionary. But for how long? "Give me a hand here."

Willie left Janet and crawled to Marshal. Willie's hand came away with dried, frothy blood, and he wiped it on his trouser leg. "Lung shot for sure."

Manny probed the dirt and let the sand sift through his fingers to age the blood. "Yesterday. Last night at the latest. Hard telling in this heat." He called to Janet over his shoulder. "And you didn't see him last night?"

"How would I see him? It was dark."

"This is the way you stormed off last night when you said you were going to find something to kill for supper."

"Well I wasn't looking for a man. I told you I shot at a deer."

"Even accidentally? Could you have shot him by accident, thinking he might be a deer?"

"Give her a break," Willie said. "It was dark and he was hidden by those cedar trees." He turned to her. "Give me your canteen."

Janet stood and cautiously walked to within arm's reach of the body as she handed Willie her canteen. She jerked her hand back and retreated a safe distance away, dropping wild-eyed and crying onto the ground. Willie poured water in the cap and trickled it over Marshal's lips. Marshal coughed, but his eyes remained closed, his body limp in that predeath manner Manny was certain was just over the horizon.

"We got to get a chopper in here."

"Good luck finding a signal." Willie flipped his cell phone open and closed it just as quick. "Not even a half bar. This man's dead."

"Not if I can help it. Can you make him comfortable until I can get help?"

"Where are you going to find help out here?"

"There." Manny pointed to a cliff a mile away and three hundred feet above the floor of the Badlands. "If I get to that spot, I might get a signal and call for a medevac."

"It makes more sense for me to go. I'm younger . . ."

"And clumsier." Manny forced a smile. "I've seen your big ass try to scramble over these hills. Besides, I'm not so old I can't still walk down a deer if I needed to. Besides, you've studied healing."

Willie's eyes widened. "Nothing like this. I can treat corns or hemorrhoids. But nothing like this."

"We got no choice. You and Janet stay here."

"Now I got to take care of Marshal *and* Janet."

"It's a curse." Manny lowered his voice. "You got another reason for keeping her here. Whoever shot Marshal might be close. You'll need another set of ears and eyes."

Willie looked back at Janet still hunched over twenty yards away. "You think it was Judge High Elk?"

Manny shrugged. "That'd be too pat now, wouldn't it, him coming here with Marshal?"

"But I don't see the judge here helping him out. If it were my hiking partner . . ."

"I know." Manny patted Willie's shoulder.

"And one other thing—Janet might have shot Marshal by accident last night." Or on purpose, Manny thought.

Manny called to Janet, "You stay with Willie. He'll need your help."

"Think he'll make it? Enough that he can tell us who shot him?"

Manny shrugged. "He just might if Willie can keep him alive and I can catch a cell signal. That being the case, you'll get a ride out of here like you wanted."

><><><><

Even at this distance, Manny saw the dust the helicopter kicked up as it lifted off. For a moment, the Chinook from Ellsworth seemed to ride a heavenly dust cloud, like some drab-colored Thunder Being carrying Marshal and Willie and Janet south along the Spirit Road.

Manny shielded his eyes, watching the helicopter disappear over the horizon. He imagined this is what the Old Ones saw when they fled to the sanctuary of the Stronghold, imagined them watching their pursuers becoming lost and succumbing to the heat, all the while telegraphing their movements by the fine dust that permeated the Badlands.

Manny had used the last of his water and tried whistling through cracked lips. *Clara will be furious with me, not even being able to kiss these lips until they heal.* He checked his watch. His own rescue chopper would be a tourist helicopter from Mt. Rushmore that was still an hour away.

He forced his mind away from his plight and thought over the investigation. Something gnawed at his mind and he needed to get a handle on it. He needed a sweat-your-ass-till-it-drops run, where he got into his zone to sort things out. His own sort of vision quest. His own special sweat.

The sun was directly overhead now, and Manny flipped up his collar to protect his neck, while his mind wandered to the bombed-out Buick that had been the grave of Moses and Ellis Lawler. He didn't believe for a moment that the pair had driven into the bombing range to pass the jar of whiskey. Ellis, maybe, but Manny has the odd feeling that Moses never drank, a feeling strong enough it sent shivers along his spine, as if the sacred man himself sat beside him on the hilltop. Something more important than booze had lured them there. Something as skillful as his shooter luring him into the night by Marshal's cabin to ambush him.

Somehow the pair was connected to Gunnar Janssen, who had hired Marshal Ten Bears to take him into the Stronghold

334 C. M. WENDELBOE

during spring break from college. Gunnar had booked Marshal under the guise of a hunting trip, but claimed to have forgotten his rifle. Had Moses and Ellis and Gunnar all been the victims of the bad rocks, with their own evil *wakan*?

Manny tucked his head between his legs, waiting for his ride off the cliff, and his thoughts drifted to Willie. Both had their own special problems with relationships: Willie fighting depression and guilt while fending off Janet's advances; Manny fighting to demonstrate he still loved Clara despite his diabetes, despite what it had done for his libido. Marshal's sudden near-death experience reinforced that a man has to be ready for whatever *Wakan Tanka* decides to throw his way. And to make amends to those he'll leave behind. Manny vowed not to leave Clara with second thoughts about their relationship when he himself departed along the Spirit Road.

>‹›‹›‹

Rotor blades cutting the air and getting louder woke Manny from his drifting stupor. He thought he saw a helicopter nearing, a helicopter bearing the orange and blue markings of the Badlands Tour Company. Just before it touched down yards from him, he imagined Lumpy emerging as the tour guide, running hunched over with water bladder in hand, frown on his florid face. Now this was one of those daymares Unc had warned him about.

>‹›‹›‹

"Willie called me an hour ago. Marshal is out of surgery at Rapid City Regional. He'll recover."

"When can I talk to him?"

Lumpy scowled. "How should I know? You want predictions, get a holy man. Like your brother. It's bad enough that I gotta sit here in the waiting room with your sorry ass."

"You don't sound very appreciative."

"Of what?"

"Us taking care of your niece."

"You two shouldn't have taken her in the first place."

"And Willie risk the ire of her uncle Leon?"

"All right, I'll say it. Thanks for keeping her in one piece. Though I still don't know how she managed to fit that much makeup and feminine things in her pack."

"That's all I wanted to hear. You can leave if you need to. I'll catch a ride from someone."

"And leave you to muck things even more? Not a chance." The Pine Ridge ER receptionist called a patient's name, and a woman stood cradling her crying baby as she disappeared through the examination room doors. "Benny Black Fox saw the judge's Suburban speeding away from the Stronghold this afternoon."

"Don't tell me he shot out another lightbulb on the KILI tower?"

Lumpy shrugged. "All we know is he was up on the Battle Creek tower when he spotted the judge's outfit driving away."

"Thought there weren't any roads that way."

"Neither did I, but Benny says there are trails there that're wide enough for a vehicle, if you know where to look."

Reuben had showed Manny a trail on his map that was once used. Perhaps Ham knew the same trail. "Then we need to find the judge fast."

Lumpy laughed. "You have been in the sun too long. The rez is five thousand square miles. If the judge don't want to be found, he won't be."

"He'll go to Sophie's house."

"Not hardly. We've learned something about police work, we lowly tribal cops. He's on the run and won't come back to his mother's. He won't want to implicate her. He might be our best suspect in Marshal's shooting—among the many others you've come up with—but he won't stick around."

The receptionist called Manny's name and he stood. Lumpy put his hand on his arm. "I got shit to do, but I'll have Pee Pee give you a lift to Rapid. It'll get him out and away from his house for the afternoon."

"Not you again." The ER physician flipped through the chart. "Says here you reinfected your leg wound from that cat. And you were pretty dehydrated when the helicopter picked you up."

"That was two hours ago—long enough that I could have knitted a sweater if I wanted. Good thing I just didn't keel over out there."

"Didn't you ever hear the Indian Health Service is just a little underfunded? Now put this gown on."

Manny winked at the ER nurse scowling at him over her half-glasses. "You just want to see my butt."

"Put it on," she ordered.

The nurse and attending physician left, and came back in a few moments. Manny could never figure out why they left the room if they were going to see you naked eventually anyway. The old nurse had it right after all.

The doctor motioned for Manny to sit on a butt-cold steel examination table that sent goose bumps up his leg and into the cat scratches. The doctor pulled up Manny's gown and peeled away the bandage. He handed Manny a prescription, one for the antibiotics, and one for balm to apply to his split lips. "I'll have the nurse clean up and dress the wound. Again. And that shoulder." He started out the door when Manny stopped him.

"How many cases of radiation poisoning have you seen here this last year?"

The doctor stopped, and Manny was unsure if he'd heard him. "What makes you think there are more than Frederick and Adelle Friend of All's kids?" he said over his shoulder.

"The cattle in that part of the reservation have always

been sickly. But more so. Their hide is pale, and blotchy from losing their hair. Like Morissa's that falls out in clumps. Like Frederick's did by just lying on his bed. And the cows abort their calves far more than healthy ones do. All the symptoms of radiation poisoning."

"You've had experience with radiation?"

"In the army. Required study in the European theater when I was in Germany. How many cases?" Manny pressed. "Surely you care enough about the number of cases, even if you're not from here. How long you got before your obligation's met?"

"Next week."

"Then where to? Beverly Hills? Upstate New York? Atlanta? Maybe the Mayo Clinic? Someplace far enough away from the reservation that you'll forget?"

The physician turned and walked back to the examination table. "What do you want me to do, violate my oath?"

"I want you to be a healer. I want you to care, and oath be dammed. There's problems here with radiation sickness, and I need your honest assessment."

The doctor rolled a chair beside the examination table and sat in front of Manny. "Look, Agent Tanno, this is none of my business . . ."

"How many?"

He sighed in resignation. "Far too many to be a coincidence. I suspect there's radiation poisoning coming from the Cheyenne River."

"Will you tell that to the EPA?"

The doctor hesitated and broke eye contact. "Only if it doesn't delay leaving Pine Ridge."

CHAPTER 35

Willie sat across the conference room table and shook his head. "The hospital will let us know when Marshal's able to talk." He sat in a clean shirt and pressed jeans for the first time in months. A piece of tissue clung to his cheek from a recent shaving cut.

"Then we'll have to do old-fashioned police work, Hot-shot." Lumpy fingered the Cuban with the pink and white Elvis cigar band. Pee Pee leaned over with his lighter, but Lumpy jerked it away. "This is the only one I got, you know that. I'm not going to let it go up in smoke."

"If you look hard enough you might find some more for sale. Sometime." Pee Pee lit his cigar and blew smoke rings toward the ceiling fan, swirling the smoke around as if to taunt Lumpy. "Now I see why the King loved these."

"Damn it, Pee Pee! How the hell did you outbid me? I assigned you to give Manny a lift home at the time the auction closed."

Pee Pee flashed a single-toothy smile, giving appropriate

meaning to the term *toothbrush*. "Wi-Fi. I made a winning bid on these cigars while we were on the road to Rapid. And a good price, too, or I wouldn't have been able to give you one out of the pure goodness of my old heart."

Lumpy swiveled his seat and faced Manny. "Let's get back to this cockamamie theory you have about Marshal and Joe Dozi and Micah all being connected to the bombing range skeletons."

Manny motioned to the Ten Bears print hanging on the wall. "I think that's Moses's vision of where the bad rocks live."

Lumpy laughed. "And did you find that place while you were doing your camping excursion?"

"Not even close," Janet volunteered. She scooted close to Lumpy.

Manny ignored her. "I think Moses knew that place was dangerous. And it had everything to do with the legend. I think he knew those rocks were radioactive."

"Uranium?"

Willie leaned across the table. "Not so far-fetched. There's been uranium mining around Edgemont for decades. And the northern Black Hills have uranium mining up the wazoo. Along with the medical problems that accompany it."

Manny walked to the picture and tapped the painting. "Look at these cattle—scraggly bleached hides. Sickly. Like we saw at that watering hole. I think we were close to finding that place. And the judge."

Lumpy joined Manny in front of the wall. "I'm not ruling him out, but you got to convince me better than that. We country Indians are real simple, so overwhelm me with your proof."

"Start with Moses Ten Bears, whom we now know was in that car with Ellis Lawler, geology professor at the School of Mines. Finding a uranium deposit in the Badlands could have meant millions, even back then."

Lumpy let Elvis's arm wrap around him as he dropped into the chair. "You figure they went there to verify their findings, and just happened to be killed in a practice bombing run? And twenty-five years later Gunnar Janssen just happened to get shot in that same car?"

"Or killed and stuffed in that old Buick."

"That'd be a coincidence. And I don't believe in coincidences."

"I don't either."

"Then what the hell are you saying?" Lumpy rolled the cigar between his thumb and forefinger, careful not to smash Elvis's picture.

"Judge High Elk ruled against mining in that part of the Badlands six times during his tenure as federal judge," Willie volunteered. He slid an open file folder across the table. Janet reached for the folder, and her hand brushed Willie's. He jerked it back. "Now either he ruled that way because it was in the best interest of the tribe, or else he knows there's uranium there. And plans to cash in on it himself."

Lumpy scanned the file and closed it. "That still doesn't prove he's anything but a person of interest."

"He might have been the last to see Gunnar alive before he disappeared in his college days." The tissue paper dropped onto the table and Willie trashed it. "And he was the last to see Marshal."

"And," Manny added, "it would take someone like the judge to drop Joe Dozi's guard. As we figured before, he wouldn't have been an easy man to kill."

Lumpy stood, looking down at Willie and shaking his head as a father does as he scolds his errant child. "You got a lot to learn. If you keep your job long enough. We don't know that Judge High Elk was even in that part of the Stronghold where you found Marshal, let alone know for certain they both set out together."

"How about Benny Black Fox spotting the judge's Suburban racing away from the Stronghold yesterday?" Janet said, making eye contact with Willie as if to convey that she agreed with him. "Maybe the judge had planned for Sonja to pick him up at the south end of the Stronghold unit."

Lumpy laughed. "We know Sophie's car's been in repairs in Gordon, just like she said. And we found the judge's Suburban at her house yesterday, after Benny Black Fox said he spotted it. But the judge didn't arrive with her. As far as I'm concerned, we'll interview the judge when we find him, but we're not actively looking for him. I called the surveillance off Sophie's house this morning."

"You did what?" Manny leaned across the table so quickly Lumpy scooted Elvis back. He groaned when he hit the wall. "The judge is missing in action. Even if he's not a suspect—which I'm still not ruling out—he may know something he's not telling us. The very least we can do is clear his name if he doesn't have anything to hide, before the confirmation hearings next week. And"—Manny pointed his finger at Lumpy—"the judge may be the next victim if he's not the killer."

Lumpy held his hands up in surrender. "All right. I'll put the BOLO back out for the judge. But not because he's a suspect, but just for a welfare check. Make sure he's all right."

"We can do better than that, Lumpy." Lumpy's face reddened but he remained silent. "I've got some more questions for Sonja Myers, like if the judge has met with her since Marshal's shooting. I'll send an agent there to talk with her again. We may luck out and find the judge at Sonja's. A man snuggling next to her in a teddy might not want to leave, huh?"

Lumpy's face flushed more, the veins throbbing across his forehead. Manny had scored another direct hit with Lumpy, one of many walking wounded left in the wake of the passing Sonja Myers. He changed the subject, turning to Pee Pee sucking on an Elvis PEZ. "You get ballistics back on Micah Crowder yet?"

"This morning." Sucking. "FBI made a positive ID on Joe Dozi's gun." Sucking. "Guess that leaves the judge off the hook for Micah's murder."

"Not yet." Janet stood, pacing. "He might have borrowed Dozi's gun. Or, as tight as Dozi and the judge were, the judge might know all about Micah's murder, right?"

Lumpy turned to Janet. "That bothers me more than a little, and it's the one thing that would explain why the judge might still be a suspect. A man with a Supreme Court nomination might do most anything to succeed in that appointment. Even covering up a homicide by his best friend." He leaned across the table at Manny. "All right, we look for the judge as a person of interest, both for knowledge of Micah's murder and for Marshal's shooting."

"And for knowledge he might have about Gunnar's death?"

"All right. We'll look for the judge. What else you want from us?"

"I want Willie to camp out in Marshal's room at Rapid City Regional until he regains consciousness. He'll tell us if the judge shot him or not."

"I'll tag along." Janet checked her mascara in her compact mirror and dropped it into her purse. "Willie might need help. He'll need company for sure. Bathroom breaks."

"You got other things to do"—Manny smiled—"If it's okay with Uncle Leon."

Lumpy nodded.

"What other things? Sit in some musty basement reading old newspapers?"

"Close." Manny forced down a smile. "I need you to go to Ellsworth Air Base. One of the agents in the Rapid City Field Office has contacts there that'll grease the wheels for you. That and your natural charm."

Janet shook her head. "What am I supposed to do?"

"I need you to find out everything you can about Senator Clayton Charles's association with the Air Corps training base during World War II."

"That's stretching it a bit, Hotshot."

Manny shook his head. "Moses and Ellis Lawler just didn't happen to drive into the bombing range by accident. And if they were passing a jar, they'd have picked a safer place than that. My guess is that Senator Charles knew about the uranium possibilities."

"What the hell's that got to do with the judge?"

"If his grandfather knew about uranium there, and arranged for the only two witnesses to be silenced . . ."

"And if Judge High Elk knew this, he'd know it would come out in the Senate hearings." Lumpy nodded.

"Those sharks digging up dirt on Judge High Elk would find it out. That's why it's important, Janet."

She rolled her eyes. "Well, at least when I'm done there I could keep Willie company at the hospital."

"Just keep the romance down," Manny said.

"And what will you be doing? Romancing your lady?"

"I'll be romancing some lady." Manny left out it just wouldn't be Clara.

CHAPTER 36

Manny adjusted the spotting scope clamped to the driver's side window of Willie's truck. He'd parked far enough from Sophie's house that he was certain he couldn't be spotted. Willie's truck had no air-conditioning, and Manny dabbed at the sweat running into his eyes with a bandanna.

But at least the truck had a tape player, and Manny adjusted the volume so the heavy tuba and accordion of the Six Fat Dutchmen sent shudders between his eardrums. It had been two hours since Willie called and said he and Manny's agent were on their way to talk with Sonja.

"I owe you," Willie had whispered over the phone, as if Lumpy was there with him in the hospital room. "Don't know how you pulled it off."

Manny smiled at his recent victory. When he'd first asked Lumpy to relieve Willie in Marshal's room, Lumpy had balked. He had no one free and Willie would have to wait until Janet finished with her Ellsworth investigation. But then Manny suggested that Sonja was certain to make a beeline to Rapid

City Regional and interview Marshal when he came around, and anyone else there with him. Manny almost felt guilty lying to Lumpy about Janet needing Willie's help. The last Manny saw of the acting chief was him with white shirt and bolo tie northbound in his new Mustang on his way to Rapid City Regional to relieve Willie. *Go get 'em tiger.*

Manny bent to the spotting scope again. Sophie, shimmering in the intense heat waves, rocked on her porch as she flattened porcupine quills between clenched teeth. The sun shone directly above her, but she seemed oblivious to it as she bent and sorted quills by color.

Ham's black Suburban, parked in back of her house, melded with Sophie's floating form. Manny expected Ham to appear any time, walking free of the shimmering afternoon heat, coming toward him with that sly smile on his face.

Sophie went into the house, coming back out within moments with a glass of water, and sat back down on her rocker. Surveillance was one of those mindless tasks he's always hated about fieldwork: waiting and staring and documenting everything that didn't matter in the case. For every moment that a criminal investigation was exciting, there were a hundred that a man had to fight to stay awake.

He wished Willie were here for company. When he'd called earlier from Ellsworth, Janet's digging into the old files of Senator Charles had mined some interesting information. The senator had been rejected as a pilot in World War I because of his eyesight, but he had remained an avid aviation fan. He had made several visits to Ellsworth for VIP tours, and had finagled a ride on every aircraft they had then, even a ride on a B-17 on several occasions.

Manny brought his face away from the powerful scope and rubbed his eyes. He was convinced Sophie had picked Ham up somewhere at the south end of the Stronghold, convinced that Ham would show himself, convinced he would

slip up just that little and confirm he was hiding inside Sophie's shack.

Manny needed to stretch his injured leg, and stepped out
into the fading light. He flexed his knee, feeling the intense
itching in the cat scratches as they healed. The staples in his
shoulder tugged, and he moved it to get the kinks out. When
he crawled back into the truck and back behind the scope,
Sophie was gone from the porch.

Manny settled back with a lukewarm diet root beer and
munched on the last of his Tanka Bar. The setting sun reflected
inside the spotting scope, and Manny adjusted it to minimize
the glare. It had been two hours since Sophie disappeared inside, and the sun had dimmed over the first treeless hill west of
Sophie's house. He'd give it another half hour for Ham to slip
up and come out, then make an approach with darkness as his
friend.

His phone vibrated and he flipped it open. Willie's voice,
frantic on the other end, sounded as if it was being filtered
through a thrashing machine, garbled and hollow. Except for
the urgency of it.

"Got crappy reception," Manny said over the phone. "Try
again."

"I talked with Sonja. Don't—" Willie was abruptly cut off.
Manny dialed his number back but it went to voice mail. He
left a message for Willie to call when he caught a decent cell
tower and dropped the phone back into his pocket.

Manny finished the rest of the bar, and secretly thanked
Janet for getting him hooked on them. He had not eaten for
hours and it hit the spot, and he washed it down with the rest
of his Hires.

The bar had been the first good vibe he'd gotten from Janet. Perhaps Reuben was right, that Manny was such a good
investigator, so adept at interviewing because *Wakan Tanka*

had given him a gift, an ability to read people, to go with his feelings.

Which brought him to all the rest of the bad vibes he had gotten from her. He'd dragged it out of Lumpy that his niece had been in trouble growing up. She was the daughter of an alcoholic father and a mother who worked sixteen hours a day cleaning motel rooms in Hot Springs. Manny wished her well, but he also knew she was poison for Willie. The longer Janet hung around Willie, the less chance he had to patch things up with Doreen Big Eagle.

He bent to the spotting scope and barely made out Sophie's house in the darkness. He reached up and took the dome light cover off and unscrewed the bulb before he opened the door and eased out. When it had been light, he'd made a mental note of the best path to Sophie's house, and he picked his way around fallen cedar trees, feeling for landmarks he'd noted in the light. He stumbled between clumps of cactus and sagebrush, around junk cars, careful not to brush his injured leg against anything.

When he reached the edge of the porch, he paused. Somewhere inside a single light shone, and Manny heard a voice. Ham's voice, faint as if he were whispering. Despite the miles of roadwork he did, his heart raced and threatened to burst from his chest. He took in slow, deep breaths, *combat breathing*, his academy instructors were fond of calling it. Manny's hand brushed against his holster on his hip and he instinctively unsnapped the thumb break.

He closed his eyes, recalling the layout of the kitchen leading into the living room and the small bedroom connected to it, reasoning that the latter would be the most likely place Ham would be waiting. He studied the porch, avoiding the board that had given him away before, and sidestepped around it, flattening himself against the side of the house. The whispering, the voice, had stopped. Silence could be a man's best friend. Or his worst enemy. Right now, it was Manny's nightmare as he waited for some noise that would mask his entry into the house. He needed a miracle. He got it.

A multicolored Chevy pickup with no muffler and two yelling kids standing in the bed hanging on to the headache rack sped along the road past Sophie's house. The roar of the motor and the screaming of the kids gave Manny the chance to lift up on the creaking screen door and slip inside the house. His rapidly beating heart was matched by the pain in his chest as he took one deep, slow breath and then another. Once again, it allowed him to function, to do what he knew he had to do.

Manny squatted and peered around the corner into the living room, the other room where Ham might be besides Sophie's bedroom. A candle illuminated the empty room, flickering light across the I love Alexander Hamilton High Elk wall, with his smiling photos and a copy of the *Argus Leader* from when he'd been appointed to the federal bench. That was the only sign of Ham.

Manny used the edge of the wall to stand. He squinted past the flickering light to the bedroom, the last room in the house. He shuffled, moving as silently as possible, unholstering his Glock, his finger shaking just outside the trigger guard. He inched his way to the bedroom, pausing long enough at the doorway to mentally rehearse his plan. He buttonhooked around the doorframe. Gun at arm's length. Focused on the front sight. Searching for Ham.

The room stood empty, except for a single bed, neatly made, with a star quilt draped almost ceremoniously on top. Several dresses were hung on a rod that had been mounted between walls. A plastic dresser, each drawer labeled, doubled as a bedstand, and a small, single lamp with an oilcloth lampshade on top was the only other thing in the room besides milk crates housing Sophie's undergarments.

Manny holstered his gun and turned. Into a rifle barrel. Sophie's face was framed by the candlelight in back of her, the light casting shadows around her, reminding Manny of photos of the Lord in the Transfiguration. But hers was not the face of an angel, but that of a demon. Deep furrows joined her eyebrows, and her too-bright teeth reflected the light in an odd, sinister way.

"You just don't give up, breaking into a person's house like you do."

"I need to talk with your son."

"He's not here."

"I just heard him."

She nodded to a tape recorder on the makeshift bedstead. "Guess the tape of his speech he made at the Alex Johnson ran out. It was a good speech. I had to listen to it again."

"I need to talk with Hamilton."

"You always need to talk with him. What about this time?"

"The murders."

"Again? You ought to know by now you can't prove he killed Gunnar Janssen. Or that Spearfish policeman that was found a few days ago."

"I was thinking of Joe Dozi."

Sophie laughed. "Now why would he kill his best friend?"

"He wouldn't. But he could lead me to the real killer."

"And who might that be?"

"You, Grandmother."

Sophie's finger tightened on the trigger and she took a step back. Manny calculated if he could draw his gun and fire before she did. Or even if he really wanted to. "Me? You figure an old woman could kill a man like Joe?"

"You've been using that rifle all your life to put meat on the table. You're a hunter. You lure prey as naturally as you lured me in here tonight with that tape recording, making me think Hamilton was here." *Like you lured me from Marshal's cabin and shot me.* But he would save that for later. If there was a later.

"Tell me your wild story about Joe Dozi." Sophie backed up another step as if reading Manny's thoughts.

"I could prove Joe ran me off the road. At least enough that I could get the case past a preliminary hearing for aggravated assault with a motor vehicle."

"Doesn't explain what Hamilton has to do with it. Or why you think I killed Dozi."

"The confirmation hearings." Manny wet his lips. That pesky breathing again, interfering with his talking his way out of Sophie shooting him. Again. "It would have come out in court that he was Hamilton's friend. Court convening right at the time of the hearings. Right when Hamilton needed bad publicity the least.

"And you protected him. Like you always did. Joe dropped his guard when you approached him, even with that .22 in your hand. His friend's mother was no danger. And it cost him. Then there was the phone call telling you about Joe's murder."

"I don't have a phone."

"I know you don't. But when I was here the other day, you told me you already knew about Joe's murder. Because you were there at the time. You had to kill Joe before it got out he killed Micah. Guess Joe was protecting Hamilton like you've been protecting him. If Micah had his way, it would get out why Hamilton's been against mining in the Badlands . . ."

"Hamilton doesn't know about Dozi killing that old policeman. Keep him out of it."

"Like he doesn't know about Gunnar Janssen's murder? Like he hasn't figured it out by now you killed him back in '69?"

"Gunnar was Hamilton's friend. Why would I want to harm him?"

Manny breathed deeply. His best weapon was his reasoning, his voice, and he needed all that, and more now, if he were to live. "Uranium. Gunnar was a geology major. He hired Marshal Ten Bears to guide him hunting, except he wasn't hunting. He was looking for the legend of where the bad rocks live. He was looking for uranium deposits.

"Hamilton wrote a paper in college against mining." Manny kept fixated on the rifle still leveled at his midsection. "Even then, even before he hit the federal bench, he knew if uranium mining was discovered in the Badlands that White men would flock to the reservation like they always had, and desecrate the Stronghold." Sophie shifted the barrel to Manny's head, and it was no longer just a .22, it was something much larger as he looked down the bore.

"Sounds like some fairy tale. You've got some imagination."

"If I'm wrong, drop that rifle."

Sophie's brows came together and she kept the gun leveled at Manny. "Hamilton intended to confront Gunnar about his uranium findings. But you found him first. You knew there'd been words between them, that Hamilton's temper would take over and he'd do something that'd prevent him from earning his degree. And prevent being accepted to law school. The thing I can't square is why you stuffed Gunnar in that car with the two other bodies."

"You're still convinced I killed Gunnar and Dozi?"

Manny rubbed his leg. "I do. Mind if I sit."

"Suit yourself." Manny sat on the couch and rubbed his throbbing leg, his shoulder muscles pulling against the staples. But if he didn't talk creatively, these pains would be minor compared to what Sophie had in mind.

"The other day I was here you had a sprig of purple sage stuck to the side of your shoe. That sage only grows in the Stronghold area where we found Joe Dozi's body. And those porcupine quills: The Game and Fish has an extensive database of DNA on just about every critter inhabiting the state. I'd bet they could match those quills with porcupines living around Marshal's cabin. Close to Dozi's murder. The best quills, from what my uncle Marion told me."

"You do have things figured out."

Manny used the arm of the couch to stand and stretch. He held out his hand. "Why don't we go someplace where we can talk, just you and me."

Sophie's knuckles whitened on the trigger and she took a step backward. "You understand, I can't allow you to leave."

Manny nodded as he said a silent prayer to God. And to *Wakan Tanka*. No sense leaving anyone out in this time of need. She intended to kill him. "I guess you can't allow the public to find out that the mother of a Supreme Court nominee had killed people just to protect her son as far back as the Vietnam War. Still, I'm fuzzy about Gunnar."

Sophie shook her head, the sneer replaced by a sad look that crossed her face for just a moment. Until she started talking about Gunnar Janssen. "Somehow Gunnar found out that Senator Charles arranged a B-17 courtesy flight to witness the Air Corps drop bombs into a target, which he insisted the crew target, the car that happened to contain Moses Ten Bears and Ellis Lawler waiting for the senator to arrive. The senator arrived all right, in the bomber, watching the bombs destroy the only two men who could rat him out about the uranium potential in the Badlands. Gunnar got my husband—Samuel—drunk one night when Hamilton and Gunnar were visiting here on college break. Samuel told Gunnar what Hannah High Elk always suspected about Clayton, that he'd died of radiation poisoning a year after the bombing. Served the greedy bastard right."

"And Gunnar would have blackmailed Hamilton—with

his connections on the Reservation—to grease the wheels for mining permits?"

Sophie nodded, the grimace returning. "Like Moses Ten Bears, Hamilton had built up a reputation as a trusted man since his Holy Rosary School days. If Hamilton endorsed mining permits to be issued to Gunnar, the tribe would have issued them. It would have been a disaster for the tribe but made Gunnar a wealthy man. And ruined Hamilton's reputation."

"So you stuffed Gunnar in that car along with Moses Ten Bears and Ellis Lawler?"

The rifle barrel drooped, moving from Manny's head to his chest, and he inched forward. Sophie snapped the barrel up, and Manny froze. "I figured if Moses and Ellis Lawler hadn't been discovered in the past twenty-five years, no one would find Gunnar for another twenty-five. I didn't count on the ordnance disposal team coming on to them."

Manny eased an inch closer, his leg cramping up, calculating if he could get out of the path of the bullet in time.

"Dozi killed Micah Crowder that day I went to Marshal's cabin," Sophie continued. "I often stayed there when I went to gather porcupine quills when Marshal wasn't around. Benny Black Fox met me on the road after changing a lightbulb on the KILI tower. Said a red Indian had been chasing an old beater Pontiac. I thought it was Hamilton chasing someone and found Joe Dozi instead. He'd already killed Micah and jumped when I come on to him. But he holstered his gun. He knew I went there often hunting porcupine and knew I wouldn't turn him in and jeopardize Hamilton's judicial appointment. Guess the thought of an old woman killing him never crossed his mind."

Manny slid his feet an inch closer. "Did you shoot Marshal?"

"You mean did I kill him?"

Manny shook his head. "He'll recover."

Sophie's eye twitched. Her jaw muscles worked against something imaginary, her ill-fitting teeth clicking, her own breaths coming faster. "What do you mean, he'll recover?"

"The bullet followed the skull cap, but just separated a skull suture. That's the odd things about .22s—they often take an odd path when they hit a body."

"You lie."

"He'll live and tell my investigator who shot him when he comes to. It'll still come out that Judge High Elk's mother shot Marshal Ten Bears, no matter what you do with me."

"I'll think of something," she said after a long pause. "Like I thought where Marshal and Hamilton would have hiked to. I took the south path, and found Marshal alone."

"In Hamilton's Suburban, because your car was still in the shop in Gordon for undercarriage damage the last time you drove to Marshal's cabin?"

"You knew?"

"I called. The mechanic said the front end was all tore up. Damned rugged roads."

Sophie nodded. "Hamilton had gone off by himself to pray and Marshal was easy pickings. Just like Joe, he didn't suspect an old woman of anything bad."

"But why Marshal? He didn't know any of this."

"He was the last one that knew just where the bad rocks live. He was with Gunnar that week when they found the uranium deposits. He would have dragged Hamilton down when all this got out. I couldn't let that happen with the Supreme Court nomination in the balance."

Manny inched closer, and his foot nudged the lamp. Sophie shouldered the gun, aiming it at his head, and Manny willed his muscles to relax, telling himself that relaxed muscles react quicker than taut ones do, telling himself he had to rush her.

He wouldn't go without fighting as had Joe Dozi and Gunnar Janssen. The candlelight bounced off her teeth that looked as if they were ready to drop out, flicked off eyes narrowed with a hatred for someone who would harm her son. In an instant, Manny knew Sophie was crazy.

He slid his foot forward. Sophie's finger tightened. The distance was too great. His heart raced. His chest pounded. A board on the porch creaked. Sophie shot a glance at the door and, in that heartbeat of time, Manny ducked and rushed her. She shot, the bullet shattering his elbow as his shoulder hit her. Manny fell to the floor atop the kicking, screaming woman clawing to get to her gun trapped underneath her.

"Don't do that!" Ham burst into the room ahead of Willie. He grabbed the rifle and kept it out of her reach as Ham picked Sophie up. She fought to get around her son, but Ham wrapped her tight in his arms.

"Benny Black Fox called me," Willie said, his eyes darting between Sophie and Manny's elbow. Blood oozed onto the floor, and Willie bent to him. "Benny told me the judge was walking out of the Stronghold. He'd been looking for Marshal. I picked the judge up walking out and filled him in."

"About what?"

"When Benny Black Fox called me, he also said it was Sophie driving away from the Stronghold in her rez rod the day he saw Joe chasing Micah. When I couldn't get you back on the phone, I came here as quick as I could."

Ham stroked Sophie's head and kissed her lightly on the temple.

Willie guided Manny into a chair and ripped his shirtsleeve away from the elbow and reached for his bandanna. "When I talked with Sonja, she told me Sophie's car had gotten tore up somewhere. I put two and three together and thought what better place to tear a car up than that area around Marshal's cabin. Those roads can be hell on four-wheel drives, let alone a rez rod on its last leg. Now let's get you to the emergency room. Again."

"What about Sophie? Who's going to bring her in?"

"The best person we can think of. A sitting federal judge."

CHAPTER 37

They all stood from the conference table when Judge Alexander Hamilton High Elk entered the room. He motioned for them to sit. "If you argue a case or testify in my court, then you can stand."

Lumpy was the last to sit, and he leaned against the table shooting smug looks at Manny. "You understand, your honor, that it wasn't the Oglala Sioux Tribe that put you on the suspect list for Joe Dozi's and Micah Crowder's murders. We got more sense than that."

Ham glanced at the Moses Ten Bears print on the wall and smiled before he took a seat. "I can see that."

"Your mother?" Manny asked. "Will she be all right?"

Ham's mouth downturned and he cleared his throat. When he spoke, it was with a clear, soft voice, as if addressing petitioners. "She'll be evaluated mentally. Given her age, she won't set foot in court for the homicides. Or see the light of day outside that mental hospital." *Maybe she'll become friends with Lizzy.*

"Sorry to hear that." Willie had put on a starched uniform, and sat clean-shaven. "I know what that's like."

Pee Pee popped a PEZ into his mouth from Elvis, and motioned around the table. Everyone declined except Ham. He held out his hand, and Precious popped one into his palm.

Ham scrunched his face up. "Never could figure what people saw in these things."

"Me neither," Pee Pee admitted, and winked at Lumpy.

They sat in silence, Manny waiting to hear what the announcement was, the one that Ham wanted those around the room to hear first. Ham cleared his throat. "I pulled out of the Senate confirmation hearings. I withdrew my name."

"I told you not to consider the judge a suspect." Lumpy pounded his fist on the table. "Now see what . . ."

Ham patted Lumpy's hand. "It's got nothing to do with the investigation, Chief."

Lumpy's chest puffed out and he sat back in Elvis as if he were grateful someone had at last recognized his rank.

"I'd be less than confident of Agent Tanno if he hadn't considered me a suspect. No, I finally realized I can do so much more for our people remaining on the federal bench just where I am."

"I hear that you've ordered the Department of Energy to investigate the Cheyenne River," Manny said.

Ham frowned, but his eyes still smiled. "After talking with doctors here, I'm convinced there's contaminates in there—and the surrounding area—that'll show radiation levels far in excess of safe tolerances. When that study comes back, then the federal government can begin cleanup. Being a federal judge with reservation jurisdiction, I'm in the best position to review mining issues. And you all know my feelings on that by now."

Willie smiled. "Then it's safe to assume permits won't be granted? That sacred men will be able to go into the Stronghold and pray when *Wakan Tanka* calls them?"

Ham smiled. "And anyone else who wants to pray there. White or Indian."

"Tell me, your honor, how was it that you didn't hear your mother shoot Marshal?"

Ham smiled at Lumpy. "Now who's still putting me on the suspect list?"

Lumpy stuttered, and Ham laughed. "Don't sweat it, Chief. Fact is, Marshal needed to do a Sending Away ceremony for his Grandfather Moses. When he stopped at where the old Buick had been, I went ahead to the rim of the Stronghold mesa, to where Chief Big Foot led his band away from the 7th Cavalry that winter of 1890, before he came into the agency, and the rest, as they say, is sad history."

Manny closed his eyes, recalling the miles between Marshal's cabin and the rim of the Stronghold. "That'd make sense. You wouldn't have been able to hear a high-powered rifle, let alone Sophie's little .22."

Ham nodded. "It was toward evening when I got back to where I'd left Marshal, but he wasn't there. I thought he'd got tired of waiting and hiked back without me. I camped overnight and humped out the next day. Now if you'll excuse me, I'm going to visit my mother before they transport her to Yankton State Hospital for her psych eval."

They all stood, and Lumpy stopped Ham. "Your withdrawal from the nomination—is this something we need to keep under our hats for now?"

Ham shook his head and smiled. "I suspect some foxy reporter from the *Rapid City Journal* will pry the story out of me somehow. I'm certain it'll hit the stands today."

Lumpy escorted Ham from the justice building, limping back into the room. He propped his feet up on the conference table, rubbing them through the boots. He winced in pain as he glared at Pee Pee.

"Don't blame me, boss. You were the one that insisted I

sell you that pair of Elvis boots. You knew they were two sizes too small for you when you bought them."

"You want them back?"

Pee Pee shook his head and picked his dentures with a paper clip. "Naw. I didn't want them in the first place."

Lumpy's face reddened, and Manny was certain he would have run around the table and choked Pee Pee. If he could have stood. "Well, at least we should charge Doreen Big Eagle for assaulting Janet."

"Can't," Willie said. "She jumped Janet in Pennington County. Not exactly the rez."

"Well, someone should prosecute Doreen."

"It was kind of self-defense." Manny walked to the coffeepot and grinned at Lumpy. "Doreen was just protecting her man."

"Still don't see why Doreen went berserk like she did."

"No? Maybe it was when Janet slipped up and told about Willie's Durango getting keyed outside the Alex Johnson. How someone had started on the front fender and ended up over the back wheel well. Willie stuck the outfit in the body shop right after that to get fixed. On your order."

"And I never mentioned anything about where the damage was to anyone except Manny," Willie added. "Now if you could testify that Janet went to the body shop . . ."

"You know I can't." Lumpy waved the thought away. A long silence followed. "You know I did what I could for that girl ever since she was little. Even then she was a handful. I thought if she got into police work that she'd be forced to walk the straight and narrow."

"More like the loopy and wide," Willie said.

Lumpy agreed. "She got herself in real deep this time. It's bad enough that she'll be charged in Rapid City for keying Willie's Durango, but also for breaking the window of his truck and stealing his flashlight."

"Guess that's out of your jurisdiction, boss," Pee Pee said, twirling a wispy strand of gray ponytail. "Can't cover for her up there."

"And her framing Henry Lone Wolf's frustrating. Framing another Lakota . . ."

"He's not Lakota," Manny smiled. "He's Italian."

Lumpy dropped his feet onto the floor and winced. "How's that? Henry's lived here all his life."

"My uncle Marion said Henry's family came here to work on a WPA crew and left Henry when the jobs ran out. He looked Indian enough—and talked Indian enough—everyone just figured him to be Lakota. His real name is Domanali."

"A pant-shitting Italian. Damn him."

Willie smiled. "Let's say this is the day for benevolence. I won't press charges for Janet breaking my truck window and stealing my flashlight if you tell Rapid City PD you don't want prosecution for her keying my Durango."

Lumpy smiled and sat up straight in Elvis. "You'd do that for her?"

"That and the promise that she'll never set foot in a police car again."

Lumpy paused, his eyes concentrating on the ceiling, mulling over the proposition.

"You going to get a better offer today?"

"Okay. Done. We won't pursue charges. And I'll see to it she doesn't climb in a patrol car again. At least not one that she's driving."

><><><

Willie parked the Durango on the hill overlooking Marshal's house. "You sure you'll be all right, with that arm? And you're still gimpy from the cat. By the way, you never mentioned what you did with him."

Manny rubbed the itching leg as if the cat were clawing

him right this moment. "He got better and just left the garage last night."

"Left or was helped?"

"Let's just say if Elvis were here, he would have been the one helping the cat out the garage."

"Elvis, as in Tony Lama Elvis?"

Manny nodded and got out of the Dodge, holding his arm in a sling from where the bullet had shattered it. "And I may be stoved in, but Marshal just got out of intensive care last week. He's on the mend worse than I am. Besides, he called me because he wanted to show me something, not to ambush me."

Manny started to close the door when Willie stopped him. "Just so you know, I appreciate it."

"Appreciate what?"

"The help. I would have fallen on my face . . ."

Manny started to speak, but Willie held up his hand. "Let me say this while I can. Thanks for steering me right. If I'd have stumbled, Lieutenant Looks Twice would have replaced me. Even if Janet wasn't in the picture anymore."

Manny smiled. "Call it selfish on my part. The better investigator you become, the less I have to do."

Manny stumbled on popcorn gravel along the trail leading to the Ten Bears cabin. Marshal watched him from his porch, sitting in an Adirondack chair and smoking a briar pipe with a copy of *Cowboys and Indians* open on his lap.

Manny nodded to the magazine. "Ever think what it would have been like to be one of those cowboys instead of an Indian?"

Marshal pointed to the bandage encircling his torso. "Couldn't have been any less painful, what with getting this old shack ready to move across from Billy Mills Hall."

"I heard you decided to donate it for the Cultural Center. I figured you'd eventually want others to see where your Grandfather Moses lived and did his work."

"And could have been rich if he'd wanted."

Manny nodded. "Could have been quite wealthy, from what art historians say about his works."

"Well, someone will be wealthy."

"How's that?"

Marshal used the arms of the chair to stand. "I'll show you." He paused a moment to catch his breath as he rubbed his stomach and the bandages constricting his chest. He led Manny into the cabin and chin-pointed to the wall that Moses had covered with wood, the wall that had held out the mighty west wind. Manny squinted, allowing his eyes to adjust to the dim light. Marshal lit a kerosene lamp and handed it to Manny. "There."

Manny stepped close to the wall and held the light up. Paintings, some on canvas, some on deer or elk hides, had been sandwiched between the outer wall and the inner wood layer. Other paintings had been laid on the bunks. Moses's visions.

"When I decided to donate it to the tribe, I decided I'd like them to have it in the condition Grandfather originally had it—with no inner walls to hold out the wind. Grandfather had nailed up scrap wood over the inner walls, but the wood had rotted and came away with little effort. Grandfather used the paintings people didn't want for insulation."

Manny nodded, thinking of Sophie's shack with newspapers stuffed inside the walls, and the cabin he and Unc lived in when Manny was a boy. "People used most anything they could back in the day to keep out the wind." He played the light around the pictures. "These must be all the missing Ten Bears paintings. They're worth millions. You're rich."

Marshal shook his head, a smile crossing his weathered face, a smile Manny had not seen before. "I'm going to donate them to the tribe, with the caveat they display them. So people can get insight into Moses Ten Bears the sacred man."

"I thought that's what you wanted—enough to live comfortably?"

"When I was laying in that hospital room, unconscious, I could hear things, could think things, even though I couldn't move. I got to appreciate the life I had before Sophie High Elk shot me. I swore if I ever recovered enough that I could live life again—really live—that money wouldn't be my main pursuit."

Manny had his own revelation, mending in the hospital with Clara doting over him. He made an appointment that day—or rather asked Clara to make it—and, between his diabetes medicine and the little blue pill, he was confident that his relationship with Clara would work out.

"The paintings would have the potential of bringing the tribe great wealth. Enough that they won't have to even consider money from uranium mining."

"Oh I don't think they have to worry about that, not with Hamilton remaining on the federal bench."

"You know about his decision to withdraw his name?"

Marshal nodded. "We both decided on our walkabout that we'd prefer the Stronghold left just as Grandfather Moses wanted it—untouched and unscathed by the *wasicu*."

CHAPTER 38

DECEMBER 1944

Moses, cramped in the seat beside Ellis Lawler, wriggled to get comfortable. He couldn't. They just didn't make cars to fit him.

"When the hell are we going to get to the center of the deposit?"

Pissy little man. "Too soon. Did you know that men do not come back from where the bad rocks live?"

"Like, nothing leaves the Stronghold?" Ellis took another pull from his mason jar of whiskey. "Another of your silly Oglala legends?" Ellis laughed, but Moses detected nervousness in that laugh. "We'll just get this trip over and done with, and you and me won't have to go anywhere else together again."

Moses wanted to clap, but he held his emotions. A sacred man must always hold his emotions. Even for pissy little men.

The Buick hit a rock that threatened to ram through the

floorboard. "Damned godforsaken country. If this wasn't so lucrative, I'd have told Clayton to shove it. Just can't figure out why you're here—Clayton tells me you don't want any money."

"He is my friend. And for everything he has done to destroy our friendship, I trust him."

"Then you trust a snake." Ellis turned his attention back to driving the game trail.

"There." Moses pointed to a path leading between two tall buttes, making the area look like a saddle on a pony.

Ellis slowed the car and double-clutched into a lower gear to get them onto the floor of the Badlands in one piece.

"Stop here."

Ellis stopped the car in a clearing. "This where Clayton's supposed to meet us?"

"It is." Though Moses knew better. For the past two years, Clayton had been planning for outside companies to mine uranium in the Stronghold. Moses had known Clayton since that first night of that barn dance fight in Imlay, through all the years of peddling booze to the Oglala, and for promises made, promises broken, promises from Clayton that he'd help the tribe. But hadn't.

Moses had no illusions about the uranium mining. He'd shown Clayton and Ellis the place where the bad rocks live, and obtained mining permits. And regretted it. He knew Clayton had been biding his time until he could arrange for Moses to be out of the picture. *His* vision had told him that.

"This isn't part of the bombing range, is it?"

Moses shook his head. "Used to be. But they have not used this part for over a year."

As if to call attention to Moses's statement, the throp-throp-throp of a large aircraft cooking off speed filled their ears as it neared.

"I don't like the sound of that."

But Moses did. His vision had told him Clayton would be in that bomber. Told him that soon he and Ellis would be left to the winds in the Sheltering Place. And Clayton would roam the Stronghold, roam the place where the bad rocks live, the greatest concentration of uranium in the west lying just feet under the ground. Close enough they would also claim Clayton. Soon.

As the B-17 made its final run toward the car-target, Moses shut out Ellis's screams. Wakan Tanka *accept me in this place. This Oonagazhee. This place where I'll die and with me, the place where the bad rocks live.*

EPILOGUE

The bleachers at the powwow grounds groaned under Willie's weight when he leaned against them. "Took me long enough to find you here, dark as it is."

"Quiet this time of night."

"Can't argue there." Willie sat beside Manny and followed his gaze up to the sky. "I like it best when there's no moon. Makes the Old Ones wink so much brighter."

Manny turned away and ran his shirtsleeve across his cheeks to dry them. "The *Wanagi Tacanku* has got one more free spirit up there tonight."

"I heard Morissa Friend Of All passed this afternoon."

Manny fought to control the shake in his voice. "I failed her."

"She knows you did a lot for her and all the others that will come after her here on the rez."

Manny turned to Willie, giving up hiding his sorrow. "And just what did I accomplish? The little girl is dead and nothing's been done."

Willie leaned over and grabbed a pebble. He skipped it across an imaginary pond in front of the bleachers. "Judge High Elk has ordered an investigation of water quality in the Cheyenne River."

"So he said."

"And the tribe's appointed a man to start up a unit to investigate pollution and hazardous complaints on a tribal level. Someone Lt. Looks Twice knows he can count on."

Manny recognized the smile on Willie's face, that same smile he had when he bragged that Lumpy had appointed him tribal criminal investigator. "You?"

Willie nodded.

"Guess we won't be working together on other cases."

Willie shook his head. "Oh, we'll be working together again."

"But I thought you said . . ."

"I said I was to head up an environmental enforcement unit. But that's in addition to my criminal investigator duties."

"Be harder for you to drink, what with all the time you'll spend working."

Willie looked down at his feet. "You know about that?"

"I do."

"Did Lt. Looks Twice tell you I was drinking my way into oblivion?"

"Didn't have to. It was obvious."

"Did he tell you I've been going to AA meetings in Hot Springs?"

"No."

"Sometimes when I was supposed to be working?"

"That where you sneaked off to sometimes when I couldn't get hold of you?"

Willie nodded. "The meetings. Other times to a shrink in Rapid I've been seeing for my depression."

Manny patted him on the back. "Well, between the meetings and the shrink, something's working."

Willie smoothed his shirtfront, a starched double-breasted Western shirt. Even in the darkness the faux pearl snaps twinkled. The old Willie was back. "I take things one day at a time now. Lt. Looks Twice is determined to keep me too busy to think about Aunt Lizzy and too busy to backslide."

Manny caught a shooting star out of the corner of his eye. "Now all you got to do is patch things up with Doreen."

"I did." Willie grabbed his Copenhagen can and pinched a lip full. "Lt. Looks Twice got hold of her and said I'd insisted Janet get into some other line of work away from the rez."

"So you lied to her?"

"Lt. Looks Twice lied to her. I just didn't tell her otherwise. Regardless, Doreen thinks I'm a hero for sending Janet packing. And speaking about packing, I see you've packed your bags and moved out of my apartment. Going somewhere?"

"Back to Clara's. After I saw the doc and got on medication for my diabetes, I figure the libido will come sneaking back. We think we'll be able to make a go of it."

They sat in silence, Manny's attention returning to the night sky, wondering which winking star was the little girl from Cheyenne River.

Willie seemed to read his mind. "You know, what you did for the Morissas on Pine Ridge won't go unnoticed. You brought attention to the pollution here. Doreen and I will one day have children and not worry if pollution or radiation sickness will kill them prematurely."

Manny nodded, the tears drying, looking skyward. "There." He smiled and pointed to the Milky Way. "Let's say that bright one's Morissa."

"Sure." Willie draped his arm around Manny's shoulder. "Let's say it is."